THE HOUND OF THE BASKERVILLES
with
"THE ADVENTURE OF THE SPECKLED BAND"

broadview editions
series editor: L.W. Conolly

p. 322.

"HOLMES EMPTIED FIVE BARRELS OF HIS REVOLVER INTO THE CREATURE'S SIDE."

Frontispiece: Sidney Paget's black-and-white illustration of "The Death of the Hound" from *The Strand Magazine*'s serialized edition of *The Hound of the Baskervilles*, reproduced in George Newnes's book edition (1902). The melancholy of the creature is different from the fierceness with which he is usually imagined and a reminder that, when Watson first experiences the calling of the Hound, it is a "long, low moan, indescribably sad" (p. 117) that he hears.

THE HOUND OF THE BASKERVILLES

Another Adventure of Sherlock Holmes

with
"THE ADVENTURE OF THE SPECKLED BAND"

Arthur Conan Doyle

edited by Francis O'Gorman

broadview editions

Library and Archives Canada Cataloguing in Publication

Doyle, Arthur Conan, 1859–1930.
    The hound of the Baskervilles : another adventure of Sherlock Holmes ; with,
The adventure of the speckled band / Arthur Conan Doyle ; edited by Francis O'Gorman.

(Broadview editions)
Includes bibliographical references.
ISBN 1-55111-722-3

    I. O'Gorman, Francis   II. Title.   III. Title: Adventure of the speckled band.
IV. Series.

PR4622.H69 2005   823′.8   C2005-905925-7

Broadview Editions
The Broadview Editions series represents the ever-changing canon of literature in English by bringing together texts long regarded as classics with valuable lesser-known works.

Advisory editor for this volume: Jennie Rubio

Broadview Press Ltd. is an independent, international publishing house, incorporated in 1985. Broadview believes in shared ownership, both with its employees and with the general public; since the year 2000 Broadview shares have traded publicly on the Toronto Venture Exchange under the symbol BDP.

We welcome comments and suggestions regarding any aspect of our publications— please feel free to contact us at the addresses below or at broadview@broadviewpress.com.

North America
Post Office Box 1243, Peterborough, Ontario, Canada K9J 7H5
3576 California Road, Post Office Box 1015, Orchard Park, NY, USA 14127
Tel: (705) 743-8990; Fax: (705) 743-8353;
email: customerservice@broadviewpress.com

UK, Ireland, and continental Europe
NBN Plymbridge, Estover Road, Plymouth PL6 7PY UK
Tel: 44 (0) 1752 202301   Fax: 44 (0) 1752 202331
Fax Order Line: 44 (0) 1752 202333
Customer Service: cservs@nbnplymbridge.com Orders: orders@nbnplymbridge.com

Australia and New Zealand
UNIREPS, University of New South Wales
Sydney, NSW, 2052 Australia
Tel: 61 2 9664 0999; Fax: 61 2 9664 5420
email: info.press@unsw.edu.au

www.broadviewpress.com

Typesetting and assembly: True to Type Inc., Mississauga, Canada.

PRINTED IN CANADA

For Katy Mullin

Contents

Acknowledgements

I have been reading *The Hound of the Baskervilles* since I was a child: I'm delighted to have been able to spend some of my professional life editing it. I am particularly gratified now to own the original editions of *The Strand Magazine* in which I first discovered Sherlock Holmes, and thank my parents for them. My first acknowledgments as an editor must be to other Holmes scholars, including previous editors. Thanks also to the following individuals who have helped me with specific information: Professor Dinah Birch on natural history; the Cocker Spaniel Club of Great Britain on spaniels; Professor David Fairer on eighteenth-century handwriting; Professor Ann Heilmann on Laura Lyons's matrimonial position; Dr Tom Lockwood on typefaces and handwriting; Dr Gail Marshall on London; Dr Rory McTurk on Irish derivations and Professor Challenger; John O'Gorman on forensics; The Revd Canon David Peacock on the setting of the novel; and Dr John Whale on natural history. Alistair Stead was typically generous in sharing some of his ideas about *The Hound* with me and I have profited from them; Professor Andrew Wawn, Dr Katy Mullin, and Dr Jane Wood also pointed me in useful directions about, variously, Sabine Baring-Gould, Norse derivations, and science and spiritualism. Dr Sonny Kandola directed me to a critical study I would otherwise have missed.

Rebecca Gowers, whose *The Swamp of Death: A True Tale of Victorian Lies and Murder* (2004), is as gripping as any fictional detective story, carefully read this edition in first draft and generously made suggestions for its improvement, which I have incorporated. The Bodleian Library (Oxford), the British Library, and the Brotherton Library (University of Leeds), have been invaluable, as has the internet. My parents, Joyce and John O'Gorman, and my brother and sister-in-law, Chris and Michelle O'Gorman, have been interested listeners to my narratives about this book. Emily Curtis-Rouse told me about Devon, Dartmoor, and—with one eye on Cordelion, her cat—dogs, and patiently tracked Sir Henry's footsteps around Central London. Thank you. Dr Mark Batty, Dr Bridget Escolme, Dr John McLeod, Dr Clare Pettitt, Dr Cristiano Ristuccia, Dr Helen Small, and Dr Juliette Taylor have been more than hospitable. I'm grateful to Nicola Wildman and Sue Baker for the most professional and friendly of administrative support in the School of English at the University of Leeds which helped me in my other duties while editing these adventures. Dr Tracy Hargreaves has set aside her own work to read the completed draft of this edition with an eye both generous and astute and I am grateful to her.

Any remaining errors, omissions, and awkward expressions in the editorial matter are, however, mine.

Abbreviations

Baring-Gould   William S. Baring-Gould, ed., *The Annotated Sherlock Holmes*, 2 vols (London: Murray, 1968)

CSH   *The Penguin Complete Sherlock Holmes*, with a preface by Christopher Morley (Harmondsworth: Penguin, 1981)

Dakin   D. Martin Dakin, *A Sherlock Holmes Commentary* (Newton Abbot: David and Charles, 1972)

Exploits   *Exploits of Brigadier Gerard* [1896], from Arthur Conan Doyle, *The Conan Doyle Historical Romances* 2 vols. (London: Murray, 1932)

Frayling   Arthur Conan Doyle, *The Hound of the Baskervilles*, ed. Christopher Frayling (Harmondsworth: Penguin, 2001)

OED   *Oxford English Dictionary* (2nd ed)

Robson   Arthur Conan Doyle, *The Hound of the Baskervilles*, ed. W. W. Robson (Oxford: Oxford UP, 1993)

All quotations in the notes from the Bible are from the King James version (1611), but with modern spelling for ease of reading.

Editor's Caution to the Readers

Both the Introduction and the notes to this edition are obliged—usually in order to point up ironies—to disclose the identity of the criminals before Conan Doyle does.

Introduction

The Hound of the Baskervilles is Sherlock Holmes's most famous case.

How easy it is to say that, as if the novel really recounted an actual episode of Victorian crime. The serialization of *The Hound* in *The Strand Magazine* from August 1901 to April 1902 was swiftly followed by book publication (from George Newnes, who also published *The Strand*) and it has never been out of print since.[1] Filmed for cinema and television, dramatized for radio, and recorded for audiobooks, *The Hound* has lived as much beyond the pages of Conan Doyle's novel as it has within them.

The fiction of his reality is well sustained. In 1951, the Sherlock Holmes exhibition, held in 221 Baker Street—the closest that could be got to the nonexistent 221B—as part of the Festival of Britain, presented exhibit after exhibit that documented the material reality of his life. It included—readers of *The Hound* will want to know—a cast of the creature's footprint together with the sorrowful head of the animal, patched with a phosphorescence. They remain on display in the Sherlock Holmes Inn on Northumberland Street in Central London. Delightfully transgressing the barriers between fiction and fact, this strange pub contains much of the original 1951 material: the interior of Holmes's sitting room, with "VR"[2] neatly

---

1   Readers looking for significant early reviews of *The Hound* will, however, find little of substance, despite its popularity (hence the absence of reviews from the appendices of the present edition). Detective fiction as a whole received sparse attention from the literary journals at the beginning of the twentieth century.

2   "VR" was the abbreviation used to signify, on official documents and inscriptions, that the reigning monarch was Queen Victoria (from the Latin *Victoria Regina*). Holmes was being unusually patriotic—and eccentric.

pocked by bullets from "The Musgrave Ritual" (1893), the gun and rock tied with string from "The Problem of Thor Bridge" (1922), the bust of Holmes with a bullet hole in his forehead from "The Adventure of the Empty House" (1903). It is a vivid example of an extraordinary and continuing cultural reluctance to treat Sherlock Holmes as a literary figure. He survives in the popular imagination—with the largely mythical deerstalker, cape, and meerschaum pipe—with a reality that is tangible.

Writers on Holmes have been impatient with this fictionality. Arthur Conan Doyle's detective stories have attracted, to be sure, the attention of a number of literary critics, some distinguished—Ian Ousby, Ronald Thomas, John Carey, W.W. Robson, John Kerrigan, Joseph Kestner[1]—who have explored the cultural and literary significance of the Holmes narratives. But much of the writing now and from the recent past on Conan Doyle's Sherlock Holmes starts from a different place. Publications from the Holmesians (in the UK) and Sherlockians (in the US) have been predicated on a half-belief in, an undeclared acceptance of, his reality.

Their productions, usually in the form of commentaries (which the internet has further developed) have worked with puzzles that derive from an unspoken agreement about his half-historical truth. Empirical problems are their substance and they are addressed in the manner of Holmes. The territory of the *hors texte* is open here. Which college did Holmes attend? In which limb was Dr Watson injured by that Jezail bullet? Where *was* 221B Baker Street, the home of the sleuth? "[It] is clear," writes D. Martin Dakin, a Holmesian/Sherlockian of distinction, in his *A Sherlock Holmes Commentary* (1972), "that Watson disguised the number, possibly in deference to Holmes's dislike of publicity."[2] It is a characteristic reply from this substantial corpus of learned, affectionate but eccentric scholars who reveal the cultural power of Conan Doyle's creation to tread out of the bounds of fiction into fact.

The Hound is now so widely known that it has become central to the popular knowledge of Holmes and his methods. It is appropriate that it should have been the adventure that inspired the best of all Holmes films. John Thaw (1942–2002) so suited the role of Colin Dexter's Inspector Morse in the UK's Independent Televi-

---

1   See Selected Further Reading (p. 297).

2   D. Martin Dakin, *A Sherlock Holmes Commentary* (Newton Abbot: David and Charles, 1972), 13.

sion series (1987–2000) that Dexter modified his original rather unlikeable hero's character in response to Thaw on set. The actor, despite considerable success in earlier roles, became intimately associated with Morse and he lent a palpable credibility to Dexter's Oxford tales. Indeed, the association was so real that Morse constricted Thaw as an actor in the short period of life left to him beyond the role. Basil Rathbone (1892–1967), starring in the first of his many Sherlock Holmes films in the 1939 version of *The Hound of the Baskervilles* (directed by Sidney Lanfield), became for many then and now definitively Conan Doyle's creation— although in fact he was the tenth actor to play the detective in sound films, after around 115 silent Holmes films with a variety of different actors (some of whom were unknown). Appearance, character, voice, and mood all fitted with uncanny accuracy the man of the tale so that Rathbone seemed to manifest permanently an actual, available, and observable embodiment of the character himself. Many other actors have played the role and there have certainly been sharper Watsons than Nigel Bruce's amiable, brave, loyal, but plodding companion. But none, despite their manifest abilities, has quite attained the authority of Rathbone—ironically, a great dog lover—to portray Conan Doyle's consulting detective. Holmes's implausible reality—Rathbone came to dislike the character, wishing he had been more human and fallible[1]—has been half-accepted, half-hoped for by many a reader of the adventures and by many more a non-reader. Rathbone's films offered, with cinematic *éclat*, a new, and paradoxical, way in which Holmes seemed to live as flesh and blood.[2]

The disinclination of the twentieth century to keep Sherlock Holmes in the realm of fiction reveals both the strength of Conan Doyle's imagination and a wider cultural reluctance to live without the kind of reassurance that Holmes's character embodies. The unimpassioned certainty that order will be restored, that crime will be solved, that the criminal will leave behind a recoverable trail of evidence that will enable the forces of justice to trace him, that the rational mind will triumph over the messy, cruel

---

1   See Basil Rathbone, *In and Out of Character* (New York: Limelight, 1989 [originally published 1962]), 412.

2   Conan Doyle himself thought that Holmes's appearances on stage during his life time intensified the impression that the detective was "a real person of flesh and blood," *Memories and Adventures* (Oxford: Oxford UP, 1989), 101.

events of human life: it is not hard to see why believing in Holmes comes from the best of motives. Conan Doyle understood the living force of his creation, the reality which he was accorded, and, were he inclined to overlook it, his correspondents reminded him. But that reality was double-edged. Conan Doyle had hoped for literary fame of a less populist kind. He regretted—as Rathbone differently did—that Holmes had changed his life. Anticipating in the earlier years of his career that readers would regard him as the author of historical novels, Conan Doyle came to think he would be better without his distracting detective and killed him off in mid career. Shrewdly, however, he described the event in such a way that, since "no coroner had pronounced upon the remains" (*CSH* [983]), Conan Doyle would be able to revive him without difficulty if necessary. In "The Final Problem" (1893) the detective and his antagonist Professor Moriarty apparently drop to their deaths in the Reichenbach Falls. In so slaying his most famous character, Conan Doyle was hoping to redirect readers' attention to his higher literary activities. But he was also endeavouring—drastically—to break the spell of Holmes's reality, demonstrating to his readers and to himself that the fictional character with whom he had lived for a long time was subject to the absolute power of the novelist-creator. The shock of that death to Holmes's readers was overwhelming. Conan Doyle was not allowed to forget it. In due course, he was obliged by public pressure to bring his hero back and take up once again his career as the author of Sherlock Holmes. Conan Doyle had succeeded neither in turning attention to his other fiction nor in getting rid of the succubus. When Holmes returns in "The Adventure of the Empty House," he appears in disguise as a man loaded with books. It was Conan Doyle's wry comment on the literary burden of Holmes on him.

Holmes's extraordinary history of the crossing of fiction with fact, his reluctance to stay in what Conan Doyle called the "fairy kingdom of romance" (*CSH* 984), has been unlike that of any other novelistic character in English literature. It is both highly ironic and peculiarly appropriate that it should be so. The irony exists in the fact that the sleuth's transformation into half-accepted factuality stands at odds with his firmest principles. The detective's task, as Conan Doyle presents it, is to seek out the empirical from the fanciful, the reliable from the imagined, despite the fact that the two become so wonderfully confused in the history of his own reception. Sherlock Holmes brings the clarity of forensic intelligence to the solving of mysteries, insisting on the certainty of his "data," his empirical facts, as fundamental to clearing up the problems he faces. That hunt for the empirically certain is essential to all the stories but it acquires startling significance in the apparent confrontation between the logical and the supernatural that forms the core of *The Hound of the Baskervilles*. As Holmes, hearing from Dr Mortimer[1] the tale of the Baskervilles' curse, seems to face the prospect of countering an unearthly foe, the question of what is credible, of what demonstrable veracity is behind the illusory, reaches a new level of challenge. "In a modest way," Holmes says, with self-deprecation, "I have combated evil, but to take on the Father of Evil himself would, perhaps, be too ambitious a task" (pp. 71-72). The "perhaps" is a nice touch. Holmes's triumph in this novel is to reveal with the aid of cool scientific inquiry that the case offers a supernatural explanation no home. Science exalts over the exploitation of superstition and the cynical manipulation of mysteries. The Hound's footprints are material. The criminal and his crime prove wholly so. Stapleton's plot involves the make-believe of the uncanny—the fiery-faced hell-hound—for an all-too material plan to acquire Baskerville Hall. Beaten by the hard-nosed persistence of Holmes, Stapleton's malevolence yields to the benign force of the supposedly rational mind. "We have not yet grasped the results which the reason alone can attain," Holmes remarks in "The Five Orange Pips" (1891) (*CSH* 225). Reason in *The Hound* triumphantly restores— or at least appears to—a reassuringly material logic to a community that thought itself possessed.

The Hound of the Baskervilles proclaims what Conan Doyle would like his readers to understand as a great modern truth. It confidently asserts that human progress from darkness to light occurs with the wise application of scientific procedure. The plot sees a movement from the primitive world of Neolithic huts, the savage moor, the spectral hound, the gothic spookiness of Baskerville Hall, and the brutal schemes of Stapleton, to the order and justice attained by Holmes's mind, aided by Dr Watson (a professional man of science of a different kind). The novel plots the return of stability to the rural community, the legitimate land owner's restoration to his ancestral domains, the securing of the

---

1 Mortimer tells Holmes that he is "Mister" not "Doctor" (p. 55) but I follow the convention of referring to him by his honorary title.

local social hierarchy, and the swallowing up of the criminal—murderer, wife beater, possibly violent burglar—by a force of nature seemingly in league with Holmes. It is a remarkable celebration of a power that the novel invites us to see as scientific reason or, as Holmes puts it, borrowing words from the prominent Victorian scientist John Tyndall (1820–93), "the scientific use of the imagination."[1]

When Watson and Sir Henry have been out on the moor looking for Selden, the escaped convict in the sub-plot of the novel, Watson with a thrill sees a figure high on the moor. "The moon was low upon the right," he writes,

> and the jagged pinnacle of a granite tor stood up against the lower curve of its silver disc. There, outlined as black as an ebony statue on that shining background, I saw the figure of a man upon the tor. Do not think that it was a delusion, Holmes. I assure you that I have never in my life seen anything more clearly. As far as I could judge, the figure was that of a tall, thin man. He stood with his legs a little separated, his arms folded, his head bowed, as if he were brooding over that enormous wilderness of peat and granite which lay before him. He might have been the very spirit of that terrible place. (pp. 144–45)

This is no spirit. The figure is Holmes himself who has injudiciously allowed the moon to rise behind him. But, while he is not indeed the spiritual embodiment of that "terrible place," he is its secular guardian. Holmes's acquaintance with Dartmoor begins by contemplation of a large-scale map. He narrates to Watson his hovering over the land as if he had become a disembodied mind, an incorporeal observing eye, while his body is left behind, consuming "in [his] absence two large pots of coffee and an incredible amount of tobacco" (p. 75). It is a comic moment. But it is also one that hints at the nature of Sherlock Holmes's intellectual power that *The Hound* will so widely celebrate. He is offered as a reasoning, observing scientific mind of convincing omnipresence. Standing alone on the dark moor watching its events, the novel advances Holmes, as Watson perceives him, as the tutelary power of the moors. We glimpse in that tall carved figure with the

---

1 See p. 83, note 2.

silver disk behind him the haloed secular divinity whose powers are not spiritual but mental.

For regular readers of *The Strand*, *The Hound*'s tribute to scientific reasoning was pronounced. Serialization of Conan Doyle's novel overlapped briefly with the closing numbers of H.G. Wells's *The First Men in the Moon* (1901), a text not destined to become his most popular. The plot hardly relates to Conan Doyle's, but the handling of scientific knowledge does. Wells's narration concerns the discovery by the obsessed scientist Cavor of a substance (Cavorite) that is opaque to gravity: once created, it closes off the pull of Earth's gravity to anything above it. After a disastrous trial in the laboratory during which a large part of the landscape is obliterated, Cavor and Bedford, the narrator, construct a space ship in which they are able to voyage far beyond Earth and, finally, reach the Moon. The lunar landscape turns out to be home to a variety of creatures who are, partly by accident, brought into conflict with their terrestrial visitors, forcing Cavor and Bedford to separate. After recovering the temporarily lost space capsule, Bedford speeds back to Earth where he is later to learn that Cavor, to his surprise, is sending messages from the Moon to a small observatory on the St Gothard in the Alps. Cavor reveals that he has been able to communicate successfully with some of the lunar dwellers (Selenites) and their leader (the Grand Lunar), but has made the grave error of telling them, firstly, that human beings are insatiably aggressive, and, secondly, that it was on himself alone that any possibility of future human visits to the Moon depends. The Selenites discover themselves in possession of the only creature who might allow visitations from a dismal combative race and it is no surprise that, after such a realization, Cavor's chances of returning to Earth alive are nil.

Bedford's final thought, as he hears the last of the distorted messages barely audible in the Alpine observatory, is of his erstwhile companion and fellow traveller as he imagines him suffering the most gruesome of fates for his injudicious revelation:

> For my own part [Bedford says] a vivid dream has come to my help, and I see, almost as plainly as though I had seen it in actual fact, a blue-lit shadowy dishevelled Cavor struggling in the grip of these insect Selenites, struggling ever more desperately and hopelessly as they press upon him, shouting, expostulating, perhaps even at last fighting, and being forced backwards step by step out of all speech or sign of his fellows, for

evermore into the Unknown—into the dark, into that silence that has no end.[1]

Wells's novel closes with the destruction of the scientist who, though matchless in his inventive capacity, has a "disastrous want of vulgar common sense."[2] Presenting a form of science that is of unique potential and exceptional danger; that leads to knowledge but also death; that brings to an apparently peaceful lunar community curiosity and slaughter; that is, at least in the person of Cavor himself, unattached to worthy virtues, *The First Men in the Moon* is fretful about the nature of scientific singlemindedness and of man's role as science's custodian. No reader of *The Strand* at the beginning of 1901 could fail to observe that *The Hound of the Baskervilles*, by the beginning of 1902, was making a sharply different claim. Conan Doyle's novel was offered as an acknowledgement of the illuminating power of scientific reason which was not dedicated to the risky probing of the secrets of the universe, but to the untangling, for the greater good, of the knots of human crime. Wells's obsessive scientist tells his lunar interlocutor of the nature of life on Earth, of its "war [...], of all the strength and irrational violence of men, of their insatiable aggressions, their tireless futility of conflict."[3] Holmes belongs in another world in which he applies his so-called scientific method to banish violence (violence to women in particular is conspicuous in both the adventures in this edition) and punish the desire of men to kill for illegitimate gain. "'It is evidently a case of extraordinary interest,'" Holmes declares to Mortimer on hearing the details of Sir Charles's death, "'and one which present[s] immense opportunities to the scientific expert'" (p. 71). In *The Hound*, it is a greatly restorative science that seizes those opportunities.

Or, at least, it is the *appearance* of science. Sherlock Holmes insists on the revelatory powers of his empirical methods and *The Hound*'s tribute to their guiding power is part of its core. But Holmes is a mythic figure nevertheless. Here is the first of the twists in the history of Holmes, his meaning and reality. Offered as the quintessence of reason, he is determined by fantasy. He functions as the defender of the material explanation against the supernatural but it is only through illusion that he belongs to the world

---

1 H.G. Wells, *The First Men in the Moon* (London: Corgi, 1957), 222.
2 Ibid., 221.
3 Ibid.

of logic. Conan Doyle always said—there is a film of him saying it—that he took inspiration for his detective from Dr Joseph Bell at Edinburgh, an actual man of science,[1] but Holmes's implausible deductions and unreal plots ensure that he is a creature of the imagination. Manipulating the world in answer to Holmes's mind, Conan Doyle offers in *The Hound*, as in the adventures altogether, a texture of plot that strikes the reader as so unlikely even amid the novel's counter-claims that it is no such thing. *The Hound* conjures the improbable and unfeasible: from Holmes's impossible deduction about Dr Mortimer's smoking habits to the improbable ignorance of the coroners' court, the motiveless following by Stapleton of Sir Henry through London, the strange uselessness of the warrant Lestrade brings to Dartmoor, to the far-fetched accounts Holmes offers at the end to explain how the villain would have taken possession of his inheritance. "The Adventure of the Speckled Band" (1892), also included in this edition, achieves no less implausibility. The material of the story, looked at with that merely rational eye, is untenable. It involves an improbably inobservant victim and her equally unnoticing sister; a crazed and irrational villain who invents such a complex scheme to commit a double murder that it requires a world famous detective to solve it; an incompetent local police force and coroner; a snake that defies the understanding of zoology to obey a whistle, to climb a rope, and to live in what appears to be the darkness of an airless safe; a detective who chooses the most hazardous of available ways to catch the murderer and who endangers his own life and that of his companion by needlessly angering a deadly serpent that is precariously (in fact impossibly) clinging to a rope a few feet away from him. Holmes identifies the creature at the end of the adventure. "'It is a swamp adder!'" he proclaims with horror; "the deadliest snake in India" (p. 235). The identification is apt in such an improbable story. There is no such animal.

Of course, rational probability is hardly a necessity for detective fiction of stature and it would be absurd to think otherwise.

---

1 Dr Joseph Bell (1837–1911), surgeon and medical educationalist, provided Conan Doyle—according to his own account—with the initial inspiration for Sherlock Holmes. Bell's methods of deduction about the nature and diseases of patients lie partly behind Holmes's techniques but in stressing Bell's role in Holmes's genesis, Conan Doyle was in part distracting readers from his more obvious literary debt to Poe's M. Dupin. See Appendix F, pp. 271–76. Conan Doyle wrote about his enthusiasm for Poe in chapter VI of *Through the Magic Door*.

The pleasures of Conan Doyle's Holmes stories lie elsewhere. Yet there is significance in their unreason and identifying its presence is not merely pedantry. Real Victorian detectives had, to be sure, even at the end of the period, limited forensic texts and it is true that Conan Doyle was not, in the pages of the Holmes narratives, eschewing forms of science that actually existed in the real policing of Britain. He asked his reader to accept the self-evident violation of reason and probability nevertheless.[1] The centrality of "science" as the agent of human progress is proclaimed across the adventures, and with apparent triumphalism in *The Hound*, yet they work with illusions. A high point of Holmes's dealing with the empirical, *The Hound* banishes the appearance of the supernatural in favour of the dispensation of material logic, but it does so by upsetting the reality it commends. That which is hailed as science is present in Dr Conan Doyle's tales from beginning to end. Yet what is really to be celebrated in the stories of Sherlock Holmes is not scientific reason but Conan Doyle's power to create an engaging simulacrum of it; what is important is not the application of logic but the pleasure that a reader may take from a writer's fantasy of it. *The Hound of the Baskervilles* heartens us with its answers and cheers with its restorations; it is eminently a consoling narration (though readers will deplore the treatment of the hound). If one of literature's possibilities *qua* literature is to achieve imagined resolutions that readers are denied in life beyond the page, then *The Hound* is an exceptional example of a crime writer's ability to exploit that enchanting power to the full.

Conan Doyle shapes the world of the adventures so it answers to Holmes's "logic." In *The Hound* that world is adapted more conspicuously and in more ways than usual. The construction of the novel's setting is suggestive. It is a feature of Conan Doyle's imaginative contouring of the tale—at one level, of its unreality; at another, of its literariness—that the landscape of the moors should speak back richly to the thematic preoccupations of the novel. And if it is not a symbolic setting, it is certainly one which is inextricable from the text's inner workings. The eerie moor is, as is instantly apparent, the ideal location for a tale of a spectral hound, a gothic manor, an escaped convict, and Sir Charles's vio-

---

1 Conan Doyle was breezy about these problems in his autobiography: "I have never been nervous about details," he remarked, by way of defence of the Holmes stories, "and one must be masterful sometimes" (*Memories and Adventures*, 108).

lent death, and it is introduced to Sir Henry, fresh from a brighter, "modern" Canada, with the full power of the pathetic fallacy: "behind the peaceful and sunlit countryside there rose ever, dark against the evening sky, the long, gloomy curve of the moor, broken by the jagged and sinister hills" (p. 105). To be sure, the tale has something of the city dweller's prejudices against wild open land and the far reaches of England only relatively recently made accessible from London by train. It is a preference glimpsed in the novel's treatment of the local police force as largely invisible and of the local coroner's court as incompetent. But Holmes had expressed his doubts about the moral state of rural England and its distance from the agents of justice long before we hear of Dr Mortimer bringing him to Dartmoor. "'It is my belief,'" Holmes says to Watson as they travel into Hampshire in "The Adventure of the Copper Beeches" (1892),

["]that the lowest and vilest alleys in London do not present a more dreadful record of sin than does the smiling and beautiful countryside... There is no lane so vile that the scream of a tortured child, or the thud of a drunkard's blow, does not beget sympathy and indignation among the neighbours, and then the whole machinery of justice is ever so close to that a word of complaint can set it going, and there is but a step between the crime and the dock. But look at these lonely houses, each in its own fields, filled for the most part with poor ignorant folk who know little of the law. Think of the deeds of hellish cruelty, the hidden wickedness which may go on, year in, year out, in such places, and none the wiser." (*CSH* 323)

The Hound was built on that opinion.

On Dartmoor, countryside and crime are bound together, but there is more to this than Holmes admits in "The Copper Beeches." The barren primitiveness of terrain in *The Hound* resonates with a lingering question about human nature and the criminal. Baskerville Hall stands in lands marked by still preserved ancient human dwellings from pre-history. Basil Rathbone's film briefly transported what looks like Stonehenge from Salisbury Plain (in Wiltshire) to Dartmoor (in Devon) to make the point of ancient habitation forcibly. Conan Doyle's text does not need such help. Stapleton explains to Dr Watson the nature of the strange huts on the landscape: "'...they are,'" he says, "'the homes of our worthy ancestors. Prehistoric man lived thickly on the moor, and as no one in particular has lived there since, we find all his little arrangements exactly as he left them. These are his wigwams with the roofs off. You can even see his hearth and his couch if you have the curiosity to go inside'" (p. 118). The ancient homes serve, certainly, as a creepy backdrop to the events of the moor. But they also prompt speculation about how far those who now inhabit the landscape have advanced from the primitiveness of early life. Selden, the Notting Hill murderer, is, for one, suggested as a throw-back to a far more brutal, animalistic existence.[1] Living, no doubt, in a hut on the moor, he is in neat counterpoint to Holmes, similarly accommodated. As Watson and Sir Henry travel out on the rocky wastes in search of the truth about Barrymore's signal, they suddenly see the escaped prisoner:

> Over the rocks, in the crevice of which the candle burned, there was thrust out an evil yellow face, a terrible animal face, all seamed and scored with vile passions. Foul with Mire, with a bristling beard, and hung with matted hair, it might well have belonged to one of those old savages who dwelt in the burrows on the hillsides. The light beneath him was reflected in his small, cunning eyes which peered fiercely to right and left through the darkness like a crafty and savage animal who has heard the steps of the hunters. (pp. 143–44)

Dr Mortimer's publications—as we learn from Watson's *Medical Directory*—are on throw-backs. He has written "Is Disease a Reversion?," "Some Freaks of Atavism," and "Do We Progress?" They are relevant titles. Selden, as Watson sees him, is a freak of atavism, a reversion to a former state of being "seamed and scored with vile passions." Figured for a moment as the vile beast from whom modern humanity has developed, Selden is at once an indication of how far men have progressed and a discomforting reminder that all have such brutal forebears.

Conan Doyle provocatively allows a link between modern human beings and their ancient animal-like ancestors as he invites his reader to consider how widespread the advance of civilization has been. It is part of Dr Mortimer's paper: *do we progress?* Of course, Conan Doyle is not offering a simply deterministic view

---

1 On the Victorians and prehistory in general, see A. Bowdoin Van Riper, *Men Among the Mammoths: Victorian Science and the Discovery of Human Prehistory* (Chicago: U of Chicago P, 1993).

of human nature; he is not merely saying that we are determined by our inheritances. To take but one example, Selden's sister (now Mrs Barrymore) makes this clear. Free from the taint of her brother's nature, she contests any simplistic notion of crime as an inescapable quality of a family legacy. "Was it possible that this stolidly respectable person was of the same blood as one of the most notorious criminals in the country?" Dr Watson asks (p. 140). Yes, it is. But if Mrs Barrymore disproves crude biological determinism (notably, she offers a social account for her brother's crime), there is another of the country's most notorious criminals who seems to have been unable to escape the weight of biological history in which the novel is so interested. Stapleton appears a man of good quality, a civilized being. But he proves to possess the soul of a savage. The perceived brutality of the Neolith is manifest in him; he is also, in words used to describe Selden, "a man of violence, half animal and half demon" (p. 179), however much his true nature is hidden beneath manners and learning. His inhuman character becomes obvious by the close of the story but Conan Doyle offers hints earlier in representing him as part of the animal world. Initially, this seems barely of consequence. Watson, on first meeting Stapleton, sees him run crazily after a butterfly with his collector's net: "His gray clothes and jerky, zigzag, irregular progress made him not unlike some huge moth himself" (p. 119). On the verge of trapping Stapleton at the end of the adventure, Holmes turns Watson's observation into more threatening terms by thinking of the naturalist not as a free but a transfixed specimen: "'before tomorrow night he will be fluttering in our net as helpless as one of his own butterflies. A pin, a cork, and a card, and we add him to the Baker Street collection!'" (p. 183). A moth or a butterfly hardly suggest Stapleton's vicious inner nature—but the leakage between the world of man and animals has begun. The comparison becomes more suggestive in Holmes's view of Stapleton as a predator, a "'big, lean-jawed pike'" (p. 186) soon to be caught. But when Watson and Holmes discover Stapleton's wife bound, gagged, and beaten with a "clear red weal of a whip-lash across her neck," the text climatically announces Stapleton's affiliation with the non-human world. "'The brute!' cried Holmes" (p. 196). Stapleton is unmasked as a beast in his deepest nature: "desperate and dangerous" (p. 206), he is the real hound of the Baskervilles.

A throw-back to the ancestral inheritance of human barbarism, Stapleton is a figure like Stevenson's Dr Jekyll: his brutish, animalistic inner self is peculiarly alive. But one need not look so far along his family line for another grim heritage. The more recent past and the appalling nature of Hugo Baskerville, through whom the curse of the family began, are found in Stapleton too. For all his amateur and professional concern with the question of human inheritances—of particular prominence to the Victorians after Darwin's evolutionary biology—Dr Mortimer has never spotted that a picture of Hugo hanging in Baskerville Hall is uncommonly like Stapleton. "'It might be his portrait,'" declares Watson when Holmes points it out: "'Yes, it is an interesting instance of a throw-back,'" the detective composedly replies, "'which appears to be both physical and spiritual'" (p. 183). This, indeed, it is. Form and character have taken a leap backwards to the figure of Hugo Baskerville and Stapleton proves in another way that he is the expression of a contaminated blood line. Mrs Barrymore indicates that family legacies are not everything; Sir Charles and Sir Henry have inherited nothing of Sir Hugo's nature. But Stapleton is the embodiment of all that is bad about his history. And he, like Selden, must die.

Stapleton expires without pity. It is one with the binding moral logic and criminological thinking of Holmes's world. Part of the reassurance of Conan Doyle's stories lies in the assumption that responsibility for crime is always to be found in individuals who can be caught and punished. The crime is over, in this imaginative domain, when the criminal is apprehended; the forces of justice triumph in his capture or, as here, in his death (the sentence he would undoubtedly have received from the early twentieth-century English court). Contemporary detective fiction's darker concern with crime that is endemic, larger always than the single perpetrator, and never to be eradicated by the simple capture of individuals, is far from Conan Doyle's individual-centred thinking about the limiting and limits of foul play. Far too from *The Hound* is any notion, despite its concern with the determining power of ancestry, that the criminal can be easily absolved of personal responsibility for his actions. Stapleton's bloodline may be corrupt but he is guilty nevertheless; a bad inheritance offers no grounds for exculpation. Indeed, only insanity relieves a man, to any degree, of responsibility. Selden, a violent murderer, is condemned by the plot, if not by the law, to die—his attempted escape abroad, which his family had planned, is destroyed. The viciousness of the Notting Hill murderer is never overlooked and Holmes senses no remorse in laughing with relief over his corpse, momentarily mistaken for Sir Henry's. Selden and Stapleton are alike in their brutality and their fate, but they are different in one respect, for there is uncertainty about the state of Selden's mind. The formal commutation of his death sentence by the court is due to "doubts as to his complete sanity, so atrocious was his conduct" (p. 106). That equivocation makes possible a small but significant pause in the text's moral revulsion against the man who committed a crime of "wanton brutality" (p. 106) in North West London. Regarding Mrs Barrymore's distress at the news of her brother's death, Watson notices and does not deny the pity she feels: "To all the world," Watson notes, "he was the man of violence, half animal and half demon; but to her he always remained the little wilful boy of her own girlhood, the child who had clung to her hand. Evil indeed is the man who has not one woman to mourn him" (p. 179). Jack Stapleton has no such griever. Dreadfully sane, the text gives him total responsibility for his deeds.

Selden's emblematic role in the novel is to point up its conflict between civilization and brutality, a duality brought together in the person of Stapleton. Processes of civilization are in the foreground in this novel, and, to a lesser extent, so are those of modernization. If *The Hound* thinks about man's ethical movement from his origins to the present, it also considers questions of more local improvement. At the opening of the text, the Baskerville family is in a precarious position. Sir Charles had inherited an ancestral home in disarray. Only his newly found South African money—the Baskerville estate proves to be worth nearly a million pounds made largely from investments—provides a timely injection of cash into a faltering manorial economy. It is, in turn-of-the-century terms, enormous wealth and Sir Charles is no miser, intending to put his money to wise use as philanthropist, landowner, and tenant of a great house. "[It] is common talk," Dr Mortimer tells Holmes and Watson at the beginning, reading from the newspaper,

["]how large were those schemes of reconstruction and improvement which have been interrupted by his death. Being himself childless, it was his openly expressed desire that the whole countryside should, within his own lifetime, profit by his good fortune, and many will have personal reasons for bewailing his untimely end. His generous donations to local and county charities have been frequently chronicled in these columns" (p. 63).

Possessed of fortune made from imperial industry, Sir Charles dies before he is able to use it as he hoped. Financially strong, he is physically weak, and he is also childless. Again, it is from overseas that aid for the English landowning family comes: in the figure of Sir Henry, the endangered prospects of Baskerville Hall and the rural community dependent on its wellbeing find renewed hope. Sir Henry is English, but he has been made by the New World—his "By thunder" vocabulary amusingly and gauchely tries to insist on his North American upbringing. Conan Doyle was partly intending to please his New World audience, whose enjoyment of Sherlock Holmes was equal to England's, by importing a character from Canada, a country Conan Doyle admired. But Sir Henry also hints at a broader cultural point about the reconfiguration of international allegiances that, to Conan Doyle's mind, will fortify post-Victorian England (it is hard to see, as Catherine Wynne would have it, that the real subtext of this novel is Ireland).[1] Ancient English social hierarchies are restored at the close of *The Hound*; the old ancestral home is occupied again, ready to be brought back to serviceable life, and, one assumes, Sir Charles's sense of responsibility to communities around him will be honoured by his nephew. The local Dartmoor economy will be strengthened once Holmes has vanquished Stapleton. Guaranteeing English rural stability, the detective is an agent for the restoration of established values and traditional patterns of life. But it is a North American-trained baronet spending South African money who will complete his work and rejuvenate a squiral family that, without help from Holmes and from abroad, would most likely have perished or been radically corrupted.

The modern world will come to Baskerville Hall, though it will take more than the "row of electric lamps" (p. 107) Sir Henry

---

1 Here is a sample of her argument: "*The Hound of the Baskervilles* is preoccupied with a collision between the forces of 'backwardness' and 'advancement,' a superstitious past in conflict with a supposedly progressive and rational future. It is reminiscent, then, of contemporaneous Ireland ... Just as the Irish landscape is populated with dangerous and violent agrarian societies, Dartmoor also features an escaped convict with murderous propinquities [*propensities?*]. It is notable, too, that the Land League progenitor Michael Davitt had been imprisoned for six years in Dartmoor in the 1870s for involvement in Fenian activities in England," *The Colonial Conan Doyle: British Imperialism, Irish Nationalism, and the Gothic* (Westport: Greenwood, 2002), 69.

cheerfully believes will transform his home. The conclusion of "The Adventure of the Speckled Band" is not so ambitious. No glimpse of the restoration of a whole community's social order is perceived in the death of Dr Grimesby Roylott, even if his demise means that Miss Stoner may safely marry Percy Armitage and inherit substantial wealth. Holmes's agency for good is more limited in Stoke Moran than on Dartmoor. But the tale has, nevertheless, a quietly suggestive ending in its presentation of Holmes not only as detective but also implicitly as judge, jury, and executioner. At the close of the later "Adventure of the Abbey Grange" (1904), Holmes's thinking about the by-passing of official law is configured in searching moral terms. Privileging justice over the narrower demands of the law, the tale opens up a question about the relationship between the statute books and mercy, between the law and generosity. Holmes has before him at the finish of this adventure a man who has struck down another, in protection of a woman he loves (miserably married to the now murdered man). The slain individual is a violent drunkard who is despised by his wife, and in this distinctive case, Holmes perceives that a greater injustice would occur in turning the murderer over to the police than in allowing him to go free. In the seclusion of 221B Baker Street, Holmes proposes his own mini-trial:

["]Watson, you are a British jury, and I never met a man who was more eminently fitted to represent one. I am the judge. Now, gentleman of the jury, you have heard the evidence. Do you find the prisoner guilty or not guilty?"
"Not guilty, my lord," said I.
"*Vox populi, vox Dei.* You are acquitted, Captain Crocker. So long as the law does not find some other victim you are safe from me. Come back to this lady in a year, and may her future and yours justify us in the judgment which we have pronounced this night!" (*CSH* 650)

The moment is a significant one in the adventures not only because it affirms with clarity the blunt nature of the law as an instrument of justice in the complex affairs of human beings but also because it permits Conan Doyle's opening up of Holmes's moral being. "Once or twice in my career," the detective tells Watson, in a self-reflective moment, justifying his alternative trial, "I feel that I have done more real harm by my discovery of the criminal than ever he had done by his crime. I have learned caution now, and I had rather play tricks with the law of England than with my own conscience" (*CSH* 646). Recognizing the grave ill that legal judgment may—legally—bring into being, "The Abbey Grange" narrativizes an exceptional moral occasion when rule must be short-circuited in favour of the ethical. In the context of the broader cultural perception in the later nineteenth century that most actual detectives were themselves semi-criminals,[1] Conan Doyle's depiction of the law-bending Holmes working in the service of a higher justice is a neat upset to a widely circulating stereotype. Through Holmes's imagined conscience, Conan Doyle deftly disturbs a commonplace to propose a consequential question about the limits of legal judgment in a genre, a series of adventures, which has customarily depended on coincidence between the law and justice.[2]

The conclusion of "The Speckled Band" is dominated by a different conception of Holmes. Belonging to another side of Conan Doyle's representation of his detective, it approaches no equivalent level of thoughtfulness about the nature of justice, it inserts no wedge between what is legal and what is moral, and it offers no access to a complex ethical conscience at work in Sherlock Holmes. Rather, in differently allowing the detective to act in place of the agents of the law, it invites recognition of Conan Doyle's faith in Holmes, in 1892, as a national figure whose trust is in the established procedures and institutions of national life. Striking the alleged swamp adder with his stick, Holmes forces it to return to its owner where it fatally attacks him. Watson can do no good to save Roylott (he does not even verify that he is dead) and Holmes is left to concede that he has been the man who, saving the criminal from the gallows, has occasioned his demise by other means and anticipated the judgment of the court. But this is no matter for regret: "'I am[,] no doubt,'" the detective says, "'indirectly responsible for Dr. Grimesby Roylott's death, and I cannot say that it is likely to weigh very heavily upon my conscience'" (p. 237). To a modern reader—particularly in countries where the death sentence has been abolished—it is an uncomfortable moment. But it is indicative of the nature and representative force which Holmes possesses at this point in his literary career so that, sufficiently expressive of the best values of his

---

1 See Stephan Petrow, "The Rise of the Detective in London, 1869–1914," *Criminal Justice History*, 14 (1993): 91–108.

2 See also the end of "The Adventure of the Illustrious Client" (1924).

nation, the detective—even in a matter of life and death—may stand in for its whole system of justice. In *The Hound of the Baskervilles*, Conan Doyle has Holmes act to secure an established element of the nation's social order and hierarchy in the rejuvenation of an ancestral house on Dartmoor; in "The Speckled Band," the detective's association with another defining feature of the nation's social order is such that Conan Doyle makes him a substitute for it entirely.

Holmes is imagined as a national figure, rooted, most evidently in *The Hound*, in the affirmation of long-lasting values and active in their reform. No wonder at the end of "His Last Bow: An Epilogue of Sherlock Holmes" (1917), the detective—in a story that opens on the day after the outbreak of World War I and two days before Britain's entry into the conflict—is allowed bardic words of national prophecy. He speaks for the whole kingdom and heartens it with an assurance of the improving consequences of even the darkest days to come. Contemplating the power of Germany to rock the stability of a continent, Holmes, looking out to a moonlit sea, remarks solemnly that an "east wind is coming." Watson, missing Holmes's metaphor, corrects him: "'I think not, Holmes. It is very warm.'" Watson's winningly literalist misunderstanding prompts the detective's famous verge-of-a-new-nation reply that hails a process by which, however painfully, England will be made fitter:

> "Good old Watson! You are the one fixed point in a changing age. There's an east wind coming all the same, such a wind as never blew on England yet. It will be cold and bitter, Watson, and a good many of us may wither before its blast. But it's God's own wind none the less, and a cleaner, better, stronger land will lie in the sunshine when the storm has cleared.["]
> (*CSH* 980)

They are challengingly optimistic words in 1917. Given Conan Doyle's investiture of Holmes as a tutelary power over the nation's wellbeing, as its encourager at points of national trial, and as a Burkean defender and restorer of its traditions (Holmes's origins in Conan Doyle's memory of Dr Bell, the Scottish surgeon [see p. 21, note 1], are far gone in this multiple sense of his Englishness), it is tempting to read a number of earlier tales, including "The Speckled Band," in terms of broader nationalist discourses. Holmes's national status suggests at times that some of the adventures work to test English virtues against other nations. "The Speckled Band" certainly could offer itself in this frame as a subdued imperial drama. Sherlock Holmes may be perceived—the "home" of his name offering obvious significance—as elegantly representative of an orderly law-abiding England who triumphs over a criminal closely associated with a nation at the far-flung reaches of the empire. From such a reading, India—where Dr Roylott worked, married, and had his daughters—emerges coded in almost tiresomely familiar Orientalist terms of violence, danger, and death. Dr Roylott's first murder (or manslaughter, probably) occurs here and it is in India that his transformation from successful medical practitioner to the "morose and disappointed man" (p. 215) who gloomily returns to England is effected. All forms of menace belong with the sub-continent in this narrative: aside, obviously, from Dr Roylott, there is the baboon and the cheetah, of which the local community is in continual fear, and the literal perpetrator of the crime, the *soi-disant* swamp adder. When Holmes remarks that "The idea of using a form of poison which could not possibly be discovered by any chemical test" (i.e., from the deadly snake), was just what "would occur to a clever and ruthless man who had had an Eastern training" (p. 236), the link in the person of Dr Roylott between Asia and deadly power is clinched.

The principled, orderly English mind of Holmes vanquishes the mysterious and deadly power of the orient. It is not hard to see why such a description may seem apt for the imperial confrontation lying beneath this tale. Yet there must be caution. The *sum* of Conan Doyle's thoughts about the Indian sub-continent, or the role of Great Britain in her governance, is not to be found comprehensively inscribed in so slender a thing as the subtext of a brief adventure; how much less his views on empire or the East altogether.[1] Writers may use locations on the globe without necessarily dramatizing the full range of their views on international

---

1 Readers may want to turn, for example, to Conan Doyle's *The Green Flag and Other Stories of War and Sport* (London: Smith, Elder, 1900), *The Great Boer War* (Leipzig: Tauchnitz, 1900), and *The Crime of the Congo* (London: Hutchinson, 1909) for a fuller picture of the author's thinking about empire in the middle period of his life. *The Mystery of Cloomber* (1889) is about a British general cursed for killing a Buddhist holy man which carefully avoids a simplistic privileging of West over East.

politics. And it is worth recalling a humbler fact. India is an imperial possession for Conan Doyle's readers but it is also, of course, simply a distant location. There are many such throughout the Holmes canon. Requiring, for the mystery to function, a form of poison that is unknown to the British coroner's court, the narrative imports it (in fact invents it) from a vaguely conceived India (*The Mystery of Cloomber* was an early story to look in the same direction). Such a straightforward solution to a crime writer's problem cannot bear the pressure of too much scrutiny. Holmes, moreover, may be closely associated with the defence and improvement of his country but the broader reflection on English wellbeing in "The Speckled Band"—if that is what it is—is hardly buoyant. There is no straightforward confrontation between an orderly healthy England and the deadly knowledge of the East. Even more gloomily than in *The Hound*, "The Speckled Band" evokes an England in decline, an ancient aristocratic family, a line once the pride of the ruling class, which has crumbled. The moral bankruptcy of a name formerly "among the richest in England" (p. 214) is climatically reached in Dr Roylott who has inherited the family curse rather than its long-lost prestige, possessing a "Violence of temper approaching to mania [that is] hereditary in the men of the family" (p. 215). Holmes may conquer the vicious doctor but he can do nothing, unlike in *The Hound*, to revive the fortunes of that decaying family. Even Helen Stoner, the central female character, dies shortly after the events of the tale: family extinction is at hand. Conan Doyle's figuration of the fitness of the ruling classes of the new imperial power in this narrative is nothing but ominous (see Adam Badeau, Appendix H, pp. 277–82).

It is not on the workings of an imperial subtext that I want to close this account of two of the most widely read Holmes adventures but on the possibilities of another, and to its author more important, subtextual engagement. Sir Arthur Conan Doyle may be most remembered firstly for his creation of Sherlock Holmes, and secondly for Professor Challenger, yet he is also recalled— rarely sympathetically, often with bafflement, not infrequently with embarrassment—for his commitment, made clear later in his life, to spiritualism. In the 1939 Hollywood version of *The Hound*, that interest is acknowledged in a way which is suggestive not just of Conan Doyle's mind but also of an inner debate in the novel itself. During dinner with the Stapletons—Sir Henry, both host and hostess, and Dr and Mrs Mortimer are present—Sidney Lanfield has Mrs Mortimer introduced as a medium who has allegedly been in contact with the spirit of Sir Charles. After some delay, she agrees to a séance. The film, which was a remarkable achievement for a director whose name was made as a vaudeville entertainer and gag writer, appears poised on the verge of committing itself one way or another to the possibility of spiritualist powers. Will Mrs Mortimer successfully call up the ghost of Sir Charles? Will a hint of the criminal's identity be learned from beyond the grave? Shrewdly avoiding making any statement, the film has the séance broken up by the distant howl of the hound (whose status at this point in the movie—real or supernatural?—is appropriately open-ended). Lanfield's use of a medium and the film's drawing back from a judgment of her capacity is apt and so is his decision to make her the wife of Dr Mortimer, the man of science. For the novel itself has a hidden sub-theme about the possibilities of the supernatural, which is not simply part of the gothic *frisson* of the tale. Rather, it is a matter of importance to Conan Doyle himself, a man of science and one increasingly concerned with the nature of the paranormal.

Writing his two-volume *The History of Spiritualism* (1926), Conan Doyle, by then President of the London Spiritualist Alliance and the British College of Psychic Science, as well as President d'Honneur de la Fédèration Spirite Internationale, remarked that he had been pursuing questions about the nature of the spirit world for "nearly forty years," during which he had "attended innumerable séances in many lands."[1] Beginning as a "convinced materialist,"[2] he told his readers in 1918, a scientist intolerant of any suggestion of the supernatural, his innate curiosity had led him to investigate the credibility of spiritualist experience despite the public risk to his reputation. Applying the scientific method, as he saw it, to supernatural data, he joined the Society for Psychical Research, gradually recognizing what he believed to be the factuality of the paranormal in the face of widespread institutional ridicule. In 1917, Conan Doyle at last "declared [himself] to be satisfied with the evidence"[3] and in 1918 brought out *The New Revelation*, the first of his spiritualist books (see Appendix J, pp. 289–95). Many regarded Conan Doyle

---

1   Arthur Conan Doyle, *The History of Spiritualism*, 2 vols in one (New York: Arno, 1975), I. 23.

2   Arthur Conan Doyle, *The New Revelation* (London: Hodder and Stoughton, 1918), 17.

3   Ibid., 16.

as having abandoned his scientific principles to believe in fantasy (even more so with the case of the Cottingley fairies).[1] But Conan Doyle saw a common search for indisputable evidence, guaranteed by the sustained integrity of the searcher, united the scientific method with spiritualist conviction. In inscribing *The History of Spiritualism* to the physicist, educational administrator, and spiritualist Sir Oliver Lodge,[2] Conan Doyle was making the point even from the dedication page that science and spiritualism could, under the right circumstances, live together.

But it was more often a hostile relationship. Conan Doyle noted with irritation the rejection of spiritualism by the nineteenth-century panoply of Huxley, Tyndall, Spencer, and Darwin in *The New Revelation*[3]; and in *The History* he was generally vexed with empiricist narrow-mindedness. "British science," he wrote, recounting the history of early North American mediums, "and, indeed, science the world over, has shown the same intolerance and want of elasticity which marked those early days."[4] It was intolerance whose force he understood because it had once been his own position. But in the middle of his career, neither intolerant nor wholly a believer, Conan Doyle was sufficiently immersed in a search for what he saw as reliable fact about the Other Side that subtle traces marked his imaginative writing. *The Hound of the Baskervilles*, written from the midst of this process, registers in the antechambers of its ideas Conan Doyle's interests, figuring anxieties about how his developing notions might be received and, with a revealing silence,

---

1 See Arthur Conan Doyle: *The Coming of the Fairies* (London: Hodder and Stoughton, 1922). The photographs of the fairies—supposedly taken by two girls, Elsie Wright and Frances Griffiths, in 1917—were to be revealed as frauds in the early 1980s, long after Conan Doyle's death.

2 The eminent physicist, Sir Oliver Lodge (1851–1940), was the first Principal of the University of Birmingham. A specialist in x-rays, radio waves, and telegraphy, he was also seriously interested in the application of scientific methods to understanding the paranormal, becoming President of the Society of Psychical Research after Frederic William Henry Myers (1843–1901), distinguished essayist and one of the Society's founders. Lodge's book, *Raymond: or, Life and Death: With Examples of the Evidence for Survival of Memory and Affection after Death* (1916), about the death of his son in World War I and contact with him through mediums, attained great popularity. It is widely discussed in *The New Revelation*.

3 Conan Doyle, *The New Revelation*, 23.

4 Conan Doyle, *The History of Spiritualism*, I.138.

refraining from any adjudication between materialist and super-naturalist understandings of knowledge's limits.

The Hound's responsiveness to Conan Doyle's private dilemma obtains signal clarity in places. After Dr Mortimer has revealed the fact of the giant hound's footprints and recounted the chilling story of the family curse, Holmes and he are confronted by a question of supernatural explanations. Mortimer explains why he had not called in Holmes promptly to investigate Sir Charles's death. "'There is,'" he remarks, inaugurating the discussion in which Holmes and Mortimer conflict:

["]a realm in which the most acute and most experienced of detectives is helpless."

"You mean that the thing is supernatural?"

"I did not positively say so."

"No, but you evidently think it."

"Since the tragedy, Mr. Holmes, there have come to my ears several incidents which are hard to reconcile with the settled order of Nature."

"For example?"

"I find that before the terrible event occurred several people had seen a creature upon the moor which corresponds with this Baskerville demon, and which could not possibly be any animal known to science. They all agreed that it was a huge creature, luminous, ghastly, and spectral. I have cross-examined these men, one of them a hard-headed countryman, one a farrier, and one a moorland farmer, who all tell the same story of this dread-ful apparition, exactly corresponding to the hell-hound of the legend. I assure you that there is a reign of terror in the district, and that it is a hardy man who will cross the moor at night."

"And you, a trained man of science, believe it to be supernat-ural?"

"I do not know what to believe."

Holmes shrugged his shoulders.

"I have hitherto confined my investigations to this world," said he. "In a modest way I have combated evil, but to take on the Father of Evil himself would, perhaps, be too ambitious a task. Yet you must admit that the footmark is material."

"The original hound was material enough to tug a man's throat out, and yet he was diabolical as well."

"I see that you have quite gone over to the supernaturalists [...]" (pp. 71–72)

At one level, *The Hound* appears to map the triumph of the scientific mind over the supernatural explanation. The moorland farmers' beliefs are, by the end, revealed as misplaced, the apparently settled order of Nature reaffirmed, and Dr Mortimer is reconverted from the side of the supernaturalists (if that is where he was) in understanding the malign but human force that slayed his friend. In appearing to exalt the material over the supernatural, the novel might well seem to answer Conan Doyle's private questions unequivocally.

"'And you, a trained man of science, believe [in the] supernatural?'" Holmes asks Dr Mortimer with surprise. This question is also implicitly addressed to Conan Doyle himself, and the exchange covertly processes a little of its author's own complicated internal debate, painfully conscious as he was of the habitual reception of spiritualism by much of the scientific community. Recollection of the collapse of a number of scientific reputations in the nineteenth century offered no encouragement: the chemist Sir William Crookes (1832–1919) forfeited his scientific credibility on his acknowledgment of spiritualism; the physician and friend of Dickens, John Elliotson (1791–1868), in accepting the authenticity of mesmerism and then of the spirit world, was deprived orthodoxy's recognition. Falls from grace gave Conan Doyle pause as he considered the vulnerability of his own position and men like Crookes would always symbolize to him the difficulties scientists who believed in spiritualism would face.[1] Later, he would extensively dramatize a shift from scientific scorn to acceptance, a Thomasian movement of doubt to faith, in the Professor Challenger story, *The Land of Mists* (1926). Refracting a fretful position as man of science and increasingly convinced member of séances, Conan Doyle, well before that campaigning but touching novel, constructs a scene in *The Hound*'s opening stages that has Holmes as one of his creator's own antagonists, a figure charged with a rebuke he (Conan Doyle) knew he was susceptible to himself.[2]

1   Cf. Arthur Conan Doyle, *The Land of Mists* (New York: Doubleday, Doran, 1933), 8, 61–65.
2   In thinking about the role of science in relationship to unknown powers, it is worth bearing in mind that even a novel as early as *The Mystery of Cloomber* was intrigued by what science could not grasp. "For what is science?," the narrator inquires at the end: "Science is the consensus of opinion of scientific men, and history has shown that it is slow to accept truth. Science sneered at Newton for twenty years. Science proved mathematically that an iron ship could not swim, and science declared that a steamship could not cross the Atlantic" (*The Mystery of Cloomber* [Thirsk: Stratus, 2003], 152).

But this is not *The Hound*'s only statement about the limits of human knowledge or its sole engagement with its author's secret history. The plot, like Sidney Lanfield's film, leaves open a door that matters, though it is easily missed. Stapleton's hound proves to be material, the crime terrestrial, but what is really discredited in *The Hound* is not the supernatural but a supernatural explanation. There is, as we have learnt by the end, nothing paranormal occurring on Dartmoor at the close of the nineteenth century but, rather, the corrupt manipulation of an illusion of it. Holmes's scientific mind—its fabricated nature set to one side for a moment—banishes not the uncanny but the mimicry of it. The chance of supernatural events that are not fraudulent but real, not staged but true, remains as intriguingly possible at the beginning of the novel as at its end. Discarding Stapleton, the text jettisons the fraudster—but not the man of authentic paranormal powers. The novel acts like the convinced spiritualist of Conan Doyle's psychic histories to reject "fraudulent mediums"[1] from the phoney séance; it half anticipates the debunking of the false Silas Linden, impostor supernaturalist, in *The Land of Mists*.[2] Speaking obliquely of what would become the most important belief of its author's life, *The Hound of the Baskervilles* shapes Conan Doyle's trepidation about the response of the scientific community to the claims of supernaturalism; but, despite the tempting appearance otherwise, refuses to discredit the experiential possibility, somewhere, some time, of the authentically paranormal. "'How often have I said to you,'" Holmes remarks to Watson in *The Sign of Four* (1890), "'that when you have eliminated the impossible, whatever remains, *however improbable*, must be the truth?'"[3] Conan Doyle, by 1917, would say the same in deducing certainty from the seemingly improbable evidence for the spirits. The process by which he arrived at that unpopular conviction was etched into the subtext of his most famous novel.

Sherlock Holmes continues to exist between the world of literature and actuality. In the "Preface" to *The Case-Book of Sherlock Holmes* (1927), Conan Doyle hoped that his detective would find rest at the end of his labours in "some fantastic limbo for the children of imagination, some strange, impossible place" (*CSH* [983]). It has not happened, and Holmes continues his vivid life

---

1   Conan Doyle, *The New Revelation*, 19.
2   See Conan Doyle, *The Land of Mists*, chapter IX.
3   *CSH* 111. Italic original.

both in and out of his original textual locations. How appropriate it is that *The Hound of the Baskervilles*, Conan Doyle's most appealing Holmes story, should include within its narrative and thematic range a consideration of identities that are not what they seem, and invite, at its centre, an unobtrusive but weighty question about what forms of being, what shapes of existence, the world has space for. Holmes crosses from the fictional into the actual with pleasing disregard for his proper realm. Conan Doyle came to believe in the possibility of other more important border crossings, between our world and the Other Side, and it is unexpectedly coherent with the developing pattern of his thought that his most successful Holmes story, celebrated the world over, should, among its many other interests, transact with the matter he would one day come radiantly to call the New Revelation. *The Hound* spoke quietly of Conan Doyle's argument with himself. In the uncertain fate of Stapleton—has he really drowned in the mire? might he, like the apparently once-slain Holmes, have escaped and be ready to return in another adventure?—the novel focuses for a brief and unsettling moment on a question about survival beyond the tomb that suggests the great issue of what may happen not to a fictional character but a living human after death. Conan Doyle had once brought Holmes back from the dead as perhaps he may have thought of bringing Stapleton: the first readers of *The Hound* were, at the broadest level, silently compelled to ask a question about the detective's survival and whether the novel signified the *return* of Sherlock Holmes from the apparently fatal Reichenbach Falls. But at a far deeper level, the possibility of truly living beyond the grave was to be an issue of the most conspicuous value in the spiritual life of Arthur Conan Doyle. In making contact with a matter of such substance for its author's inner self, this outstanding novel acquired flecks of personal seriousness that added autobiographical consequence to its already enthralling narrative power.

A Note on the Authorship of *The Hound of the Baskervilles*

There is a question about the composition of *The Hound* and the role of the journalist and novelist (Bertram) Fletcher Robinson (1872–1907). Robinson went on holiday with Conan Doyle— recently back, frayed, from medical duties in the Boer War—in March 1901 to Norfolk. He seems to have discussed legends of spectral dogs with Conan Doyle who, by the end of the month, had taken up the idea for a new story, which presently became a Holmes adventure (it did not begin as one). In the first instalment of *The Hound* in *The Strand Magazine*, the creator of Sherlock Holmes remarked: "This story owes its inception to my friend, Mr. Fletcher Robinson, who has helped me both in the general plot and in the local details."[1] In the first English book edition, this was changed to a letter which declared:

> Mr Dear Robinson
> It was your account of a West-Country legend that this tale owes its inception. For this and for your help in the details all thanks.[2]

It was slightly less of an acknowledgement. In the first American edition, Conan Doyle wrote:

> Mr Dear Robinson
> It was your account of a west country legend which first suggested the idea of this little tale to my mind.
> For this, and for the help which you have given me in its evolution, all thanks.[3]

Robinson's contribution is now telling a story that *suggested* to Conan Doyle a novel. Conan Doyle made his final public statement in the 1929 edition of the complete long stories, saying that *The Hound* had arisen

> from a remark by that fine fellow whose premature death was a loss to the world, Fletcher Robinson, that there was spectral dog near his house on Dartmoor. That remark was the inception of the book, but I should add that the plot and every word of the actual narrative was my own.[4]

The narrative implied by these changing acknowledgements is not wholly clear and further complicated by private letters. For example, Conan Doyle informed his mother in April 1901 (before seri-

---

1 *The Strand Magazine*, xxii (August 1901): [123].
2 Dedication, A. Conan Doyle, *The Hound of the Baskervilles* (London: Newnes, 1902).
3 Quoted in Baring Gould, II.113.
4 Ibid.

alization began in August) that the "highly dramatic idea" for the forthcoming tale was "owe[d] to Robinson" (Robson, xii) and the editor of the *Strand*, before the tale was received, was told that "I must do it with my friend Fletcher Robinson, and his name must appear with mine. I can answer for the yarn being all my own, my own style without dilution, since your readers like that. But he gave me the central idea and the local colour, and I feel his name must appear" (Robson, xii–xiii).

Some have sensed a scandal behind all this, suggesting that Conan Doyle improperly, if not illegally, deprived his friend of both the prestige and the income from joint authorship. Rodger Garrick-Steele in the exceptionally poorly produced *The House of the Baskervilles* (2003)—which obtained some media and TV coverage—infamously went much further to suggest that Conan Doyle had his friend murdered so as to disguise the truth about his real share in the novel. There is no hard evidence that Robinson wrote any of *The Hound*. Conan Doyle, certainly, allowed S.S. McClure to disperse the original manuscript around North America using individual framed pages as advertisements and would not have done so if it revealed another's (unacknowledged) hand.[1] There is no reason why a principled man such as Conan Doyle would have committed an offence against his friend, let alone have him killed. The notion is ridiculous. What is likely is that in the first excitement about ideas for a new story, Conan Doyle felt the as-yet-unwritten text would indeed be partly Robinson's because they had talked much about its possibilities and Robinson had suggested a key detail of its plot from his knowledge of folklore. It might be added, however, that tales of phantom dogs in the English countryside, the black shucks of legend, are widely-known staples of folk tales: Robinson hardly deserves credit for passing specialized information to Conan Doyle.[2] As Conan Doyle worked out the details of the novel later, however, turning it from suggestive idea to solid plot, the narrative became more

1 Only one complete chapter of the ms is known to survive: "The Man on the Tor," Chapter XI, is now in the New York Public Library.
2 Benjamin J. Fisher notes some other ways in which Conan Doyle may have acquired knowledge that helped him writing *The Hound* in Benjamin F. Fisher, "*The Hound of the Baskervilles* 100 Years After: A Review Essay," *English Literature in Transition (1880-1920)*, 47 (2004): 185 and 190n.

his own; by the time he had actually written it, his initial thoughts about co-ownership seemed impossibly generous. He quite properly thanked Robinson for being involved in the inception but he was the only person who had, and could have, written the tale as we have it.

Arthur Conan Doyle: A Brief Chronology

22 May 1859
>Arthur Ignatius Conan Doyle born at 11 Picardy Place, Edinburgh, eldest son of the artist, draughtsman, and eventual alcoholic Charles Altamont Doyle (1832–1893) and his Irish wife Mary, *née* Foley (1838–1921).

1868–70 Hodder preparatory school (Roman Catholic)
1870–75 Stonyhurst College, Clitheroe, Lancashire; Catholic faith eroded.
1875–76 Continues education at Feldkirch, Austria.
1876 Enters Edinburgh University medical school.

6 September 1879
>First published story, "The Mystery of Sasassa Valley," *Chambers's Edinburgh Journal*.

February–September 1880
>Serves as a ship's doctor on the Greenland whaler *Hope*.

October 1881–January 1882
>Served on the steamer SS *Mayumba* on its voyage to west Africa; meets dying anti-slavery leader Henry Highland Garnet (1815–82). Tells mother that he is no longer a Catholic. After unsuccessful attempt at general practice in Plymouth, he is more successful in Southsea, Portsmouth. Publishes a number of stories including "J. Habakuk Jephson's Statement" (1884) about, and to some extent creating, the mystery of the *Mary Celeste* (which Conan Doyle called the *Marie Celeste*).

1885 Receives MD from the University of Edinburgh. On 6 August, marries Louisa/Louise (but usually called Touie) Hawkins (1856/7–1906).

1887 Publication of the first Sherlock Holmes adventure, *A Study in Scarlet.*

1889 Daughter, Mary, born; *Micah Clarke: His Statement as made to his Three Grandchildren, Joseph, Gervas and Reuben, during the Hard Winter of 1734*; *The Mystery of Cloomber*.

1890	*The Sign of Four; The Firm of Girdlestone.*
1891	*The White Company;* moves to London; gives up a poor specialist eye practice to concentrate on writing.
1892	Son, Alleyne Kingsley, born; *The Adventures of Sherlock Holmes; The Great Shadow.*
1893	"The Final Problem;" Louisa diagnosed with tuberculosis. Death of Charles Altamont Doyle; by now Conan Doyle is a member of the Society for Psychical Research and attending many séances.
1894	Lecture tour of the United States.
1896	*The Exploits of Brigadier Gerard.*
1897	Meets and falls in love with Jean Leckie (later his second wife).
1898	*The Tragedy of Korosko.*
1900	Serves as doctor in South Africa (the Boer War); *The Great Boer War;* Unionist and Tariff Reform candidate for Parliament at Edinburgh (unsuccessful).
1901	Serialization of *The Hound of the Baskervilles* begins in *The Strand Magazine.*
1902	*The War in South Africa: Its Cause and Conduct;* knighted for work in South Africa.
1903	*Adventures of Gerard;* Sherlock Holmes returns in "The Adventure of the Empty House;" release of earliest known and very brief "film" of Sherlock Holmes (made 1900) called "Sherlock Holmes Baffled."
1905	*The Return of Sherlock Holmes.*
1906	Involved in movement for Divorce Law Reform; death of Lady Conan Doyle from tuberculosis; *Sir Nigel;* candidate for Parliament (unsuccessful again).
1907	Marries Jean Leckie; *Through the Magic Door.*
1909	Son Denis born.
1910	Son Adrian born; "The Speckled Band" successfully performed as play in London.
1912	Daughter Jean Lena Annette born, later to become head of the Women's Royal Air Force; *The Lost World,* the most popular of the Professor Challenger stories.
1914	Serialization of *The Valley of Fear* begins; Great War begins.
1918	Captain Kingsley Conan Doyle dies from influenza after being wounded in battle; *The New Revelation;* Armistice, 11 November.

1920	*British Campaign in France and Flanders* (6 vols).
1921	*The Wanderings of a Spiritualist.*
1922	*The Coming of the Fairies*; lecturing in America.
1926	*The History of Spiritualism* (2 vols).
1927	*The Case-Book of Sherlock Holmes*; *Poems*.
1930	*Edge of the Unknown*; dies at "Windlesham," his home in Crowborough in Sussex on 7 July; buried in his rose garden; in 1953, after the sale of "Windlesham," Sir Arthur and his second wife (died 1940) are reburied in the churchyard of All Saints' Church, Minstead, in the New Forest, Hampshire. His grave stone is headed with the motto "Steel True/Blade Straight" and commemorates him simply as "Patriot, Physician, Man of Letters."

A Note on the Text

The Hound of the Baskervilles
The novel was first published in serial form in *The Strand Magazine* (August 1901–April 1902); the text used here is that of the first English book edition, published in London by George Newnes on 25 March 1902. I have silently corrected one or two obvious errors. Some textual variants are recorded in the notes but it should be observed that none is of real significance for the meaning of the published forms. Sidney Paget (1860–1908) provided black-and-white illustrations for *The Strand* edition, some of which were retained in the book version. One is reproduced here as the frontispiece.

"The Adventure of the Speckled Band"
The text used here is that of the first publication of the story in *The Strand Magazine*, February 1892, pp. 142–57. Sidney Paget illustrated this narrative too (illustrations not reproduced here).

The Hound of the Baskervilles
Another Adventure of Sherlock Homes

My dear Robinson

It was to your account of a West-Country legend that this tale owes its inception. For this and for your help in the details all thanks.

Yours most truly,

A. Conan Doyle

Hindhead
Haslemere[1]

---

1   See "Note on The Authorship of *The Hound of the Baskervilles*," pp. 39–42.

Chapter I

Mr. Sherlock Holmes

Mr. Sherlock Holmes, who was usually very late in the mornings, save upon those not infrequent occasions when he stayed up all night,[1] was seated at the breakfast table. I stood upon the hearth-rug and picked up the stick which our visitor had left behind him the night before. It was a fine, thick piece of wood, bulbous-headed, of the sort which is known as a "Penang lawyer."[2] Just under the head was a broad silver band nearly an inch across. "To James Mortimer, M.R.C.S.,[3] from his friends of the C.C.H.," was engraved upon it, with the date "1884."[4] It was just such a stick as the old-fashioned family practitioner used to carry—dignified, solid, and reassuring.

"Well, Watson,[5] what do you make of it?"

Holmes was sitting with his back to me, and I had given him no sign of my occupation.

"How did you know what I was doing? I believe you have eyes in the back of your head."

"I have, at least, a well-polished, silver-plated coffee-pot in front of me," said he.[6] "But, tell me, Watson, what do you make

---

1 An example straightaway of the carelessness with details in Conan Doyle's Holmes stories. Dr Watson's first impressions of the detective in *A Study in Scarlet* (1887) recorded instead that "Holmes was certainly not a difficult man to live with. He was quiet in his ways, and his habits were regular. It was rare for him to be up after ten at night, and he had invariably breakfasted and gone out before I rose in the morning" (*CSH*, 20).

2 A kind of walking-stick, formed from the stem of the dwarf palm (*Licuala acutifolia*), growing natively in Singapore and Penang.

3 Member of the Royal College of Surgeons, the diploma in basic surgery from the Royal College of Surgeons at Lincoln's Inn Fields, London.

4 See p. 53, note 2.

5 Surnames-only modes of address signified, at this point in English conversational history, friendship.

6 This episode has a comic and parodic element when set beside other set piece incidents where Holmes seems to read Watson's mind. See, for instance, the opening of "The Adventure of the Cardboard Box" (1893) where Holmes, after apparently disregarding Watson for some time in favour of a letter, remarks suddenly "'You are right, Watson ... It does

(continued on page 50)

of our visitor's stick? Since we have been so unfortunate as to miss him and have no notion of his errand, this accidental souvenir becomes of importance. Let me hear you reconstruct the man by an examination of it."

"I think," said I, following as far as I could the methods of my companion, "that Dr. Mortimer is a successful, elderly medical man, well-esteemed since those who know him give him this mark of their appreciation."

"Good!" said Holmes. "Excellent!"

"I think also that the probability is in favour of his being a country practitioner who does a great deal of his visiting on foot."

"Why so?"

"Because this stick, though originally a very handsome one has been so knocked about that I can hardly imagine a town practitioner carrying it. The thick-iron ferrule[1] is worn down, so it is evident that he has done a great amount of walking with it."

"Perfectly sound!" said Holmes.

---

seem a most preposterous way of settling a dispute'" (*CSH* 888) before providing a long account of what led him to this statement. The procedure is itself a recollection of the method of Edgar Allan Poe's detective, C. Auguste Dupin. Consider Dupin's deduction in "The Murders of the Rue Morgue" (1841) that his unnamed companion, as they have been walking in silence down a Parisian street, has been thinking about the actor Chantilly and the theatre. "'He is a very little fellow, that's true,'" Dupin suddenly says, apparently with telepathic insight into his friend's mind, "'and would be better for the *Théâtre des Varieties*'" (Edgar Allan Poe, *Tales of Mystery and Imagination* [London: Dent, 1993], 416). A lengthy narrative of Dupin's observations of his friend's behaviour that led to this conclusion is then provided. In *A Study in Scarlet* (1887)—Holmes's first appearance—he repudiates Dupin for precisely this form of showmanship: he is "a very inferior fellow. That trick of his of breaking in on his friends' thought with an apropos remark after a quarter of an hour's silence is really very showy and superficial. He had some analytical genius, no doubt; but he was by no means such a phenomenon as Poe appeared to imagine" (*CSH* 24). But then Conan Doyle decided to allow Holmes to do exactly the same thing and, while explaining his reasoning in "The Cardboard Box," has him draw explicit attention to the fact that he is "constantly in the habit of doing the same thing [as Poe's remarkable hero]" (*CSH* 888). There is another example at the beginning of "The Adventure of the Dancing Men" (1903). See Appendix F, pp. 271–76.

1 A ring or cap of metal placed around the end of a walking stick to prevent splitting and reduce wearing.

"And then again, there is the 'friends of the C.C.H.' I should guess that to be the Something Hunt, the local hunt to whose members he has possibly given some surgical assistance, and which has made him a small presentation in return."

"Really, Watson, you excel yourself," said Holmes, pushing back his chair and lighting a cigarette. "I am bound to say that in all the accounts which you have been so good as to give of my own small achievements you have habitually underrated your own abilities. It may be that you are not yourself luminous, but you are a conductor of light.[1] Some people without possessing genius have a remarkable power of stimulating it. I confess, my dear fellow, that I am very much in your debt."

He had never said as much before, and I must admit that his words gave me keen pleasure, for I had often been piqued by his indifference to my admiration and to the attempts which I had made to give publicity to his methods. I was proud, too, to think that I had so far mastered his system as to apply it in a way which earned his approval. He now took the stick from my hands and examined it for a few minutes with his naked eyes. Then with an expression of interest he laid down his cigarette, and carrying the cane to the window, he looked over it again with a convex lens.

"Interesting, though elementary,"[2] said he as he returned to his favourite corner of the settee.[3] "There are certainly one or two indications upon the stick. It gives us the basis for several deductions."

"Has anything escaped me?" I asked with some self-importance. "I trust that there is nothing of consequence which I have overlooked?"

---

1 Cf. Falstaff in Shakespeare, *Henry IV* Part 2, I.ii, "I am not only witty in myself, but the cause that wit is in other men." The word "luminous" is to become of significance in the tale as it is a key descriptor of the Hound. As Mortimer tells Holmes, the animal on the moor has been described as a "huge creature, luminous, ghastly, and spectral" (p. 71) and its luminosity will be the subject of some speculation. It is typical of the Holmes stories that one cannot be sure that Conan Doyle—writing these adventures with some indifference—deliberately chose "luminous" in Holmes's double-edged compliment to Watson because of its aptness or whether it was accidental and its relevance unnoticed.

2 Holmes, of course, never actually says the famous line credited to him— "Elementary, my dear Watson"—in any of the adventures. But this is an example of how close he gets.

3 By the beginning of the twentieth century, a synonym for sofa.

"I am afraid, my dear Watson, that most of your conclusions were erroneous. When I said that you stimulated me I meant, to be frank, that in noting your fallacies I was occasionally guided towards the truth. Not that you are entirely wrong in this instance. The man is certainly a country practitioner. And he walks a good deal."

"Then I was right."

"To that extent."

"But that was all."

"No, no, my dear Watson, not all—by no means all. I would suggest, for example, that a presentation to a doctor is more likely to come from a hospital than from a hunt, and that when the initials 'C.C.' are placed before that hospital the words 'Charing Cross'[1] very naturally suggest themselves."

"You may be right."

"The probability lies in that direction. And if we take this as a working hypothesis we have a fresh basis from which to start our construction of this unknown visitor."

"Well, then, supposing that 'C.C.H.' does stand for 'Charing Cross Hospital,' what further inferences may we draw?"

"Do none suggest themselves? You know my methods. Apply them!"

"I can only think of the obvious conclusion that the man has practised in town before going to the country."

"I think that we might venture a little farther than this. Look at it in this light. On what occasion would it be most probable that such a presentation would be made? When would his friends unite to give him a pledge of their good will? Obviously at the moment when Dr. Mortimer withdrew from the service of the hospital in order to start in practice for himself. We know there has been a presentation. We believe there has been a change from a town hospital to a country practice. Is it, then, stretching our inference too far to say that the presentation was on the occasion of the change?"

"It certainly seems probable."

"Now, you will observe that he could not have been on the *staff* of the hospital, since only a man well-established in a London practice could hold such a position, and such a one would not

---

1   The Charing Cross Hospital Medical School, at Charing Cross Hospital in Central London, was established in 1823. In 1984 it merged with the Westminster Hospital Medical School to become the Charing Cross and Westminster Medical School.

drift into the country. What was he, then? If he was in the hospital and yet not on the staff[1] he could only have been a house-surgeon or a house-physician—little more than a senior student. And he left five years ago—the date is on the stick.[2] So your grave, middle-aged family practitioner vanishes into thin air, my dear Watson, and there emerges a young fellow under thirty, amiable, unambitious, absent-minded, and the possessor of a favourite dog, which I should describe roughly as being larger than a terrier and smaller than a mastiff."

I laughed incredulously as Sherlock Holmes leaned back in his settee and blew little wavering rings of smoke up to the ceiling.

"As to the latter part, I have no means of checking you," said I, "but at least it is not difficult to find out a few particulars about the man's age and professional career." From my small medical shelf I took down the Medical Directory and turned up the name. There were several Mortimers, but only one who could be our visitor. I read his record aloud.

"Mortimer, James, M.R.C.S., 1882, Grimpen, Dartmoor, Devon. House-surgeon,[3] from 1882 to 1884, at Charing Cross Hospital. Winner of the Jackson prize for Comparative Pathology, with essay entitled 'Is Disease a Reversion?' Corresponding member [4] of the Swedish Pathological Society. Author of 'Some Freaks of Atavism' (*Lancet*[5] 1882). 'Do We Progress?' (*Journal of Psy-*

---

1 Not with a permanent position.

2 The date at which *The Hound* is set is not consistently established across the novel and readers' suggestions have ranged from 1886 onwards: see Baring-Gould, II.5. When Frankland announces the forthcoming case of Frankland *v.* Regina (see p. 162), it is a pointer, certainly, to the Victorian setting of the novel. What was on Conan Doyle's mind in disguising the exact date of the narrative (he is relatively precise in other stories) was the question of whether it was set before Holmes's supposed death in 1891 ("The Final Problem" [1893]) or after his reappearance in 1894 (revealed in "The Adventure of the Empty House" [1903]). *The Hound*, of course, appeared before the publication of "The Empty House" and so readers would have wanted to know if the new novel signified that Holmes had not in fact perished with Professor Moriarty in the Reichenbach Falls. Conan Doyle avoids satisfying their curiosity.

3 A position for a junior doctor in a hospital.

4 That is, one who lives remote from the Society headquarters and corresponds with it by letter.

5 The leading medical journal by the end of the nineteenth century, founded in 1823 as a radical organ by the doctor and MP Thomas Wakley (1795–1862).

chology, March, 1883).[1] Medical Officer for the parishes of Grimpen, Thorsley, and High Barrow."

"No mention of that local hunt, Watson," said Holmes with a mischievous smile, "but a country doctor, as you very astutely observed. I think that I am fairly justified in my inferences. As to the adjectives, I said, if I remember right, amiable, unambitious, and absent-minded. It is my experience that it is only an amiable man in this world who receives testimonials, only an unambitious one who abandons a London career for the country, and only an absent-minded one who leaves his stick and not his visiting-card after waiting an hour in your room."

"And the dog?"

"Has been in the habit of carrying this stick behind his master. Being a heavy stick the dog has held it tightly by the middle, and the marks of his teeth are very plainly visible. The dog's jaw, as shown in the space between these marks, is too broad in my opinion for a terrier and not broad enough for a mastiff. It may have been—yes, by Jove, it *is* a curly-haired spaniel."[2]

He had risen and paced the room as he spoke. Now he halted in the recess of the window. There was such a ring of conviction in his voice that I glanced up in surprise.

"My dear fellow, how can you possibly be so sure of that?"

"For the very simple reason that I see the dog himself on our very door-step, and there is the ring of its owner. Don't move, I beg you, Watson. He is a professional brother of yours, and your presence may be of assistance to me. Now is the dramatic moment of fate, Watson, when you hear a step upon the stair which is walking into your life, and you know not whether for good or ill. What does Dr. James Mortimer, the man of science, ask of Sherlock Holmes, the specialist in crime? Come in!"

The appearance of our visitor was a surprise to me, since I had expected a typical country practitioner. He was a very tall, thin man, with a long nose like a beak, which jutted out between two keen, gray eyes, set closely together and sparkling brightly from behind a pair of gold-rimmed glasses. He was clad in a professional but rather slovenly fashion, for his frock-coat was dingy and his trousers frayed. Though young, his long back was already bowed, and he walked with a forward thrust of his head and a

---

1 On Mortimer's essays, see the Introduction, p. 24.
2 Not an official breed name: most likely a cocker spaniel. Appropriately for this tale of pursuit, the cocker spaniel is a hunting dog.

general air of peering benevolence. As he entered his eyes fell upon the stick in Holmes's hand, and he ran towards it with an exclamation of joy. "I am so very glad," said he. "I was not sure whether I had left it here or in the Shipping Office. I would not lose that stick for the world."

"A presentation, I see," said Holmes.

"Yes, sir."

"From Charing Cross Hospital?"

"From one or two friends there on the occasion of my marriage."

"Dear, dear, that's bad!" said Holmes, shaking his head.

Dr. Mortimer blinked through his glasses in mild astonishment.

"Why was it bad?"

"Only that you have disarranged our little deductions. Your marriage, you say?"

"Yes, sir. I married, and so left the hospital, and with it all hopes of a consulting practice. It was necessary to make a home of my own."

"Come, come, we are not so far wrong, after all," said Holmes. "And now, Dr. James Mortimer—"

"Mister, sir, Mister—a humble M.R.C.S."[1]

"And a man of precise mind, evidently."

"A dabbler in science, Mr. Holmes, a picker up of shells on the shores of the great unknown ocean.[2] I presume that it is Mr. Sherlock Holmes whom I am addressing and not—"

"No, this is my friend Dr. Watson."

"Glad to meet you, sir. I have heard your name mentioned in connection with that of your friend. You interest me very much, Mr. Holmes. I had hardly expected so dolichocephalic[3] a skull or

---

1   The medical degree of MD—which Dr Watson possesses—would properly allow the title of Doctor. But Mortimer might, were he to possess a less "precise mind," allow himself the courtesy title, as most English doctors today, without the actual possession of a doctorate.

2   Mortimer's words are a cliché but they echo Isaac Newton's remark "I seem to have been only like a boy playing on the sea-shore, and diverting myself in now and then finding a smoother pebble or prettier shell than ordinary, whilst the great ocean of truth lay all undiscovered before me," David Brewster, *Memoirs of the Life, Writings, and Discoveries of Sir Isaac Newton*, 2 vols (Edinburgh: Constable, 1855), II.407.

3   Long-headed: referring to skulls of which the breadth is either less than four-fifths or, according to some authorities, three-fourths, of the length.

such well-marked supra-orbital[1] development. Would you have any objection to my running my finger along your parietal fissure?[2] A cast of your skull, sir, until the original is available, would be an ornament to any anthropological museum.[3] It is not my intention to be fulsome, but I confess that I covet your skull."

Sherlock Holmes waved our strange visitor into a chair. "You are an enthusiast in your line of thought, I perceive, sir, as I am in mine," said he. "I observe from your forefinger[4] that you make your own cigarettes. Have no hesitation in lighting one."

The man drew out paper and tobacco and twirled the one up in the other with surprising dexterity. He had long, quivering fingers as agile and restless as the antennae of an insect.

Holmes was silent, but his little darting glances showed me the interest which he took in our curious companion.

"I presume, sir," said he at last, "that it was not merely for the purpose of examining my skull that you have done me the honour to call here last night and again to-day?"

"No, sir, no; though I am happy to have had the opportunity of doing that as well. I came to you, Mr. Holmes, because I recognized that I am myself an unpractical man and because I am suddenly confronted with a most serious and extraordinary problem. Recognizing, as I do, that you are the second highest expert in Europe—"

"Indeed, sir! May I inquire who has the honour to be the first?" asked Holmes, with some asperity.

---

1 Above the orbit of the eye.

2 Division between principal bones of the skull.

3 Anthropology is the branch of science that concerned itself with, in a description from 1861, "the principal characters of our species, its perfection, its accidental degradations, its unity, its races, and the manner in which it has been classified." It emerged in the Victorian period as a dominant scientific discipline for understanding the divisions of human "races." Anthropological museums accordingly were relatively new when Mortimer considers the shape of Holmes's skull; Lieutenant General Pitt Rivers, for instance, gave his remarkable anthropological collection to the University of Oxford in 1884, the year Mortimer leaves London, to found the important Pitt Rivers Museum there, still existing.

4 It is possible to tell if a person *smokes* from nicotine stains on their fingers but not that they roll their own cigarettes.

"To the man of precisely scientific mind the work of Monsieur Bertillon[1] must always appeal strongly."

"Then had you not better consult him?"

"I said, sir, to the precisely scientific mind. But as a practical man of affairs it is acknowledged that you stand alone. I trust, sir, that I have not inadvertently—"

"Just a little," said Holmes. "I think, Dr. Mortimer, you would do wisely if without more ado you would kindly tell me plainly what the exact nature of the problem is in which you demand my assistance."

Chapter II

The Curse of the Baskervilles

"I have in my pocket a manuscript," said Dr. James Mortimer.

"I observed it as you entered the room," said Holmes.

"It is an old manuscript."

"Early eighteenth century, unless it is a forgery."

"How can you say that, sir?"

"You have presented an inch or two of it to my examination all the time that you have been talking. It would be a poor expert who could not give the date of a document within a decade or so. You may possibly have read my little monograph upon the subject. I put that at 1730."

"The exact date is 1742." Dr. Mortimer drew it from his breast-pocket. "This family paper was committed to my care by

---

1 Alphonse Bertillon (1853–1914), French criminologist, creator of the identification system known as anthropometry, or the Bertillon system, or bertillonage, which used physiological measurements, including of scars, facial features, and finger-characteristics, to document human individualities and types. Bertillon was the author of *La Photographie judiciaire, avec un appendice sur la classification et l'identification anthropométriques* (1890) and *Identification anthropométrique* (1893), the "idée maîtresse" of which was similarly "l'application des procédés de l'anatomie anthropométrique aux questions d'identifications judicaire," *Identifications anthropométrique: instructions signalétiques* (Mecun: Imprimerie Administrative, 1893), i. For Francis Galton's related work on *composite* photography, see Appendix B, pp. 245–49.

Sir Charles Baskerville,[1] whose sudden and tragic death some three months ago created so much excitement in Devonshire.[2] I may say that I was his personal friend as well as his medical attendant. He was a strong-minded man, sir, shrewd, practical, and as unimaginative as I am myself. Yet he took this document very seriously, and his mind was prepared for just such an end as did eventually overtake him."

Holmes stretched out his hand for the manuscript and flattened it upon his knee.

"You will observe, Watson, the alternative use of the long *s* and the short. It is one of several indications which enabled me to fix the date."[3]

I looked over his shoulder at the yellow paper and the faded script. At the head was written: "Baskerville Hall," and below in large, scrawling figures: "1742."

"It appears to be a statement of some sort."

"Yes, it is a statement of a certain legend which runs in the Baskerville family."

---

1   When Conan Doyle visited Dartmoor to investigate the future setting of this novel, it seems that his coachman was called Harry Baskerville but this may well have been a coincidence rather than the source of the family name.

2   Now more frequently "Devon." Much work has been spent on linking, or endeavouring to link, the locations in *The Hound* with actual sites on Dartmoor. I have given a small number of these as indicative in the following notes but readers wishing to know more about this aspect of Conan Doyle's imagination should consult Philip Weller, *The Dartmoor Locations of* The Hound of the Baskervilles: *A Practical Guide to the Sherlock Holmes Locations,* 2nd edition (Hornsea: Sherlock Publications, 1992). It is not only Dartmoor that has been suggested. Some have argued—and this is proclaimed on internet tourist material and in the entry on Conan Doyle in the new *Oxford Dictionary of National Biography* (2004)—that Stonyhurst College, where Conan Doyle was educated, was the setting for Baskerville Hall. The countryside around Skipton is another candidate.

3   Confusing. The long ∫ was never used exclusively, and was most often present, in the eighteenth century, as a character in a double-s; this practice continued, albeit it unevenly, well into the Victorian period and is no secure way of identifying as precise a date as Holmes manages. But, since the use of the double-s formations did gradually recede through the eighteenth century, perhaps Conan Doyle is—somewhat fancifully—imagining Holmes seeing in this manuscript both "ss" and "∫s"/ "s∫" forms as an exemplum of transition.

"But I understand that it is something more modern and practical upon which you wish to consult me?"

"Most modern. A most practical, pressing matter, which must be decided within twenty-four hours. But the manuscript is short and is intimately connected with the affair. With your permission I will read it to you."

Holmes leaned back in his chair, placed his finger-tips together, and closed his eyes, with an air of resignation. Dr. Mortimer turned the manuscript to the light and read in a high, crackling voice the following curious, old-world narrative:

"Of the origin of the Hound of the Baskervilles there have been many statements, yet as I come in a direct line from Hugo Baskerville, and as I had the story from my father, who also had it from his, I have set it down with all belief that it occurred even as is here set forth. And I would have you believe, my sons, that the same Justice which punishes sin may also most graciously forgive it, and that no ban is so heavy but that by prayer and repentance it may be removed. Learn then from this story not to fear the fruits of the past, but rather to be circumspect in the future, that those foul passions whereby our family has suffered so grievously may not again be loosed to our undoing.

"Know then that in the time of the Great Rebellion[1] (the history of which by the learned Lord Clarendon[2] I most earnestly commend to your attention) this Manor of Baskerville was held by Hugo of that name, nor can it be gainsaid that he was a most wild, profane, and godless man. This, in truth, his neighbours might have pardoned, seeing that saints have never flourished in those parts, but there was in him a certain wanton and cruel humour which made his name a byword through the West. It chanced that this Hugo came to love (if, indeed, so dark a passion may be known under so bright a name) the daughter of a yeoman who held lands near the Baskerville estate. But the young maiden, being discreet and of good repute, would ever avoid him, for she feared his evil name. So it came to pass that

---

1 The English Civil War, 1642–49, between the Republican forces of
   Oliver Cromwell (1599–1658) and Royalist forces of the monarchy.

2 Edward Hyde, 1st Earl of Clarendon (1609–74), author of *The History
   of the Rebellion and Civil Wars in England, begun in 1641, with the precedent
   passages and actions that contributed thereto, and the happy end and conclusion thereof by the King's blessed restoration, etc* (1702–1704).

one Michaelmas[1] this Hugo, with five or six of his idle and wicked companions, stole down upon the farm and carried off the maiden, her father and brothers being from home, as he well knew. When they had brought her to the Hall the maiden was placed in an upper chamber, while Hugo and his friends sat down to a long carouse, as was their nightly custom. Now, the poor lass upstairs was like to have her wits turned at the singing and shouting and terrible oaths which came up to her from below, for they say that the words used by Hugo Baskerville, when he was in wine, were such as might blast the man who said them. At last in the stress of her fear she did that which might have daunted the bravest or most active man, for by the aid of the growth of ivy which covered (and still covers) the south wall she came down from under the eaves, and so homeward across the moor, there being three leagues betwixt the Hall and her father's farm.

"It chanced that some little time later Hugo left his guests to carry food and drink—with other worse things, perchance[2]—to his captive, and so found the cage empty and the bird escaped. Then, as it would seem, he became as one that hath a devil, for, rushing down the stairs into the dining-hall, he sprang upon the great table, flagons[3] and trenchers[4] flying before him, and he cried aloud before all the company that he would that very night render his body and soul to the Powers of Evil if he might but overtake the wench.[5] And while the revellers stood aghast at the fury of the man, one more wicked or, it may be, more drunken than the rest, cried out that they should put the hounds upon her. Whereat Hugo ran from the house, crying to his grooms that they should saddle his mare and unkennel the pack, and giving the hounds a kerchief[6] of the maid's, he swung them to the line,[7] and so off full cry in the moonlight over the moor.

"Now, for some space the revellers stood agape, unable to

---

1 At or around the time of the feast of St Michael and All Angels, 29 September.
2 We are meant to assume—if we hadn't already—that Hugo's intentions are sexual.
3 Large bottles containing wine.
4 Flat pieces of wood for serving and cutting meat.
5 A parodic version of the Faustian pact—where rather less is asked for.
6 A cloth used to cover a woman's head.
7 Brought them into order, ready for the chase.

understand all that had been done in such haste. But anon[1] their bemused wits awoke to the nature of the deed which was like to be done upon the moorlands. Everything was now in an uproar, some calling for their pistols, some for their horses, and some for another flask of wine. But at length some sense came back to their crazed minds, and the whole of them, thirteen in number, took horse and started in pursuit. The moon shone clear above them, and they rode swiftly abreast, taking that course which the maid must needs have taken if she were to reach her own home.

"They had gone a mile or two when they passed one of the night shepherds upon the moorlands, and they cried to him to know if he had seen the hunt. And the man, as the story goes, was so crazed with fear that he could scarce speak, but at last he said that he had indeed seen the unhappy maiden, with the hounds upon her track. 'But I have seen more than that,' said he, 'for Hugo Baskerville passed me upon his black mare, and there ran mute behind him such a hound of hell as God forbid should ever be at my heels.' So the drunken squires cursed the shepherd and rode onward. But soon their skins turned cold, for there came a galloping across the moor, and the black mare, dabbled with white froth, went past with trailing bridle and empty saddle. Then the revellers rode close together, for a great fear was on them, but they still followed over the moor, though each, had he been alone, would have been right glad to have turned his horse's head. Riding slowly in this fashion they came at last upon the hounds. These, though known for their valour and their breed, were whimpering in a cluster at the head of a deep dip or goyal,[2] as we call it, upon the moor, some slinking away and some, with starting hackles and staring eyes, gazing down the narrow valley before them.

"The company had come to a halt, more sober men, as you may guess, than when they started. The most of them would by no means advance, but three of them, the boldest, or it may be the most drunken, rode forward down the goyal. Now, it opened into a broad space in which stood two of those great stones, still to be seen there, which were set by certain forgotten peoples in the days of old. The moon was shining bright upon the clearing, and there in the centre lay the unhappy maid where she had fall-

---

1 "Gradually" (this is a misuse, technically, though a common one. "Anon" properly means "immediately").
2 Usually "goyle": a deep trench.

en, dead of fear and of fatigue. But it was not the sight of her body, nor yet was it that of the body of Hugo Baskerville lying near her, which raised the hair upon the heads of these three daredevil roysterers, but it was that, standing over Hugo, and plucking at his throat, there stood a foul thing, a great, black beast, shaped like a hound, yet larger than any hound that ever mortal eye has rested upon. And even as they looked the thing tore the throat out of Hugo Baskerville, on which, as it turned its blazing eyes and dripping jaws upon them, the three shrieked with fear and rode for dear life, still screaming, across the moor. One, it is said, died that very night of what he had seen, and the other twain were but broken men for the rest of their days.

"Such is the tale, my sons, of the coming of the hound which is said to have plagued the family so sorely ever since. If I have set it down it is because that which is clearly known hath less terror than that which is but hinted at and guessed. Nor can it be denied that many of the family have been unhappy in their deaths, which have been sudden, bloody, and mysterious. Yet may we shelter ourselves in the infinite goodness of Providence, which would not forever punish the innocent beyond that third or fourth generation which is threatened in Holy Writ.[1] To that Providence, my sons, I hereby commend you, and I counsel you by way of caution to forbear from crossing the moor in those dark hours when the powers of evil are exalted.

"[This from Hugo Baskerville to his sons Rodger and John, with instructions that they say nothing thereof to their sister Elizabeth.]"

When Dr. Mortimer had finished reading this singular narrative he pushed his spectacles up on his forehead and stared across at Mr. Sherlock Holmes. The latter yawned and tossed the end of his cigarette into the fire.

"Well?" said he.

"Do you not find it interesting?"

"To a collector of fairy tales."

Dr. Mortimer drew a folded newspaper out of his pocket.

---

1 See Exodus 34.6–7: "And the Lord passed by before him, and proclaimed, The Lord, The Lord God, merciful and gracious, long suffering, and abundant in goodness and truth, Keeping mercy for thousands, forgiving iniquity and transgression and sin, and that will by no means clear the guilty, visiting the iniquity of the fathers upon the children, and upon the children's children, unto the third and to the fourth generation."

"Now, Mr. Holmes, we will give you something a little more recent. This is the *Devon County Chronicle*[1] of June 14th of this year. It is a short account of the facts elicited at the death of Sir Charles Baskerville which occurred a few days before that date." My friend leaned a little forward and his expression became intent. Our visitor readjusted his glasses and began:

"The recent sudden death of Sir Charles Baskerville, whose name has been mentioned as the probable Liberal candidate for Mid-Devon at the next election, has cast a gloom over the county. Though Sir Charles had resided at Baskerville Hall for a comparatively short period his amiability of character and extreme generosity had won the affection and respect of all who had been brought into contact with him. In these days of *nouveaux riches*[2] it is refreshing to find a case where the scion[3] of an old county family which has fallen upon evil days is able to make his own fortune and to bring it back with him to restore the fallen grandeur of his line. Sir Charles, as is well known, made large sums of money in South African speculation.[4] More wise than those who go on until the wheel turns against them, he realized his gains and returned to England with them. It is only two years since he took up his residence at Baskerville Hall, and it is common talk how large were those schemes of reconstruction and improvement which have been interrupted by his death. Being himself childless, it was his openly expressed desire that the whole countryside should, within his own lifetime, profit by his good fortune, and many will have personal reasons for bewailing his untimely end. His generous donations to local and county charities have been frequently chronicled in these columns.

---

1 Not a real newspaper.
2 Those whose money is recently acquired. Sir Charles's money is very recent, as we are about to find out, but the journalist allows it with a neat dodge because of the ancient lineage of his family.
3 Heir, descendant.
4 British investment and speculation in the profits of South African natural resources—one of "great treasure chests of the world," Conan Doyle remarked in *The Great Boer War* (1900), p. 12—generated, for some, huge fortunes towards the end of the nineteenth century. Cecil Rhodes's De Beers Mining Company (1880), followed by the De Beers Consolidated Mines (1888), and the British South Africa Company, organized in 1889, might be taken as prominent examples. Sir Charles is intended, presumably, to have had money in these or others like them.

"The circumstances connected with the death of Sir Charles cannot be said to have been entirely cleared up by the inquest, but at least enough has been done to dispose of those rumours to which local superstition has given rise. There is no reason whatever to suspect foul play, or to imagine that death could be from any but natural causes. Sir Charles was a widower, and a man who may be said to have been in some ways of an eccentric habit of mind. In spite of his considerable wealth he was simple in his personal tastes, and his indoor servants at Baskerville Hall consisted of a married couple named Barrymore, the husband acting as butler and the wife as housekeeper. Their evidence, corroborated by that of several friends, tends to show that Sir Charles's health has for some time been impaired, and points especially to some affection of the heart, manifesting itself in changes of colour, breathlessness, and acute attacks of nervous depression. Dr. James Mortimer, the friend and medical attendant of the deceased, has given evidence to the same effect.

"The facts of the case are simple. Sir Charles Baskerville was in the habit every night before going to bed of walking down the famous Yew Alley of Baskerville Hall. The evidence of the Barrymores shows that this had been his custom. On the fourth of June Sir Charles had declared his intention of starting next day for London, and had ordered Barrymore to prepare his luggage. That night he went out as usual for his nocturnal walk, in the course of which he was in the habit of smoking a cigar. He never returned. At twelve o'clock Barrymore, finding the hall door still open, became alarmed, and, lighting a lantern, went in search of his master. The day had been wet, and Sir Charles's footmarks were easily traced down the alley. Halfway down this walk there is a gate which leads out on to the moor. There were indications that Sir Charles had stood for some little time here. He then proceeded down the alley, and it was at the far end of it that his body was discovered.

"One fact which has not been explained is the statement of Barrymore that his master's footprints altered their character from the time that he passed the moor-gate, and that he appeared from thence onward to have been walking upon his toes. One Murphy, a gipsy horse-dealer, was on the moor at no great distance at the time, but he appears by his own confession to have been the worse for drink. He declares that he heard cries but is unable to state from what direction they came. No signs of violence were to be discovered upon Sir Charles's person, and though the doctor's evidence pointed to an almost incredible facial distortion—so great that Dr. Mortimer refused at first to believe that it was indeed his friend and patient who lay before him—it was explained that that is a symptom which is not unusual in cases of dyspnœa[1] and death from cardiac exhaustion. This explanation was borne out by the post-mortem examination, which showed long-standing organic disease, and the coroner's jury[2] returned a verdict in accordance with the medical evidence.

It is well that this is so, for it is obviously of the utmost importance that Sir Charles's heir should settle at the Hall and continue the good work which has been so sadly interrupted. Had the prosaic finding of the coroner not finally put an end to the romantic stories which have been whispered in connection with the affair, it might have been difficult to find a tenant[3] for Baskerville Hall. It is understood that the next of kin is Mr. Henry Baskerville, if he be still alive, the son of Sir Charles Baskerville's younger brother. The young man when last heard of was in America, and inquiries are being instituted with a view to informing him of his good fortune."

Dr. Mortimer refolded his paper and replaced it in his pocket.

"Those are the public facts, Mr. Holmes, in connection with the death of Sir Charles Baskerville."

"I must thank you," said Sherlock Holmes, "for calling my attention to a case which certainly presents some features of interest. I had observed some newspaper comment at the time, but I was exceedingly preoccupied by that little affair of the Vatican[4] cameos, and in my anxiety to oblige the Pope[5] I lost touch with several interesting English cases. This article, you say, contains all the public facts?"

"It does."

"Then let me have the private ones." He leaned back, put his

---

1 Difficult, laborious breathing.

2 In English law, a coroner's court, consisting of a magistrate (called the coroner) and twelve jurymen who undertake an inquest or investigation as to the cause of a death where it is required. The peculiar circumstances of Sir Charles's death—it is *prima facie* unclear whether he has died of natural causes or by human intervention—would necessitate one.

3 Not someone to rent the Hall but someone who, owning it, lives there.

4 City state in the centre of Rome, official residence of the Pope. Conan Doyle did not write a story about Holmes and the Vatican cameos, alas.

5 At the time, Leo XIII, Pope from 1878 to 1903.

finger-tips together, and assumed his most impassive and judicial expression.

"In doing so," said Dr. Mortimer, who had begun to show signs of some strong emotion, "I am telling that which I have not confided to anyone. My motive for withholding it from the coroner's inquiry is that a man of science shrinks from placing himself in the public position of seeming to indorse a popular superstition. I had the further motive that Baskerville Hall, as the paper says, would certainly remain untenanted if anything were done to increase its already rather grim reputation. For both these reasons I thought that I was justified in telling rather less than I knew, since no practical good could result from it, but with you there is no reason why I should not be perfectly frank.

"The moor is very sparsely inhabited, and those who live near each other are thrown very much together. For this reason I saw a good deal of Sir Charles Baskerville. With the exception of Mr. Frankland, of Lafter Hall, and Mr. Stapleton, the naturalist, there are no other men of education within many miles. Sir Charles was a retiring man, but the chance of his illness brought us together, and a community of interests in science kept us so. He had brought back much scientific information from South Africa, and many a charming evening we have spent together discussing the comparative anatomy of the Bushman and the Hottentot.[1]

"Within the last few months it became increasingly plain to me that Sir Charles's nervous system was strained to the breaking point. He had taken this legend which I have read you exceedingly to heart—so much so that, although he would walk in his own grounds, nothing would induce him to go out upon the moor at night. Incredible as it may appear to you, Mr. Holmes, he was honestly convinced that a dreadful fate overhung his family, and certainly the records which he was able to give of his ancestors were not encouraging. The idea of some ghastly presence constantly haunted him, and on more than one occasion he has asked me whether I had on my medical journeys at night ever seen any

---

1 Now racially offensive terms, but for Conan Doyle the familiar language of Victorian and early twentieth-century racial taxonomy. Hottentot is described—in the old-fashioned words of the *OED*—as "one of the two sub-races of the Khoisanid race (the other being the Sanids or Bushmen), characterized by short stature, yellow-brown skin colour, and tightly curled hair. They are of mixed Bushman-Hamite descent with some Bantu admixture, and are now found principally in South-West Africa."

strange creature or heard the baying of a hound. The latter question he put to me several times, and always with a voice which vibrated with excitement.

"I can well remember driving up to his house in the evening some three weeks before the fatal event. He chanced to be at his hall door. I had descended from my gig[1] and was standing in front of him, when I saw his eyes fix themselves over my shoulder and stare past me with an expression of the most dreadful horror. I whisked round and had just time to catch a glimpse of something which I took to be a large black calf passing at the head of the drive. So excited and alarmed was he that I was compelled to go down to the spot where the animal had been and look around for it. It was gone, however, and the incident appeared to make the worst impression upon his mind. I stayed with him all the evening, and it was on that occasion, to explain the emotion which he had shown, that he confided to my keeping that narrative which I read to you when first I came. I mention this small episode because it assumes some importance in view of the tragedy which followed, but I was convinced at the time that the matter was entirely trivial and that his excitement had no justification.

"It was at my advice that Sir Charles was about to go to London. His heart was, I knew, affected, and the constant anxiety in which he lived, however chimerical[2] the cause of it might be, was evidently having a serious effect upon his health. I thought that a few months among the distractions of town would send him back a new man. Mr. Stapleton, a mutual friend who was much concerned at his state of health, was of the same opinion. At the last instant came this terrible catastrophe.

"On the night of Sir Charles's death Barrymore the butler who made the discovery, sent Perkins the groom on horseback to me, and as I was sitting up late I was able to reach Baskerville Hall within an hour of the event. I checked and corroborated all the facts which were mentioned at the inquest. I followed the footsteps down the Yew Alley, I saw the spot at the moor-gate where he seemed to have waited, I remarked the change in the shape of the prints after that point, I noted that there were no other footsteps save those of Barrymore on the soft gravel, and finally I carefully examined the body, which had not been touched until my arrival. Sir Charles lay on his face, his arms out, his fingers

1 A light two-wheeled one-horse carriage.
2 Illusory.

dug into the ground, and his features convulsed with some strong emotion to such an extent that I could hardly have sworn to his identity. There was certainly no physical injury of any kind. But one false statement was made by Barrymore at the inquest. He said that there were no traces upon the ground round the body. He did not observe any. But I did—some little distance off, but fresh and clear."

"Footprints?"

"Footprints."

"A man's or a woman's?"

Dr. Mortimer looked strangely at us for an instant, and his voice sank almost to a whisper as he answered:

"Mr. Holmes, they were the footprints of a gigantic hound!"[1]

---

1 The first instalment of *The Strand* edition ended here. Many commentators have objected to the fact that it is impossible to tell the breed of a dog from its prints: Mortimer could not know this was a hound. But it is clear throughout the novel that "hound" is used simply as a synonym for "large dog." The word is not breed specific but it does have the advantage of calling to mind the idea of spectral creatures, the hell-hounds. Perhaps somewhere at the back of Conan Doyle's mind—he was brought up a Catholic, educated as a schoolboy at Stonyhurst—and distantly informing the imaginative shape of this creature and the experience of being hunted down was the poem by the Catholic writer Francis Thompson (1859–1907) on the believer's tormented relationship with the divine, "The Hound of Heaven." Its arresting opening—

> I fled Him, down the nights and down the days;
> I fled Him, down the arches of the years;
> I fled Him, down the labyrinthine ways
> Of my own mind [...]
> (ll.1–4 from *The Poems of Francis Thompson* [London: Hollis and Carter, 1946], p. 101)

—offers the Christian as the man relentlessly pursued by a tireless hound that is not of the Earth. Thompson's Hound is God; Conan Doyle calls up one from the depths of Hell with a ghastly intent. But its pursuit is as relentless and inescapable. Holmes later says of Sir Charles, "He was running, Watson—running desperately, running for his life, running until he burst his heart—and fell dead upon his face" (p. 77). There is perhaps a far distant echo of Thompson's poem in that, transformed from religion to murder. By an amusing irony—perhaps Newnes's joke as he organized the layout of the edition—the first instalment of *The Hound* in *The Strand* ended on p. 132 and facing it on 133 was the beginning of Lenore Van der Veer's "A School of Animal Painting" and a photograph of the artist with his very large but amiable dog at his feet.

Chapter III

The Problem

I confess at these words a shudder passed through me. There was a thrill in the doctor's voice which showed that he was himself deeply moved by that which he told us. Holmes leaned forward in his excitement and his eyes had the hard, dry glitter which shot from them when he was keenly interested.

"You saw this?"

"As clearly as I see you."

"And you said nothing?"

"What was the use?"

"How was it that no one else saw it?"

"The marks were some twenty yards from the body and no one gave them a thought. I don't suppose I should have done so had I not known this legend."

"There are many sheep-dogs on the moor?"

"No doubt, but this was no sheep-dog."

"You say it was large?"

"Enormous."

"But it had not approached the body?"

"No."

"What sort of night was it?"

"Damp and raw."

"But not actually raining?"

"No."

"What is the alley like?"

"There are two lines of old yew hedge, twelve feet high and impenetrable. The walk in the centre is about eight feet across."

"Is there anything between the hedges and the walk?"

"Yes, there is a strip of grass about 6ft. broad on either side."

"I understand that the yew hedge is penetrated at one point by a gate?"

"Yes, the wicket-gate which leads on to the moor."

"Is there any other opening?"

"None."

"So that to reach the Yew Alley one either has to come down it from the house or else to enter it by the moor-gate?"

"There is an exit through a summer-house at the far end."

"Had Sir Charles reached this?"

"No; he lay about fifty yards from it."

"Now, tell me, Dr. Mortimer—and this is important—the

marks which you saw were on the path and not on the grass?"

"No marks could show on the grass."

"Were they on the same side of the path as the moor-gate?"

"Yes; they were on the edge of the path on the same side as the moor-gate."

"You interest me exceedingly. Another point. Was the wicket-gate[1] closed?"

"Closed and padlocked."

"How high was it?"

"About four feet high."

"Then anyone could have got over it?"

"Yes."

"And what marks did you see by the wicket-gate?"

"None in particular."

"Good heaven! Did no one examine?"

"Yes, I examined, myself."

"And found nothing?"

"It was all very confused. Sir Charles had evidently stood there for five or ten minutes."

"How do you know that?"

"Because the ash had twice dropped from his cigar."

"Excellent! This is a colleague, Watson, after our own heart.[2] But the marks?"

---

1 Small gate for those on foot.

2 See *The Sign of Four* (1890) where Holmes refers to his own monograph *Upon the Distinction between the Ashes of the Various Tobaccos*. In it, Holmes tells Watson, "I enumerate a hundred and forty forms of cigar, cigarette, and pipe tobacco, with coloured plates illustrating the difference in the ash. It is a point which is continually turning up in criminal trials, and which is sometimes of supreme importance as a clue. If you can say definitely, for example, that some murder had been done by a man who was smoking an Indian *lunkah*, it obviously narrows your field of search. To the trained eye there is as much difference between the black ash of a Trichinopoly, and the white fluff of bird's-eye as there is between a cabbage and a potato," *CSH* 91. Readers will want to know that a *lunkah* is a kind of strong cigar; Trichinopoly, a tobacco that took its name from what was, in 1901, a city and district of British India, in the Madras area; and bird's-eye a more common form of tobacco in which the ribs of the leaves were cut along with the fibre. Discerning Trichinopoly ash is one of Holmes's observations in his very first appearance, *A Study in Scarlet* (1887).

"He had left his own marks all over that small patch of gravel. I could discern no others."

Sherlock Holmes struck his hand against his knee with an impatient gesture.

"If I had only been there!" he cried. "It is evidently a case of extraordinary interest, and one which presented immense opportunities to the scientific expert. That gravel page upon which I might have read so much has been long ere this smudged by the rain and defaced by the clogs of curious peasants. Oh, Dr. Mortimer, Dr. Mortimer, to think that you should not have called me in! You have indeed much to answer for."

"I could not call you in, Mr. Holmes, without disclosing these facts to the world, and I have already given my reasons for not wishing to do so. Besides, besides—"

"Why do you hesitate?"

"There is a realm in which the most acute and most experienced of detectives is helpless."

"You mean that the thing is supernatural?"

"I did not positively say so."

"No, but you evidently think it."

"Since the tragedy, Mr. Holmes, there have come to my ears several incidents which are hard to reconcile with the settled order of Nature."

"For example?"

"I find that before the terrible event occurred several people had seen a creature upon the moor which corresponds with this Baskerville demon, and which could not possibly be any animal known to science. They all agreed that it was a huge creature, luminous, ghastly, and spectral. I have cross-examined these men, one of them a hard-headed countryman, one a farrier,[1] and one a moorland farmer, who all tell the same story of this dreadful apparition, exactly corresponding to the hell-hound of the legend. I assure you that there is a reign of terror in the district, and that it is a hardy man who will cross the moor at night."

"And you, a trained man of science, believe it to be supernatural?"

"I do not know what to believe."

Holmes shrugged his shoulders.

"I have hitherto confined my investigations to this world," said he. "In a modest way I have combated evil, but to take on the

---

1 A man who shoes horses.

Father of Evil himself would, perhaps, be too ambitious a task. Yet you must admit that the footmark is material."

"The original hound was material enough to tug a man's throat out, and yet he was diabolical as well."

"I see that you have quite gone over to the supernaturalists. But now, Dr. Mortimer, tell me this. If you hold these views why have you come to consult me at all? You tell me in the same breath that it is useless to investigate Sir Charles's death, and that you desire me to do it."

"I did not say that I desired you to do it."

"Then, how can I assist you?"

"By advising me as to what I should do with Sir Henry Baskerville, who arrives at Waterloo Station"[1]—Dr. Mortimer looked at his watch—"in exactly one hour and a quarter."

"He being the heir?"

"Yes. On the death of Sir Charles we inquired for this young gentleman and found that he had been farming in Canada. From the accounts which have reached us he is an excellent fellow in every way. I speak now not as a medical man but as a trustee and executor of Sir Charles's will."

"There is no other claimant, I presume?"

"None. The only other kinsman whom we have been able to trace was Rodger Baskerville, the youngest of three brothers of whom poor Sir Charles was the elder. The second brother, who died young, is the father of this lad Henry. The third, Rodger, was the black sheep of the family. He came of the old masterful Baskerville strain and was the very image, they tell me, of the family picture of old Hugo.[2] He made England too hot to hold him, fled to Central America, and died there in 1876 of yellow fever. Henry is the last of the Baskervilles[3] In one hour and five

---

1 The first mainline station in London, opened on 11 July 1848 by the London and South Western Railway.

2 A throw-back (with which the novel is variously preoccupied); another visual throw-back will in due course help clinch the solution for Holmes. See Introduction, pp. 25–26.

3 A resonant phrase, perhaps calling to mind anxieties about extinction in the nineteenth century that were focused around Charles Darwin's account of biological evolution. It has literary echoes too, such as James Fenimore Cooper's *The Last of the Mohicans* (1826) and Edward Bulwer-Lytton's *The Last of the Barons* (1843). Being the "last of" a particular race provides a moment of comedy in chapter 11, volume 1, of Anthony

minutes I meet him at Waterloo Station. I have had a wire[1] that he arrived at Southampton this morning. Now, Mr. Holmes, what would you advise me to do with him?"

"Why should he not go to the home of his fathers?"

"It seems natural, does it not? And yet, consider that every Baskerville who goes there meets with an evil fate. I feel sure that if Sir Charles could have spoken with me before his death he would have warned me against bringing this, the last of the old race, and the heir to great wealth, to that deadly place. And yet it cannot be denied that the prosperity of the whole poor, bleak countryside depends upon his presence. All the good work which has been done by Sir Charles will crash to the ground if there is no tenant of the Hall. I fear lest I should be swayed too much by my own obvious interest in the matter, and that is why I bring the case before you and ask for your advice."

Holmes considered for a little time.

"Put into plain words, the matter is this," said he. "In your opinion there is a diabolical agency which makes Dartmoor an unsafe abode for a Baskerville—that is your opinion?"

"At least I might go the length of saying that there is some evidence that this may be so."

"Exactly. But surely, if your supernatural theory be correct, it could work the young man evil in London as easily as in Devonshire. A devil with merely local powers like a parish vestry[2] would be too inconceivable a thing."

"You put the matter more flippantly, Mr. Holmes, than you would probably do if you were brought into personal contact with these things. Your advice, then, as I understand it, is that the young man will be as safe in Devonshire as in London. He comes in fifty minutes. What would you recommend?"

"I recommend, sir, that you take a cab, call off your spaniel

---

Trollope's *Barchester Towers* (1857) where Dr Proudie, the vague Bishop of Barchester, is introduced to a child of half-Italian parentage who is heralded as the last of the Neros: "The bishop had heard of the last of the Visigoths, and had floating in his brain some indistinct idea of the last of the Mohicans, but to have the last of the Neros thus brought before him for a blessing was very staggering" (Anthony Trollope, *Barchester Towers* [Harmondsworth: Penguin, 1982], 87).

1 Colloquial word for telegram which was a message sent by electric telegraph, a system for transmitting signals through cables over distance.

2 That is, the meeting of the officers of a parish church to decide on parochial business.

who is scratching at my front door, and proceed to Waterloo to meet Sir Henry Baskerville."

"And then?"

"And then you will say nothing to him at all until I have made up my mind about the matter."

"How long will it take you to make up your mind?"

"Twenty-four hours. At ten o'clock to-morrow, Dr. Mortimer, I will be much obliged to you if you will call upon me here, and it will be of help to me in my plans for the future if you will bring Sir Henry Baskerville with you."

"I will do so, Mr. Holmes." He scribbled the appointment on his shirt-cuff and hurried off in his strange, peering, absentminded fashion. Holmes stopped him at the head of the stair.

"Only one more question, Dr. Mortimer. You say that before Sir Charles Baskerville's death several people saw this apparition upon the moor?"

"Three people did."

"Did any see it after?"

"I have not heard of any."

"Thank you. Good-morning."

Holmes returned to his seat with that quiet look of inward satisfaction which meant that he had a congenial task before him.

"Going out, Watson?"

"Unless I can help you."

"No, my dear fellow, it is at the hour of action that I turn to you for aid. But this is splendid, really unique from some points of view. When you pass Bradley's,[1] would you ask him to send up a pound of the strongest shag tobacco?[2] Thank you. It would be as well if you could make it convenient not to return before evening. Then I should be very glad to compare impressions as to this most interesting problem which has been submitted to us this morning."

I knew that seclusion and solitude were very necessary for my friend in those hours of intense mental concentration during which he weighed every particle of evidence, constructed alternative theories, balanced one against the other, and made up his mind as to which points were essential and which immaterial. I therefore spent the day at my club and did not return to Baker Street until evening. It was nearly nine o'clock when I found myself in the sitting-room once more.

My first impression as I opened the door was that a fire had

---

1   A fictitious—if plausible sounding—tobacconist.

2   A strong tobacco cut into fine shreds.

broken out, for the room was so filled with smoke that the light of the lamp upon the table was blurred by it. As I entered, however, my fears were set at rest, for it was the acrid fumes of strong coarse tobacco which took me by the throat and set me coughing. Through the haze I had a vague vision of Holmes in his dressing-gown coiled up in an armchair with his black clay pipe between his lips. Several rolls of paper lay around him.

"Caught cold, Watson?" said he.

"No, it's this poisonous atmosphere."

"I suppose it *is* pretty thick, now that you mention it."

"Thick! It is intolerable."

"Open the window, then! You have been at your club all day, I perceive."

"My dear Holmes!"

"Am I right?"

"Certainly, but how—?"

He laughed at my bewildered expression.

"There is a delightful freshness about you, Watson, which makes it a pleasure to exercise any small powers which I possess at your expense. A gentleman goes forth on a showery and miry day. He returns immaculate in the evening with the gloss still on his hat and his boots. He has been a fixture therefore all day. He is not a man with intimate friends. Where, then, could he have been? Is it not obvious?"

"Well, it is rather obvious."

"The world is full of obvious things which nobody by any chance ever observes. Where do you think that I have been?"

"A fixture also."

"On the contrary, I have been to Devonshire."

"In spirit?"

"Exactly. My body has remained in this armchair and has, I regret to observe, consumed in my absence two large pots of coffee and an incredible amount of tobacco. After you left I sent down to Stanford's[1] for the Ordnance map[2] of this portion of the

---

1 The cartographer and printer Edward Stanford (1827–1904)—the name was given as *Stamford's* in the *Strand* edition—founded a map maker's shop in London in 1852; the business is still active and now advertises itself as the world's leading privately owned map and travel book seller. The word was changed to "Stanford's" in the first English book edition.

2 The business of forming accurate maps of the United Kingdom for strategic purposes began in the modern era with George II who commissioned a military survey of the Scottish highlands in 1746; in 1841

(continued on page 76)

moor, and my spirit has hovered over it all day. I flatter myself that I could find my way about."

"A large scale map, I presume?"

"Very large." He unrolled one section and held it over his knee. "Here you have the particular district which concerns us. That is Baskerville Hall in the middle."

"With a wood round it?"

"Exactly. I fancy the Yew Alley, though not marked under that name, must stretch along this line, with the moor, as you perceive, upon the right of it. This small clump of buildings here is the hamlet of Grimpen, where our friend Dr. Mortimer has his headquarters. Within a radius of five miles there are, as you see, only a very few scattered dwellings. Here is Lafter Hall, which was mentioned in the narrative. There is a house indicated here which may be the residence of the naturalist—Stapleton, if I remember right, was his name. Here are two moorland farmhouses, High Tor[1] and Foulmire. Then fourteen miles away the great convict prison[2] of Princetown.[3] Between and around these scattered points extends the desolate, lifeless moor. This, then, is the stage upon which tragedy has been played, and upon which we may help to play it again."

"It must be a wild place."

"Yes, the setting is a worthy one. If the devil did desire to have a hand in the affairs of men—"

"Then you are yourself inclining to the supernatural explanation."

---

the Ordnance Survey Act gave surveyors rights to enter any land in the country and greatly facilitated the continued business of charting the nation. By 1863, scales of six inches and twenty-five inches to the mile had been approved for mountain and moorland, and rural areas respectively; by 1895 the twenty-five inch survey was complete. Holmes merely says that his map is of "very large" scale.

1   A tor is a rock pile on a high location, particularly in Devon, Cornwall, and Derbyshire. There is a Higher Tor on Dartmoor. See Baring-Gould, II.18.

2   The tautology stresses the prison's grimness.

3   Princetown prison was begun in 1806 to house French prisoners from the Napoleonic wars; in 1850 it was adapted to hold long-term inmates. "Dartmoor Prison" features significantly in "How the King Held the Brigadier" in *The Exploits of Brigadier Gerard*.

"The devil's agents may be of flesh and blood, may they not?[1] There are two questions waiting for us at the outset. The one is whether any crime has been committed at all; the second is, what is the crime and how was it committed? Of course, if Dr. Mortimer's surmise should be correct, and we are dealing with forces outside the ordinary laws of Nature, there is an end of our investigation. But we are bound to exhaust all other hypotheses before falling back upon this one. I think we'll shut that window again, if you don't mind. It is a singular thing, but I find that a concentrated atmosphere helps a concentration of thought. I have not pushed it to the length of getting into a box to think, but that is the logical outcome of my convictions. Have you turned the case over in your mind?"

"Yes, I have thought a good deal of it in the course of the day."

"What do you make of it?"

"It is very bewildering."

"It has certainly a character of its own. There are points of distinction about it. That change in the footprints, for example. What do you make of that?"

"Mortimer said that the man had walked on tiptoe down that portion of the alley."

"He only repeated what some fool had said at the inquest. Why should a man walk on tiptoe down the alley?"

"What then?"

"He was running, Watson—running desperately, running for his life, running until he burst his heart and fell dead upon his face."

"Running from what?"

"There lies our problem. There are indications that the man was crazed with fear before ever he began to run."

"How can you say that?"

"I am presuming that the cause of his fears came to him across the moor. If that were so, and it seems most probable only a man who had lost his wits would have run *from* the house instead of

---

1   A rare hint at something of Holmes's theological views. Cf. his reflections at the end of "The Adventure of the Cardboard Box" (1893): "What object is served by this circle of misery and violence and fear? It must tend to some end, or else our universe is ruled by chance, which is unthinkable. But what end? There is the great standing perennial problem to which human reason is as far from an answer as ever" (*CSH* 901).

towards it. If the gipsy's evidence may be taken as true, he ran with cries for help in the direction where help was least likely to be. Then, again, whom was he waiting for that night, and why was he waiting for him in the Yew Alley rather than in his own house?"

"You think that he was waiting for someone?"

"The man was elderly and infirm.[1] We can understand his taking an evening stroll, but the ground was damp and the night inclement. Is it natural that he should stand for five or ten minutes, as Dr. Mortimer, with more practical sense than I should have given him credit for,[2] deduced from the cigar ash?"

"But he went out every evening."

"I think it unlikely that he waited at the moor-gate every evening. On the contrary, the evidence is that he avoided the moor. That night he waited there. It was the night before he made his departure for London. The thing takes shape, Watson. It becomes coherent. Might I ask you to hand me my violin, and we will postpone all further thought upon this business until we have had the advantage of meeting Dr. Mortimer and Sir Henry Baskerville in the morning."

Chapter IV

Sir Henry Baskerville

Our breakfast-table was cleared early, and Holmes waited in his dressing-gown for the promised interview. Our clients were punctual to[3] their appointment, for the clock had just struck ten when Dr. Mortimer was shown up, followed by the young baronet.[4] The latter was a small, alert, dark-eyed man about thirty years of age, very sturdily built, with thick black eyebrows and a strong, pugnacious face. He wore a ruddy-tinted tweed suit and had the weather-beaten appearance of one who has spent most of his time

---

1   And therefore, one would have thought, a singularly unlikely candidate for an MP at the next election.

2   That is, "with more practical sense than I would otherwise have given him credit for."

3   Modern English would have "for."

4   A baronet is the lowest rung of the hereditary titles—passing here from uncle to nephew—in the English aristocracy, allowing the use of "Sir" before the name.

in the open air, and yet there was something in his steady eye and the quiet assurance of his bearing which indicated the gentleman.

"This is Sir Henry Baskerville," said Dr. Mortimer.

"Why, yes," said he, "and the strange thing is, Mr. Sherlock Holmes, that if my friend here had not proposed coming round to you this morning I should have come on my own account. I understand that you think out little puzzles, and I've had one this morning which wants more thinking out than I am able to give it."

"Pray take a seat, Sir Henry. Do I understand you to say that you have yourself had some remarkable experience since you arrived in London?"

"Nothing of much importance, Mr. Holmes. Only a joke, as like as not. It was this letter, if you can call it a letter, which reached me this morning."

He laid an envelope upon the table, and we all bent over it. It was of common quality, grayish in colour.[1] The address, "Sir Henry Baskerville, Northumberland Hotel,"[2] was printed in rough characters; the post-mark "Charing Cross," and the date of posting the preceding evening.

"Who knew that you were going to the Northumberland Hotel?" asked Holmes, glancing keenly across at our visitor.

---

1 Although no longer common, grey notepaper was a familiar Victorian colour choice.

2 There is a Northumberland Street and a Northumberland Avenue in central London; the former connects the latter with The Strand, close to Trafalgar Square and the Charing Cross area. It has often been said that the Hotel at which Sir Henry stays was on Northumberland Street in a building now known as The Sherlock Holmes [Inn] (it contains many "relics" of Sherlock Holmes, see Introduction, pp. 13–14). But there were hotels on Northumberland Avenue also which Conan Doyle might have had in mind, if he had anywhere particular in mind. If the Northumberland Hotel was in either of these locations, it would have been near to Great Scotland Yard, which, between 1829 and 1890, contained the headquarters of the London police. In 1861, there was a scandal at 16 Northumberland Street (which was demolished in 1874 to make way for the present Northumberland Avenue): the fatal wounding of William James Roberts. This widely-discussed crime would have given a Northumberland Street/Avenue address a little hint of sensation for those with long memories in 1901/02 (see Richard Altick's account of the murder in *Deadly Encounters: Two Victorian Sensations* [Philadelphia: U of Pennsylvania P, 1986]).

"No one could have known. We only decided after I met Dr. Mortimer."

"But Dr. Mortimer was no doubt already stopping there?"

"No, I had been staying with a friend," said the doctor. "There was no possible indication that we intended to go to this hotel."

"Hum! Someone seems to be very deeply interested in your movements." Out of the envelope he took a half-sheet of foolscap[1] paper folded into four. This he opened and spread flat upon the table. Across the middle of it a single sentence had been formed by the expedient of pasting printed words upon it. It ran: "As you value your life or your reason keep away from the moor." The word "moor" only was printed in ink.

"Now," said Sir Henry Baskerville, "perhaps you will tell me, Mr. Holmes, what in thunder is the meaning of that, and who it is that takes so much interest in my affairs?"

"What do you make of it, Dr. Mortimer? You must allow that there is nothing supernatural about this, at any rate?"

"No, sir, but it might very well come from someone who was convinced that the business is supernatural."

"What business?" asked Sir Henry sharply. "It seems to me that all you gentlemen know a great deal more than I do about my own affairs."

"You shall share our knowledge before you leave this room, Sir Henry. I promise you that," said Sherlock Holmes. "We will confine ourselves for the present with your permission to this very interesting document, which must have been put together and posted yesterday evening. Have you yesterday's *Times*,[2] Watson?"

"It is here in the corner."

"Might I trouble you for it—the inside page, please, with the leading articles?" He glanced swiftly over it, running his eyes up and down the columns.

"Capital article this on free trade. Permit me to give you an extract from it. 'You may be cajoled into imagining that your own special trade or your own industry will be encouraged by a protective tariff, but it stands to reason that such legislation must in the long run keep away wealth from the country, diminish the value of our imports, and lower the general conditions of life in this island.'

---

1 A paper size, though no exact standard of measurement was ever fixed.

2 Founded in 1788, *The Times* newspaper maintained its position as the most respected national newspaper throughout the nineteenth century.

"What do you think of that, Watson?" cried Holmes in high glee, rubbing his hands together with satisfaction. "Don't you think that is an admirable sentiment?"

Dr. Mortimer looked at Holmes with an air of professional interest,[1] and Sir Henry Baskerville turned a pair of puzzled dark eyes upon me.

"I don't know much about the tariff and things of that kind," said he, "but it seems to me we've got a bit off the trail so far as that note is concerned."

"On the contrary, I think we are particularly hot upon the trail, Sir Henry. Watson here knows more about my methods than you do, but I fear that even he has not quite grasped the significance of this sentence."

"No, I confess that I see no connection."

"And yet, my dear Watson, there is so very close a connection that the one is extracted out of the other. 'You,' 'your,' 'your,' 'life,' 'reason,' 'value,' 'keep away,' 'from the.' Don't you see now whence these words have been taken?"

"By thunder, you're right! Well, if that isn't smart!" cried Sir Henry.

"If any possible doubt remained it is settled by the fact that 'keep away' and 'from the' are cut out in one piece."

"Well, now—so it is!"

"Really, Mr. Holmes, this exceeds anything which I could have imagined," said Dr. Mortimer, gazing at my friend in amazement. "I could understand anyone saying that the words were from a newspaper; but that you should name which, and add that it came from the leading article, is really one of the most remarkable things which I have ever known. How did you do it?"

"I presume, Doctor, that you could tell the skull of a negro from that of an Esquimau?"[2]

"Most certainly."

"But how?"

"Because that is my special hobby. The differences are obvious. The supra-orbital crest, the facial angle, the maxillary[3] curve, the—"

"But this is my special hobby, and the differences are equally

---

1 That is, Holmes's sanity appears in doubt, of interest to a doctor.

2 Later to be spelled "Eskimo," and now a racially offensive term; to Conan Doyle merely neutrally descriptive of Inuit peoples.

3 Of the jawbone.

obvious. There is as much difference to my eyes between the lead-ed bourgeois[1] type of a *Times* article and the slovenly print of an evening halfpenny[2] paper as there could be between your negro and your Esquimaux. The detection of types[3] is one of the most elementary branches of knowledge to the special expert in crime, though I confess that once when I was very young I confused the *Leeds Mercury* with the *Western Morning News*.[4] But a *Times* leader is entirely distinctive, and these words could have been taken from nothing else. As it was done yesterday the strong probabili-ty was that we should find the words in yesterday's issue."

"So far as I can follow you, then, Mr. Holmes," said Sir Henry Baskerville, "someone cut out this message with a scissors—"[5]

"Nail-scissors," said Holmes. "You can see that it was a very short-bladed scissors, since the cutter had to take two snips over "keep away.'"

"That is so. Someone, then, cut out the message with a pair of short-bladed scissors, pasted it with paste—"

"Gum," said Holmes.

"With gum on to the paper. But I want to know why the word 'moor' should have been written?"

---

1 A size of printing type, technically that between Long Primer and Brevi-er, used by *The Times*. It is pronounced to rhyme with "rejoice." "Lead-ed" meant that the lines of type had, between them, narrow strips of lead, which gave a neat appearance, different from the "slovenly" quality of the unleaded presses.

2 Pronounced "hay'penny."

3 This is a little joke about criminological theories that sought to identify criminal *types*—that is, for instance, Francis Galton's composite portraits of criminals. See Appendix B, pp. 245–49.

4 As other commentators have pointed out, this was a considerable error, given, for much of the nineteenth century, the two papers looked thor-oughly different. W. W. Robson makes a sensible observation: "There is no reason to believe ACD was acquainted with [the *Leeds Mercury*]: he just might have seen a copy in 1878, when he was briefly a medical assistant in Sheffield. But it probably stems from the two rival Plymouth dailies, the *Western Morning News* and the *Western Daily Mercury*, both launched in 1860 in vehement professional and political rivalry, which could certainly have made their confusion a social solecism for (say) the neophyte Dr Conan Doyle in Plymouth in early 1882" (Robson, 176). There are reproductions of extracts from both the *Leeds Mercury* and *Western Morning News* in Baring-Gould, II.23.

5 Modern English no longer uses the indefinite article (a).

"Because he could not find it in print. The other words were all simple and might be found in any issue, but 'moor' would be less common."

"Why, of course, that would explain it. Have you read anything else in this message, Mr. Holmes?"

"There are one or two indications, and yet the utmost pains have been taken to remove all clues. The address, you observe, is printed in rough characters. But the *Times* is a paper which is seldom found in any hands but those of the highly educated. We may take it, therefore, that the letter was composed by an educated man[1] who wished to pose as an uneducated one, and his effort to conceal his own writing suggests that that writing might be known, or come to be known, by you. Again, you will observe that the words are not gummed on in an accurate line, but that some are much higher than others. 'Life,' for example is quite out of its proper place. That may point to carelessness or it may point to agitation and hurry upon the part of the cutter. On the whole I incline to the latter view, since the matter was evidently important, and it is unlikely that the composer of such a letter would be careless. If he were in a hurry it opens up the interesting question why he should be in a hurry, since any letter posted up to early morning would reach Sir Henry before he would leave his hotel. Did the composer fear an interruption—and from whom?"

"We are coming now rather into the region of guesswork," said Dr. Mortimer.

"Say, rather, into the region where we balance probabilities and choose the most likely. It is the scientific use of the imagination,[2] but we have always some material basis on which to start our speculation. Now, you would call it a guess, no doubt, but I am almost certain that this address has been written in a hotel."

"How in the world can you say that?"

"If you examine it carefully you will see that both the pen and the ink have given the writer trouble. The pen has spluttered twice in a single word and has run dry three times in a short

1 Holmes will later reveal he was being a fraction disingenuous in this identification of sex.

2 A phrase borrowed from extensive mid-Victorian discussions about the place of imagination in empirical science, the most prominent contribution of which was John Tyndall's *On the Scientific Use of the Imagination: A Discourse Delivered before the British Association at Liverpool on* [...] *16th Sept. 1870* (London: Longmans, Green, 1870).

address, showing that there was very little ink in the bottle. Now, a private pen or ink-bottle is seldom allowed to be in such a state, and the combination of the two must be quite rare. But you know the hotel ink and the hotel pen, where it is rare to get anything else. Yes, I have very little hesitation in saying that could we examine the waste-paper baskets of the hotels around Charing Cross until we found the remains of the mutilated *Times* leader we could lay our hands straight upon the person who sent this singular message. Halloa! Halloa![1] What's this?"

He was carefully examining the foolscap, upon which the words were pasted, holding it only an inch or two from his eyes.

"Well?"

"Nothing," said he, throwing it down. "It is a blank half-sheet of paper, without even a water-mark[2] upon it. I think we have drawn as much as we can from this curious letter; and now, Sir Henry, has anything else of interest happened to you since you have been in London?"

"Why, no, Mr. Holmes. I think not."

"You have not observed anyone follow or watch you?"

"I seem to have walked right into the thick of a dime novel,"[3] said our visitor. "Why in thunder should anyone follow or watch me?"

"We are coming to that. You have nothing else to report to us before we go into this matter?"

"Well, it depends upon what you think worth reporting."

"I think anything out of the ordinary routine of life well worth reporting."

Sir Henry smiled.

"I don't know much of British life yet, for I have spent nearly all my time in the States and in Canada. But I hope that to lose one of your boots is not part of the ordinary routine of life over here."

"You have lost one of your boots?"

"My dear sir," cried Dr. Mortimer, "it is only mislaid. You will find it when you return to the hotel. What is the use of troubling Mr. Holmes with trifles of this kind?"

---

1 One of the late Victorian spellings of "Hello" and not pronounced differently from it (cf. "cocoa" today).

2 A crest or initials or some form of device added by the paper maker in some forms of—often expensive—writing paper: most watermarks are visible only when holding the paper to the light.

3 Cheap sensation novel.

"Well, he asked me for anything outside the ordinary routine."

"Exactly," said Holmes, "however foolish the incident may seem. You have lost one of your boots, you say?"

"Well, mislaid it, anyhow. I put them both outside my door last night, and there was only one in the morning. I could get no sense out of the chap who cleans them. The worst of it is that I only bought the pair last night in the Strand,[1] and I have never had them on."

"If you have never worn them, why did you put them out to be cleaned?"

"They were tan boots and had never been varnished. That was why I put them out."

"Then I understand that on your arrival in London yesterday you went out at once and bought a pair of boots?"

"I did a good deal of shopping. Dr. Mortimer here went round with me. You see, if I am to be squire down there I must dress the part, and it may be that I have got a little careless in my ways out West. Among other things I bought these brown boots—gave six dollars for them—and had one stolen before ever I had them on my feet."

"It seems a singularly useless thing to steal," said Sherlock Holmes. "I confess that I share Dr. Mortimer's belief that it will not be long before the missing boot is found."

"And, now, gentlemen," said the baronet with decision, "it seems to me that I have spoken quite enough about the little that I know. It is time that you kept your promise and gave me a full account of what we are all driving at."

"Your request is a very reasonable one," Holmes answered. "Dr. Mortimer, I think you could not do better than to tell your story as you told it to us."

Thus encouraged, our scientific friend drew his papers from his pocket and presented the whole case as he had done upon the morning before. Sir Henry Baskerville listened with the deepest attention and with an occasional exclamation of surprise.

"Well, I seem to have come into an inheritance with a vengeance," said he when the long narrative was finished. "Of course, I've heard of the hound ever since I was in the nursery. It's the pet story of the family,[2] though I never thought of taking it seriously before. But as to my uncle's death—well, it all seems

1 Major London road, connecting Trafalgar Square with the City.
2 A dreadful (and accidental?) anti-pun.

boiling up in my head, and I can't get it clear yet. You don't seem quite to have made up your mind whether it's a case for a policeman or a clergyman."

"Precisely."

"And now there's this affair of the letter to me at the hotel. I suppose that fits into its place."

"It seems to show that someone knows more than we do about what goes on upon the moor," said Dr. Mortimer.

"And also," said Holmes, "that someone is not ill-disposed towards you, since they warn you of danger."

"Or it may be that they wish, for their own purposes, to scare me away."

"Well, of course, that is possible also. I am very much indebted to you, Dr. Mortimer, for introducing me to a problem which presents several interesting alternatives. But the practical point which we now have to decide, Sir Henry, is whether it is or is not advisable for you to go to Baskerville Hall."

"Why should I not go?"

"There seems to be danger."

"Do you mean danger from this family fiend or do you mean danger from human beings?"

"Well, that is what we have to find out."

"Whichever it is, my answer is fixed. There is no devil in hell, Mr. Holmes, and there is no man upon earth who can prevent me from going to the home of my own people, and you may take that to be my final answer." His dark brows knitted and his face flushed to a dusky red as he spoke. It was evident that the fiery temper of the Baskervilles was not extinct in this their last representative. "Meanwhile," said he, "I have hardly had time to think over all that you have told me. It's a big thing for a man to have to understand and to decide at one sitting. I should like to have a quiet hour by myself to make up my mind. Now, look here, Mr. Holmes, it's half-past eleven now and I am going back right away to my hotel. Suppose you and your friend, Dr. Watson, come round and lunch with us at two. I'll be able to tell you more clearly then how this thing strikes me."

"Is that convenient to you, Watson?"

"Perfectly."

"Then you may expect us. Shall I have a cab called?"

"I'd prefer to walk, for this affair has flurried me rather."

"I'll join you in a walk, with pleasure," said his companion.

"Then we meet again at two o'clock. Au revoir, and good-morning!"

We heard the steps of our visitors descend the stair and the bang of the front door. In an instant Holmes had changed from the languid dreamer to the man of action.

"Your hat and boots, Watson, quick! Not a moment to lose!" He rushed into his room in his dressing-gown and was back again in a few seconds in a frock-coat. We hurried together down the stairs and into the street. Dr. Mortimer and Baskerville were still visible about two hundred yards ahead of us in the direction of Oxford Street.[1]

"Shall I run on and stop them?"

"Not for the world, my dear Watson. I am perfectly satisfied with your company if you will tolerate mine. Our friends are wise, for it is certainly a very fine morning for a walk."

He quickened his pace until we had decreased the distance which divided us by about half. Then, still keeping a hundred yards behind, we followed into Oxford Street and so down Regent Street. Once our friends stopped and stared into a shop window, upon which Holmes did the same. An instant afterwards he gave a little cry of satisfaction, and, following the direction of his eager eyes, I saw that a hansom cab[2] with a man inside which had halted on the other side of the street was now proceeding slowly onward again.

"There's our man, Watson! Come along! We'll have a good look at him, if we can do no more."

At that instant I was aware of a bushy black beard and a pair of piercing eyes turned upon us through the side window of the cab. Instantly the trapdoor at the top flew up, something was screamed to the driver, and the cab flew madly off down Regent Street. Holmes looked eagerly round for another, but no empty one was in sight. Then he dashed in wild pursuit amid the stream of the traffic, but the start was too great, and already the cab was out of sight.

"There now!" said Holmes bitterly as he emerged panting and white with vexation from the tide of vehicles. "Was ever such bad luck and such bad management, too? Watson, Watson, if you are an honest man you will record this also and set it against my successes!"

"Who was the man?"

---

1 Central London fashionable commercial street.

2 The standard London cab, a low-hung, two-wheeled, horse-drawn cabriolet, seating two, with a driver mounted on the outside.

"I have not an idea."

"A spy?"

"Well, it was evident from what we have heard that Baskerville has been very closely shadowed by someone since he has been in town. How else could it be known so quickly that it was the Northumberland Hotel which he had chosen? If they had followed him the first day I argued that they would follow him also the second.[1] You may have observed that I twice strolled over to the window while Dr. Mortimer was reading his legend."

"Yes, I remember."

"I was looking out for loiterers in the street, but I saw none. We are dealing with a clever man, Watson. This matter cuts very deep, and though I have not finally made up my mind whether it is a benevolent or a malevolent agency which is in touch with us, I am conscious always of power and design. When our friends left I at once followed them in the hopes of marking down their invisible attendant. So wily was he that he had not trusted himself upon foot, but he had availed himself of a cab so that he could loiter behind or dash past them and so escape their notice. His method had the additional advantage that if they were to take a cab he was all ready to follow them. It has, however, one obvious disadvantage."

"It puts him in the power of the cabman."

"Exactly."

"What a pity we did not get the number!"

"My dear Watson, clumsy as I have been, you surely do not seriously imagine that I neglected to get the number? 2704 is our man. But that is no use to us for the moment."

"I fail to see how you could have done more."

"On observing the cab I should have instantly turned and walked in the other direction. I should then at my leisure have hired a second cab and followed the first at a respectful distance, or, better still, have driven to the Northumberland Hotel and waited there. When our unknown had followed Baskerville home we should have had the opportunity of playing his own game upon himself and seeing where he made for. As it is, by an indiscreet eagerness, which was taken advantage of with extraordinary quickness and energy by our opponent, we have betrayed ourselves and lost our man."

We had been sauntering slowly down Regent Street during this

---

1   It is never clear why the spy should do so.

conversation, and Dr. Mortimer, with his companion, had long vanished in front of us.

"There is no object in our following them," said Holmes. "The shadow has departed and will not return. We must see what further cards we have in our hands and play them with decision. Could you swear to that man's face within the cab?"

"I could swear only to the beard."

"And so could I—from which I gather that in all probability it was a false one. A clever man upon so delicate an errand has no use for a beard save to conceal his features.[1] Come in here, Watson!"

He turned into one of the district messenger offices,[2] where he was warmly greeted by the manager.

"Ah, Wilson, I see you have not forgotten the little case in which I had the good fortune to help you?"

"No, sir, indeed I have not. You saved my good name, and perhaps my life."

"My dear fellow, you exaggerate. I have some recollection, Wilson, that you had among your boys a lad named Cartwright, who showed some ability during the investigation."

"Yes, sir, he is still with us."

"Could you ring him up?—thank you! And I should be glad to have change of this five-pound note."

A lad of fourteen, with a bright, keen face, had obeyed the summons of the manager. He stood now gazing with great reverence at the famous detective.

"Let me have the Hotel Directory," said Holmes. "Thank you! Now, Cartwright, there are the names of twenty-three hotels here, all in the immediate neighbourhood of Charing Cross. Do you see?"

"Yes, sir."

"You will visit each of these in turn."

"Yes, sir."

"You will begin in each case by giving the outside porter one shilling. Here are twenty-three shillings."

---

1 Conan Doyle's hurried pace of working encourages him here to write one of Holmes's most absurd remarks, though it perhaps should be said that beards were no longer as fashionable at the end of the nineteenth century as they had been in the middle of Victoria's reign.

2 From which telegrams could be sent or phone calls made in the absence of many domestic telephones.

"Yes, sir."

"You will tell him that you want to see the waste-paper of yesterday. You will say that an important telegram has miscarried and that you are looking for it. You understand?"

"Yes, sir."

"But what you are really looking for is the centre page of the *Times* with some holes cut in it with scissors. Here is a copy of the *Times*. It is this page. You could easily recognize it, could you not?"

"Yes, sir."

"In each case the outside porter will send for the hall porter, to whom also you will give a shilling. Here are twenty-three shillings. You will then learn in possibly twenty cases out of the twenty-three that the waste of the day before has been burned or removed. In the three other cases you will be shown a heap of paper and you will look for this page of the *Times* among it. The odds are enormously against your finding it. There are ten shillings over in case of emergencies. Let me have a report by wire at Baker Street before evening. And now, Watson, it only remains for us to find out by wire the identity of the cabman, No. 2704, and then we will drop into one of the Bond Street picture-galleries[1] and fill in the time until we are due at the hotel."

---

1   The Grosvenor Gallery was the most famous of galleries in this area (on New Bond Street, in fact). Under the management of Sir Coutts Lindsay (1824–1913), it had become a centre for modern painting, late Pre-Raphaelitism, and the work of the Aesthetic Movement: paintings included canvases by Edward Burne-Jones (1833–98), John Everett Millais (1829–96), Lawrence Alma Tadema (1836–1912), Frederick Leighton (1830–96), and James Abbott McNeill Whistler (1834–1903). In the summer of 1877 it had also become the focus of an artistic *cause célèbre*. The art and social critic John Ruskin (1819–1900), in his monthly public letter published under the title *Fors Clavigera* (1871–84), had memorably denounced Whistler's work, saying "I have seen, and heard, much of Cockney impudence before now; but never expected to hear a coxcomb ask two hundred guineas for flinging a pot of paint in the public's face" (*The Complete Works of John Ruskin* ed. by E.T. Cook and Alexander Wedderburn, 39 vols [London: Allen, 1903–12], xxix.160). Whistler took Ruskin to court in 1878, an important event in the history of the Aesthetic Movement. Whistler technically won his libel case but was awarded derisory damages of a farthing (a quarter of one penny), making him feel that, in truth, he had lost. Holmes, as we find out at the beginning of the next chapter, has, according to Dr Watson, the "crudest ideas" about art. Having apparently "crude ideas" and the exhibitions of the Grosvenor Gallery were, thanks to Whistler's vexation with Ruskin, intimately connected at the end of the century.

Chapter V

Three Broken Threads

Sherlock Holmes had, in a very remarkable degree, the power of detaching his mind at will. For two hours the strange business in which we had been involved appeared to be forgotten, and he was entirely absorbed in the pictures of the modern Belgian masters.[1] He would talk of nothing but art, of which he had the crudest ideas,[2] from our leaving the gallery until we found ourselves at the Northumberland Hotel.

"Sir Henry Baskerville is upstairs expecting you," said the clerk. "He asked me to show you up at once when you came."

"Have you any objection to my looking at your register?" said Holmes.

"Not in the least."

The book showed that two names had been added after that of Baskerville. One was Theophilus Johnson and family, of Newcastle; the other Mrs. Oldmore and maid, of High Lodge, Alton.[3]

"Surely that must be the same Johnson whom I used to know," said Holmes to the porter. "A lawyer, is he not, gray-headed, and walks with a limp?"

"No, sir, this is Mr. Johnson, the coal-owner,[4] a very active gentleman, not older than yourself."

---

1 Presumably, as has been often suggested, the work of the Brussels *Groupe des XX* [vingt], including Félicien Rops (1833–98) and James Ensor (1860–1949). If so, one wonders what Conan Doyle thought Holmes might have made of the sexualized art of Rops' *La Tentation de Saint-Antoine* (1878) or *Pornokrates* (1878).

2 Holmes is carefully separated from anyone with refined artistic judgment and, more specifically, from the Aesthete here. In fact, in "The Greek Interpreter" (1893), we learn (*CSH* 435) that Holmes had artistic blood in his family: his grandmother was, it is implied, the sister of the (real) French artist Claude-Joseph Vernet (1714–89). On the broader cultural question of Holmes, masculinity, and the *fin de siècle*, see Joseph Kestner, *Sherlock's Men: Masculinity, Conan Doyle and Cultural History* (Aldershot and Burlington, VT: Ashgate, 1997) and Diana Barsham, *Arthur Conan Doyle and the Meaning of Masculinity* (Aldershot and Burlington, VT: Ashgate, 2000).

3 Newcastle on Tyne, a substantial city in north eastern England (rather than the much smaller Midlands town of Newcastle under Lyne); Alton is a town in Hampshire, near Basingstoke.

4 Newcastle on Tyne is (proverbially) famous for coal.

"Surely you are mistaken about his trade?"

"No, sir! he has used this hotel for many years, and he is very well known to us."

"Ah, that settles it. Mrs. Oldmore, too; I seem to remember the name. Excuse my curiosity, but often in calling upon one friend one finds another."

"She is an invalid lady, sir. Her husband was once Mayor of Gloucester.[1] She always comes to us when she is in town."

"Thank you; I am afraid I cannot claim her acquaintance. We have established a most important fact by these questions, Watson," he continued in a low voice as we went upstairs together. "We know now that the people who are so interested in our friend have not settled down in his own hotel. That means that while they are, as we have seen, very anxious to watch him, they are equally anxious that he should not see them. Now, this is a most suggestive fact."

"What does it suggest?"

"It suggests—halloa, my dear fellow, what on earth is the matter?"

As we came round the top of the stairs we had run up against Sir Henry Baskerville himself. His face was flushed with anger, and he held an old and dusty boot in one of his hands. So furious was he that he was hardly articulate, and when he did speak it was in a much broader and more Western dialect than any which we had heard from him in the morning.

"Seems to me they are playing me for a sucker[2] in this hotel," he cried. "They'll find they've started in to monkey with the wrong man unless they are careful. By thunder, if that chap can't find my missing boot there will be trouble. I can take a joke with the best, Mr. Holmes, but they've got a bit over the mark this time."

"Still looking for your boot?"

"Yes, sir, and mean to find it."

"But, surely, you said that it was a new brown boot?"

"So it was, sir. And now it's an old black one."

"What! you don't mean to say?"

---

1 Cathedral city in the south west of England.

2 A simpleton. Conan Doyle is attempting to make Sir Henry sound like a turn-of-the-century American (he says "By thunder" a little later, and periodically thereafter, which is meant to have the same effect). See Introduction, p. 28.

"That's just what I do mean to say. I only had three pairs in the world—the new brown, the old black, and the patent leathers, which I am wearing. Last night they took one of my brown ones, and to-day they have sneaked one of the black. Well, have you got it? Speak out, man, and don't stand staring!"

An agitated German waiter had appeared upon the scene.

"No, sir; I have made inquiry all over the hotel, but I can hear no word of it."

"Well, either that boot comes back before sundown or I'll see the manager and tell him that I go right straight out of this hotel."

"It shall be found, sir—I promise you that if you will have a little patience it will be found."

"Mind it is, for it's the last thing of mine that I'll lose in this den of thieves. Well, well, Mr. Holmes, you'll excuse my troubling you about such a trifle—"

"I think it's well worth troubling about."

"Why, you look very serious over it."

"How do you explain it?"

"I just don't attempt to explain it. It seems the very maddest, queerest thing that ever happened to me."

"The queerest, perhaps—" said Holmes thoughtfully.

"What do you make of it yourself?"

"Well, I don't profess to understand it yet. This case of yours is very complex, Sir Henry. When taken in conjunction with your uncle's death I am not sure that of all the five hundred cases of capital importance which I have handled there is one which cuts so deep. But we hold several threads in our hands, and the odds are that one or other of them guides us to the truth.[1] We may waste time in following the wrong one, but sooner or later we must come upon the right."

We had a pleasant luncheon in which little was said of the business which had brought us together. It was in the private sitting-room to which we afterwards repaired that Holmes asked Baskerville what were his intentions.

---

1 Holmes's metaphor—picking up on the title of the chapter—works in its own terms as a description of the investigation but also recalls familiar images of the ancient classical goddesses, the three Fates, who held the threads of men's lives (in detail, Clotho spun them, Lachesis measured their allotted length, and Atropos cut them when the time for death was reached). Holmes's superior, god-like position as the dealer of justice and arbiter of life and death is subtly suggested.

"To go to Baskerville Hall."

"And when?"

"At the end of the week."

"On the whole," said Holmes, "I think that your decision is a wise one. I have ample evidence that you are being dogged[1] in London, and amid the millions[2] of this great city it is difficult to discover who these people are or what their object can be. If their intentions are evil they might do you a mischief, and we should be powerless to prevent it. You did not know, Dr. Mortimer, that you were followed this morning from my house?"

Dr. Mortimer started violently.

"Followed! By whom?"

"That, unfortunately, is what I cannot tell you. Have you among your neighbours or acquaintances on Dartmoor any man with a black, full beard?"

"No—or, let me see—why, yes. Barrymore, Sir Charles's butler, is a man with a full, black beard."

"Ha! Where is Barrymore?"

"He is in charge of the Hall."

"We had best ascertain if he is really there, or if by any possibility he might be in London."

"How can you do that?"

"Give me a telegraph form. 'Is all ready for Sir Henry?' That will do. Address to Mr. Barrymore, Baskerville Hall. What is the nearest telegraph-office? Grimpen. Very good, we will send a second wire to the postmaster, Grimpen: 'Telegram to Mr. Barrymore, to be delivered into his own hand. If absent, please return wire to Sir Henry Baskerville, Northumberland Hotel.' That should let us know before evening whether Barrymore is at his post in Devonshire or not."

"That's so," said Baskerville. "By the way, Dr. Mortimer, who is this Barrymore, anyhow?"

"He is the son of the old caretaker, who is dead. They have looked after the Hall for four generations now. So far as I know, he and his wife are as respectable a couple as any in the county."

"At the same time," said Baskerville, "it's clear enough that so

---

1   The first—almost *too* appropriate—use of a canine metaphor in the text. There are many more to come, though one wonders if Conan Doyle noticed all of them.

2   By the time of the death of Queen Victoria in 1901, there were over six million inhabitants of London.

long as there are none of the family at the Hall these people have a mighty fine home and nothing to do."

"That is true."

"Did Barrymore profit at all by Sir Charles's will?" asked Holmes.

"He and his wife had five hundred pounds each."

"Ha! Did they know that they would receive this?"

"Yes; Sir Charles was very fond of talking about the provisions of his will."

"That is very interesting."

"I hope," said Dr. Mortimer, "that you do not look with suspicious eyes upon everyone who received a legacy from Sir Charles, for I also had a thousand pounds left to me."

"Indeed! And anyone else?"

"There were many insignificant sums to individuals, and a large number of public charities. The residue all went to Sir Henry."

"And how much was the residue?"

"Seven hundred and forty thousand pounds."

Holmes raised his eyebrows in surprise. "I had no idea that so gigantic a sum was involved," said he.

"Sir Charles had the reputation of being rich, but we did not know how very rich he was until we came to examine his securities.[1] The total value of the estate was close on to a million."

"Dear me! It is a stake for which a man might well play a desperate game. And one more question, Dr. Mortimer. Supposing that anything happened to our young friend here—you will forgive the unpleasant hypothesis!—who would inherit the estate?"

"Since Rodger Baskerville, Sir Charles's younger brother, died unmarried, the estate would descend to the Desmonds, who are distant cousins. James Desmond is an elderly clergyman in Westmorland.[2]

"Thank you. These details are all of great interest. Have you met Mr. James Desmond?"

"Yes; he once came down to visit Sir Charles. He is a man of venerable appearance and of saintly life. I remember that he refused to accept any settlement from Sir Charles, though he pressed it upon him."

---

1 Certificates confirming any form of investment.
2 Mountainous lakeland county in the north west of England.

"And this man of simple tastes would be the heir to Sir Charles's thousands."

"He would be the heir to the estate because that is entailed. He would also be the heir to the money unless it were willed otherwise by the present owner, who can, of course, do what he likes with it."

"And have you made your will, Sir Henry?"

"No, Mr. Holmes, I have not. I've had no time, for it was only yesterday that I learned how matters stood. But in any case I feel that the money should go with the title and estate. That was my poor uncle's idea. How is the owner going to restore the glories of the Baskervilles if he has not money enough to keep up the property? House, land, and dollars must go together."

"Quite so. Well, Sir Henry, I am of one mind with you as to the advisability of your going down to Devonshire without delay. There is only one provision which I must make. You certainly must not go alone."

"Dr. Mortimer returns with me."

"But Dr. Mortimer has his practice to attend to, and his house is miles away from yours. With all the good will in the world he may be unable to help you. No, Sir Henry, you must take with you someone, a trusty man, who will be always by your side."

"Is it possible that you could come yourself, Mr. Holmes?"

"If matters came to a crisis I should endeavour to be present in person; but you can understand that, with my extensive consulting practice and with the constant appeals which reach me from many quarters, it is impossible for me to be absent from London for an indefinite time. At the present instant one of the most revered names in England is being besmirched by a blackmailer, and only I can stop a disastrous scandal. You will see how impossible it is for me to go to Dartmoor."

"Whom would you recommend, then?"

Holmes laid his hand upon my arm.

"If my friend would undertake it there is no man who is better worth having at your side when you are in a tight place. No one can say so more confidently than I."

The proposition took me completely by surprise, but before I had time to answer, Baskerville seized me by the hand and wrung it heartily.

"Well, now, that is real kind of you, Dr. Watson," said he. "You see how it is with me, and you know just as much about the matter as I do. If you will come down to Baskerville Hall and see me through I'll never forget it."

The promise of adventure had always a fascination for me, and I was complimented by the words of Holmes and by the eagerness with which the baronet hailed me as a companion.

"I will come, with pleasure," said I. "I do not know how I could employ my time better."

"And you will report very carefully to me," said Holmes. "When a crisis comes, as it will do, I will direct how you shall act. I suppose that by Saturday all might be ready?"

"Would that suit Dr. Watson?"

"Perfectly."

"Then on Saturday, unless you hear to the contrary, we shall meet at the ten-thirty train from Paddington."[1]

We had risen to depart when Baskerville gave a cry, of triumph, and diving into one of the corners of the room he drew a brown boot from under a cabinet.

"My missing boot!" he cried.

"May all our difficulties vanish as easily!" said Sherlock Holmes.

"But it is a very, singular thing," Dr. Mortimer remarked. "I searched this room carefully before lunch."

"And so did I," said Baskerville. "Every inch of it."

"There was certainly no boot in it then."

"In that case the waiter must have placed it there while we were lunching."

The German was sent for but professed to know nothing of the matter, nor could any inquiry clear it up. Another item had been added to that constant and apparently purposeless series of small mysteries which had succeeded each other so rapidly. Setting aside the whole grim story of Sir Charles's death, we had a line of inexplicable incidents all within the limits of two days, which included the receipt of the printed letter, the black-bearded spy in the hansom, the loss of the new brown boot, the loss of the old black boot, and now the return of the new brown boot. Holmes sat in silence in the cab as we drove back to Baker Street, and I knew from his drawn brows and keen face that his mind, like my own, was busy in endeavouring to frame some scheme into which all these strange and apparently disconnected episodes could be

---

1 Paddington Station, London, was built 1852–54 as the capital's terminal of the Great Western Railway, which ran initially to Bristol, and later to Plymouth, and was therefore the gateway to Devon, Somerset, and Cornwall. There seems to have been a 10.30 train to Plymouth in 1901—but only on Sundays.

fitted. All afternoon and late into the evening he sat lost in tobacco and thought.

Just before dinner two telegrams were handed in. The first ran:

"Have just heard that Barrymore is at the Hall.—BASKERVILLE."

The second:

"Visited twenty-three hotels as directed, but sorry to report unable to trace cut sheet of *Times*—CARTWRIGHT."

"There go two of my threads, Watson. There is nothing more stimulating than a case where everything goes against you. We must cast round for another scent."[1]

"We have still the cabman who drove the spy."

"Exactly. I have wired to get his name and address from the Official Registry. I should not be surprised if this were an answer to my question."

The ring at the bell proved to be something even more satisfactory than an answer, however, for the door opened and a rough-looking fellow entered who was evidently the man himself.

"I got a message from the head office that a gent at this address had been inquiring for 2704," said he. "I've driven my cab this seven years and never a word of complaint. I came here straight from the Yard to ask you to your face what you had against me."

"I have nothing in the world against you, my good man," said Holmes. "On the contrary, I have half a sovereign for you if you will give me a clear answer to my questions."

"Well, I've had a good day and no mistake," said the cabman with a grin. "What was it you wanted to ask, sir?"

"First of all your name and address, in case I want you again."

"John Clayton, 3, Turpey Street, the Borough.[2] My cab is out of Shipley's Yard, near Waterloo Station."

Sherlock Holmes made a note of it.

"Now, Clayton, tell me all about the fare who came and watched this house at ten o'clock this morning and afterwards followed the two gentlemen down Regent Street."

The man looked surprised and a little embarrassed.

"Why there's no good my telling you things, for you seem to know as much as I do already," said he. "The truth is that the gentleman told me that he was a detective and that I was to say nothing about him to anyone."

---

1 Holmes imagines himself and Watson as tracker dogs.
2 District in London, south of the Thames, just east of Southwark.

"My good fellow; this is a very serious business, and you may find yourself in a pretty bad position if you try to hide anything from me. You say that your fare told you that he was a detective?"

"Yes, he did."

"When did he say this?"

"When he left me."

"Did he say anything more?"

"He mentioned his name."

Holmes cast a swift glance of triumph at me. "Oh, he mentioned his name, did he? That was imprudent. What was the name that he mentioned?"

"His name," said the cabman, "was Mr. Sherlock Holmes."

Never have I seen my friend more completely taken aback than by the cabman's reply. For an instant he sat in silent amazement. Then he burst into a hearty laugh.

"A touch, Watson—an undeniable touch!" said he.[1] "I feel a foil[2] as quick and supple as my own.[3] He got home upon me very prettily that time. So his name was Sherlock Holmes, was it?"

"Yes, sir, that was the gentleman's name."

"Excellent! Tell me where you picked him up, and all that occurred."

"He hailed me at half-past nine in Trafalgar Square. He said that he was a detective, and he offered me two guineas[4] if I would do exactly what he wanted all day and ask no questions. I was glad enough to agree. First we drove down to the Northumberland Hotel and waited there until two gentlemen came out and took a cab from the rank. We followed their cab until it pulled up somewhere near here."

---

1   A "touch" is a term from fencing; Holmes is remembering Laertes in *Hamlet* 5.2.285: "A touch, a touch, I do confess." Although not very frequently, Holmes now and again admits to an awareness of literature. In *The Sign of Four*, for example, he quotes (in German) from Goethe whom he calls "always pithy" (*CSH* 115), and tells Watson that "There is much food for thought in Richter" (*CSH* 121). Watson is accordingly rather hard on Holmes when, at the start of their relationship in *A Study in Scarlet*, he lists "Sherlock Holmes—his limits 1. Knowledge of Literature.—Nil..." (*CSH* 21).

2   A light flexible sword, used in fencing.

3   There is a little joke here in response to someone who has used Sherlock Holmes's own name against him.

4   1 guinea = 1 pound and 1 shilling = £1.05. Two make a substantial sum indeed for a cab driver.

"This very door," said Holmes.

"Well, I couldn't be sure of that, but I dare say my fare knew all about it. We pulled up halfway down the street and waited an hour and a half. Then the two gentlemen passed us, walking, and we followed down Baker Street and along—"

"I know," said Holmes.

"Until we got three-quarters down Regent Street. Then my gentleman threw up the trap, and he cried that I should drive right away to Waterloo Station as hard as I could go. I whipped up the mare and we were there under the ten minutes. Then he paid up his two guineas, like a good one, and away he went into the station. Only just as he was leaving he turned round and he said: 'It might interest you to know that you have been driving Mr. Sherlock Holmes.' That's how I come to know the name."

"I see. And you saw no more of him?"

"Not after he went into the station."

"And how would you describe Mr. Sherlock Holmes?"

The cabman scratched his head. "Well, he wasn't altogether such an easy gentleman to describe. I'd put him at forty years of age, and he was of a middle height, two or three inches shorter than you, sir. He was dressed like a toff,[1] and he had a black beard, cut square at the end, and a pale face. I don't know as I could say more than that."

"Colour of his eyes?"

"No, I can't say that."

"Nothing more that you can remember?"

"No, sir; nothing."

"Well, then, here is your half-sovereign. There's another one waiting for you if you can bring any more information. Good night!"

"Good night, sir, and thank you!"

John Clayton departed chuckling, and Holmes turned to me with a shrug of his shoulders and a rueful smile.

"Snap goes our third thread, and we end where we began," said he. "The cunning rascal! He knew our number, knew that Sir Henry Baskerville had consulted me, spotted who I was in Regent Street, conjectured that I had got the number of the cab and would lay my hands on the driver, and so sent back this audacious message. I tell you, Watson, this time we have got a foeman who

---

1 Working-class term for someone well dressed or well spoken of a higher class.

is worthy of our steel.[1] I've been checkmated in London. I can only wish you better luck in Devonshire. But I'm not easy in my mind about it."

"About what?"

"About sending you. It's an ugly business, Watson, an ugly dangerous business, and the more I see of it the less I like it. Yes, my dear fellow, you may laugh, but I give you my word that I shall be very glad to have you back safe and sound in Baker Street once more."

---

1   Cf. Sir Walter Scott, *The Lady of the Lake* (1810):

> Fitz-James was brave. Though to his heart
> The life-blood thrill'd with sudden start,
> He mann'd himself with dauntless air,
> Return'd the Chief his haughty stare,
> His back against a rock he bore,
> And firmly placed his foot before:
> "Come one, come all! this rock shall fly
> From its firm base as soon as I."
> Sir Roderick mark'd, and in his eyes
> Respect was mingled with surprise,
> And the stern joy which warriors feel
> In foemen worthy of their steel.
>
> J. Logie Robertson, ed., *The Poetical Works of Sir Walter Scott*
> (Oxford: Oxford UP, 1904), 253.

Compare also the parody in Act 2 of Gilbert and Sullivan's operetta *The Pirates of Penzance, or, The Slave of Duty* (1880):

> When the foeman bares his steel,
> Tarantara! tarantara!
> We uncomfortable feel,
> Tarantara!
> And we find the wisest thing,
> Tarantara! tarantara!
> Is to slap our chests and sing,
> Tarantara!
>
> Ian Bradley, ed.,
> *The Complete Annotated Gilbert and Sullivan*
> (Oxford: Oxford UP, 1996),
> 231–32.

Chapter VI

Baskerville Hall

Sir Henry Baskerville and Dr. Mortimer were ready upon the appointed day, and we started as arranged for Devonshire. Mr. Sherlock Holmes drove with me to the station and gave me his last parting injunctions and advice.

"I will not bias your mind by suggesting theories or suspicions, Watson," said he; "I wish you simply to report facts in the fullest possible manner to me, and you can leave me to do the theorizing."

"What sort of facts?" I asked.

"Anything which may seem to have a bearing however indirect upon the case, and especially the relations between young Baskerville and his neighbours or any fresh particulars concerning the death of Sir Charles. I have made some inquiries myself in the last few days, but the results have, I fear, been negative. One thing only appears to be certain, and that is that Mr. James Desmond, who is the next heir, is an elderly gentleman of a very amiable disposition, so that this persecution does not arise from him. I really think that we may eliminate him entirely from our calculations. There remain the people who will actually surround Sir Henry Baskerville upon the moor."

"Would it not be well in the first place to get rid of this Barrymore couple?"

"By no means. You could not make a greater mistake. If they are innocent it would be a cruel injustice, and if they are guilty we should be giving up all chance of bringing it home to them. No, no, we will preserve them upon our list of suspects. Then there is a groom at the Hall, if I remember right. There are two moorland farmers. There is our friend Dr. Mortimer, whom I believe to be entirely honest, and there is his wife, of whom we know nothing.[1] There is this naturalist, Stapleton, and there is his sister, who is said to be a young lady of attractions. There is Mr. Frankland, of Lafter Hall, who is also an unknown factor, and there are one or two other neighbours. These are the folk who must be your very special study."

"I will do my best."

---

1 And never find out more.

"You have arms, I suppose?"

"Yes, I thought it as well to take them."

"Most certainly. Keep your revolver near you night and day, and never relax your precautions."

Our friends had already secured a first-class carriage and were waiting for us upon the platform.

"No, we have no news of any kind," said Dr. Mortimer in answer to my friend's questions. "I can swear to one thing, and that is that we have not been shadowed during the last two days. We have never gone out without keeping a sharp watch, and no one could have escaped our notice."

"You have always kept together, I presume?"

"Except yesterday afternoon. I usually give up one day to pure amusement when I come to town, so I spent it at the Museum of the College of Surgeons."

"And I went to look at the folk in the park," said Baskerville. "But we had no trouble of any kind."

"It was imprudent, all the same," said Holmes, shaking his head and looking very grave. "I beg, Sir Henry, that you will not go about alone. Some great misfortune will befall you if you do. Did you get your other boot?"

"No, sir, it is gone forever."

"Indeed. That is very interesting. Well, good-bye," he added as the train began to glide down the platform. "Bear in mind, Sir Henry, one of the phrases in that queer old legend which Dr. Mortimer has read to us and avoid the moor in those hours of darkness when the powers of evil are exalted."

I looked back at the platform when we had left it far behind and saw the tall, austere figure of Holmes standing motionless and gazing after us.

The journey was a swift and pleasant one, and I spent it in making the more intimate acquaintance of my two companions and in playing with Dr. Mortimer's spaniel. In a very few hours the brown earth had become ruddy,[1] the brick had changed to granite, and red cows grazed in well-hedged fields where the lush grasses and more luxuriant vegetation spoke of a richer, if a damper, climate. Young Baskerville stared eagerly out of the window and cried aloud with delight as he recognized the familiar features of the Devon scenery.

---

1 Devon is distinguished by redder soil, a very obvious marker of the change in counties in the journey south west.

"I've been over a good part of the world since I left it, Dr. Watson," said he; "but I have never seen a place to compare with it."

"I never saw a Devonshire man who did not swear by his county," I remarked.

"It depends upon the breed of men quite as much as on the county," said Dr. Mortimer. "A glance at our friend here reveals the rounded head of the Celt, which carries inside it the Celtic enthusiasm and power of attachment. Poor Sir Charles's head was of a very rare type, half Gaelic, half Ivernian[1] in its characteristics. But you were very young when you last saw Baskerville Hall, were you not?"

"I was a boy in my teens at the time of my father's death and had never seen the Hall, for he lived in a little cottage on the South Coast. Thence I went straight to a friend in America. I tell you it is all as new to me as it is to Dr. Watson, and I'm as keen as possible to see the moor."

"Are you? Then your wish is easily granted, for there is your first sight of the moor," said Dr. Mortimer, pointing out of the carriage window.

Over the green squares of the fields and the low curve of a wood there rose in the distance a gray, melancholy hill, with a strange jagged summit, dim and vague in the distance, like some fantastic landscape in a dream. Baskerville sat for a long time his eyes fixed upon it, and I read upon his eager face how much it meant to him, this first sight of that strange spot where the men of his blood had held sway so long and left their mark so deep. There he sat, with his tweed suit and his American accent, in the corner of a prosaic railway-carriage, and yet as I looked at his dark and expressive face I felt more than ever how true a descendant he was of that long line of high-blooded, fiery, and masterful men. There were pride, valour, and strength in his thick brows, his sensitive nostrils, and his large hazel eyes. If on that forbidding moor a difficult and dangerous quest should lie before us, this was at least a comrade for whom one might venture to take a risk with the certainty that he would bravely share it.

The train pulled up at a small wayside station[2] and we all descended. Outside, beyond the low, white fence, a wagonette

---

1 Victorian/early twentieth-century term for "of Ireland"/Hibernian.
2 Baring-Gould suggests this might have been Coryton Station, near to Princetown (See Baring-Gould, II.38).

with a pair of cobs[1] was waiting. Our coming was evidently a great event, for station-master and porters clustered round us to carry out our luggage. It was a sweet, simple country spot, but I was surprised to observe that by the gate there stood two soldierly men in dark uniforms who leaned upon their short rifles and glanced keenly at us as we passed. The coachman, a hard-faced, gnarled little fellow,[2] saluted Sir Henry Baskerville, and in a few minutes we were flying swiftly down the broad, white road. Rolling pasture lands curved upward on either side of us, and old gabled houses peeped out from amid the thick green foliage, but behind the peaceful and sunlit countryside there rose ever, dark against the evening sky, the long, gloomy curve of the moor, broken by the jagged and sinister hills.

The wagonette swung round into a side road, and we curved upward through deep lanes worn by centuries of wheels, high banks on either side, heavy with dripping moss and fleshy hart's-tongue ferns. Bronzing bracken and mottled bramble gleamed in the light of the sinking sun. Still steadily rising, we passed over a narrow granite bridge and skirted a noisy stream which gushed swiftly down, foaming and roaring amid the gray boulders. Both road and stream wound up through a valley dense with scrub oak and fir. At every turn Baskerville gave an exclamation of delight, looking eagerly about him and asking countless questions. To his eyes all seemed beautiful, but to me a tinge of melancholy lay upon the countryside, which bore so clearly the mark of the waning year. Yellow leaves carpeted the lanes and fluttered down upon us as we passed. The rattle of our wheels died away as we drove through drifts of rotting vegetation—sad gifts, as it seemed to me, for Nature to throw before the carriage of the returning heir of the Baskervilles.

"Halloa!" cried Dr. Mortimer, "what is this?"

A steep curve of heath-clad land, an outlying spur of the moor, lay in front of us. On the summit, hard and clear like an equestrian statue upon its pedestal, was a mounted soldier, dark and stern, his rifle poised ready over his forearm. He was watching the road along which we travelled.

---

1 A stout, short-legged variety of horse capable of bearing riders of heavy weight.

2 Christopher Frayling makes the useful point: "If this *was* a description of Fletcher Robinson's coachman Harry Baskerville, he can't have been amused by it" (179).

"What is this, Perkins?" asked Dr. Mortimer.

Our driver half turned in his seat.

"There's a convict escaped from Princetown, sir. He's been out three days now, and the warders watch every road and every station, but they've had no sight of him yet. The farmers about here don't like it, sir, and that's a fact."

"Well, I understand that they get five pounds if they can give information."

"Yes, sir, but the chance of five pounds is but a poor thing compared to the chance of having your throat cut. You see, it isn't like any ordinary convict. This is a man that would stick at nothing."

"Who is he, then?"

"It is Selden, the Notting Hill[1] murderer."

I remembered the case well, for it was one in which Holmes had taken an interest on account of the peculiar ferocity of the crime and the wanton brutality which had marked all the actions of the assassin. The commutation of his death sentence had been due to some doubts as to his complete sanity, so atrocious was his conduct.[2] Our wagonette had topped a rise and in front of us rose the huge expanse of the moor, mottled with gnarled and craggy cairns and tors. A cold wind swept down from it and set us shivering. Somewhere there, on that desolate plain, was lurking this fiendish man, hiding in a burrow like a wild beast, his heart full of malignancy against the whole race which had cast him out.[3] It needed but this to complete the grim suggestiveness of the barren waste, the chilling wind, and the darkling sky. Even Baskerville fell silent and pulled his overcoat more closely around him.

---

1   In the Victorian period, a largely working-class area of West London. Perhaps this is an acknowledgement of an important precursor in English detective fiction, Charles Felix's *The Notting Hill Mystery: Compiled by Charles Felix from the Papers of the Late R.. Henderson, Esq.* (London: Saunders, Otley, 1865). This is a curious tale with no other obvious relation to *The Hound*. Unlike the Holmes stories, it offers no definitive solution to the crimes it suggests, in their "nature and execution almost too horrible to contemplate" (284), and no prosecution of any individual responsible.

2   Perhaps some shadow of the events of Poe's "The Murders in the Rue Morgue" (1841) flit across this description. See Appendix F, pp. 271–76.

3   The first of the many double-edged accounts of Selden (see Introduction, pp. 24–27): here he is at once a criminal of peculiar brutality and also, with a hint of pity, a man cast out by his race.

We had left the fertile country behind and beneath us. We looked back on it now, the slanting rays of a low sun turning the streams to threads of gold and glowing on the red earth new turned by the plough and the broad tangle of the woodlands. The road in front of us grew bleaker and wilder over huge russet and olive slopes, sprinkled with giant boulders. Now and then we passed a moorland cottage, walled and roofed with stone, with no creeper to break its harsh outline. Suddenly we looked down into a cuplike depression, patched with stunted oaks and firs which had been twisted and bent by the fury of years of storm. Two high, narrow towers rose over the trees. The driver pointed with his whip.

"Baskerville Hall," said he.

Its master had risen and was staring with flushed cheeks and shining eyes. A few minutes later we had reached the lodge-gates, a maze of fantastic tracery in wrought iron, with weather-bitten pillars on either side, blotched with lichens, and surmounted by the boars' heads of the Baskervilles. The lodge was a ruin of black granite and bared ribs of rafters, but facing it was a new building, half constructed, the first fruit of Sir Charles's South African gold.

Through the gateway we passed into the avenue, where the wheels were again hushed amid the leaves, and the old trees shot their branches in a sombre tunnel over our heads. Baskerville shuddered as he looked up the long, dark drive to where the house glimmered like a ghost at the farther end.

"Was it here?" he asked in a low voice.

"No, no, the Yew Alley is on the other side."

The young heir glanced round with a gloomy face.

"It's no wonder my uncle felt as if trouble were coming on him in such a place as this," said he. "It's enough to scare any man. I'll have a row of electric lamps[1] up here inside of six months, and you won't know it again, with a thousand candle-power Swan and Edison[2] right here in front of the hall door."

---

1 A modern notion, of course. Commercial domestic lighting powered by electricity had been used for the first time—at the Central Station, New York—in 1882.

2 Sir Humphry Davy (1778–1829) had first produced an electric light in 1800; the English physicist Sir Joseph Wilson Swan (1828–1914), looking to construct a durable and practical electric light in the 1860s, used carbon paper filaments, demonstrating new electric lamps in 1878 in Newcastle. Thomas Edison (1847–1931), the inventor, in the United States, developed this work, eventually manufacturing a bulb that glowed for more than 1500 hours before this was overtaken after the perfection, in 1910, of a revolutionary tungsten filament.

The avenue opened into a broad expanse of turf, and the house lay before us. In the fading light I could see that the centre was a heavy block of building from which a porch projected. The whole front was draped in ivy, with a patch clipped bare here and there where a window or a coat of arms broke through the dark veil. From this central block rose the twin towers, ancient, crenellated, and pierced with many loopholes. To right and left of the turrets were more modern wings of black granite. A dull light shone through heavy mullioned windows, and from the high chimneys which rose from the steep, high-angled roof there sprang a single black column of smoke.

"Welcome, Sir Henry! Welcome to Baskerville Hall!"

A tall man had stepped from the shadow of the porch to open the door of the wagonette. The figure of a woman was silhouetted against the yellow light of the hall. She came out and helped the man to hand down our bags.

"You don't mind my driving straight home, Sir Henry?" said Dr. Mortimer. "My wife is expecting me."

"Surely you will stay and have some dinner?"

"No, I must go. I shall probably find some work awaiting me. I would stay to show you over the house, but Barrymore will be a better guide than I. Good-bye, and never hesitate night or day to send for me if I can be of service."

The wheels died away down the drive while Sir Henry and I turned into the hall, and the door clanged heavily behind us. It was a fine apartment in which we found ourselves, large, lofty, and heavily raftered with huge baulks of age-blackened oak. In the great old-fashioned fireplace behind the high iron dogs[1] a log-fire crackled and snapped. Sir Henry and I held out our hands to it, for we were numb from our long drive. Then we gazed round us at the high, thin window of old stained glass, the oak panelling, the stags' heads, the coats of arms upon the walls, all dim and sombre in the subdued light of the central lamp.

"It's just as I imagined it," said Sir Henry. "Is it not the very picture of an old family home? To think that this should be the same hall in which for five hundred years my people have lived. It strikes me solemn to think of it."

I saw his dark face lit up with a boyish enthusiasm as he gazed about him. The light beat upon him where he stood, but long

---

1 Part of the iron construction of the fire basket in which logs burn. But also another touch of canine vocabulary.

shadows trailed down the walls and hung like a black canopy above him. Barrymore had returned from taking our luggage to our rooms. He stood in front of us now with the subdued manner of a well-trained servant. He was a remarkable-looking man, tall, handsome, with a square black beard and pale, distinguished features.

"Would you wish dinner to be served at once, sir?"

"Is it ready?"

"In a very few minutes, sir. You will find hot water in your rooms. My wife and I will be happy, Sir Henry, to stay with you until you have made your fresh arrangements, but you will understand that under the new conditions this house will require a considerable staff."

"What new conditions?"

"I only meant, sir, that Sir Charles led a very retired life, and we were able to look after his wants. You would, naturally, wish to have more company, and so you will need changes in your household."

"Do you mean that your wife and you wish to leave?"

"Only when it is quite convenient to you, sir."

"But your family have been with us for several generations, have they not? I should be sorry to begin my life here by breaking an old family connection."

I seemed to discern some signs of emotion upon the butler's white face.

"I feel that also, sir, and so does my wife. But to tell the truth, sir, we were both very much attached to Sir Charles and his death gave us a shock and made these surroundings very painful to us. I fear that we shall never again be easy in our minds at Baskerville Hall."

"But what do you intend to do?"

"I have no doubt, sir, that we shall succeed in establishing ourselves in some business. Sir Charles's generosity has given us the means to do so. And now, sir, perhaps I had best show you to your rooms."

A square balustraded gallery ran round the top of the old hall, approached by a double stair. From this central point two long corridors extended the whole length of the building, from which all the bedrooms opened. My own was in the same wing as Baskerville's and almost next door to it. These rooms appeared to be much more modern than the central part of the house, and the bright paper and numerous candles did something to remove the sombre impression which our arrival had left upon my mind.

But the dining-room which opened out of the hall was a place of shadow and gloom. It was a long chamber with a step separating the dais where the family sat from the lower portion reserved for their dependents. At one end a minstrels' gallery overlooked it. Black beams shot across above our heads, with a smoke-darkened ceiling beyond them. With rows of flaring torches to light it up, and the colour and rude hilarity of an old-time banquet, it might have softened; but now, when two black-clothed gentlemen sat in the little circle of light thrown by a shaded lamp, one's voice became hushed and one's spirit subdued. A dim line of ancestors, in every variety of dress, from the Elizabethan knight[1] to the buck of the Regency,[2] stared down upon us and daunted us by their silent company. We talked little, and I for one was glad when the meal was over and we were able to retire into the modern billiard-room[3] and smoke a cigarette.

"My word, it isn't a very cheerful place," said Sir Henry. "I suppose one can tone down to it, but I feel a bit out of the picture at present. I don't wonder that my uncle got a little jumpy if he lived all alone in such a house as this. However, if it suits you, we will retire early to-night, and perhaps things may seem more cheerful in the morning."

I drew aside my curtains before I went to bed and looked out from my window. It opened upon the grassy space which lay in front of the hall door. Beyond, two copses of trees moaned and swung in a rising wind. A half moon broke through the rifts of racing clouds. In its cold light I saw beyond the trees a broken fringe of rocks, and the long, low curve of the melancholy moor. I closed the curtain, feeling that my last impression was in keeping with the rest.

And yet it was not quite the last. I found myself weary and yet wakeful, tossing restlessly from side to side, seeking for the sleep which would not come. Far away a chiming clock struck out the quarters of the hours, but otherwise a deathly silence lay upon the

---

1 From the period of Elizabeth I, Queen of England 1558–1603.
2 Literally, the period 1810–20 when the future George IV reigned as Prince Regent consequent on the madness of King George III. More loosely, it refers to the "early nineteenth century."
3 Billiards is often thought to have its clearest origin in royal lawn games of fourteenth-century Europe. By the Victorian period it was an extremely popular men's pastime and many large homes including manor and squiral houses were designed with or adapted to contain rooms especially dedicated to it.

old house. And then suddenly, in the very dead of the night, there came a sound to my ears, clear, resonant, and unmistakable. It was the sob of a woman, the muffled, strangling gasp of one who is torn by an uncontrollable sorrow. I sat up in bed and listened intently. The noise could not have been far away and was certainly in the house. For half an hour I waited with every nerve on the alert, but there came no other sound save the chiming clock and the rustle of the ivy on the wall.

Chapter VII

The Stapletons of Merripit House

The fresh beauty of the following morning did something to efface from our minds the grim and gray impression which had been left upon both of us by our first experience of Baskerville Hall. As Sir Henry and I sat at breakfast the sunlight flooded in through the high mullioned windows, throwing watery patches of colour from the coats of arms which covered them. The dark panelling glowed like bronze in the golden rays, and it was hard to realize that this was indeed the chamber which had struck such a gloom into our souls upon the evening before.

"I guess it is ourselves and not the house that we have to blame!" said the baronet. "We were tired with our journey and chilled by our drive, so we took a gray view of the place. Now we are fresh and well, so it is all cheerful once more."

"And yet it was not entirely a question of imagination," I answered. "Did you, for example, happen to hear someone, a woman I think, sobbing in the night?"

"That is curious, for I did when I was half asleep fancy that I heard something of the sort. I waited quite a time, but there was no more of it, so I concluded that it was all a dream."

"I heard it distinctly, and I am sure that it was really the sob of a woman."

"We must ask about this right away." He rang the bell and asked Barrymore whether he could account for our experience. It seemed to me that the pallid features of the butler turned a shade paler still as he listened to his master's question.

"There are only two women in the house, Sir Henry," he answered. "One is the scullery-maid, who sleeps in the other wing. The other is my wife, and I can answer for it that the sound could not have come from her."

And yet he lied as he said it, for it chanced that after breakfast I met Mrs. Barrymore in the long corridor with the sun full upon her face. She was a large, impassive, heavy-featured woman with a stern set expression of mouth. But her telltale eyes were red and glanced at me from between swollen lids. It was she, then, who wept in the night, and if she did so her husband must know it. Yet he had taken the obvious risk of discovery in declaring that it was not so. Why had he done this? And why did she weep so bitterly? Already round this pale-faced, handsome, black-bearded man there was gathering an atmosphere of mystery and of gloom. It was he who had been the first to discover the body of Sir Charles, and we had only his word for all the circumstances which led up to the old man's death. Was it possible that it was Barrymore, after all, whom we had seen in the cab in Regent Street? The beard might well have been the same. The cabman had described a somewhat shorter man, but such an impression might easily have been erroneous. How could I settle the point forever? Obviously the first thing to do was to see the Grimpen postmaster and find whether the test telegram had really been placed in Barrymore's own hands. Be the answer what it might, I should at least have something to report to Sherlock Holmes.

Sir Henry had numerous papers to examine after breakfast, so that the time was propitious for my excursion. It was a pleasant walk of four miles along the edge of the moor, leading me at last to a small gray hamlet, in which two larger buildings, which proved to be the inn and the house of Dr. Mortimer, stood high above the rest. The postmaster, who was also the village grocer, had a clear recollection of the telegram.

"Certainly, sir," said he, "I had the telegram delivered to Mr. Barrymore exactly as directed."

"Who delivered it?"

"My boy here. James, you delivered that telegram to Mr. Barrymore at the Hall last week, did you not?"

"Yes, father, I delivered it."

"Into his own hands?" I asked.

"Well, he was up in the loft at the time, so that I could not put it into his own hands, but I gave it into Mrs. Barrymore's hands, and she promised to deliver it at once."

"Did you see Mr. Barrymore?"

"No, sir; I tell you he was in the loft."

"If you didn't see him, how do you know he was in the loft?"

"Well, surely his own wife ought to know where he is," said the postmaster testily. "Didn't he get the telegram? If there is any mistake it is for Mr. Barrymore himself to complain."

It seemed hopeless to pursue the inquiry any farther, but it was clear that in spite of Holmes's ruse we had no proof that Barrymore had not been in London all the time. Suppose that it were so—suppose that the same man had been the last who had seen Sir Charles alive, and the first to dog the new heir when he returned to England. What then? Was he the agent of others or had he some sinister design of his own? What interest could he have in persecuting the Baskerville family? I thought of the strange warning clipped out of the leading article of the *Times*. Was that his work or was it possibly the doing of someone who was bent upon counteracting his schemes? The only conceivable motive was that which had been suggested by Sir Henry, that if the family could be scared away a comfortable and permanent home would be secured for the Barrymores. But surely such an explanation as that would be quite inadequate to account for the deep and subtle scheming which seemed to be weaving an invisible net round the young baronet. Holmes himself had said that no more complex case had come to him in all the long series of his sensational investigations. I prayed, as I walked back along the gray, lonely road, that my friend might soon be freed from his preoccupations and able to come down to take this heavy burden of responsibility from my shoulders.

Suddenly my thoughts were interrupted by the sound of running feet behind me and by a voice which called me by name. I turned, expecting to see Dr. Mortimer, but to my surprise it was a stranger who was pursuing me. He was a small, slim, clean-shaven, prim-faced man, flaxen-haired and lean-jawed, between thirty and forty years of age, dressed in a gray suit and wearing a straw hat. A tin box for botanical specimens hung over his shoulder and he carried a green butterfly-net in one of his hands.

"You will, I am sure, excuse my presumption, Dr. Watson," said he as he came panting up to where I stood. "Here on the moor we are homely folk and do not wait for formal introductions. You may possibly have heard my name from our mutual friend,[1] Mortimer. I am Stapleton, of Merripit House."[2]

"Your net and box would have told me as much," said I,[3] "for I knew that Mr. Stapleton was a naturalist. But how did you know me?"

"I have been calling on Mortimer, and he pointed you out to me from the window of his surgery as you passed. As our road lay the same way I thought that I would overtake you and introduce myself. I trust that Sir Henry is none the worse for his journey?"

"He is very well, thank you."

"We were all rather afraid that after the sad death of Sir Charles the new baronet might refuse to live here. It is asking much of a wealthy man to come down and bury himself in a place of this kind,[4] but I need not tell you that it means a very great deal to the countryside. Sir Henry has, I suppose, no superstitious fears in the matter?"

"I do not think that it is likely."

"Of course you know the legend of the fiend dog which haunts the family?"

"I have heard it."

"It is extraordinary how credulous the peasants are about here! Any number of them are ready to swear that they have seen such a creature upon the moor." He spoke with a smile, but I seemed to read in his eyes that he took the matter more seriously. "The story took a great hold upon the imagination of Sir Charles, and I have no doubt that it led to his tragic end."

"But how?"

"His nerves were so worked up that the appearance of any dog

---

1 Charles Dickens published his last complete novel, *Our Mutual Friend*, in serialized parts 1864–65. W. W. Robson judiciously remarks: "a coy Dickensian allusion by which Stapleton flickers his academic status and displays himself as a person of cultivation. His touch of snobbery is not the least of his notable qualities. 'Our common friend' is the correct term" (Robson, 180-81).

2 There is a Higher Merripit House on Dartmoor. *Merri*pit and Frankland's residence, *Lafter* Hall, offer a (deliberately?) incongruous vocabulary of mirth to the novel.

3 Watson tries out Holmes's deduction techniques, this time more accurately than with Dr Mortimer's stick.

4 A phrase that, as only Stapleton could know, is grimly double in meaning.

might have had a fatal effect upon his diseased heart. I fancy that he really did see something of the kind upon that last night in the Yew Alley. I feared that some disaster might occur, for I was very fond of the old man, and I knew that his heart was weak."

"How did you know that?"

"My friend Mortimer told me."

"You think, then, that some dog pursued Sir Charles, and that he died of fright in consequence?"

"Have you any better explanation?"

"I have not come to any conclusion."

"Has Mr. Sherlock Holmes?"

The words took away my breath for an instant but a glance at the placid face and steadfast eyes of my companion showed that no surprise was intended.

"It is useless for us to pretend that we do not know you, Dr. Watson," said he. "The records of your detective have reached us here,[1] and you could not celebrate him without being known yourself. When Mortimer told me your name he could not deny your identity. If you are here, then it follows that Mr. Sherlock Holmes is interesting himself in the matter, and I am naturally curious to know what view he may take."

"I am afraid that I cannot answer that question."

"May I ask if he is going to honour us with a visit himself?"

"He cannot leave town at present. He has other cases which engage his attention."

"What a pity! He might throw some light on that which is so dark to us. But as to your own researches, if there is any possible way in which I can be of service to you I trust that you will command me. If I had any indication of the nature of your suspicions or how you propose to investigate the case, I might perhaps even now give you some aid or advice."

"I assure you that I am simply here upon a visit to my friend, Sir Henry, and that I need no help of any kind."

"Excellent!" said Stapleton. "You are perfectly right to be wary and discreet. I am justly reproved for what I feel was an unjustifiable intrusion, and I promise you that I will not mention the matter again."

We had come to a point where a narrow grassy path struck off from the road and wound away across the moor. A steep,

---

1   A knowing recognition of how far Conan Doyle's fame as the author of the Holmes stories had spread.

boulder-sprinkled hill lay upon the right which had in bygone days been cut into a granite quarry. The face which was turned towards us formed a dark cliff, with ferns and brambles growing in its niches. From over a distant rise there floated a gray plume of smoke.

"A moderate walk along this moor-path brings us to Merripit House," said he. "Perhaps you will spare an hour that I may have the pleasure of introducing you to my sister."

My first thought was that I should be by Sir Henry's side. But then I remembered the pile of papers and bills with which his study table was littered. It was certain that I could not help with those. And Holmes had expressly said that I should study the neighbours upon the moor. I accepted Stapleton's invitation, and we turned together down the path.

"It is a wonderful place, the moor," said he, looking round over the undulating downs, long green rollers, with crests of jagged granite foaming up into fantastic surges. "You never tire of the moor. You cannot think the wonderful secrets which it contains.[1] It is so vast, and so barren, and so mysterious."

"You know it well, then?"

"I have only been here two years. The residents would call me a new-comer. We came shortly after Sir Charles settled. But my tastes led me to explore every part of the country round, and I should think that there are few men who know it better than I do."

"Is it hard to know?"

"Very hard. You see, for example, this great plain to the north here with the queer hills breaking out of it. Do you observe anything remarkable about that?"

"It would be a rare place for a gallop."

"You would naturally think so and the thought has cost several their lives before now. You notice those bright green spots scattered thickly over it?"

"Yes, they seem more fertile than the rest."

Stapleton laughed.

"That is the great Grimpen Mire,"[2] said he. "A false step yon-

---

1 Stapleton is taking a risk with this rather revealing statement. Is he testing out how much Dr Watson knows?

2 There is a Grimspound area on Dartmoor (a Bronze Age settlement). There is a popular association in the early history of the word "grim" with the devil.

der means death to man or beast. Only yesterday I saw one of the moor ponies wander into it. He never came out. I saw his head for quite a long time craning out of the bog-hole, but it sucked him down at last. Even in dry seasons it is a danger to cross it, but after these autumn rains it is an awful place. And yet I can find my way to the very heart of it and return alive. By George, there is another of those miserable ponies!"

Something brown was rolling and tossing among the green sedges. Then a long, agonized, writhing neck shot upward and a dreadful cry echoed over the moor. It turned me cold with horror, but my companion's nerves seemed to be stronger than mine.

"It's gone!" said he. "The Mire has him. Two in two days, and many more, perhaps, for they get in the way of going there in the dry weather and never know the difference until the Mire has them in its clutches. It's a bad place, the great Grimpen Mire."

"And you say you can penetrate it?"

"Yes, there are one or two paths which a very active man can take. I have found them out."

"But why should you wish to go into so horrible a place?"

"Well, you see the hills beyond? They are really islands cut off on all sides by the impassable Mire, which has crawled round them in the course of years. That is where the rare plants and the butterflies are, if you have the wit to reach them."

"I shall try my luck some day."

He looked at me with a surprised face.

"For God's sake put such an idea out of your mind," said he. "Your blood would be upon my head. I assure you that there would not be the least chance of your coming back alive. It is only by remembering certain complex landmarks that I am able to do it."

"Halloa!" I cried. "What is that?"

A long, low moan, indescribably sad,[1] swept over the moor. It filled the whole air, and yet it was impossible to say whence it came. From a dull murmur it swelled into a deep roar, and then sank back into a melancholy, throbbing murmur once again. Stapleton looked at me with a curious expression in his face.

---

1   Sidney Paget, Conan Doyle's illustrator for the novel in both serial and book form, certainly developed the idea that the Hound was sad rather than fierce. His illustration of the death of the Hound—see frontispiece—offers the most melancholy of creatures, as if reminding us that he had been cruelly used by Stapleton.

"Queer place, the moor!" said he.

"But what is it?"

"The peasants say it is the Hound of the Baskervilles calling for its prey. I've heard it once or twice before, but never quite so loud."

I looked round, with a chill of fear in my heart, at the huge swelling plain, mottled with the green patches of rushes. Nothing stirred over the vast expanse save a pair of ravens, which croaked loudly from a tor behind us.

"You are an educated man. You don't believe such nonsense as that?" said I. "What do you think is the cause of so strange a sound?"

"Bogs make queer noises sometimes. It's the mud settling, or the water rising, or something."

"No, no, that was a living voice."

"Well, perhaps it was. Did you ever hear a bittern booming?"

"No, I never did."

"It's a very rare bird—practically extinct[1]—in England now, but all things are possible upon the moor. Yes, I should not be surprised to learn that what we have heard is the cry of the last of the bitterns."[2]

"It's the weirdest, strangest thing that ever I heard in my life."

"Yes, it's rather an uncanny place altogether. Look at the hillside yonder. What do you make of those?"

The whole steep slope was covered with gray circular rings of stone, a score of them at least.

"What are they? Sheep-pens?"

"No, they are the homes of our worthy ancestors. Prehistoric man lived thickly on the moor, and as no one in particular has lived there since, we find all his little arrangements exactly as he left them. These are his wigwams with the roofs off. You can even see his hearth and his couch if you have the curiosity to go inside."

"But it is quite a town. When was it inhabited?"

---

1 The Great Bittern, *Botaurus stellaris*, is a kind of thick set heron, with bright, pale, buff-brown plumage marked by darker bars and streaks. It still survives in England. Stapleton is offering a rather fanciful theory— bitterns do not live on moor land and they only boom in the spring. Perhaps he is (again) testing Watson, this time with bad natural history.

2 See pp. 72–73, note 3.

"Neolithic[1] man—no date."

"What did he do?"

"He grazed his cattle on these slopes, and he learned to dig for tin when the bronze sword began to supersede the stone axe. Look at the great trench in the opposite hill. That is his mark. Yes, you will find some very singular points about the moor, Dr. Watson. Oh, excuse me an instant! It is surely Cyclopides."[2]

A small fly or moth had fluttered across our path, and in an instant Stapleton was rushing with extraordinary energy and speed in pursuit of it. To my dismay the creature flew straight for the great Mire, and my acquaintance never paused for an instant, bounding from tuft to tuft behind it, his green net waving in the air. His gray clothes and jerky, zigzag, irregular progress made him not unlike some huge moth himself. I was standing watching his pursuit with a mixture of admiration for his extraordinary activity and fear lest he should lose his footing in the treacherous Mire when I heard the sound of steps and, turning round, found a woman near me upon the path. She had come from the direction in which the plume of smoke indicated the position of Merripit House, but the dip of the moor had hid her until she was quite close.

I could not doubt that this was the Miss Stapleton of whom I had been told, since ladies of any sort must be few upon the moor, and I remembered that I had heard someone describe her as being a beauty. The woman who approached me was certainly that, and of a most uncommon type. There could not have been a greater contrast between brother and sister,[3] for Stapleton was neutral tinted, with light hair and gray eyes, while she was darker than any brunette whom I have seen in England—slim, elegant, and tall. She had a proud, finely cut face, so regular that it might have seemed impassive were it not for the sensitive mouth and the beautiful dark, eager eyes. With her perfect figure and elegant dress she was, indeed, a strange apparition upon a lonely moor-

---

1 In England, roughly 6000–5500 BCE.

2 Not an English butterfly, but the generic name for several South African skippers, or moth-like butterflies, of the family *Hesperiidae*. This is either an inaccurate reference on the part of Conan Doyle, or a hint to the knowledge that Stapleton is untrustworthy or that, once more, he is trying Watson out.

3 The force of this statement only becomes clear when Holmes and Watson are reunited.

land path. Her eyes were on her brother as I turned, and then she quickened her pace towards me. I had raised my hat and was about to make some explanatory remark when her own words turned all my thoughts into a new channel.

"Go back!" she said. "Go straight back to London, instantly."

I could only stare at her in stupid surprise. Her eyes blazed at me, and she tapped the ground impatiently with her foot.

"Why should I go back?" I asked.

"I cannot explain." She spoke in a low, eager voice, with a curious lisp in her utterance. "But for God's sake do what I ask you. Go back and never set foot upon the moor again."

"But I have only just come."

"Man, man!" she cried. "Can you not tell when a warning is for your own good? Go back to London! Start to-night! Get away from this place at all costs! Hush, my brother is coming! Not a word of what I have said. Would you mind getting that orchid for me among the mare's-tails[1] yonder? We are very rich in orchids on the moor, though, of course, you are rather late to see the beauties of the place."[2]

Stapleton had abandoned the chase and came back to us breathing hard and flushed with his exertions.

"Halloa, Beryl!" said he, and it seemed to me that the tone of his greeting was not altogether a cordial one.

"Well, Jack, you are very hot."

"Yes, I was chasing a Cyclopides. He is very rare and seldom found in the late autumn. What a pity that I should have missed him!" He spoke unconcernedly, but his small light eyes glanced incessantly from the girl to me.

"You have introduced yourselves, I can see."

"Yes. I was telling Sir Henry that it was rather late for him to see the true beauties of the moor."

"Why, who do you think this is?"

"I imagine that it must be Sir Henry Baskerville."

---

1   A common flowering marsh or bog plant, *Hippuris vulgaris*, though it appears not to grow on Dartmoor.

2   The small number of orchids that do survive on Dartmoor do not flower in mid-October. W. W. Robson thinks, with some plausibility, that we are asked to believe Beryl Stapleton is imagining a flower of her native Costa Rica (Robson, 181).

"No, no," said I. "Only a humble commoner,[1] but his friend. My name is Dr. Watson."

A flush of vexation passed over her expressive face. "We have been talking at cross purposes," said she.

"Why, you had not very much time for talk," her brother remarked with the same questioning eyes.

"I talked as if Dr. Watson were a resident instead of being merely a visitor," said she. "It cannot much matter to him whether it is early or late for the orchids. But you will come on, will you not, and see Merripit House?"

A short walk brought us to it, a bleak moorland house, once the farm of some grazier in the old prosperous days, but now put into repair and turned into a modern dwelling. An orchard surrounded it, but the trees, as is usual upon the moor, were stunted and nipped, and the effect of the whole place was mean and melancholy. We were admitted by a strange, wizened, rusty-coated old manservant, who seemed in keeping with the house. Inside, however, there were large rooms furnished with an elegance in which I seemed to recognize the taste of the lady. As I looked from their windows at the interminable granite-flecked moor rolling unbroken to the farthest horizon I could not but marvel at what could have brought this highly educated man and this beautiful woman to live in such a place.

"Queer spot to choose, is it not?" said he as if in answer to my thought. "And yet we manage to make ourselves fairly happy, do we not, Beryl?"

"Quite happy," said she, but there was no ring of conviction in her words.

"I had a school," said Stapleton. "It was in the north country. The work to a man of my temperament was mechanical and uninteresting, but the privilege of living with youth, of helping to mould those young minds, and of impressing them with one's own character and ideals was very dear to me.[2] However, the

---

1   So is Sir Henry, in fact, for the term "Commoner" includes all except peers (those holding the rank of duke, marquis, earl, viscount, or baron): Sir Henry is merely a baronet.

2   Stapleton deliberately, but with ironic effect, speaks language echoing that of the great reforming headmaster of Rugby School, Dr Thomas Arnold (1795–1842), who memorably injected English public school life with a higher seriousness and a model of modern Christian manliness. Arnold's work was popularly celebrated in Thomas Hughes's successful novel, *Tom Brown's School Days* (1857).

fates were against us. A serious epidemic broke out in the school and three of the boys died. It never recovered from the blow, and much of my capital was irretrievably swallowed up.[1] And yet, if it were not for the loss of the charming companionship of the boys, I could rejoice over my own misfortune, for, with my strong tastes for botany and zoology, I find an unlimited field of work here, and my sister is as devoted to Nature as I am. All this, Dr. Watson, has been brought upon your head by your expression as you surveyed the moor out of our window."

"It certainly did cross my mind that it might be a little dull—less for you, perhaps, than for your sister."

"No, no, I am never dull," said she quickly.

"We have books, we have our studies, and we have interesting neighbours. Dr. Mortimer is a most learned man in his own line. Poor Sir Charles was also an admirable companion. We knew him well and miss him more than I can tell. Do you think that I should intrude if I were to call this afternoon and make the acquaintance of Sir Henry?"

"I am sure that he would be delighted."

"Then perhaps you would mention that I propose to do so. We may in our humble way do something to make things more easy for him until he becomes accustomed to his new surroundings. Will you come upstairs, Dr. Watson, and inspect my collection of Lepidoptera?[2] I think it is the most complete one in the south-west of England. By the time that you have looked through them lunch will be almost ready."

But I was eager to get back to my charge. The melancholy of the moor, the death of the unfortunate pony, the weird sound which had been associated with the grim legend of the Baskervilles—all these things tinged my thoughts with sadness. Then on the top of these more or less vague impressions there had come the definite and distinct warning of Miss Stapleton, delivered with such intense earnestness that I could not doubt that some grave and deep reason lay behind it. I resisted all pressure to stay for lunch, and I set off at once upon my return journey, taking the grass-grown path by which we had come.

It seems, however, that there must have been some short cut for those who knew it, for before I had reached the road I was astounded to see Miss Stapleton sitting upon a rock by the side

---

1   An ironic choice of words, as will later turn out.

2   The order of butterflies and moths

of the track. Her face was beautifully flushed with her exertions and she held her hand to her side.

"I have run all the way in order to cut you off, Dr. Watson," said she. "I had not even time to put on my hat. I must not stop, or my brother may miss me. I wanted to say to you how sorry I am about the stupid mistake I made in thinking that you were Sir Henry. Please forget the words I said, which have no application whatever to you."

"But I can't forget them, Miss Stapleton," said I. "I am Sir Henry's friend, and his welfare is a very close concern of mine. Tell me why it was that you were so eager that Sir Henry should return to London."

"A woman's whim, Dr. Watson. When you know me better you will understand that I cannot always give reasons for what I say or do."

"No, no. I remember the thrill in your voice. I remember the look in your eyes. Please, please, be frank with me, Miss Stapleton, for ever since I have been here I have been conscious of shadows all round me. Life has become like that great Grimpen Mire, with little green patches everywhere into which one may sink and with no guide to point the track. Tell me then what it was that you meant, and I will promise to convey your warning to Sir Henry."

An expression of irresolution passed for an instant over her face, but her eyes had hardened again when she answered me.

"You make too much of it, Dr. Watson," said she. "My brother and I were very much shocked by the death of Sir Charles. We knew him very intimately, for his favourite walk was over the moor to our house. He was deeply impressed with the curse which hung over the family, and when this tragedy came I naturally felt that there must be some grounds for the fears which he had expressed. I was distressed therefore when another member of the family came down to live here, and I felt that he should be warned of the danger which he will run. That was all which I intended to convey."

"But what is the danger?"

"You know the story of the hound?"

"I do not believe in such nonsense."

"But I do. If you have any influence with Sir Henry, take him away from a place which has always been fatal to his family. The world is wide. Why should he wish to live at the place of danger?"

"Because it *is* the place of danger. That is Sir Henry's nature. I fear that unless you can give me some more definite information than this it would be impossible to get him to move."

"I cannot say anything definite, for I do not know anything definite."

"I would ask you one more question, Miss Stapleton. If you meant no more than this when you first spoke to me, why should you not wish your brother to overhear what you said? There is nothing to which he, or anyone else, could object."

"My brother is very anxious to have the Hall inhabited, for he thinks it is for the good of the poor folk upon the moor. He would be very angry if he knew that I have said anything which might induce Sir Henry to go away. But I have done my duty now and I will say no more. I must go back, or he will miss me and suspect that I have seen you. Good-bye!"

She turned and had disappeared in a few minutes among the scattered boulders, while I, with my soul full of vague fears, pursued my way to Baskerville Hall.

Chapter VIII

First Report of Dr. Watson

From this point onward I will follow the course of events by transcribing my own letters to Mr. Sherlock Holmes which lie before me on the table. One page is missing,[1] but otherwise they are exactly as written and show my feelings and suspicions of the moment more accurately than my memory, clear as it is upon these tragic events, can possibly do.

Baskerville Hall, October 13th.

My dear Holmes,

My previous letters and telegrams have kept you pretty well up-to-date as to all that has occurred in this most God-forsaken corner of the world. The longer one stays here the more does the spirit of the moor sink into one's soul, its vastness, and also its grim charm. When you are once out upon its bosom you have left all traces of modern England behind you, but, on the other hand, you are conscious everywhere of the homes and the work of the prehistoric people. On all sides of you as you walk are the houses

---

1 Is it? It's not clear where.

of these forgotten folk, with their graves and the huge monoliths[1] which are supposed to have marked their temples. As you look at their gray stone huts against the scarred hillsides you leave your own age behind you, and if you were to see a skin-clad, hairy man crawl out from the low door fitting a flint-tipped arrow on to the string of his bow, you would feel that his presence there was more natural than your own.[2] The strange thing is that they should have lived so thickly on what must always have been most unfruitful soil. I am no antiquarian, but I could imagine that they were some unwarlike and harried race who were forced to accept that which none other would occupy.

All this, however, is foreign to the mission on which you sent me and will probably be very uninteresting to your severely practical mind. I can still remember your complete indifference as to whether the sun moved round the earth or the earth round the sun. Let me, therefore, return to the facts concerning Sir Henry Baskerville.

If you have not had any report within the last few days it is because up to to-day there was nothing of importance to relate. Then a very surprising circumstance occurred, which I shall tell you in due course. But, first of all, I must keep you in touch with some of the other factors in the situation.

One of these, concerning which I have said little, is the escaped convict upon the moor. There is strong reason now to believe that he has got right away, which is a considerable relief to the lonely householders of this district. A fortnight has passed since his flight, during which he has not been seen and nothing has been heard of him. It is surely inconceivable that he could have held out upon the moor during all that time. Of course, so far as his concealment goes there is no difficulty at all. Any one of these stone huts would give him a hiding-place. But there is nothing to eat unless he were to catch and slaughter one of the moor sheep. We think, therefore, that he has gone, and the outlying farmers sleep the better in consequence.

We are four able-bodied men in this household, so that we could take good care of ourselves, but I confess that I have had uneasy moments when I have thought of the Stapletons. They live

---

1 Boulders or large shaped stones of prehistoric origin, of uncertain purpose.
2 Cf. the appearance of Seldon on pp. 143–44.

miles from any help. There are one maid, an old manservant, the sister, and the brother, the latter not a very strong man. They would be helpless in the hands of a desperate fellow like this Notting Hill criminal if he could once effect an entrance. Both Sir Henry and I were concerned at their situation, and it was suggested that Perkins the groom should go over to sleep there, but Stapleton would not hear of it.

The fact is that our friend, the baronet, begins to display a considerable interest in our fair neighbour. It is not to be wondered at, for time hangs heavily in this lonely spot to an active man like him, and she is a very fascinating and beautiful woman. There is something tropical and exotic about her which forms a singular contrast to her cool and unemotional brother. Yet he also gives the idea of hidden fires. He has certainly a very marked influence over her, for I have seen her continually glance at him as she talked as if seeking approbation for what she said. I trust that he is kind to her. There is a dry glitter in his eyes and a firm set of his thin lips, which goes with a positive and possibly a harsh nature. You would find him an interesting study.

He came over to call upon Baskerville on that first day, and the very next morning he took us both to show us the spot where the legend of the wicked Hugo is supposed to have had its origin. It was an excursion of some miles across the moor to a place which is so dismal that it might have suggested the story. We found a short valley between rugged tors which led to an open, grassy space flecked over with the white cotton grass.[1] In the middle of it rose two great stones, worn and sharpened at the upper end until they looked like the huge corroding fangs of some monstrous beast. In every way it corresponded with the scene of the old tragedy. Sir Henry was much interested and asked Stapleton more than once whether he did really believe in the possibility of the interference of the supernatural in the affairs of men. He spoke lightly, but it was evident that he was very much in earnest. Stapleton was guarded in his replies, but it was easy to see that he said less than he might, and that he would not express his whole opinion out of consideration for the feelings of the baronet. He told us of similar cases, where families had suffered from some evil influence, and he left us with the impression that he shared the popular view upon the matter.

---

1 A familiar name for a species of grass, with heads of long white silky hairs.

On our way back we stayed for lunch at Merripit House, and it was there that Sir Henry made the acquaintance of Miss Stapleton. From the first moment that he saw her he appeared to be strongly attracted by her, and I am much mistaken if the feeling was not mutual. He referred to her again and again on our walk home, and since then hardly a day has passed that we have not seen something of the brother and sister. They dine here to-night, and there is some talk of our going to them next week. One would imagine that such a match would be very welcome to Stapleton, and yet I have more than once caught a look of the strongest disapproval in his face when Sir Henry has been paying some attention to his sister. He is much attached to her, no doubt, and would lead a lonely life without her, but it would seem the height of selfishness if he were to stand in the way of her making so brilliant a marriage. Yet I am certain that he does not wish their intimacy to ripen into love, and I have several times observed that he has taken pains to prevent them from being *tête-à-tête*.[1] By the way, your instructions to me never to allow Sir Henry to go out alone will become very much more onerous if a love affair were to be added to our other difficulties. My popularity would soon suffer if I were to carry out your orders to the letter.

The other day—Thursday, to be more exact—Dr. Mortimer lunched with us. He has been excavating a barrow[2] at Long Down and has got a prehistoric skull which fills him with great joy. Never was there such a single-minded enthusiast as he! The Stapletons came in afterwards, and the good doctor took us all to the Yew Alley at Sir Henry's request to show us exactly how everything occurred upon that fatal night. It is a long, dismal walk, the Yew Alley, between two high walls of clipped hedge, with a narrow band of grass upon either side. At the far end is an old tumble-down summer-house. Halfway down is the moor-gate, where the old gentleman left his cigar-ash. It is a white wooden gate with a latch. Beyond it lies the wide moor. I remembered your theory of the affair and tried to picture all that had occurred. As the old man stood there he saw something coming across the moor, something which terrified him so that he lost his wits and ran and ran until he died of sheer horror and exhaustion. There was the long, gloomy tunnel down which he fled. And from what? A sheep-dog of the moor? Or a spectral hound, black, silent, and

---

1   Head-to-head/face-to-face (French).

2   A grass-covered mound of a pre-historic grave.

monstrous? Was there a human agency in the matter? Did the pale, watchful Barrymore know more than he cared to say? It was all dim and vague, but always there is the dark shadow of crime behind it.

One other neighbour I have met since I wrote last. This is Mr. Frankland, of Lafter Hall, who lives some four miles to the south of us. He is an elderly man, red-faced, white-haired, and choleric.[1] His passion is for the British law, and he has spent a large fortune in litigation. He fights for the mere pleasure of fighting and is equally ready to take up either side of a question, so that it is no wonder that he has found it a costly amusement. Sometimes he will shut up a right of way and defy the parish to make him open it. At others he will with his own hands tear down some other man's gate and declare that a path has existed there from time immemorial, defying the owner to prosecute him for trespass. He is learned in old manorial and communal rights, and he applies his knowledge sometimes in favour of the villagers of Fernworthy[2] and sometimes against them, so that he is periodically either carried in triumph down the village street or else burned in effigy, according to his latest exploit. He is said to have about seven lawsuits upon his hands at present, which will probably swallow up the remainder of his fortune and so draw his sting and leave him harmless for the future. Apart from the law he seems a kindly, good-natured person, and I only mention him because you were particular that I should send some description of the people who surround us. He is curiously employed at present, for, being an amateur astronomer, he has an excellent telescope, with which he lies upon the roof of his own house and sweeps the moor all day in the hope of catching a glimpse of the escaped convict. If he would confine his energies to this all would be well, but there are rumours that he intends to prosecute Dr. Mortimer for opening a grave without the consent of the next of kin because he dug up the neolithic skull in the barrow on Long Down. He helps to keep our lives from being monotonous and gives a little comic relief where it is badly needed.

And now, having brought you up to date in[3] the escaped con-

---

1 Hot-tempered, inclined to anger.
2 Once a village situated off what is now the B3212, near Chagford; now under a reservoir. Like many a Dartmoor village, it was close to prominent pre-historic earthworks and stones.
3 Changed to "on" in some versions.

vict, the Stapletons, Dr. Mortimer, and Frankland, of Lafter Hall, let me end on that which is most important and tell you more about the Barrymores, and especially about the surprising development of last night.

First of all about the test telegram, which you sent from London in order to make sure that Barrymore was really here. I have already explained that the testimony of the postmaster shows that the test was worthless and that we have no proof one way or the other. I told Sir Henry how the matter stood, and he at once, in his downright fashion, had Barrymore up and asked him whether he had received the telegram himself. Barrymore said that he had.

"Did the boy deliver it into your own hands?" asked Sir Henry.

Barrymore looked surprised, and considered for a little time.

"No," said he, "I was in the box-room[1] at the time, and my wife brought it up to me."

"Did you answer it yourself?"

"No; I told my wife what to answer and she went down to write it."

In the evening he recurred to the subject of his own accord.

"I could not quite understand the object of your questions this morning, Sir Henry," said he. "I trust that they do not mean that I have done anything to forfeit your confidence?"

Sir Henry had to assure him that it was not so and pacify him by giving him a considerable part of his old wardrobe, the London outfit having now all arrived.

Mrs. Barrymore is of interest to me. She is a heavy, solid person, very limited, intensely respectable, and inclined to be puritanical. You could hardly conceive a less emotional subject. Yet I have told you how, on the first night here, I heard her sobbing bitterly, and since then I have more than once observed traces of tears upon her face. Some deep sorrow gnaws ever at her heart. Sometimes I wonder if she has a guilty memory which haunts her, and sometimes I suspect Barrymore of being a domestic tyrant. I have always felt that there was something singular and questionable in this man's character, but the adventure of last night brings all my suspicions to a head.

And yet it may seem a small matter in itself. You are aware that I am not a very sound sleeper, and since I have been on guard in this house my slumbers have been lighter than ever. Last night,

1 We'd first been told—p. 112—he was in the loft.

about two in the morning, I was aroused by a stealthy step passing my room. I rose, opened my door, and peeped out. A long black shadow was trailing down the corridor. It was thrown by a man who walked softly down the passage with a candle held in his hand. He was in shirt and trousers, with no covering to his feet. I could merely see the outline, but his height told me that it was Barrymore. He walked very slowly and circumspectly, and there was something indescribably guilty and furtive in his whole appearance.

I have told you that the corridor is broken by the balcony which runs round the hall, but that it is resumed upon the farther side. I waited until he had passed out of sight and then I followed him. When I came round the balcony he had reached the end of the farther corridor, and I could see from the glimmer of light through an open door that he had entered one of the rooms. Now, all these rooms are unfurnished and unoccupied so that his expedition became more mysterious than ever. The light shone steadily as if he were standing motionless. I crept down the passage as noiselessly as I could and peeped round the corner of the door.

Barrymore was crouching at the window with the candle held against the glass. His profile was half turned towards me, and his face seemed to be rigid with expectation as he stared out into the blackness of the moor. For some minutes he stood watching intently. Then he gave a deep groan and with an impatient gesture he put out the light. Instantly I made my way back to my room, and very shortly came the stealthy steps passing once more upon their return journey. Long afterwards when I had fallen into a light sleep I heard a key turn somewhere in a lock, but I could not tell whence the sound came. What it all means I cannot guess, but there is some secret business going on in this house of gloom which sooner or later we shall get to the bottom of. I do not trouble you with my theories, for you asked me to furnish you only with facts. I have had a long talk with Sir Henry this morning, and we have made a plan of campaign founded upon my observations of last night. I will not speak about it just now, but it should make my next report interesting reading.

Chapter IX

[Second Report of Dr. Watson]
The Light upon the Moor

Baskerville Hall, October 15th.

My dear Holmes—If I was compelled to leave you without much news during the early days of my mission you must acknowledge that I am making up for lost time, and that events are now crowding thick and fast upon us. In my last report I ended upon my top note with Barrymore at the window, and now I have quite a budget[1] already which will, unless I am much mistaken, considerably surprise you. Things have taken a turn which I could not have anticipated. In some ways they have within the last forty-eight hours become much clearer and in some ways they have become more complicated. But I will tell you all and you shall judge for yourself.

Before breakfast on the morning following my adventure I went down the corridor and examined the room in which Barrymore had been on the night before. The western window through which he had stared so intently has, I noticed, one peculiarity above all other windows in the house—it commands the nearest outlook on to the moor. There is an opening between two trees which enables one from this point of view to look right down upon it, while from all the other windows it is only a distant glimpse which can be obtained. It follows, therefore, that Barrymore, since only this window would serve the purpose, must have been looking out for something or somebody upon the moor. The night was very dark, so that I can hardly imagine how he could have hoped to see anyone. It had struck me that it was possible that some love intrigue was on foot. That would have accounted for his stealthy movements and also for the uneasiness of his wife. The man is a striking-looking fellow, very well equipped to steal the heart of a country girl, so that this theory seemed to have something to support it. That opening of the door which I had heard after I had returned to my room might mean that he had gone out to keep some clandestine appointment. So I reasoned with myself in the morning, and I tell you the direction of my sus-

---

1 A collection or stock, especially of news.

picions, however much the result may have shown that they were unfounded.

But whatever the true explanation of Barrymore's movements might be, I felt that the responsibility of keeping them to myself until I could explain them was more than I could bear. I had an interview with the baronet in his study after breakfast, and I told him all that I had seen. He was less surprised than I had expected.

"I knew that Barrymore walked about nights, and I had a mind to speak to him about it," said he. "Two or three times I have heard his steps in the passage, coming and going, just about the hour you name."

"Perhaps then he pays a visit every night to that particular window," I suggested.

"Perhaps he does. If so, we should be able to shadow him and see what it is that he is after. I wonder what your friend Holmes would do if he were here."

"I believe that he would do exactly what you now suggest," said I. "He would follow Barrymore and see what he did."

"Then we shall do it together."

"But surely he would hear us."

"The man is rather deaf, and in any case we must take our chance of that. We'll sit up in my room to-night and wait until he passes." Sir Henry rubbed his hands with pleasure, and it was evident that he hailed the adventure as a relief to his somewhat quiet life upon the moor.

The baronet has been in communication with the architect who prepared the plans for Sir Charles, and with a contractor from London, so that we may expect great changes to begin here soon. There have been decorators and furnishers up from Plymouth,[1] and it is evident that our friend has large ideas and means to spare no pains or expense to restore the grandeur of his family. When the house is renovated and refurnished, all that he will need will be a wife to make it complete. Between ourselves there are pretty clear signs that this will not be wanting if the lady is willing, for I have seldom seen a man more infatuated with a woman than he is with our beautiful neighbour, Miss Stapleton. And yet the course of true love does not run quite as smoothly as one would under the circumstances expect. To-day, for example, its surface was broken by a very unexpected ripple, which has caused our friend considerable perplexity and annoyance.

---

1 Major coastal port on the south coast of Devon.

After the conversation which I have quoted about Barrymore, Sir Henry put on his hat and prepared to go out. As a matter of course I did the same.

"What, are *you* coming, Watson?" he asked, looking at me in a curious way.

"That depends on whether you are going on the moor," said I.

"Yes, I am."

"Well, you know what my instructions are. I am sorry to intrude, but you heard how earnestly Holmes insisted that I should not leave you, and especially that you should not go alone upon the moor."

Sir Henry put his hand upon my shoulder, with a pleasant smile.

"My dear fellow," said he, "Holmes, with all his wisdom, did not foresee some things which have happened since I have been on the moor. You understand me? I am sure that you are the last man in the world who would wish to be a spoil-sport. I must go out alone."

It put me in a most awkward position. I was at a loss what to say or what to do, and before I had made up my mind he picked up his cane and was gone.

But when I came to think the matter over my conscience reproached me bitterly for having on any pretext allowed him to go out of my sight. I imagined what my feelings would be if I had to return to you and to confess that some misfortune had occurred through my disregard for your instructions. I assure you my cheeks flushed at the very thought. It might not even now be too late to overtake him, so I set off at once in the direction of Merripit House.

I hurried along the road at the top of my speed without seeing anything of Sir Henry, until I came to the point where the moor path branches off. There, fearing that perhaps I had come in the wrong direction after all, I mounted a hill from which I could command a view—the same hill which is cut into the dark quarry. Thence I saw him at once. He was on the moor path about a quarter of a mile off, and a lady was by his side who could only be Miss Stapleton. It was clear that there was already an understanding between them and that they had met by appointment. They were walking slowly along in deep conversation, and I saw her making quick little movements of her hands as if she were very earnest in what she was saying, while he listened intently, and once or twice shook his head in strong dissent. I stood among the rocks watching them, very much puzzled as to what I should do next. To follow them and break into their intimate conversation seemed to be an outrage, and yet my clear duty was never for an instant to let him out of my sight. To act the spy upon a friend was a hateful task. Still, I could see no better course than to observe him from the hill, and to clear my conscience by confessing to him afterwards what I had done. It is true that if any sudden danger had threatened him I was too far away to be of use, and yet I am sure that you will agree with me that the position was very difficult, and that there was nothing more which I could do.

Our friend, Sir Henry, and the lady had halted on the path and were standing deeply absorbed in their conversation, when I was suddenly aware that I was not the only witness of their interview. A wisp of green floating in the air caught my eye, and another glance showed me that it was carried on a stick by a man who was moving among the broken ground. It was Stapleton with his butterfly-net. He was very much closer to the pair than I was, and he appeared to be moving in their direction. At this instant Sir Henry suddenly drew Miss Stapleton to his side. His arm was round her, but it seemed to me that she was straining away from him with her face averted. He stooped his head to hers, and she raised one hand as if in protest. Next moment I saw them spring apart and turn hurriedly round. Stapleton was the cause of the interruption. He was running wildly towards them, his absurd net dangling behind him. He gesticulated and almost danced with excitement in front of the lovers. What the scene meant I could not imagine, but it seemed to me that Stapleton was abusing Sir Henry, who offered explanations, which became more angry as the other refused to accept them. The lady stood by in haughty silence. Finally Stapleton turned upon his heel and beckoned in a peremptory way to his sister, who, after an irresolute glance at Sir Henry, walked off by the side of her brother. The naturalist's angry gestures showed that the lady was included in his displeasure. The baronet stood for a minute looking after them, and then he walked slowly back the way that he had come, his head hanging, the very picture of dejection.

What all this meant I could not imagine, but I was deeply ashamed to have witnessed so intimate a scene without my friend's knowledge. I ran down the hill therefore and met the baronet at the bottom. His face was flushed with anger and his brows were wrinkled, like one who is at his wit's ends what to do.

"Halloa, Watson! Where have you dropped from?" said he. "You don't mean to say that you came after me in spite of all?"

I explained everything to him: how I had found it impossible to remain behind, how I had followed him, and how I had witnessed all that had occurred. For an instant his eyes blazed at me, but my frankness disarmed his anger, and he broke at last into a rather rueful laugh.

"You would have thought the middle of that prairie a fairly safe place for a man to be private," said he, "but, by thunder, the whole country-side seems to have been out to see me do my wooing—and a mighty poor wooing at that! Where had you engaged a seat?"

"I was on that hill."

"Quite in the back row, eh? But her brother was well up to the front. Did you see him come out on us?"

"Yes, I did."

"Did he ever strike you as being crazy—this brother of hers?"

"I can't say that he ever did."

"I dare say not. I always thought him sane enough until to-day, but you can take it from me that either he or I ought to be in a straitjacket. What's the matter with me, anyhow? You've lived near me for some weeks, Watson. Tell me straight, now! Is there anything that would prevent me from making a good husband to a woman that I loved?"

"I should say not."

"He can't object to my worldly position, so it must be myself that he has this down on. What has he against me? I never hurt man or woman in my life that I know of. And yet he would not so much as let me touch the tips of her fingers."

"Did he say so?"

"That, and a deal more. I tell you, Watson, I've only known her these few weeks, but from the first I just felt that she was made for me, and she, too—she was happy when she was with me, and that I'll swear. There's a light in a woman's eyes that speaks louder than words. But he has never let us get together and it was only to-day for the first time that I saw a chance of having a few words with her alone. She was glad to meet me, but when she did it was not love that she would talk about, and she wouldn't have let me talk about it either if she could have stopped it. She kept coming back to it that this was a place of danger, and that she would never be happy until I had left it. I told her that since I had seen her I was in no hurry to leave it, and that if she really wanted me to go, the only way to work it was for her to arrange to go with me. With that I offered in as many words to marry her, but before she could answer, down came this brother of hers, running at us with a face on him like a madman. He was just white with rage, and those light eyes of his were blazing with fury. What was I doing with the lady? How dared I offer her attentions which were distasteful to her? Did I think that because I was a baronet I could do what I liked? If he had not been her brother I should have known better how to answer him. As it was I told him that my feelings towards his sister were such as I was not ashamed of, and that I hoped that she might honour me by becoming my wife. That seemed to make the matter no better, so then I lost my temper too, and I answered him rather more hotly than I should perhaps, considering that she was standing by. So it ended by his going off with her, as you saw, and here am I as badly puzzled a man as any in this county. Just tell me what it all means, Watson, and I'll owe you more than ever I can hope to pay."

I tried one or two explanations, but, indeed, I was completely puzzled myself. Our friend's title, his fortune, his age, his character, and his appearance are all in his favour, and I know nothing against him unless it be this dark fate which runs in his family. That his advances should be rejected so brusquely without any reference to the lady's own wishes and that the lady should accept the situation without protest is very amazing. However, our conjectures were set at rest by a visit from Stapleton himself that very afternoon. He had come to offer apologies for his rudeness of the morning, and after a long private interview with Sir Henry in his study the upshot of their conversation was that the breach is quite healed, and that we are to dine at Merripit House next Friday as a sign of it.

"I don't say now that he isn't a crazy man," said Sir Henry "I can't forget the look in his eyes when he ran at me this morning, but I must allow that no man could make a more handsome apology than he has done."

"Did he give any explanation of his conduct?"

"His sister is everything in his life, he says. That is natural enough, and I am glad that he should understand her value. They have always been together, and according to his account he has been a very lonely man with only her as a companion, so that the thought of losing her was really terrible to him. He had not understood, he said, that I was becoming attached to her, but when he saw with his own eyes that it was really so, and that she might be taken away from him, it gave him such a shock that for a time he was not responsible for what he said or did. He was very sorry for all that had passed, and he recognized how foolish and how selfish it was that he should imagine that he could hold a beautiful woman like his sister to himself for her whole life. If she had to leave him he had rather it was to a neighbour like myself than to anyone else. But in any case it was a blow to him and it would take him some time before he could prepare himself to meet it. He would withdraw all opposition upon his part if I would promise for three months to let the matter rest and to be content with cultivating the lady's friendship during that time without claiming her love. This I promised, and so the matter rests."

So there is one of our small mysteries cleared up. It is something to have touched bottom anywhere in this bog in which we are floundering.[1] We know now why Stapleton looked with disfavour upon his sister's suitor—even when that suitor was so eligible a one as Sir Henry. And now I pass on to another thread which I have extricated out of the tangled skein, the mystery of the sobs in the night, of the tear-stained face of Mrs. Barrymore, of the secret journey of the butler to the western lattice window. Congratulate me, my dear Holmes, and tell me that I have not disappointed you as an agent—that you do not regret the confidence which you showed in me when you sent me down. All these things have by one night's work been thoroughly cleared.

I have said "by one night's work," but, in truth, it was by two nights' work, for on the first we drew entirely blank. I sat up with Sir Henry in his rooms until nearly three o'clock in the morning, but no sound of any sort did we hear except the chiming clock upon the stairs. It was a most melancholy vigil and ended by each of us falling asleep in our chairs. Fortunately we were not discouraged, and we determined to try again. The next night we lowered the lamp and sat smoking cigarettes without making the least sound. It was incredible how slowly the hours crawled by, and yet we were helped through it by the same sort of patient interest which the hunter must feel as he watches the trap into which he hopes the game may wander. One struck, and two, and we had almost for the second time given it up in despair when in an instant we both sat bolt upright in our chairs with all our weary senses keenly on the alert once more. We had heard the creak of a step in the passage.

Very stealthily we heard it pass along until it died away in the distance. Then the baronet gently opened his door and we set out in pursuit. Already our man had gone round the gallery and the

---

1 An apt image of course, and to become more so.

corridor was all in darkness. Softly we stole along until we had come into the other wing. We were just in time to catch a glimpse of the tall, black-bearded figure, his shoulders rounded as he tip-toed down the passage. Then he passed through the same door as before, and the light of the candle framed it in the darkness and shot one single yellow beam across the gloom of the corridor. We shuffled cautiously towards it, trying every plank before we dared to put our whole weight upon it. We had taken the precaution of leaving our boots behind us, but, even so, the old boards snapped and creaked beneath our tread. Sometimes it seemed impossible that he should fail to hear our approach. However, the man is for-tunately rather deaf, and he was entirely preoccupied in that which he was doing. When at last we reached the door and peeped through we found him crouching at the window, candle in hand, his white, intent face pressed against the pane, exactly as I had seen him two nights before.

We had arranged no plan of campaign, but the baronet is a man to whom the most direct way is always the most natural. He walked into the room, and as he did so Barrymore sprang up from the window with a sharp hiss of his breath and stood, livid and trembling, before us. His dark eyes, glaring out of the white mask of his face, were full of horror and astonishment as he gazed from Sir Henry to me.

"What are you doing here, Barrymore?"

"Nothing, sir." His agitation was so great that he could hardly speak, and the shadows sprang up and down from the shaking of his candle. "It was the window, sir. I go round at night to see that they are fastened."

"On the second floor?"

"Yes, sir, all the windows."

"Look here, Barrymore," said Sir Henry sternly, "we have made up our minds to have the truth out of you, so it will save you trouble to tell it sooner rather than later. Come, now! No lies! What were you doing at that window?"

The fellow looked at us in a helpless way, and he wrung his hands together like one who is in the last extremity of doubt and misery.

"I was doing no harm, sir. I was holding a candle to the window."

"And why were you holding a candle to the window?"

"Don't ask me, Sir Henry—don't ask me! I give you my word, sir, that it is not my secret, and that I cannot tell it. If it concerned no one but myself I would not try to keep it from you."

A sudden idea occurred to me, and I took the candle from the trembling hand of the butler.

"He must have been holding it as a signal," said I. "Let us see if there is any answer." I held it as he had done, and stared out into the darkness of the night. Vaguely I could discern the black bank of the trees and the lighter expanse of the moor, for the moon was behind the clouds. And then I gave a cry of exultation, for a tiny pin-point of yellow light had suddenly transfixed the dark veil, and glowed steadily in the centre of the black square framed by the window.

"There it is!" I cried.

"No, no, sir, it is nothing—nothing at all!" the butler broke in; "I assure you, sir—"

"Move your light across the window, Watson!" cried the baronet. "See, the other moves also! Now, you rascal, do you deny that it is a signal? Come, speak up! Who is your confederate out yonder, and what is this conspiracy that is going on?"

The man's face became openly defiant.

"It is my business, and not yours. I will not tell."

"Then you leave my employment right away."

"Very good, sir. If I must I must."

"And you go in disgrace. By thunder, you may well be ashamed of yourself. Your family has lived with mine for over a hundred years under this roof, and here I find you deep in some dark plot against me."

"No, no, sir; no, not against you!"

It was a woman's voice, and Mrs. Barrymore, paler and more horror-struck than her husband, was standing at the door. Her bulky figure in a shawl and skirt might have been comic were it not for the intensity of feeling upon her face.

"We have to go, Eliza. This is the end of it. You can pack our things," said the butler.

"Oh, John, John, have I brought you to this? It is my doing, Sir Henry—all mine. He has done nothing except for my sake and because I asked him."

"Speak out, then! What does it mean?"

"My unhappy brother is starving on the moor. We cannot let him perish at our very gates. The light is a signal to him that food is ready for him, and his light out yonder is to show the spot to which to bring it."

"Then your brother is—"

"The escaped convict, sir—Selden, the criminal."

"That's the truth, sir," said Barrymore. "I said that it was not my secret and that I could not tell it to you. But now you have heard it, and you will see that if there was a plot it was not against you."

This, then, was the explanation of the stealthy expeditions at night and the light at the window. Sir Henry and I both stared at the woman in amazement. Was it possible that this stolidly respectable person was of the same blood as one of the most notorious criminals in the country?

"Yes, sir, my name was Selden, and he is my younger brother. We humoured him too much when he was a lad and gave him his own way in everything until he came to think that the world was made for his pleasure, and that he could do what he liked in it.[1] Then as he grew older he met wicked companions, and the devil entered into him[2] until he broke my mother's heart and dragged our name in the dirt. From crime to crime he sank lower and lower until it is only the mercy of God which has snatched him from the scaffold; but to me, sir, he was always the little curly-headed boy that I had nursed and played with as an elder sister would. That was why he broke prison, sir. He knew that I was here and that we could not refuse to help him. When he dragged himself here one night, weary and starving, with the warders hard at his heels, what could we do? We took him in and fed him and cared for him.[3] Then you returned, sir, and my brother thought he would be safer on the moor than anywhere else until the hue and cry was over, so he lay in hiding there. But every second night we made sure if he was still there by putting a light in the window, and if there was an answer my husband took out some bread and meat to him. Every day we hoped that he was gone, but as long as he was there we could not desert him. That is the whole truth, as I am an honest Christian woman and you will see that if there is blame in the matter it does not lie with my husband but with me, for whose sake he has done all that he has."

The woman's words came with an intense earnestness which carried conviction with them.

---

1 Cf. the description of Mrs Barrymore as "puritanical" (p. 129). Certainly, these lines hint at a severe Protestant suspicion of the material world and its pleasures in their explanation of the genesis of Selden's criminality.

2 In tension with Dr Watson's general representation of Selden as naturally corrupt, Mrs Barrymore offers a social theory his criminality. See Introduction, pp. 24–25.

3 Perhaps this is what Barrymore was intended to be doing in the box room/loft.

"Is this true, Barrymore?"

"Yes, Sir Henry. Every word of it."

"Well, I cannot blame you for standing by your own wife. Forget what I have said. Go to your room, you two, and we shall talk further about this matter in the morning."

When they were gone we looked out of the window again. Sir Henry had flung it open, and the cold night wind beat in upon our faces. Far away in the black distance there still glowed that one tiny point of yellow light.

"I wonder he dares," said Sir Henry.

"It may be so placed as to be only visible from here."

"Very likely. How far do you think it is?"

"Out by the Cleft Tor, I think."

"Not more than a mile or two off."

"Hardly that."

"Well, it cannot be far if Barrymore had to carry out the food to it. And he is waiting, this villain, beside that candle. By thunder, Watson, I am going out to take that man!"

The same thought had crossed my own mind. It was not as if the Barrymores had taken us into their confidence. Their secret had been forced from them. The man was a danger to the community, an unmitigated scoundrel for whom there was neither pity nor excuse. We were only doing our duty in taking this chance of putting him back where he could do no harm. With his brutal and violent nature, others would have to pay the price if we held our hands. Any night, for example, our neighbours the Stapletons might be attacked by him, and it may have been the thought of this which made Sir Henry so keen upon the adventure.

"I will come," said I.

"Then get your revolver and put on your boots. The sooner we start the better, as the fellow may put out his light and be off."

In five minutes we were outside the door, starting upon our expedition. We hurried through the dark shrubbery, amid the dull moaning of the autumn wind and the rustle of the falling leaves. The night air was heavy with the smell of damp and decay. Now and again the moon peeped out for an instant, but clouds were driving over the face of the sky, and just as we came out on the moor a thin rain began to fall. The light still burned steadily in front.

"Are you armed?" I asked.

"I have a hunting-crop."[1]

---

1 A small, sometimes weighted, stock or whip handle with a loop for the insertion of a lash.

"We must close in on him rapidly, for he is said to be a desperate fellow. We shall take him by surprise and have him at our mercy before he can resist."

"I say, Watson," said the baronet, "what would Holmes say to this? How about that hour of darkness in which the power of evil is exalted?"

As if in answer to his words there rose suddenly out of the vast gloom of the moor that strange cry which I had already heard upon the borders of the great Grimpen Mire. It came with the wind through the silence of the night, a long, deep mutter then a rising howl, and then the sad moan in which it died away. Again and again it sounded, the whole air throbbing with it, strident, wild, and menacing. The baronet caught my sleeve and his face glimmered white through the darkness.

"My God, what's that, Watson?"

"I don't know. It's a sound they have on the moor. I heard it once before."

It died away, and an absolute silence closed in upon us. We stood straining our ears, but nothing came.

"Watson," said the baronet, "it was the cry of a hound."

My blood ran cold in my veins, for there was a break in his voice which told of the sudden horror which had seized him.

"What do they call this sound?" he asked.

"Who?"

"The folk on the country-side."[1]

"Oh, they are ignorant people. Why should you mind what they call it?"

"Tell me, Watson. What do they say of it?"

I hesitated but could not escape the question.

"They say it is the cry of the Hound of the Baskervilles."

He groaned and was silent for a few moments.

"A hound it was," he said at last, "but it seemed to come from miles away, over yonder, I think."

"It was hard to say whence it came."

"It rose and fell with the wind. Isn't that the direction of the great Grimpen Mire?"

"Yes, it is."

"Well, it was up there. Come now, Watson, didn't you think yourself that it was the cry of a hound? I am not a child. You need not fear to speak the truth."

---

1 Modern English would have "of" for "on."

"Stapleton was with me when I heard it last. He said that it might be the calling of a strange bird."

"No, no, it was a hound. My God, can there be some truth in all these stories? Is it possible that I am really in danger from so dark a cause? You don't believe it, do you, Watson?"

"No, no."

"And yet it was one thing to laugh about it in London, and it is another to stand out here in the darkness of the moor and to hear such a cry as that. And my uncle! There was the footprint of the hound beside him as he lay. It all fits together. I don't think that I am a coward, Watson, but that sound seemed to freeze my very blood. Feel my hand!"

It was as cold as a block of marble.

"You'll be all right to-morrow."

"I don't think I'll get that cry out of my head. What do you advise that we do now?"

"Shall we turn back?"

"No, by thunder; we have come out to get our man, and we will do it. We are after the convict, and a hell-hound, as likely as not, after us. Come on! We'll see it through if all the fiends of the pit were loose upon the moor."

We stumbled slowly along in the darkness, with the black loom of the craggy hills around us, and the yellow speck of light burning steadily in front. There is nothing so deceptive as the distance of a light upon a pitch-dark night, and sometimes the glimmer seemed to be far away upon the horizon and sometimes it might have been within a few yards of us. But at last we could see whence it came, and then we knew that we were indeed very close. A guttering candle was stuck in a crevice of the rocks which flanked it on each side so as to keep the wind from it and also to prevent it from being visible, save in the direction of Baskerville Hall. A boulder of granite concealed our approach, and crouching behind it we gazed over it at the signal light. It was strange to see this single candle burning there in the middle of the moor, with no sign of life near it—just the one straight yellow flame and the gleam of the rock on each side of it.

"What shall we do now?" whispered Sir Henry.

"Wait here. He must be near his light. Let us see if we can get a glimpse of him."

The words were hardly out of my mouth when we both saw him. Over the rocks, in the crevice of which the candle burned, there was thrust out an evil yellow face, a terrible animal face, all seamed and scored with vile passions. Foul with mire, with a bristling beard, and hung with matted hair, it might well have belonged to one of those old savages who dwelt in the burrows on the hillsides. The light beneath him was reflected in his small, cunning eyes which peered fiercely to right and left through the darkness like a crafty and savage animal who has heard the steps of the hunters.

Something had evidently aroused his suspicions. It may have been that Barrymore had some private signal which we had neglected to give, or the fellow may have had some other reason for thinking that all was not well, but I could read his fears upon his wicked face. Any instant he might dash out the light and vanish in the darkness. I sprang forward therefore, and Sir Henry did the same. At the same moment the convict screamed out a curse at us and hurled a rock which splintered up against the boulder which had sheltered us. I caught one glimpse of his short, squat, strongly built figure as he sprang to his feet and turned to run. At the same moment by a lucky chance the moon broke through the clouds. We rushed over the brow of the hill, and there was our man running with great speed down the other side, springing over the stones in his way with the activity of a mountain goat. A lucky long shot of my revolver might have crippled him, but I had brought it only to defend myself if attacked and not to shoot an unarmed man who was running away.

We were both fair runners and in good condition,[1] but we soon found that we had no chance of overtaking him. We saw him for a long time in the moonlight until he was only a small speck moving swiftly among the boulders upon the side of a distant hill. We ran and ran until we were completely blown, but the space between us grew ever wider. Finally we stopped and sat panting on two rocks, while we watched him disappearing in the distance.

And it was at this moment that there occurred a most strange and unexpected thing. We had risen from our rocks and were turning to go home, having abandoned the hopeless chase. The moon was low upon the right, and the jagged pinnacle of a granite tor stood up against the lower curve of its silver disc. There, outlined as black as an ebony statue on that shining background, I saw the figure of a man upon the tor. Do not think that it was a delusion, Holmes. I assure you that I have never in my life seen anything more clearly. As far as I could judge, the figure was that of a tall, thin man. He stood with his legs a little separated, his arms fold-

---

1   A somewhat implausible claim. The first American edition (1902) has "We were both swift runners and in fairly good training," but in either case the sentence raises the question of what exercise the two men do.

ed, his head bowed, as if he were brooding over that enormous wilderness of peat and granite which lay before him. He might have been the very spirit of that terrible place. It was not the convict. This man was far from the place where the latter had disappeared. Besides, he was a much taller man. With a cry of surprise I pointed him out to the baronet, but in the instant during which I had turned to grasp his arm the man was gone. There was the sharp pinnacle of granite still cutting the lower edge of the moon, but its peak bore no trace of that silent and motionless figure.

I wished to go in that direction and to search the tor, but it was some distance away. The baronet's nerves were still quivering from that cry, which recalled the dark story of his family, and he was not in the mood for fresh adventures. He had not seen this lonely man upon the tor and could not feel the thrill which his strange presence and his commanding attitude had given to me. "A warder, no doubt," said he. "The moor has been thick with them since this fellow escaped." Well, perhaps his explanation may be the right one, but I should like to have some further proof of it. To-day we mean to communicate to the Princetown people where they should look for their missing man, but it is hard lines that we have not actually had the triumph of bringing him back as our own prisoner. Such are the adventures of last night, and you must acknowledge, my dear Holmes, that I have done you very well in the matter of a report. Much of what I tell you is no doubt quite irrelevant, but still I feel that it is best that I should let you have all the facts and leave you to select for yourself those which will be of most service to you in helping you to your conclusions. We are certainly making some progress. So far as the Barrymores go, we have found the motive of their actions, and that has cleared up the situation very much. But the moor with its mysteries and its strange inhabitants remains as inscrutable as ever. Perhaps in my next I may be able to throw some light upon this also. Best of all would it be if you could come down to us.

Chapter X

Extract from the Diary of Dr. Watson

So far I have been able to quote from the reports which I have forwarded during these early days to Sherlock Holmes. Now, however, I have arrived at a point in my narrative where I am compelled to abandon this method and to trust once more to my recollections, aided by the diary which I kept at the time. A few extracts from the latter will carry me on to those scenes which are indelibly fixed in every detail upon my memory. I proceed, then, from the morning which followed our abortive chase of the convict and our other strange experiences upon the moor.

October 16th—A dull and foggy day with a drizzle of rain. The house is banked in with rolling clouds, which rise now and then to show the dreary curves of the moor, with thin, silver veins upon the sides of the hills, and the distant boulders gleaming where the light strikes upon their wet faces. It is melancholy outside and in. The baronet is in a black reaction after the excitements of the night. I am conscious myself of a weight at my heart and a feeling of impending danger—ever present danger, which is the more terrible because I am unable to define it.

And have I not cause for such a feeling? Consider the long sequence of incidents which have all pointed to some sinister influence which is at work around us. There is the death of the last occupant of the Hall, fulfilling so exactly the conditions of the family legend, and there are the repeated reports from peasants of the appearance of a strange creature upon the moor. Twice I have with my own ears heard the sound which resembled the distant baying of a hound. It is incredible, impossible, that it should really be outside the ordinary laws of nature. A spectral hound which leaves material footmarks and fills the air with its howling is surely not to be thought of. Stapleton may fall in with such a superstition, and Mortimer also, but if I have one quality upon earth it is common sense, and nothing will persuade me to believe in such a thing. To do so would be to descend to the level of these poor peasants, who are not content with a mere fiend dog but must needs describe him with hell-fire shooting from his mouth and eyes. Holmes would not listen to such fancies, and I am his agent. But facts are facts, and I have twice heard this crying upon the moor. Suppose that there were really some huge hound loose upon it; that would go far to explain everything. But where could such a hound lie concealed, where did it get its food, where did it come from, how was it that no one saw it by day? It must be confessed that the natural explanation offers almost as many difficulties as the other. And always, apart from the hound, there is the fact of the human agency in London, the man in the cab, and the letter which warned Sir Henry against the moor. This at least was real, but it might have been the work of a protecting friend as easily as of an enemy. Where is that friend or enemy now? Has he remained in London, or has he followed us down here? Could he—could he be the stranger whom I saw upon the Tor?

It is true that I have had only the one glance at him, and yet there are some things to which I am ready to swear. He is no one whom I have seen down here, and I have now met all the neighbours. The figure was far taller than that of Stapleton, far thinner than that of Frankland. Barrymore it might possibly have been, but we had left him behind us, and I am certain that he could not have followed us. A stranger then is still dogging us, just as a stranger dogged us in London.[1] We have never shaken him off. If I could lay my hands upon that man, then at last we might find ourselves at the end of all our difficulties. To this one purpose I must now devote all my energies.

My first impulse was to tell Sir Henry all my plans. My second and wisest one is to play my own game and speak as little as possible to anyone. He is silent and distrait.[2] His nerves have been strangely shaken by that sound upon the moor. I will say nothing to add to his anxieties, but I will take my own steps to attain my own end.

We had a small scene this morning after breakfast. Barrymore asked leave to speak with Sir Henry, and they were closeted in his study some little time. Sitting in the billiard-room I more than once heard the sound of voices raised, and I had a pretty good idea what the point was which was under discussion. After a time the baronet opened his door and called for me.

"Barrymore considers that he has a grievance," he said. "He thinks that it was unfair on our part to hunt his brother-in-law down when he, of his own free will, had told us the secret."

The butler was standing very pale but very collected before us.

"I may have spoken too warmly, sir," said he, "and if I have, I am sure that I beg your pardon. At the same time, I was very much surprised when I heard you two gentlemen come back this morning and learned that you had been chasing Selden. The poor fellow has enough to fight against without my putting more upon his track."

"If you had told us of your own free will it would have been a different thing," said the baronet. "You only told us, or rather your wife only told us, when it was forced from you and you could not help yourself."

---

1 Note canine vocabulary again.

2 Distressed, upset (French).

"I didn't think you would have taken advantage of it, Sir Henry—indeed I didn't."

"The man is a public danger. There are lonely houses scattered over the moor, and he is a fellow who would stick at nothing. You only want to get a glimpse of his face to see that. Look at Mr. Stapleton's house, for example, with no one but himself to defend it. There's no safety for anyone until he is under lock and key."

"He'll break into no house, sir. I give you my solemn word upon that. But he will never trouble anyone in this country again. I assure you, Sir Henry, that in a very few days the necessary arrangements will have been made and he will be on his way to South America. For God's sake, sir, I beg of you not to let the police know that he is still on the moor. They have given up the chase there, and he can lie quiet until the ship is ready for him. You can't tell on him without getting my wife and me into trouble. I beg you, sir, to say nothing to the police."

"What do you say, Watson?"

I shrugged my shoulders. "If he were safely out of the country it would relieve the tax-payer of a burden."

"But how about the chance of his holding someone up before he goes?"

"He would not do anything so mad, sir. We have provided him with all that he can want. To commit a crime would be to show where he was hiding."

"That is true," said Sir Henry. "Well, Barrymore—"

"God bless you, sir, and thank you from my heart! It would have killed my poor wife had he been taken again."

"I guess we are aiding and abetting a felony,[1] Watson? But, after what we have heard I don't feel as if I could give the man up, so there is an end of it. All right, Barrymore, you can go."

With a few broken words of gratitude the man turned, but he hesitated and then came back.

"You've been so kind to us, sir, that I should like to do the best I can for you in return. I know something, Sir Henry, and perhaps I should have said it before, but it was long after the inquest that I found it out. I've never breathed a word about it yet to mortal man. It's about poor Sir Charles's death."

The baronet and I were both upon our feet. "Do you know how he died?"

---

1   Under English law, a technical formulation for assisting in a crime.

"No, sir, I don't know that."

"What then?"

"I know why he was at the gate at that hour. It was to meet a woman."

"To meet a woman! He?"

"Yes, sir."

"And the woman's name?"

"I can't give you the name, sir, but I can give you the initials. Her initials were L.L."

"How do you know this, Barrymore?"

"Well, Sir Henry, your uncle had a letter that morning. He had usually a great many letters, for he was a public man and well known for his kind heart, so that everyone who was in trouble was glad to turn to him. But that morning, as it chanced, there was only this one letter, so I took the more notice of it. It was from Coombe Tracey,[1] and it was addressed in a woman's hand."

"Well?"

"Well, sir, I thought no more of the matter, and never would have done had it not been for my wife. Only a few weeks ago she was cleaning out Sir Charles's study—it had never been touched since his death—and she found the ashes of a burned letter in the back of the grate. The greater part of it was charred to pieces, but one little slip, the end of a page, hung together, and the writing could still be read, though it was gray on a black ground. It seemed to us to be a postscript at the end of the letter and it said: 'Please, please, as you are a gentleman, burn this letter, and be at the gate by ten o'clock. Beneath it were signed the initials L.L.'"

"Have you got that slip?"

"No, sir, it crumbled all to bits after we moved it."

"Had Sir Charles received any other letters in the same writing?"

"Well, sir, I took no particular notice of his letters. I should not have noticed this one, only it happened to come alone."

"And you have no idea who L.L. is?"

"No, sir. No more than you have. But I expect if we could lay our hands upon that lady we should know more about Sir Charles's death."

---

1   A Devon-sounding name but not a real place. Probably put together from the real Combe, on the eastern edge of Dartmoor, and Bovey Tracey (pronounced Bovvey Tracey), a couple of miles south.

"I cannot understand, Barrymore, how you came to conceal this important information."

"Well, sir, it was immediately after that our own trouble came to us. And then again, sir, we were both of us very fond of Sir Charles, as we well might be considering all that he has done for us. To rake this up couldn't help our poor master, and it's well to go carefully when there's a lady in the case. Even the best of us—"

"You thought it might injure his reputation?"

"Well, sir, I thought no good could come of it. But now you have been kind to us, and I feel as if it would be treating you unfairly not to tell you all that I know about the matter."

"Very good, Barrymore; you can go." When the butler had left us Sir Henry turned to me. "Well, Watson, what do you think of this new light?"

"It seems to leave the darkness rather blacker than before."

"So I think. But if we can only trace L.L. it should clear up the whole business. We have gained that much. We know that there is someone who has the facts if we can only find her. What do you think we should do?"

"Let Holmes know all about it at once. It will give him the clue for which he has been seeking. I am much mistaken if it does not bring him down."

I went at once to my room and drew up my report of the morning's conversation for Holmes. It was evident to me that he had been very busy of late, for the notes which I had from Baker Street were few and short, with no comments upon the information which I had supplied and hardly any reference to my mission. No doubt his blackmailing case is absorbing all his faculties. And yet this new factor must surely arrest his attention and renew his interest. I wish that he were here.

October 17th—All day to-day the rain poured down, rustling on the ivy and dripping from the eaves. I thought of the convict out upon the bleak, cold, shelterless moor. Poor fellow! Whatever his crimes, he has suffered something to atone for them. And then I thought of that other one—the face in the cab, the figure against the moon. Was he also out in that deluged—the unseen watcher, the man of darkness? In the evening I put on my waterproof and I walked far upon the sodden moor, full of dark imaginings, the rain beating upon my face and the wind whistling about my ears. God help those who wander into the Great Mire now, for even the firm uplands are becoming a morass. I found the black Tor upon which I had seen the solitary watcher, and from its craggy summit I looked out myself across the melancholy downs. Rain squalls drifted across their russet face, and the heavy, slate-coloured clouds hung low over the landscape, trailing in gray wreaths down the sides of the fantastic hills. In the distant hollow on the left, half hidden by the mist, the two thin towers of Baskerville Hall rose above the trees. They were the only signs of human life which I could see, save only those prehistoric huts which lay thickly upon the slopes of the hills. Nowhere was there any trace of that lonely man whom I had seen on the same spot two nights before.

As I walked back I was overtaken by Dr. Mortimer driving in his dog-cart[1] over a rough moorland track which led from the outlying farmhouse of Foulmire. He has been very attentive to us, and hardly a day has passed that he has not called at the Hall to see how we were getting on. He insisted upon my climbing into his dog-cart, and he gave me a lift homeward. I found him much troubled over the disappearance of his little spaniel. It had wandered on to the moor and had never come back. I gave him such consolation as I might, but I thought of the pony on the Grimpen Mire, and I do not fancy that he will see his little dog again.

"By the way, Mortimer," said I as we jolted along the rough road, "I suppose there are few people living within driving distance of this whom you do not know?"

"Hardly any, I think."

"Can you, then, tell me the name of any woman whose initials are L.L.?"

He thought for a few minutes.

"No," said he. "There are a few gipsies and labouring folk for whom I can't answer, but among the farmers or gentry there is no one whose initials are those. Wait a bit though," he added after a pause. "There is Laura Lyons—her initials are L.L.—but she lives in Coombe Tracey."

"Who is she?" I asked.

"She is Frankland's daughter."

"What? Old Frankland the crank?"

"Exactly. She married an artist named Lyons, who came sketching on the moor. He proved to be a blackguard and deserted her. The fault, from what I hear, may not have been entirely on

---

1 "A cart with a box under the seat for sportsmen's dogs; subsequently, an open vehicle for ordinary driving, with two transverse seats back to back, the hinder of these originally made to shut up so as to form a box for dogs" (*OED*).

one side. Her father refused to have anything to do with her because she had married without his consent and perhaps for one or two other reasons as well. So, between the old sinner and the young one the girl has had a pretty bad time."

"How does she live?"

"I fancy old Frankland allows her a pittance, but it cannot be more, for his own affairs are considerably involved. Whatever she may have deserved one could not allow her to go hopelessly to the bad. Her story got about, and several of the people here did something to enable her to earn an honest living. Stapleton did for one, and Sir Charles for another. I gave a trifle myself. It was to set her up in a type-writing business."[1]

He wanted to know the object of my inquiries, but I managed to satisfy his curiosity without telling him too much, for there is no reason why we should take anyone into our confidence. To-morrow morning I shall find my way to Coombe Tracey, and if I can see this Mrs. Laura Lyons, of equivocal reputation, a long step will have been made towards clearing one incident in this chain of mysteries. I am certainly developing the wisdom of the serpent, for when Mortimer pressed his questions to an inconvenient extent I asked him casually to what type Frankland's skull belonged, and so heard nothing but craniology[2] for the rest of our drive. I have not lived for years with Sherlock Holmes for nothing.

I have only one other incident to record upon this tempestuous and melancholy day. This was my conversation with Barrymore just now, which gives me one more strong card which I can play in due time.

Mortimer had stayed to dinner, and he and the baronet played écarté[3] afterwards. The butler brought me my coffee into the library, and I took the chance to ask him a few questions.

"Well," said I, "has this precious relation of yours departed, or is he still lurking out yonder?"

"I don't know, sir. I hope to heaven that he has gone, for he has brought nothing but trouble here! I've not heard of him since I left out food for him last, and that was three days ago."

---

1 See p. 155, note 2.

2 The science of the human skull.

3 A French game of cards for two: Conan Doyle was particularly interested in it. An *écarté* competition—the "game of games" (*Exploits* 504)—plays a crucial role in, and gives the title to, the episode "How he held the King" from *The Exploits of Brigadier Gerard*.

"Did you see him then?"

"No, sir, but the food was gone when next I went that way."

"Then he was certainly there?"

"So you would think, sir, unless it was the other man who took it."

I sat with my coffee-cup halfway to my lips and stared at Barrymore.

"You know that there is another man then?"

"Yes, sir; there is another man upon the moor."

"Have you seen him?"

"No, sir."

"How do you know of him then?"

"Selden told me of him, sir, a week ago or more. He's in hiding, too, but he's not a convict as far as I can make out. I don't like it, Dr. Watson—I tell you straight, sir, that I don't like it." He spoke with a sudden passion of earnestness.

"Now, listen to me, Barrymore! I have no interest in this matter but that of your master. I have come here with no object except to help him. Tell me, frankly, what it is that you don't like."

Barrymore hesitated for a moment, as if he regretted his outburst or found it difficult to express his own feelings in words.

"It's all these goings-on, sir," he cried at last, waving his hand towards the rain-lashed window which faced the moor. "There's foul play somewhere, and there's black villainy brewing, to that I'll swear! Very glad I should be, sir, to see Sir Henry on his way back to London again!"

"But what is it that alarms you?"

"Look at Sir Charles's death! That was bad enough, for all that the coroner said. Look at the noises on the moor at night. There's not a man would cross it after sundown if he was paid for it. Look at this stranger hiding out yonder, and watching and waiting! What's he waiting for? What does it mean? It means no good to anyone of the name of Baskerville, and very glad I shall be to be quit of it all on the day that Sir Henry's new servants are ready to take over the Hall."

"But about this stranger," said I. "Can you tell me anything about him? What did Selden say? Did he find out where he hid, or what he was doing?"

"He saw him once or twice, but he is a deep one and gives nothing away. At first he thought that he was the police, but soon he found that he had some lay of his own.[1] A kind of gentleman

---

1 Some other preoccupation of his own.

he was, as far as he could see, but what he was doing he could not make out."

"And where did he say that he lived?"

"Among the old houses on the hillside—the stone huts where the old folk used to live."

"But how about his food?"

"Selden found out that he has got a lad who works for him and brings all he needs. I dare say he goes to Coombe Tracey for what he wants."

"Very good, Barrymore. We may talk further of this some other time."

When the butler had gone I walked over to the black window, and I looked through a blurred pane at the driving clouds and at the tossing outline of the wind-swept trees. It is a wild night indoors, and what must it be in a stone hut upon the moor. What passion of hatred can it be which leads a man to lurk in such a place at such a time! And what deep and earnest purpose can he have which calls for such a trial! There, in that hut upon the moor, seems to lie the very centre of that problem which has vexed me so sorely. I swear that another day shall not have passed before I have done all that man can do to reach the heart of the mystery.

Chapter XI

The Man on the Tor

The extract from my private diary which forms the last chapter has brought my narrative up to the 18th of October, a time when these strange events began to move swiftly towards their terrible conclusion. The incidents of the next few days are indelibly graven upon my recollection, and I can tell them without reference to the notes made at the time. I start them from the day which succeeded that upon which I had established two facts of great importance, the one that Mrs. Laura Lyons of Coombe Tracey had written to Sir Charles Baskerville and made an appointment with him at the very place and hour that he met his death, the other that the lurking man upon the moor was to be found among the stone huts upon the hillside. With these two facts in my possession I felt that either my intelligence or my courage must be deficient if I could not throw some further light upon these dark places.

I had no opportunity to tell the baronet what I had learned about Mrs. Lyons upon the evening before, for Dr. Mortimer remained with him at cards until it was very late. At breakfast, however, I informed him about my discovery and asked him whether he would care to accompany me to Coombe Tracey.[1] At first he was very eager to come, but on second thoughts it seemed to both of us that if I went alone the results might be better. The more formal we made the visit the less information we might obtain. I left Sir Henry behind, therefore, not without some prickings of conscience, and drove off upon my new quest.

When I reached Coombe Tracey I told Perkins to put up the horses, and I made inquiries for the lady whom I had come to interrogate. I had no difficulty in finding her rooms, which were central and well appointed. A maid showed me in without ceremony, and as I entered the sitting-room a lady, who was sitting before a Remington typewriter,[2] sprang up with a pleasant smile of welcome.[3] Her face fell, however, when she saw that I was a stranger, and she sat down again and asked me the object of my visit.

The first impression left by Mrs. Lyons was one of extreme beauty. Her eyes and hair were of the same rich hazel colour, and her cheeks, though considerably freckled, were flushed with the exquisite bloom of the brunette, the dainty pink which lurks at the heart of the sulphur rose.[4] Admiration was, I repeat, the first

---

1 From the surviving ms of this chapter—the only one so to survive—it's clear that Conan Doyle originally located Mrs Lyons in "Newton Abbott." Newton Abbot [sic] is a real place in Devon; Coombe Tracey fictional.

2 The gun-maker E. Remington & Sons—oddly enough—made the first commercially successful typewriter—the "Remington No. 2"—in 1878 in New York: presumably Mrs Lyons is using one of them. It is worth stressing for the contemporary reader that being in the typewriting business, like Mrs Lyons, was a very modern—and for some slightly disreputable—way of living for a woman in 1901/02. It suited the pages of the new, commercially-driven Strand, however, not least because it included many advertisements in each edition for the latest products. In the instalment that included this chapter, The Strand published adverts for the Blickensderfer, Chicago, Siècle, Empire, Yost, and Remington typewriters, as well as Taylor's Typewriter Company shop. Sidney Paget illustrated Mrs Lyons at her machine.

3 Dr Watson is described as being admitted "without ceremony"—the maid did not take his name nor announce it to her mistress—so Mrs Lyons must think that it is Stapleton who has come to see her.

4 With double yellow blooms, Rosa Hemisphaerica, is native to Southwest Asia.

impression. But the second was criticism. There was something subtly wrong with the face,[1] some coarseness of expression, some hardness, perhaps, of eye, some looseness of lip which marred its perfect beauty. But these, of course, are afterthoughts. At the moment I was simply conscious that I was in the presence of a very handsome woman, and that she was asking me the reasons for my visit. I had not quite understood until that instant how delicate my mission was.

"I have the pleasure," said I, "of knowing your father." It was a clumsy introduction, and the lady made me feel it.

"There is nothing in common between my father and me," she said. "I owe him nothing, and his friends are not mine. If it were not for the late Sir Charles Baskerville and some other kind hearts I might have starved for all that my father cared."

"It was about the late Sir Charles Baskerville that I have come here to see you."

The freckles started out on the lady's face.

"What can I tell you about him?" she asked, and her fingers played nervously over the stops[2] of her typewriter.

"You knew him, did you not?"

"I have already said that I owe a great deal to his kindness. If I am able to support myself it is largely due to the interest which he took in my unhappy situation."

"Did you correspond with him?"

The lady looked quickly up with an angry gleam in her hazel eyes.

"What is the object of these questions?" she asked sharply.

"The object is to avoid a public scandal. It is better that I should ask them here than that the matter should pass outside our control."

She was silent and her face was still very pale. At last she looked up with something reckless and defiant in her manner.

"Well, I'll answer," she said. "What are your questions?"

"Did you correspond with Sir Charles?"

"I certainly wrote to him once or twice to acknowledge his delicacy and his generosity."

"Have you the dates of those letters?"

---

1 Watson espouses the commonplace nineteenth-century/early twentieth-century notion (not wholly discredited today) that character was written on the face.

2 Keys.

"No."

"Have you ever met him?"

"Yes, once or twice, when he came into Coombe Tracey. He was a very retiring man, and he preferred to do good by stealth."

"But if you saw him so seldom and wrote so seldom, how did he know enough about your affairs to be able to help you, as you say that he has done?"

She met my difficulty with the utmost readiness.

"There were several gentlemen who knew my sad history and united to help me. One was Mr. Stapleton, a neighbour and intimate friend of Sir Charles's. He was exceedingly kind, and it was through him that Sir Charles learned about my affairs."

I knew already that Sir Charles Baskerville had made Stapleton his almoner[1] upon several occasions, so the lady's statement bore the impress of truth upon it.

"Did you ever write to Sir Charles asking him to meet you?" I continued.

Mrs. Lyons flushed with anger again.

"Really, sir, this is a very extraordinary question."

"I am sorry, madam, but I must repeat it."

"Then I answer, certainly not."

"Not on the very day of Sir Charles's death?"

The flush had faded in an instant, and a deathly face was before me. Her dry lips could not speak the "No" which I saw rather than heard.

"Surely your memory deceives you," said I. "I could even quote a passage of your letter. It ran 'Please, please, as you are a gentleman, burn this letter, and be at the gate by ten o'clock.'"

I thought that she had fainted, but she recovered herself by a supreme effort.

"Is there no such thing as a gentleman?" she gasped.

"You do Sir Charles an injustice. He *did* burn the letter. But sometimes a letter may be legible even when burned. You acknowledge now that you wrote it?"

"Yes, I did write it," she cried, pouring out her soul in a torrent of words. "I did write it. Why should I deny it? I have no reason to be ashamed of it. I wished him to help me. I believed that if I had an interview I could gain his help, so I asked him to meet me."

---

1 Someone who distributes the charity of others.

"But why at such an hour?"

"Because I had only just learned that he was going to London next day and might be away for months. There were reasons why I could not get there earlier."

"But why a rendezvous in the garden instead of a visit to the house?"

"Do you think a woman could go alone at that hour to a bachelor's house?"

"Well, what happened when you did get there?"

"I never went."

"Mrs. Lyons!"

"No, I swear it to you on all I hold sacred. I never went. Something intervened to prevent my going."

"What was that?"

"That is a private matter. I cannot tell it."

"You acknowledge then that you made an appointment with Sir Charles at the very hour and place at which he met his death, but you deny that you kept the appointment."

"That is the truth."

Again and again I cross-questioned her, but I could never get past that point.

"Mrs. Lyons," said I as I rose from this long and inconclusive interview, "you are taking a very great responsibility and putting yourself in a very false position by not making an absolutely clean breast of all that you know. If I have to call in the aid of the police you will find how seriously you are compromised. If your position is innocent, why did you in the first instance deny having written to Sir Charles upon that date?"

"Because I feared that some false conclusion might be drawn from it and that I might find myself involved in a scandal."

"And why were you so pressing that Sir Charles should destroy your letter?"

"If you have read the letter you will know."

"I did not say that I had read all the letter."

"You quoted some of it."

"I quoted the postscript. The letter had, as I said, been burned and it was not all legible. I ask you once again why it was that you were so pressing that Sir Charles should destroy this letter which he received on the day of his death."

"The matter is a very private one."

"The more reason why you should avoid a public investigation."

"I will tell you, then. If you have heard anything of my unhappy history you will know that I made a rash marriage[1] and had reason to regret it."

"I have heard so much."

"My life has been one incessant persecution from a husband whom I abhor. The law is upon his side, and every day I am faced by the possibility that he may force me to live with him.[2] At the time that I wrote this letter to Sir Charles I had learned that there was a prospect of my regaining my freedom if certain expenses could be met. It meant everything to me—peace of mind, happiness, self-respect—everything. I knew Sir Charles's generosity,

---

1 Note Mrs Lyons unquestioningly views the failure of her marriage in terms of her own moral error.

2 Conan Doyle's feminist readers, and those generally legally aware, would have noted a matter of considerable importance here, an issue relatively recently (1891) tried in a high profile case in the English courts. Under the Matrimonial Causes Act of 1884, the courts could issue an order forcing a wife to return to her husband and fulfil her conjugal duties. A case—the Clitheroe case or Jackson *v* Regina—seriously tested this. Edmund Jackson married Emily in 1887 then set off to New Zealand where she arranged to join him. Instead, she wrote requesting his return. This he did, but she refused to see him. He began proceedings against her, and wrote to her, but she was adamantly against him. In March 1891, Emily was seized while leaving church in Clitheroe, forced into a carriage, and held against her will in Blackburn. The husband insisted that the law was on his side, and the lower court agreed. However, the matter then went to the Court of Appeal where, after seeing Mrs Jackson, the judges delivered a unanimous verdict which vindicated and freed her, arguing that "where a wife refuses to live with her husband he is not entitled to keep her in confinement in order to enforce restitution of conjugal rights" (quoted in Lucy Bland, *Banishing the Beast: English Feminism and Sexual Morality 1885–1914* [Harmondsworth: Penguin, 1995], 136). The ruling encountered hostility in the conservative press but feminists welcomed it as the herald of a new age in matrimonial relations as treated under law. Sarah Grand, in the *Ludgate* ("Women in the Queen's Reign," 1898, 216–17, reprinted in Ann Heilmann and Stephanie Forward, eds, *Sex, Social Purity and Sarah Grand* [London: Routledge, 2000], I.92–93) referred to it as one of "the most notable features in the progress of women during the last sixty years" (I.92) and the feminist Elizabeth Wolstenholme Elmy regarded it as "the grandest victory the women's cause has ever gained" (quoted in Bland, 136). Assuming *The Hound of the Baskervilles* is set after the Clitheroe case, Mrs Lyons would, accordingly, have had some hope that the law would not have forced her return.

and I thought that if he heard the story from my own lips he would help me."

"Then how is it that you did not go?"

"Because I received help in the interval from another source."

"Why then, did you not write to Sir Charles and explain this?"

"So I should have done had I not seen his death in the paper next morning."[1]

The woman's story hung coherently together, and all my questions were unable to shake it. I could only check it by finding if she had, indeed, instituted divorce proceedings against her husband at or about the time of the tragedy.

It was unlikely that she would dare to say that she had not been to Baskerville Hall if she really had been, for a trap would be necessary to take her there, and could not have returned to Coombe Tracey until the early hours of the morning. Such an excursion could not be kept secret. The probability was, therefore, that she was telling the truth, or, at least, a part of the truth. I came away baffled and disheartened. Once again I had reached that dead wall which seemed to be built across every path by which I tried to get at the object of my mission. And yet the more I thought of the lady's face and of her manner the more I felt that something was being held back from me. Why should she turn so pale? Why should she fight against every admission until it was forced from her? Why should she have been so reticent at the time of the tragedy? Surely the explanation of all this could not be as innocent as she would have me believe. For the moment I could proceed no farther in that direction, but must turn back to that other clue which was to be sought for among the stone huts upon the moor.

And that was a most vague direction. I realized it as I drove back and noted how hill after hill showed traces of the ancient people. Barrymore's only indication had been that the stranger lived in one of these abandoned huts, and many hundreds of them are scattered throughout the length and breadth of the moor. But I had my own experience for a guide since it had shown me the man himself standing upon the summit of the Black Tor. That, then, should be the centre of my search. From there I should explore every hut upon the moor until I lighted upon the right one. If this man were inside it I should find out

---

1 Impossibly quick work as Sir Charles's body was not discovered till midnight.

from his own lips, at the point of my revolver if necessary, who he was and why he had dogged us so long. He might slip away from us in the crowd of Regent Street, but it would puzzle him to do so upon the lonely moor. On the other hand, if I should find the hut and its tenant should not be within it I must remain there, however long the vigil, until he returned. Holmes had missed him in London. It would indeed be a triumph for me if I could run him to earth[1] where my master had failed.

Luck had been against us again and again in this inquiry, but now at last it came to my aid. And the messenger of good fortune was none other than Mr. Frankland, who was standing, gray-whiskered and red-faced, outside the gate of his garden, which opened on to the highroad along which I travelled.

"Good-day, Dr. Watson," cried he with unwonted good humour, "you must really give your horses a rest and come in to have a glass of wine and to congratulate me."

My feelings towards him were very far from being friendly after what I had heard of his treatment of his daughter, but I was anxious to send Perkins and the wagonette home, and the opportunity was a good one. I alighted and sent a message to Sir Henry that I should walk over in time for dinner. Then I followed Frankland into his dining-room.

"It is a great day for me, sir—one of the red-letter days of my life,"[2] he cried with many chuckles. "I have brought off a double event. I mean to teach them in these parts that law is law, and that there is a man here who does not fear to invoke it. I have established a right of way through the centre of old Middleton's park, slap across it, sir, within a hundred yards of his own front door. What do you think of that? We'll teach these magnates that they cannot ride roughshod over the rights of the commoners, confound them! And I've closed the wood where the Fernworthy folk used to picnic. These infernal people seem to think that there are no rights of property, and that they can swarm where they like with their papers and their bottles. Both cases decided Dr. Watson, and both in my favour. I haven't had such a day since I had

---

1   A phrase from hunting (foxes live in "earths") but suggestive in the broader context of the novel's canine vocabulary because Watson is characterising himself—it's a charming idea—as Holmes's dog.

2   A term derived from ecclesiastical calendars which give major saints' days/religious feastdays in red.

Sir John Morland[1] for trespass, because he shot in his own warren."[2]

"How on earth did you do that?"

"Look it up in the books, sir. It will repay reading—Frankland v. Morland, Court of Queen's Bench.[3] It cost me £200, but I got my verdict."

"Did it do you any good?"

"None, sir, none. I am proud to say that I had no interest in the matter. I act entirely from a sense of public duty. I have no doubt, for example, that the Fernworthy people will burn me in effigy to-night. I told the police last time they did it that they should stop these disgraceful exhibitions. The County Constabulary is in a scandalous state,[4] sir, and it has not afforded me the protection to which I am entitled. The case of Frankland v. Regina[5] will bring the matter before the attention of the public. I told them that they would have occasion to regret their treatment of me, and already my words have come true."

"How so?" I asked.

The old man put on a very knowing expression.

"Because I could tell them what they are dying to know; but nothing would induce me to help the rascals in any way."

I had been casting round for some excuse by which I could get away from his gossip, but now I began to wish to hear more of it. I had seen enough of the contrary nature of the old sinner to understand that any strong sign of interest would be the surest way to stop his confidences.

"Some poaching case, no doubt?" said I with an indifferent manner.

---

1 Perhaps Conan Doyle's reading in the history of medicine had left a distant memory of John Morland MD to suggest this name. He was the author of *A Rational Account of the Causes of Chronic Diseases* (London, c. 1780).

2 Is there a touch of Boythorn from Charles Dickens's *Bleak House* (1851–53) in the wantonly litigious Frankland?

3 The Queen's Bench/King's Bench was originally a court presided over by the monarch but in the modern judiciary, as here, simply a division of the High Court.

4 Perhaps this is why Holmes has so little time for them.

5 I.e., Frankland *v* The Queen. He is taking action against the government—represented in legal terminology by the head of state—for failing to provide adequate policing.

"Ha, ha, my boy, a very much more important matter than that! What about the convict on the moor?"

I stared. "You don't mean that you know where he is?" said I.

"I may not know exactly where he is, but I am quite sure that I could help the police to lay their hands on him. Has it never struck you that the way to catch that man was to find out where he got his food and so trace it to him?"

He certainly seemed to be getting uncomfortably near the truth. "No doubt," said I; "but how do you know that he is anywhere upon the moor?"

"I know it because I have seen with my own eyes the messenger who takes him his food."

My heart sank for Barrymore. It was a serious thing to be in the power of this spiteful old busybody. But his next remark took a weight from my mind.

"You'll be surprised to hear that his food is taken to him by a child. I see him every day through my telescope upon the roof. He passes along the same path at the same hour, and to whom should he be going except to the convict?"

Here was luck indeed! And yet I suppressed all appearance of interest. A child! Barrymore had said that our unknown was supplied by a boy. It was on his track, and not upon the convict's, that Frankland had stumbled. If I could get his knowledge it might save me a long and weary hunt. But incredulity and indifference were evidently my strongest cards.

"I should say that it was much more likely that it was the son of one of the moorland shepherds taking out his father's dinner."

The least appearance of opposition struck fire out of the old autocrat. His eyes looked malignantly at me, and his gray whiskers bristled like those of an angry cat.

"Indeed, sir!" said he, pointing out over the wide-stretching moor. "Do you see that Black Tor over yonder? Well, do you see the low hill beyond with the thornbush upon it? It is the stoniest part of the whole moor. Is that a place where a shepherd would be likely to take his station? Your suggestion, sir, is a most absurd one."

I meekly answered that I had spoken without knowing all the facts. My submission pleased him and led him to further confidences.

"You may be sure, sir, that I have very good grounds before I come to an opinion. I have seen the boy again and again with his bundle. Every day, and sometimes twice a day, I have been able—

but wait a moment, Dr. Watson. Do my eyes deceive me, or is there at the present moment something moving upon that hillside?"

It was several miles off, but I could distinctly see a small dark dot against the dull green and gray.

"Come, sir, come!" cried Frankland, rushing upstairs. "You will see with your own eyes and judge for yourself."

The telescope, a formidable instrument mounted upon a tripod, stood upon the flat leads[1] of the house. Frankland clapped his eye to it and gave a cry of satisfaction.

"Quick, Dr. Watson, quick, before he passes over the hill!"

There he was, sure enough, a small urchin with a little bundle upon his shoulder, toiling slowly up the hill. When he reached the crest I saw the ragged uncouth figure outlined for an instant against the cold blue sky. He looked round him with a furtive and stealthy air, as one who dreads pursuit. Then he vanished over the hill.

"Well! Am I right?"

"Certainly, there is a boy who seems to have some secret errand."

"And what the errand is even a county constable could guess. But not one word shall they have from me, and I bind you to secrecy also, Dr. Watson. Not a word! You understand!"

"Just as you wish."

"They have treated me shamefully—shamefully. When the facts come out in Frankland *v.* Regina I venture to think that a thrill of indignation will run through the country. Nothing would induce me to help the police in any way. For all they cared it might have been me, instead of my effigy, which these rascals burned at the stake. Surely you are not going! You will help me to empty the decanter in honour of this great occasion!"

But I resisted all his solicitations and succeeded in dissuading him from his announced intention of walking home with me. I kept the road as long as his eye was on me, and then I struck off across the moor and made for the stony hill over which the boy had disappeared. Everything was working in my favour, and I swore that it should not be through lack of energy or perseverance that I should miss the chance which fortune had thrown in my way.

---

1 A portion of the roof which is flat and protected against the weather by sheets of lead.

The sun was already sinking when I reached the summit of the hill, and the long slopes beneath me were all golden-green on one side and gray shadow on the other. A haze lay low upon the farthest sky-line, out of which jutted the fantastic shapes of Belliver and Vixen Tor. Over the wide expanse there was no sound and no movement. One great gray bird, a gull or curlew, soared aloft in the blue heaven. He and I seemed to be the only living things between the huge arch of the sky and the desert beneath it. The barren scene, the sense of loneliness, and the mystery and urgency of my task all struck a chill into my heart. The boy was nowhere to be seen. But down beneath me in a cleft of the hills there was a circle of the old stone huts, and in the middle of them there was one which retained sufficient roof to act as a screen against the weather. My heart leaped within me as I saw it. This must be the burrow where the stranger lurked. At last my foot was on the threshold of his hiding place—his secret was within my grasp.

As I approached the hut, walking as warily as Stapleton would do when with poised net he drew near the settled butterfly, I satisfied myself that the place had indeed been used as a habitation. A vague pathway among the boulders led to the dilapidated opening which served as a door. All was silent within. The unknown might be lurking there, or he might be prowling on the moor. My nerves tingled with the sense of adventure. Throwing aside my cigarette, I closed my hand upon the butt of my revolver and, walking swiftly up to the door, I looked in. The place was empty.

But there were ample signs that I had not come upon a false scent. This was certainly where the man lived. Some blankets rolled in a waterproof lay upon that very stone slab upon which neolithic man had once slumbered. The ashes of a fire were heaped in a rude grate. Beside it lay some cooking utensils and a bucket half-full of water. A litter of empty tins showed that the place had been occupied for some time, and I saw, as my eyes became accustomed to the checkered light, a pannikin[1] and a half-full bottle of spirits standing in the corner. In the middle of the hut a flat stone served the purpose of a table, and upon this stood a small cloth bundle—the same, no doubt, which I had seen through the telescope upon the shoulder of the boy. It con-

---

1 Small metal drinking vessel.

tained a loaf of bread, a tinned tongue,[1] and two tins of preserved peaches. As I set it down again, after having examined it, my heart leaped to see that beneath it there lay a sheet of paper with writing upon it. I raised it, and this was what I read, roughly scrawled in pencil—

"Dr. Watson has gone to Coombe Tracey."

For a minute I stood there with the paper in my hands thinking out the meaning of this curt message. It was I, then, and not Sir Henry, who was being dogged by this secret man. He had not followed me himself, but he had set an agent—the boy, perhaps—upon my track, and this was his report. Possibly I had taken no step since I had been upon the moor which had not been observed and reported. Always there was this feeling of an unseen force, a fine net drawn round us with infinite skill and delicacy, holding us so lightly that it was only at some supreme moment that one realized that one was indeed entangled in its meshes.

If there was one report there might be others, so I looked round the hut in search of them. There was no trace, however, of anything of the kind, nor could I discover any sign which might indicate the character or intentions of the man who lived in this singular place, save that he must be of Spartan habits and cared little for the comforts of life. When I thought of the heavy rains and looked at the gaping roof I understood how strong and immutable must be the purpose which had kept him in that inhospitable abode. Was he our malignant enemy, or was he by chance our guardian angel? I swore that I would not leave the hut until I knew.

Outside the sun was sinking low and the west was blazing with scarlet and gold. Its reflection was shot back in ruddy patches by the distant pools which lay amid the great Grimpen Mire. There were the two towers of Baskerville Hall, and there a distant blur of smoke which marked the village of Grimpen. Between the two, behind the hill, was the house of the Stapletons. All was sweet and mellow and peaceful in the golden evening light, and yet as I

---

1   The first tinned food in Britain was canned by Bryan Donkins of Bermondsey, Southwark, south London, in 1811. Tongue—usually beef—was often eaten preserved in the Victorian period, tinned, picked, or dried. Isabella Beeton (1836–65) warned the mid-century housewife "man's instinct has decided that ox-tongue is better than horse-tongue; nevertheless, the latter is frequently substituted by dishonest dealers for the former," *The Book of Household Management* (Oxford: Oxford UP, 2000 [first published in 1859]), 171.

looked at them my soul shared none of the peace of Nature but quivered at the vagueness and the terror of that interview which every instant was bringing nearer. With tingling nerves but a fixed purpose, I sat in the dark recess of the hut and waited with sombre patience for the coming of its tenant.

And then at last I heard him. Far away came the sharp clink of a boot striking upon a stone. Then another and yet another, coming nearer and nearer. I shrank back into the darkest corner and cocked the pistol in my pocket, determined not to discover myself until I had an opportunity of seeing something of the stranger. There was a long pause which showed that he had stopped. Then once more the footsteps approached and a shadow fell across the opening of the hut.

"It is a lovely evening, my dear Watson," said a well-known voice. "I really think that you will be more comfortable outside than in."

Chapter XII

Death on the Moor

For a moment or two I sat breathless, hardly able to believe my ears. Then my senses and my voice came back to me, while a crushing weight of responsibility seemed in an instant to be lifted from my soul. That cold, incisive, ironical voice could belong to but one man in all the world.

"Holmes!" I cried—"Holmes!"

"Come out," said he, "and please be careful with the revolver."

I stooped under the rude lintel, and there he sat upon a stone outside, his gray eyes dancing with amusement as they fell upon my astonished features. He was thin and worn, but clear and alert, his keen face bronzed by the sun and roughened by the wind. In his tweed suit and cloth cap he looked like any other tourist upon the moor, and he had contrived, with that catlike love of personal cleanliness which was one of his characteristics, that his chin should be as smooth and his linen as perfect as if he were in Baker Street.

"I never was more glad to see anyone in my life," said I as I wrung him by the hand.

"Or more astonished, eh?"

"Well, I must confess to it."

"The surprise was not all on one side, I assure you. I had no idea that you had found my occasional retreat, still less that you were inside it, until I was within twenty paces of the door."

"My footprint, I presume?"

"No, Watson, I fear that I could not undertake to recognize your footprint amid all the footprints of the world. If you seriously desire to deceive me you must change your tobacconist; for when I see the stub of a cigarette marked Bradley, Oxford Street, I know that my friend Watson is in the neighbourhood. You will see it there beside the path. You threw it down, no doubt, at that supreme moment when you charged into the empty hut."

"Exactly."

"I thought as much—and knowing your admirable tenacity I was convinced that you were sitting in ambush, a weapon within reach, waiting for the tenant to return. So you actually thought that I was the criminal?"

"I did not know who you were, but I was determined to find out."

"Excellent, Watson! And how did you localise me? You saw me, perhaps, on the night of the convict hunt, when I was so imprudent as to allow the moon to rise behind me?"

"Yes, I saw you then."

"And have no doubt searched all the huts until you came to this one?"

"No, your boy had been observed, and that gave me a guide where to look."

"The old gentleman with the telescope, no doubt. I could not make it out when first I saw the light flashing upon the lens." He rose and peeped into the hut. "Ha, I see that Cartwright has brought up some supplies. What's this paper? So you have been to Coombe Tracey, have you?"

"Yes."

"To see Mrs. Laura Lyons?"

"Exactly."

"Well done! Our researches have evidently been running on parallel lines, and when we unite our results I expect we shall have a fairly full knowledge of the case."

"Well, I am glad from my heart that you are here, for indeed the responsibility and the mystery were both becoming too much for my nerves. But how in the name of wonder did you come here, and what have you been doing? I thought that you were in Baker Street working out that case of blackmailing."

"That was what I wished you to think."

"Then you use me, and yet do not trust me!" I cried with some bitterness. "I think that I have deserved better at your hands, Holmes."

"My dear fellow, you have been invaluable to me in this as in many other cases, and I beg that you will forgive me if I have seemed to play a trick upon you. In truth, it was partly for your own sake that I did it, and it was my appreciation of the danger which you ran which led me to come down and examine the matter for myself. Had I been with Sir Henry and you it is confident that my point of view would have been the same as yours, and my presence would have warned our very formidable opponents to be on their guard. As it is, I have been able to get about as I could not possibly have done had I been living in the Hall, and I remain an unknown factor in the business, ready to throw in all my weight at a critical moment."

"But why keep me in the dark?"

"For you to know could not have helped us and might possibly have led to my discovery. You would have wished to tell me something, or in your kindness you would have brought me out some comfort or other, and so an unnecessary risk would be run. I brought Cartwright down with me—you remember the little chap at the express office—and he has seen after my simple wants: a loaf of bread and a clean collar. What does man want more? He has given me an extra pair of eyes upon a very active pair of feet, and both have been invaluable."

"Then my reports have all been wasted!"—My voice trembled as I recalled the pains and the pride with which I had composed them.

Holmes took a bundle of papers from his pocket.

"Here are your reports, my dear fellow, and very well thumbed, I assure you. I made excellent arrangements, and they are only delayed one day upon their way. I must compliment you exceedingly upon the zeal and the intelligence which you have shown over an extraordinarily difficult case."

I was still rather raw over the deception which had been practised upon me, but the warmth of Holmes's praise drove my anger from my mind. I felt also in my heart that he was right in what he said and that it was really best for our purpose that I should not have known that he was upon the moor.

"That's better," said he, seeing the shadow rise from my face. "And now tell me the result of your visit to Mrs. Laura Lyons—it was not difficult for me to guess that it was to see her that you had gone, for I am already aware that she is the one person in Coombe Tracey who might be of service to us in the matter. In fact, if you had not gone to-day it is exceedingly probable that I should have gone to-morrow."

The sun had set and dusk was settling over the moor. The air had turned chill and we withdrew into the hut for warmth. There sitting together in the twilight, I told Holmes of my conversation with the lady. So interested was he that I had to repeat some of it twice before he was satisfied.

"This is most important," said he when I had concluded. "It fills up a gap which I had been unable to bridge in this most complex affair. You are aware, perhaps, that a close intimacy exists between this lady and the man Stapleton?"

"I did not know of a close intimacy."

"There can be no doubt about the matter. They meet, they write, there is a complete understanding between them. Now, this puts a very powerful weapon into our hands. If I could only use it to detach his wife—"

"His wife?"

"I am giving you some information now, in return for all that you have given me. The lady who has passed here as Miss Stapleton is in reality his wife."

"Good heavens, Holmes! Are you sure of what you say? How could he have permitted Sir Henry to fall in love with her?"

"Sir Henry's falling in love could do no harm to anyone except Sir Henry. He took particular care that Sir Henry did not *make* love to her,[1] as you have yourself observed. I repeat that the lady is his wife and not his sister."

"But why this elaborate deception?"

"Because he foresaw that she would be very much more useful to him in the character of a free woman."

All my unspoken instincts, my vague suspicions, suddenly took shape and centred upon the naturalist. In that impassive colourless man, with his straw hat and his butterfly-net, I seemed to see something terrible—a creature of infinite patience and craft, with a smiling face and a murderous heart.

"It is he, then, who is our enemy—it is he who dogged us in London?"

"So I read the riddle."

"And the warning—it must have come from her!"

"Exactly."

---

1   "Make love" means "woo" or "court" here; it does not refer to having sex.

The shape of some monstrous villainy, half seen, half guessed, loomed through the darkness which had girt me so long.

"But are you sure of this, Holmes? How do you know that the woman is his wife?"

"Because he so far forgot himself as to tell you a true piece of autobiography upon the occasion when he first met you, and I dare say he has many a time regretted it since. He *was* once a schoolmaster in the north of England. Now, there is no one more easy to trace than a schoolmaster. There are scholastic agencies by which one may identify any man who has been in the profession. A little investigation showed me that a school had come to grief under atrocious circumstances, and that the man who had owned it—the name was different—had disappeared with his wife. The descriptions agreed. When I learned that the missing man was devoted to entomology[1] the identification was complete."

The darkness was rising, but much was still hidden by the shadows.

"If this woman is in truth his wife, where does Mrs. Laura Lyons come in?" I asked.

"That is one of the points upon which your own researches have shed a light. Your interview with the lady has cleared the situation very much. I did not know about a projected divorce between herself and her husband. In that case, regarding Stapleton as an unmarried man, she counted no doubt upon becoming his wife."

"And when she is undeceived?"

"Why, then we may find the lady of service. It must be our first duty to see her—both of us—to-morrow. Don't you think, Watson, that you are away from your charge rather long? Your place should be at Baskerville Hall."

The last red streaks had faded away in the west and night had settled upon the moor. A few faint stars were gleaming in a violet sky.

"One last question, Holmes," I said as I rose. "Surely there is no need of secrecy between you and me. What is the meaning of it all? What is he after?"

Holmes's voice sank as he answered:

"It is murder, Watson—refined, cold-blooded, deliberate murder. Do not ask me for particulars. My nets are closing upon him,

---

1   The branch of natural history concerned with insects.

even as his are upon Sir Henry, and with your help he is already almost at my mercy. There is but one danger which can threaten us. It is that he should strike before we are ready to do so. Another day—two at the most—and I have my case complete, but until then guard your charge as closely as ever a fond mother watched her ailing child. Your mission to-day has justified itself, and yet I could almost wish that you had not left his side—Hark!"

A terrible scream—a prolonged yell of horror and anguish burst out of the silence of the moor. That frightful cry turned the blood to ice in my veins.

"Oh, my God!" I gasped. "What is it? What does it mean?"

Holmes had sprung to his feet, and I saw his dark, athletic outline at the door of the hut, his shoulders stooping, his head thrust forward, his face peering into the darkness.

"Hush!" he whispered. "Hush!"

The cry had been loud on account of its vehemence, but it had pealed out from somewhere far off on the shadowy plain. Now it burst upon our ears, nearer, louder, more urgent than before.

"Where is it?" Holmes whispered; and I knew from the thrill of his voice that he, the man of iron, was shaken to the soul. "Where is it, Watson?"

"There, I think." I pointed into the darkness.

"No, there!"

Again the agonized cry swept through the silent night, louder and much nearer than ever. And a new sound mingled with it, a deep, muttered rumble, musical and yet menacing, rising and falling like the low, constant murmur of the sea.

"The hound!" cried Holmes. "Come, Watson, come! Great heavens, if we are too late!"

He had started running swiftly over the moor, and I had followed at his heels. But now from somewhere among the broken ground immediately in front of us there came one last despairing yell, and then a dull, heavy thud. We halted and listened. Not another sound broke the heavy silence of the windless night.

I saw Holmes put his hand to his forehead like a man distracted. He stamped his feet upon the ground.

"He has beaten us, Watson. We are too late."

"No, no, surely not!"

"Fool that I was to hold my hand. And you, Watson, see what comes of abandoning your charge! But, by Heaven, if the worst has happened we'll avenge him!"

Blindly we ran through the gloom, blundering against boulders, forcing our way through gorse bushes, panting up hills and rushing down slopes, heading always in the direction whence those dreadful sounds had come. At every rise Holmes looked eagerly round him, but the shadows were thick upon the moor, and nothing moved upon its dreary face.

"Can you see anything?"

"Nothing."

"But, hark, what is that?"

A low moan had fallen upon our ears. There it was again upon our left! On that side a ridge of rocks ended in a sheer cliff which overlooked a stone-strewn slope. On its jagged face was spread-eagled some dark, irregular object. As we ran towards it the vague outline hardened into a definite shape. It was a prostrate man face downward upon the ground, the head doubled under him at a horrible angle, the shoulders rounded and the body hunched together as if in the act of throwing a somersault. So grotesque was the attitude that I could not for the instant realize that that moan had been the passing of his soul. Not a whisper, not a rus-tle, rose now from the dark figure over which we stooped. Holmes laid his hand upon him and held it up again with an exclamation of horror. The gleam of the match which he struck shone upon his clotted fingers and upon the ghastly pool which widened slowly from the crushed skull of the victim. And it shone upon something else which turned our hearts sick and faint within us— the body of Sir Henry Baskerville!

There was no chance of either of us forgetting that peculiar ruddy tweed suit—the very one which he had worn on the first morning that we had seen him in Baker Street. We caught the one clear glimpse of it, and then the match flickered and went out, even as the hope had gone out of our souls. Holmes groaned, and his face glimmered white through the darkness.

"The brute! the brute!" I cried with clenched hands. "Oh Holmes, I shall never forgive myself for having left him to his fate."

"I am more to blame than you, Watson. In order to have my case well rounded and complete, I have thrown away the life of my client. It is the greatest blow which has befallen me in my career. But how *could* I know—how could I know—that he would risk his life alone upon the moor in the face of all my warnings?"

"That we should have heard his screams—my God, those screams!—and yet have been unable to save him! Where is this brute of a hound which drove him to his death? It may be lurking among these rocks at this instant. And Stapleton, where is he? He shall answer for this deed."

"He shall. I will see to that. Uncle and nephew have been murdered—the one frightened to death by the very sight of a beast which he thought to be supernatural, the other driven to his end in his wild flight to escape from it. But now we have to prove the connection between the man and the beast. Save from what we heard, we cannot even swear to the existence of the latter, since Sir Henry has evidently died from the fall. But, by heavens, cunning as he is, the fellow shall be in my power before another day is past!"

We stood with bitter hearts on either side of the mangled body, overwhelmed by this sudden and irrevocable disaster which had brought all our long and weary labours to so piteous an end. Then as the moon rose we climbed to the top of the rocks over which our poor friend had fallen, and from the summit we gazed out over the shadowy moor, half silver and half gloom. Far away, miles off, in the direction of Grimpen, a single steady yellow light was shining. It could only come from the lonely abode of the Stapletons. With a bitter curse I shook my fist at it as I gazed.

"Why should we not seize him at once?"

"Our case is not complete. The fellow is wary and cunning to the last degree. It is not what we know, but what we can prove. If we make one false move the villain may escape us yet."

"What can we do?"

"There will be plenty for us to do to-morrow. To-night we can only perform the last offices to our poor friend."

Together we made our way down the precipitous slope and approached the body, black and clear against the silvered stones. The agony of those contorted limbs struck me with a spasm of pain and blurred my eyes with tears.

"We must send for help, Holmes! We cannot carry him all the way to the Hall. Good heavens, are you mad?"

He had uttered a cry and bent over the body. Now he was dancing and laughing and wringing my hand. Could this be my stern, self-contained friend? These were hidden fires, indeed!

"A beard! A beard! The man has a beard!"

"A beard?"

"It is not the baronet—it is—why, it is my neighbour, the convict!"

With feverish haste we had turned the body over, and that dripping beard was pointing up to the cold, clear moon. There could be no doubt about the beetling forehead, the sunken animal eyes. It was indeed the same face which had glared upon me in the light of the candle from over the rock—the face of Selden, the criminal.

Then in an instant it was all clear to me. I remembered how the baronet had told me that he had handed his old wardrobe to Barrymore. Barrymore had passed it on in order to help Selden in his escape. Boots, shirt, cap—it was all Sir Henry's. The tragedy was still black enough, but this man had at least deserved death by the laws of his country.[1] I told Holmes how the matter stood, my heart bubbling over with thankfulness and joy.

"Then the clothes have been the poor devil's death," said he. "It is clear enough that the hound has been laid on from some article of Sir Henry's—the boot which was abstracted in the hotel, in all probability—and so ran this man down. There is one very singular thing, however: How came Selden, in the darkness, to know that the hound was on his trail?"

"He heard him."

"To hear a hound upon the moor would not work a hard man like this convict into such a paroxysm of terror that he would risk recapture by screaming wildly for help. By his cries he must have run a long way after he knew the animal was on his track. How did he know?"

"A greater mystery to me is why this hound, presuming that all our conjectures are correct—"

"I presume nothing."

"Well, then, why this hound should be loose to-night. I suppose that it does not always run loose upon the moor. Stapleton would not let it go unless he had reason to think that Sir Henry would be there."

"My difficulty is the more formidable of the two, for I think that we shall very shortly get an explanation of yours, while mine may remain forever a mystery. The question now is, what shall we do with this poor wretch's body? We cannot leave it here to the foxes and the ravens."

"I suggest that we put it in one of the huts until we can communicate with the police."

"Exactly. I have no doubt that you and I could carry it so far. Halloa, Watson, what's this? It's the man himself, by all that's wonderful and audacious! Not a word to show your suspicions—not a word, or my plans crumble to the ground."

A figure was approaching us over the moor, and I saw the dull

---

1 A frail argument: Selden's death sentence had been commuted.

red glow of a cigar. The moon shone upon him, and I could distinguish the dapper shape and jaunty walk of the naturalist. He stopped when he saw us, and then came on again.

"Why, Dr. Watson, that's not you, is it? You are the last man that I should have expected to see out on the moor at this time of night. But, dear me, what's this? Somebody hurt? Not—don't tell me that it is our friend Sir Henry!" He hurried past me and stooped over the dead man. I heard a sharp intake of his breath and the cigar fell from his fingers.

"Who—who's this?" he stammered.

"It is Selden, the man who escaped from Princetown."

Stapleton turned a ghastly face upon us, but by a supreme effort he had overcome his amazement and his disappointment. He looked sharply from Holmes to me.

"Dear me! What a very shocking affair! How did he die?"

"He appears to have broken his neck by falling over these rocks. My friend and I were strolling on the moor when we heard a cry."

"I heard a cry also. That was what brought me out. I was uneasy about Sir Henry."

"Why about Sir Henry in particular?" I could not help asking.

"Because I had suggested that he should come over. When he did not come I was surprised, and I naturally became alarmed for his safety when I heard cries upon the moor. By the way"—his eyes darted again from my face to Holmes's—"did you hear anything else besides a cry?"

"No," said Holmes; "did you?"

"No."

"What do you mean, then?"

"Oh, you know the stories that the peasants tell about a phantom hound, and so on. It is said to be heard at night upon the moor. I was wondering if there were any evidence of such a sound to-night."

"We heard nothing of the kind," said I.

"And what is your theory of this poor fellow's death?"

"I have no doubt that anxiety and exposure have driven him off his head. He has rushed about the moor in a crazy state and eventually fallen over here and broken his neck."

"That seems the most reasonable theory," said Stapleton, and he gave a sigh which I took to indicate his relief. "What do you think about it, Mr. Sherlock Holmes?"

My friend bowed his compliments.

"You are quick at identification," said he.

"We have been expecting you in these parts since Dr. Watson came down. You are in time to see a tragedy."

"Yes, indeed. I have no doubt that my friend's explanation will cover the facts. I will take an unpleasant remembrance back to London with me to-morrow."

"Oh, you return to-morrow?"

"That is my intention."

"I hope your visit has cast some light upon those occurrences which have puzzled us?"

Holmes shrugged his shoulders.

"One cannot always have the success for which one hopes. An investigator needs facts and not legends or rumours. It has not been a satisfactory case."

My friend spoke in his frankest and most unconcerned manner. Stapleton still looked hard at him. Then he turned to me.

"I would suggest carrying this poor fellow to my house, but it would give my sister such a fright that I do not feel justified in doing it. I think that if we put something over his face he will be safe until morning."

And so it was arranged. Resisting Stapleton's offer of hospitality, Holmes and I set off to Baskerville Hall, leaving the naturalist to return alone. Looking back we saw the figure moving slowly away over the broad moor, and behind him that one black smudge on the silvered slope which showed where the man was lying who had come so horribly to his end.

"We're at close grips at last," said Holmes as we walked together across the moor. "What a nerve the fellow has! How he pulled himself together in the face of what must have been a paralyzing shock when he found that the wrong man had fallen a victim to his plot. I told you in London, Watson, and I tell you now again, that we have never had a foeman more worthy of our steel."

"I am sorry that he has seen you."

"And so was I at first. But there was no getting out of it."

"What effect do you think it will have upon his plans now that he knows you are here?"

"It may cause him to be more cautious, or it may drive him to desperate measures at once. Like most clever criminals, he may be too confident in his own cleverness and imagine that he has completely deceived us."

"Why should we not arrest him at once?"

"My dear Watson, you were born to be a man of action. Your instinct is always to do something energetic. But supposing, for argument's sake, that we had him arrested to-night, what on earth the better off should we be for that? We could prove nothing against him. There's the devilish cunning of it! If he were acting through a human agent we could get some evidence, but if we were to drag this great dog to the light of day it would not help us in putting a rope round the neck of its master."

"Surely we have a case."

"Not a shadow of one—only surmise and conjecture. We should be laughed out of court if we came with such a story and such evidence."

"There is Sir Charles's death."

"Found dead without a mark upon him. You and I know that he died of sheer fright, and we know also what frightened him but how are we to get twelve stolid jurymen to know it? What signs are there of a hound? Where are the marks of its fangs? Of course we know that a hound does not bite a dead body and that Sir Charles was dead before ever the brute overtook him. But we have to *prove* all this, and we are not in a position to do it."

"Well, then, to-night?"

"We are not much better off to-night. Again, there was no direct connection between the hound and the man's death. We never saw the hound. We heard it, but we could not prove that it was running upon this man's trail. There is a complete absence of motive. No, my dear fellow; we must reconcile ourselves to the fact that we have no case at present, and that it is worth our while to run any risk in order to establish one."

"And how do you propose to do so?"

"I have great hopes of what Mrs. Laura Lyons may do for us when the position of affairs is made clear to her. And I have my own plan as well. Sufficient for to-morrow is the evil thereof;[1] but I hope before the day is past to have the upper hand at last."

I could draw nothing further from him, and he walked, lost in thought, as far as the Baskerville gates.

"Are you coming up?"

"Yes; I see no reason for further concealment. But one last word, Watson. Say nothing of the hound to Sir Henry. Let him think that Selden's death was as Stapleton would have us believe. He will have a better nerve for the ordeal which he will have to

---

1 A modification of Jesus's words from Matthew 6: 34 "Take therefore no thought for the morrow for the morrow shall take thought for the things of it self: sufficient unto the day is the evil thereof."

undergo to-morrow, when he is engaged, if I remember your report aright, to dine with these people."

"And so am I."

"Then you must excuse yourself and he must go alone. That will be easily arranged. And now, if we are too late for dinner, I think that we are both ready for our suppers."[1]

Chapter XIII

Fixing the Nets[2]

Sir Henry was more pleased than surprised to see Sherlock Holmes, for he had for some days been expecting that recent events would bring him down from London. He did raise his eyebrows, however, when he found that my friend had neither any luggage nor any explanations for its absence. Between us we soon supplied his wants, and then over a belated supper we explained to the baronet as much of our experience as it seemed desirable that he should know. But first I had the unpleasant duty of breaking the news to Barrymore and his wife. To him it may have been an unmitigated relief, but she wept bitterly in her apron. To all the world he was the man of violence, half animal and half demon; but to her he always remained the little wilful boy of her own girlhood, the child who had clung to her hand. Evil indeed is the man who has not one woman to mourn him.

"I've been moping in the house all day since Watson went off in the morning," said the baronet. "I guess I should have some credit, for I have kept my promise. If I hadn't sworn not to go about alone I might have had a more lively evening, for I had a message from Stapleton asking me over there."

"I have no doubt that you would have had a more lively evening," said Holmes drily. "By the way, I don't suppose you appreciate that we have been mourning over you as having broken your neck?"

Sir Henry opened his eyes. "How was that?"

"This poor wretch was dressed in your clothes. I fear your

---

1 The Victorian middle-class custom was to eat supper late in the evening before retiring to bed.

2 A title that emphasises how Holmes and Watson are pursuing Stapleton as Stapleton pursued the moths and butterflies.

servant who gave them to him may get into trouble with the police."

"That is unlikely. There was no mark on any of them, as far as I know."

"That's lucky for him—in fact, it's lucky for all of you, since you are all on the wrong side of the law in this matter. I am not sure that as a conscientious detective my first duty is not to arrest the whole household. Watson's reports are most incriminating documents."

"But how about the case?" asked the baronet. "Have you made anything out of the tangle? I don't know that Watson and I are much the wiser since we came down."

"I think that I shall be in a position to make the situation rather more clear to you before long. It has been an exceedingly difficult and most complicated business. There are several points upon which we still want light—but it is coming all the same."

"We've had one experience, as Watson has no doubt told you. We heard the hound on the moor, so I can swear that it is not all empty superstition. I had something to do with dogs when I was out West, and I know one when I hear one. If you can muzzle that one and put him on a chain I'll be ready to swear you are the greatest detective of all time."

"I think I will muzzle him and chain him all right if you will give me your help."

"Whatever you tell me to do I will do."

"Very good; and I will ask you also to do it blindly, without always asking the reason."

"Just as you like."

"If you will do this I think the chances are that our little problem will soon be solved. I have no doubt,—"

He stopped suddenly and stared fixedly up over my head into the air. The lamp beat upon his face, and so intent was it and so still that it might have been that of a clear-cut classical statue, a personification of alertness and expectation.

"What is it?" we both cried.

I could see as he looked down that he was repressing some internal emotion. His features were still composed, but his eyes shone with amused exultation.

"Excuse the admiration of a connoisseur,"[1] said he as he

---

1 Dr Watson thinks Holmes's ideas of art are crude: see p. 90, note 1.

waved his hand towards the line of portraits which covered the opposite wall. "Watson won't allow that I know anything of art but that is mere jealousy because our views upon the subject differ. Now, these are a really very fine series of portraits."

"Well, I'm glad to hear you say so," said Sir Henry, glancing with some surprise at my friend. "I don't pretend to know much about these things, and I'd be a better judge of a horse or a steer[1] than of a picture. I didn't know that you found time for such things."

"I know what is good when I see it, and I see it now. That's a Kneller,[2] I'll swear, that lady in the blue silk over yonder, and the stout gentleman with the wig ought to be a Reynolds.[3] They are all family portraits, I presume?"

"Every one."[4]

"Do you know the names?"

"Barrymore has been coaching me in them, and I think I can say my lessons fairly well."

"Who is the gentleman with the telescope?"

"That is Rear-Admiral Baskerville, who served under Rodney[5] in the West Indies. The man with the blue coat and the roll of paper is Sir William Baskerville, who was Chairman of Committees of the House of Commons under Pitt."[6]

---

1 Steers are beef cattle (more US vocabulary).

2 Sir Godfrey Kneller (1646–1723) was a German-born painter (originally Gottfried Kniller) who became the most prominent of portraitists in London at the end of the seventeenth century.

3 Sir Joshua Reynolds (1723–92), pre-eminent English portraitist of his time and first President of the Royal Academy (founded 1768).

4 Sir Henry confirms the identity of none of the painters. Maybe he does not know—he says that he understands little "about these things"—or perhaps Holmes is correct, or Sir Henry chooses not to respond to Holmes because the real artists are less exalted.

5 Admiral Lord George Rodney, First Baron Rodney (1719–92), fought against the French and Spanish navies in the West Indies, culminating in his victory over Admiral de Grasse at the Battle of Les Saintes on 12 April 1782.

6 Either William Pitt the Elder, 1st Earl of Chatham, British premier from 1757 to 1761 and 1766 to 1768, or William Pitt the Younger, British premier from 1783 to 1801 and 1804 to 1806.

"And this Cavalier[1] opposite to me—the one with the black velvet and the lace?"

"Ah, you have a right to know about him. That is the cause of all the mischief, the wicked Hugo, who started the Hound of the Baskervilles. We're not likely to forget him."

I gazed with interest and some surprise upon the portrait.

"Dear me!" said Holmes, "he seems a quiet, meek-mannered man enough, but I dare say that there was a lurking devil in his eyes. I had pictured him as a more robust and ruffianly person."

"There's no doubt about the authenticity, for the name and the date, 1647, are on the back of the canvas."

Holmes said little more, but the picture of the old roysterer seemed to have a fascination for him, and his eyes were continually fixed upon it during supper. It was not until later, when Sir Henry had gone to his room, that I was able to follow the trend of his thoughts. He led me back into the banqueting-hall, his bedroom candle in his hand, and he held it up against the time-stained portrait on the wall.

"Do you see anything there?"

I looked at the broad plumed hat, the curling love-locks, the white lace collar, and the straight, severe face which was framed between them. It was not a brutal countenance, but it was prim hard, and stern, with a firm-set, thin-lipped mouth, and a coldly intolerant eye.

"Is it like anyone you know?"

"There is something of Sir Henry about the jaw."

"Just a suggestion, perhaps. But wait an instant!" He stood upon a chair, and, holding up the light in his left hand, he curved his right arm over the broad hat and round the long ringlets.

"Good heavens!" I cried in amazement.

The face of Stapleton had sprung out of the canvas.

"Ha, you see it now. My eyes have been trained to examine faces and not their trimmings. It is the first quality of a criminal investigator that he should see through a disguise."

---

1   A supporter of the Royalist cause during the English Civil War 1642-9. Christopher Frayling seems to assume the novel is describing an actual household interior when he says that "since Conan Doyle spelt the word with a capital C and since the Baskervilles evidently liked to commission the best-known portraitists of their day, the most likely artist is Frans Hals (1581/5–1666) … who painted *The Laughing Cavalier* (1624), now in London's Wallace Collection" (Frayling, 191).

"But this is marvellous. It might be his portrait."

"Yes, it is an interesting instance of a throw-back, which appears to be both physical and spiritual. A study of family portraits is enough to convert a man to the doctrine of reincarnation. The fellow is a Baskerville—that is evident."[1]

"With designs upon the succession."

"Exactly. This chance of the picture has supplied us with one of our most obvious missing links. We have him, Watson, we have him, and I dare swear that before to-morrow night he will be fluttering in our net as helpless as one of his own butterflies. A pin, a cork, and a card, and we add him to the Baker Street collection!"

He burst into one of his rare fits of laughter as he turned away from the picture. I have not heard him laugh often, and it has always boded ill to somebody.[2]

I was up betimes in the morning, but Holmes was afoot earlier still, for I saw him as I dressed, coming up the drive.

"Yes, we should have a full day to-day," he remarked, and he rubbed his hands with the joy of action. "The nets are all in place, and the drag is about to begin. We'll know before the day is out whether we have caught our big, leanjawed pike, or whether he has got through the meshes."

"Have you been on the moor already?"

"I have sent a report from Grimpen to Princetown as to the death of Selden. I think I can promise that none of you will be troubled in the matter. And I have also communicated with my faithful Cartwright, who would certainly have pined away at the door of my hut, as a dog does at his master's grave,[3] if I had not set his mind at rest about my safety."

"What is the next move?"

"To see Sir Henry. Ah, here he is!"

"Good morning, Holmes," said the baronet. "You look like a general who is planning a battle with his chief of the staff."

"That is the exact situation. Watson was asking for orders."

"And so do I."

"Very good. You are engaged, as I understand, to dine with our friends the Stapletons to-night."

---

1 Dr Mortimer is interested in "throw-backs" but has obviously failed to spot this one.

2 The last time Holmes laughed in this novel (p. 174) it didn't bode anything of the sort.

3 A new variation on the canine imagery.

"I hope that you will come also. They are very hospitable people, and I am sure that they would be very glad to see you."

"I fear that Watson and I must go to London."

"To London?"

"Yes, I think that we should be more useful there at the present juncture."

The baronet's face perceptibly lengthened.

"I hoped that you were going to see me through this business. The Hall and the moor are not very pleasant places when one is alone."

"My dear fellow, you must trust me implicitly and do exactly what I tell you. You can tell your friends that we should have been happy to have come with you, but that urgent business required us to be in town. We hope very soon to return to Devonshire. Will you remember to give them that message?"

"If you insist upon it."

"There is no alternative, I assure you."

I saw by the baronet's clouded brow that he was deeply hurt by what he regarded as our desertion.

"When do you desire to go?" he asked coldly.

"Immediately after breakfast. We will drive in to Coombe Tracey, but Watson will leave his things as a pledge that he will come back to you. Watson, you will send a note to Stapleton to tell him that you regret that you cannot come."

"I have a good mind to go to London with you," said the baronet. "Why should I stay here alone?"

"Because it is your post of duty. Because you gave me your word that you would do as you were told, and I tell you to stay."

"All right, then, I'll stay."

"One more direction! I wish you to drive to Merripit House. Send back your trap, however, and let them know that you intend to walk home."

"To walk across the moor?"

"Yes."

"But that is the very thing which you have so often cautioned me not to do."

"This time you may do it with safety. If I had not every confidence in your nerve and courage I would not suggest it, but it is essential that you should do it."

"Then I will do it."

"And as you value your life do not go across the moor in any direction save along the straight path which leads from Merripit House to the Grimpen Road, and is your natural way home."

"I will do just what you say."

"Very good. I should be glad to get away as soon after breakfast as possible, so as to reach London in the afternoon."

I was much astounded by this programme, though I remembered that Holmes had said to Stapleton on the night before that his visit would terminate next day. It had not crossed my mind however, that he would wish me to go with him, nor could I understand how we could both be absent at a moment which he himself declared to be critical. There was nothing for it, however, but implicit obedience; so we bade good-bye to our rueful friend, and a couple of hours afterwards we were at the station of Coombe Tracey and had dispatched the trap upon its return journey. A small boy was waiting upon the platform.

"Any orders, sir?"

"You will take this train to town, Cartwright. The moment you arrive you will send a wire to Sir Henry Baskerville, in my name, to say that if he finds the pocketbook which I have dropped he is to send it by registered post to Baker Street."

"Yes, sir."

"And ask at the station office if there is a message for me."

The boy returned with a telegram, which Holmes handed to me. It ran—

"Wire received. Coming down with unsigned warrant. Arrive five-forty.—LESTRADE"[1]

"That is in answer to mine of this morning. He is the best of the professionals,[2] I think, and we may need his assistance. Now, Watson, I think that we cannot employ our time better than by calling upon your acquaintance, Mrs. Laura Lyons."

His plan of campaign was beginning to be evident. He would

---

1 Inspector Lestrade of Scotland Yard appears in many of the Holmes tales, sometimes as the admirer and sometimes the critic of the consulting detective. In "The Adventure of the Cardboard Box" (1893), Holmes offers the most forthright of mixed opinions: "although he is absolutely devoid of reason, he is as tenacious as a bulldog when he once understands what he has to do" (*CSH* 895). Given Lestrade is from the Yard, one wonders where the *local* police authorities are, for whom Conan Doyle seems to have little time. It is puzzling why this warrant is unsigned and therefore not of any help—or is the word misused and intended to indicate that it *is* signed but doesn't yet have the *name of the person to be arrested* written on it? That, at least, would make more sense (if legally be a gross abuse).

2 Which, as far as Holmes is concerned, is not much of a compliment.

use the baronet in order to convince the Stapletons that we were really gone, while we should actually return at the instant when we were likely to be needed. That telegram from London, if mentioned by Sir Henry to the Stapletons, must remove the last suspicions from their minds. Already I seemed to see our nets drawing closer around that leanjawed pike.[1]

Mrs. Laura Lyons was in her office, and Sherlock Holmes opened his interview with a frankness and directness which considerably amazed her.

"I am investigating the circumstances which attended the death of the late Sir Charles Baskerville," said he. "My friend here, Dr. Watson, has informed me of what you have communicated, and also of what you have withheld in connection with that matter."

"What have I withheld?" she asked defiantly.

"You have confessed that you asked Sir Charles to be at the gate at ten o'clock. We know that that was the place and hour of his death. You have withheld what the connection is between these events."

"There is no connection."

"In that case the coincidence must indeed be an extraordinary one. But I think that we shall succeed in establishing a connection, after all. I wish to be perfectly frank with you, Mrs. Lyons. We regard this case as one of murder, and the evidence may implicate not only your friend Mr. Stapleton but his wife as well."

The lady sprang from her chair.

"His wife!" she cried.

"The fact is no longer a secret. The person who has passed for his sister is really his wife."

Mrs. Lyons had resumed her seat. Her hands were grasping the arms of her chair, and I saw that the pink nails had turned white with the pressure of her grip.

"His wife!" she said again. "His wife! He is not a married man."

Sherlock Holmes shrugged his shoulders.

"Prove it to me! Prove it to me! And if you can do so—!" The fierce flash of her eyes said more than any words.

"I have come prepared to do so," said Holmes, drawing several papers from his pocket. "Here is a photograph of the couple

---

1 Large predatory freshwater fish (see Introduction, p. 25).

taken in York[1] four years ago. It is indorsed 'Mr. and Mrs. Vandeleur,' but you will have no difficulty in recognizing him, and her also, if you know her by sight. Here are three written descriptions by trustworthy witnesses of Mr. and Mrs. Vandeleur, who at that time kept St. Oliver's[2] private school. Read them and see if you can doubt the identity of these people."

She glanced at them, and then looked up at us with the set rigid face of a desperate woman.

"Mr. Holmes," she said, "this man had offered me marriage on condition that I could get a divorce from my husband. He has lied to me, the villain, in every conceivable way. Not one word of truth has he ever told me. And why—why? I imagined that all was for my own sake. But now I see that I was never anything but a tool in his hands. Why should I preserve faith with him who never kept any with me? Why should I try to shield him from the consequences of his own wicked acts? Ask me what you like, and there is nothing which I shall hold back. One thing I swear to you, and that is that when I wrote the letter I never dreamed of any harm to the old gentleman, who had been my kindest friend."

"I entirely believe you, madam," said Sherlock Holmes. "The recital of these events must be very painful to you, and perhaps it will make it easier if I tell you what occurred, and you can check me if I make any material mistake. The sending of this letter was suggested to you by Stapleton?"

"He dictated it."

"I presume that the reason he gave was that you would receive help from Sir Charles for the legal expenses connected with your divorce?"

"Exactly."

"And then after you had sent the letter he dissuaded you from keeping the appointment?"

"He told me that it would hurt his self-respect that any other man should find the money for such an object, and that though

---

1   Great cathedral city of Yorkshire, seat of the Archbishop of York, the second most powerful Anglican cleric in the country.

2   "St Oliver" in the nineteenth century (before the canonization of the seventeenth-century Irish martyr St Oliver Plunkett in 1975) referred to an obscure eleventh-century Benedictine monk, whose feast day is 3 February. Almost nothing is known of him and he seems an unlikely patron of a school.

he was a poor man himself he would devote his last penny to removing the obstacles which divided us."

"He appears to be a very consistent character. And then you heard nothing until you read the reports of the death in the paper?"

"No."

"And he made you swear to say nothing about your appointment with Sir Charles?"

"He did. He said that the death was a very mysterious one, and that I should certainly be suspected if the facts came out. He frightened me into remaining silent."

"Quite so. But you had your suspicions?"

She hesitated and looked down.

"I knew him," she said. "But if he had kept faith with me I should always have done so with him."

"I think that on the whole you have had a fortunate escape," said Sherlock Holmes. "You have had him in your power and he knew it, and yet you are alive. You have been walking for some months very near to the edge of a precipice. We must wish you good-morning now, Mrs. Lyons, and it is probable that you will very shortly hear from us again."

"Our case becomes rounded off, and difficulty after difficulty thins away in front of us," said Holmes as we stood waiting for the arrival of the express from town. "I shall soon be in the position of being able to put into a single connected narrative one of the most singular and sensational crimes of modern times. Students of criminology will remember the analogous incidents in Grodno, in Little Russia,[1] in the year '66, and of course there are the Anderson murders in North Carolina,[2] but this case possesses some features which are entirely its own. Even now we have no clear case against this very wily man. But I shall be very much surprised if it is not clear enough before we go to bed this night."

The London express came roaring into the station, and a small, wiry bulldog of a man had sprung from a first-class carriage. We all three shook hands, and I saw at once from the reverential way in which Lestrade gazed at my companion that he had learned a good deal since the days when they had first

---

1 Grodno is in Belarus.
2 Never a subject of a Holmes story. North Carolina is a state on the eastern coast of the USA, between South Carolina and Virginia; it was founded in 1653 by Virginia colonists.

worked together. I could well remember the scorn which the theories of the reasoner used then to excite in the practical man.

"Anything good?" he asked.

"The biggest thing for years," said Holmes. "We have two hours before we need think of starting. I think we might employ it in getting some dinner and then, Lestrade, we will take the London fog out of your throat by giving you a breath of the pure night-air of Dartmoor. Never been there? Ah, well, I don't suppose you will forget your first visit."

Chapter XIV

The Hound of the Baskervilles

One of Sherlock Holmes's defects—if, indeed, one may call it a defect—was that he was exceedingly loath to communicate his full plans to any other person until the instant of their fulfilment. Partly it came no doubt from his own masterful nature, which loved to dominate and surprise those who were around him. Partly also from his professional caution, which urged him never to take any chances.[1] The result, however, was very trying for those who were acting as his agents and assistants. I had often suffered under it, but never more so than during that long drive in the darkness. The great ordeal was in front of us; at last we were about to make our final effort, and yet Holmes had said nothing, and I could only surmise what his course of action would be. My nerves thrilled with anticipation when at last the cold wind upon our faces and the dark, void spaces on either side of the narrow road told me that we were back upon the moor once again. Every stride of the horses and every turn of the wheels was taking us nearer to our supreme adventure.

Our conversation was hampered by the presence of the driver of the hired waggonette,[2] so that we were forced to talk of trivial matters when our nerves were tense with emotion and anticipation. It was a relief to me, after that unnatural restraint, when we at last passed Frankland's house and knew that we were drawing

---

1 Dr Watson is rather generous to Holmes here who is taking the gravest of chances with Sir Henry's life.

2 Newnes's inconsistency. The word is spelt with a single "g" throughout Chapter VI.

near to the Hall and to the scene of action. We did not drive up to the door but got down near the gate of the avenue. The wag-gonette was paid off and ordered to return to Coombe Tracey forthwith, while we started to walk to Merripit House.

"Are you armed, Lestrade?"

The little detective smiled.

"As long as I have my trousers I have a hip-pocket, and as long as I have my hip-pocket I have something in it."

"Good! My friend and I are also ready for emergencies."

"You're mighty close about this affair, Mr. Holmes. What's the game now?"

"A waiting game."

"My word, it does not seem a very cheerful place," said the detective with a shiver, glancing round him at the gloomy slopes of the hill and at the huge lake of fog which lay over the Grimpen Mire. "I see the lights of a house ahead of us."

"That is Merripit House and the end of our journey. I must request you to walk on tiptoe and not to talk above a whisper."

We moved cautiously along the track as if we were bound for the house, but Holmes halted us when we were about two hun-dred yards from it.

"This will do," said he. "These rocks upon the right make an admirable screen."

"We are to wait here?"

"Yes, we shall make our little ambush here. Get into this hol-low, Lestrade. You have been inside the house, have you not, Wat-son? Can you tell the position of the rooms? What are those lat-ticed windows at this end?"

"I think they are the kitchen windows."

"And the one beyond, which shines so brightly?"

"That is certainly the dining-room."

"The blinds are up. You know the lie of the land best. Creep forward quietly and see what they are doing—but for heaven's sake don't let them know that they are watched!"

I tiptoed down the path and stooped behind the low wall which surrounded the stunted orchard. Creeping in its shadow I reached a point whence I could look straight through the uncur-tained window.

There were only two men in the room, Sir Henry and Staple-ton. They sat with their profiles towards me on either side of the round table. Both of them were smoking cigars, and coffee and wine were in front of them. Stapleton was talking with animation, but the baronet looked pale and distrait. Perhaps the thought of that lonely walk across the ill-omened moor was weighing heavily upon his mind.

As I watched them Stapleton rose and left the room, while Sir Henry filled his glass again and leaned back in his chair, puffing at his cigar. I heard the creak of a door and the crisp sound of boots upon gravel. The steps passed along the path on the other side of the wall under which I crouched. Looking over, I saw the naturalist pause at the door of an out-house in the corner of the orchard. A key turned in a lock, and as he passed in there was a curious scuffling noise from within. He was only a minute or so inside, and then I heard the key turn once more and he passed me and re-entered the house. I saw him rejoin his guest, and I crept quietly back to where my companions were waiting to tell them what I had seen.

"You say, Watson, that the lady is not there?" Holmes asked when I had finished my report.

"No."

"Where can she be, then, since there is no light in any other room except the kitchen?"

"I cannot think where she is."

I have said that over the great Grimpen Mire there hung a dense, white fog. It was drifting slowly in our direction and banked itself up like a wall on that side of us, low but thick and well defined. The moon shone on it, and it looked like a great shimmering ice-field, with the heads of the distant tors as rocks borne upon its surface. Holmes's face was turned towards it, and he muttered impatiently as he watched its sluggish drift.

"It's moving towards us, Watson."

"Is that serious?"

"Very serious, indeed—the one thing upon earth which could have disarranged my plans. He can't be very long, now. It is already ten o'clock. Our success and even his life may depend upon his coming out before the fog is over the path."

The night was clear and fine above us. The stars shone cold and bright, while a half-moon bathed the whole scene in a soft, uncertain light. Before us lay the dark bulk of the house, its serrated roof and bristling chimneys hard outlined against the silver-spangled sky. Broad bars of golden light from the lower windows stretched across the orchard and the moor. One of them was suddenly shut off. The servants had left the kitchen. There only remained the lamp in the dining-room where the two men, the murderous host and the unconscious guest, still chatted over their cigars.

Every minute that white woolly plain which covered one-half of the moor was drifting closer and closer to the house. Already the first thin wisps of it were curling across the golden square of the lighted window. The farther wall of the orchard was already invisible, and the trees were standing out of a swirl of white vapour. As we watched it the fog-wreaths came crawling round both corners of the house and rolled slowly into one dense bank on which the upper floor and the roof floated like a strange ship upon a shadowy sea. Holmes struck his hand passionately upon the rock in front of us and stamped his feet in his impatience.

"If he isn't out in a quarter of an hour the path will be covered. In half an hour we won't be able to see our hands in front of us."

"Shall we move farther back upon higher ground?"

"Yes, I think it would be as well."

So as the fog-bank flowed onward we fell back before it until we were half a mile from the house, and still that dense white sea, with the moon silvering its upper edge, swept slowly and inexorably on.

"We are going too far," said Holmes. "We dare not take the chance of his being overtaken before he can reach us. At all costs we must hold our ground where we are." He dropped on his knees and clapped his ear to the ground. "Thank Heaven, I think that I hear him coming."

A sound of quick steps broke the silence of the moor. Crouching among the stones we stared intently at the silver-tipped bank in front of us. The steps grew louder, and through the fog, as through a curtain, there stepped the man whom we were awaiting. He looked round him in surprise as he emerged into the clear, starlit night. Then he came swiftly along the path, passed close to where we lay, and went on up the long slope behind us. As he walked he glanced continually over either shoulder, like a man who is ill at ease.

"Hist!" cried Holmes, and I heard the sharp click of a cocking pistol. "Look out! It's coming!"

There was a thin, crisp, continuous patter from somewhere in the heart of that crawling bank. The cloud was within fifty yards of where we lay, and we glared at it, all three, uncertain what horror was about to break from the heart of it. I was at Holmes's elbow, and I glanced for an instant at his face. It was pale and exultant, his eyes shining brightly in the moonlight. But suddenly they started forward in a rigid, fixed stare, and his lips parted in amazement. At the same instant Lestrade gave a yell of terror and threw himself face downward upon the ground. I sprang to my feet, my inert hand grasping my pistol, my mind paralyzed by the dreadful shape which had sprung out upon us from the shadows of the fog. A hound it was, an enormous coal-black hound, but not such a hound as mortal eyes have ever seen. Fire burst from its open mouth, its eyes glowed with a smouldering glare, its muzzle and hackles and dewlap[1] were outlined in flickering flame. Never in the delirious dream of a disordered brain could anything more savage, more appalling, more hellish be conceived than that dark form and savage face[2] which broke upon us out of the wall of fog.[3]

With long bounds the huge black creature was leaping down the track, following hard upon the footsteps of our friend. So paralyzed were we by the apparition that we allowed him to pass before we had recovered our nerve. Then Holmes and I both fired together, and the creature gave a hideous howl, which showed that one at least had hit him. He did not pause, however, but bounded onward. Far away on the path we saw Sir Henry looking back, his face white in the moonlight, his hands raised in horror, glaring helplessly at the frightful thing which was hunting him down.

But that cry of pain from the hound had blown all our fears to the winds. If he was vulnerable he was mortal, and if we could wound him we could kill him. Never have I seen a man run as Holmes ran that night. I am reckoned fleet of foot, but he outpaced me as much as I outpaced the little professional. In front of us as we flew up the track we heard scream after scream from Sir Henry and the deep roar of the hound. I was in time to see the beast spring upon its victim, hurl him to the ground, and worry at his throat. But the next instant Holmes had emptied five barrels[4] of his revolver into the creature's flank.[5] With a last howl of agony and a vicious snap in the air, it rolled upon its back, four feet pawing furiously, and then fell limp upon its side. I stooped,

---

1 Loose skin under the throat of a dog.
2 A description hardly justified by Sidney Paget's illustrations of the Hound (see the frontispiece).
3 The eighth *Strand* instalment of *The Hound* ended here.
4 An odd error for Conan Doyle to make: he means "chambers." The revolver—unless it was an exceptionally experimental weapon—would have had only one barrel.
5 Not the best place for a fatal shot. But perhaps Conan Doyle imagined Holmes reluctant to shoot the hound in head as it was too close to Sir Henry. See the frontispiece.

panting, and pressed my pistol to the dreadful, shimmering head, but it was useless to press the trigger. The giant hound was dead.[1]

Sir Henry lay insensible where he had fallen. We tore away his collar, and Holmes breathed a prayer of gratitude when we saw that there was no sign of a wound and that the rescue had been in time. Already our friend's eyelids shivered and he made a feeble effort to move. Lestrade thrust his brandy-flask between the baronet's teeth, and two frightened eyes were looking up at us.

"My God!" he whispered. "What was it? What, in Heaven's name, was it?"

"It's dead, whatever it is," said Holmes. "We've laid the family ghost once and forever."

In mere size and strength it was a terrible creature which was lying stretched before us. It was not a pure bloodhound and it was not a pure mastiff; but it appeared to be a combination of the two—gaunt, savage, and as large as a small lioness.[2] Even now in the stillness of death, the huge jaws seemed to be dripping with a bluish flame and the small, deep-set, cruel eyes were ringed with fire. I placed my hand upon the glowing muzzle, and as I held them up my own fingers smouldered and gleamed in the darkness.

"Phosphorus," I said.[3]

"A cunning preparation of it," said Holmes, sniffing at the dead animal. "There is no smell which might have interfered with his power of scent. We owe you a deep apology, Sir Henry, for

---

1 Death scenes of giant dogs obviously grimly appealed to Conan Doyle, though he was a dog lover (perhaps Paget catches more of Conan Doyle's real feelings about the hound and his treatment?). Compare this episode to a similar one from *The Exploits of Brigadier Gerard* (1896): "The first thing that I saw as I came out into the hall was a man with a butcher's axe in his hand, lying flat upon his back, with a gaping wound across his forehead. The second was a huge dog, with two of its legs broken, twisting in agony upon the floor. As it raised itself up I saw the two broken ends flapping like flails. At the same instant I heard a cry, and there was Duroc, thrown against the wall, with the other hound's teeth in his throat. He pushed it off with his left hand, while again and again he passed his sabre through its body, but it was not until I blew out its brains with my pistol that the iron jaws relaxed, and the fierce, bloodshot eyes were glazed in death" (452).

2 The combination of bloodhound and mastiff would not produce a dog so remarkable in size. This creature may be of flesh and blood, but it is a fantasy still.

3 Pure phosphorus is deadly poisonous and would have burned the animal dreadfully. Presumably some kind of phosphoresence is meant.

having exposed you to this fright. I was prepared for a hound, but not for such a creature as this. And the fog gave us little time to receive him."

"You have saved my life."

"Having first endangered it. Are you strong enough to stand?"

"Give me another mouthful of that brandy and I shall be ready for anything. So! Now, if you will help me up. What do you propose to do?"

"To leave you here. You are not fit for further adventures to-night. If you will wait, one or other of us will go back with you to the Hall."

He tried to stagger to his feet; but he was still ghastly pale and trembling in every limb. We helped him to a rock, where he sat shivering with his face buried in his hands.

"We must leave you now," said Holmes.

"The rest of our work must be done, and every moment is of importance. We have our case, and now we only want our man.

"It's a thousand to one against our finding him at the house," he continued as we retraced our steps swiftly down the path. "Those shots must have told him that the game was up."

"We were some distance off, and this fog may have deadened them."

"He followed the hound to call him off—of that you may be certain. No, no, he's gone by this time! But we'll search the house and make sure."

The front door was open, so we rushed in and hurried from room to room to the amazement of a doddering old manservant, who met us in the passage. There was no light save in the dining-room, but Holmes caught up the lamp and left no corner of the house unexplored. No sign could we see of the man whom we were chasing. On the upper floor, however, one of the bedroom doors was locked.

"There's someone in here," cried Lestrade. "I can hear a movement. Open this door!"

A faint moaning and rustling came from within. Holmes struck the door just over the lock with the flat of his foot and it flew open. Pistol in hand, we all three rushed into the room.

But there was no sign within it of that desperate and defiant villain whom we expected to see. Instead we were faced by an object so strange and so unexpected that we stood for a moment staring at it in amazement.

The room had been fashioned into a small museum, and the walls were lined by a number of glass-topped cases full of that collection of butterflies and moths the formation of which had been the relaxation of this complex and dangerous man. In the centre of this room there was an upright beam, which had been placed at some period as a support for the old worm-eaten baulk of timber which spanned the roof. To this post a figure was tied, so swathed and muffled in the sheets which had been used to secure it that one could not for the moment tell whether it was that of a man or a woman. One towel passed round the throat and was secured at the back of the pillar. Another covered the lower part of the face, and over it two dark eyes—eyes full of grief and shame and a dreadful questioning—stared back at us. In a minute we had torn off the gag, unswathed the bonds, and Mrs. Stapleton sank upon the floor in front of us. As her beautiful head fell upon her chest I saw the clear red weal of a whiplash across her neck.

"The brute!" cried Holmes. "Here, Lestrade, your brandy-bottle![1] Put her in the chair! She has fainted from ill-usage and exhaustion."

She opened her eyes again.

"Is he safe?" she asked. "Has he escaped?"

"He cannot escape us, madam."

"No, no, I did not mean my husband. Sir Henry? Is he safe?"

"Yes."

"And the hound?"

"It is dead."

She gave a long sigh of satisfaction.

"Thank God! Thank God! Oh, this villain! See how he has treated me!" She shot her arms out from her sleeves, and we saw with horror that they were all mottled with bruises. "But this is nothing—nothing! It is my mind and soul that he has tortured and defiled. I could endure it all, ill-usage, solitude, a life of deception, everything, as long as I could still cling to the hope that I had his love, but now I know that in this also I have been his dupe and his tool." She broke into passionate sobbing as she spoke.

"You bear him no good will, madam," said Holmes. "Tell us then where we shall find him. If you have ever aided him in evil, help us now and so atone."

---

1 See p. 218, note 2 to "The Speckled Band."

"There is but one place where he can have fled," she answered. "There is an old tin mine on an island in the heart of the Mire. It was there that he kept his hound and there also he had made preparations so that he might have a refuge. That is where he would fly."

The fog-bank lay like white wool against the window. Holmes held the lamp towards it.

"See," said he. "No one could find his way into the Grimpen Mire to-night."

She laughed and clapped her hands. Her eyes and teeth gleamed with fierce merriment

"He may find his way in, but never out," she cried. "How can he see the guiding wands[1] to-night? We planted them together, he and I, to mark the pathway through the Mire. Oh, if I could only have plucked them out to-day. Then indeed you would have had him at your mercy!"

It was evident to us that all pursuit was in vain until the fog had lifted. Meanwhile we left Lestrade in possession of the house while Holmes and I went back with the baronet to Baskerville Hall. The story of the Stapletons could no longer be withheld from him, but he took the blow bravely when he learned the truth about the woman whom he had loved. But the shock of the night's adventures had shattered his nerves, and before morning he lay delirious in a high fever under the care of Dr. Mortimer. The two of them were destined to travel together round the world before Sir Henry had become once more the hale, hearty man that he had been before he became master of that ill-omened estate.[2]

And now I come rapidly to the conclusion of this singular narrative, in which I have tried to make the reader share those dark fears and vague surmises which clouded our lives so long

---

1 Some form of markers fashioned from sticks. On first describing his prowess in being able to cross the Mire, the deceiving Stapleton tells Dr Watson that "It is only by remembering certain complex landmarks that I am able to do it" (p. 117). Now we discover he has provided himself with assistance.

2 Dr Watson's wife—while she was alive—was almost as invisible as Mrs Mortimer (the notable exception being *The Sign of Four*, which is where Dr Watson meets her).

and ended in so tragic a manner. On the morning after the death of the hound the fog had lifted and we were guided by Mrs. Stapleton to the point where they had found a pathway through the bog. It helped us to realize the horror of this woman's life when we saw the eagerness and joy with which she laid us on her husband's track. We left her standing upon the thin peninsula of firm, peaty soil which tapered out into the widespread bog. From the end of it a small wand planted here and there showed where the path zigzagged from tuft to tuft of rushes among those green-scummed pits and foul quagmires which barred the way to the stranger. Rank reeds and lush, slimy water-plants sent an odour of decay and a heavy miasmatic vapour onto our faces, while a false step plunged us more than once thigh-deep into the dark, quivering Mire, which shook for yards in soft undulations around our feet. Its tenacious grip plucked at our heels as we walked, and when we sank into it it was as if some malignant hand was tugging us down into those obscene depths, so grim and purposeful was the clutch in which it held us. Once only we saw a trace that someone had passed that perilous way before us. From amid a tuft of cotton grass which bore it up out of the slime some dark thing was projecting. Holmes sank to his waist as he stepped from the path to seize it, and had we not been there to drag him out he could never have set his foot upon firm land again. He held an old black boot in the air. "Meyers, Toronto," was printed on the leather inside.

"It is worth a mud bath," said he. "It is our friend Sir Henry's missing boot."

"Thrown there by Stapleton in his flight."

"Exactly. He retained it in his hand after using it to set the hound upon the track. He fled when he knew the game was up, still clutching it. And he hurled it away at this point of his flight. We know at least that he came so far in safety."

But more than that we were never destined to know, though there was much which we might surmise. There was no chance of finding footsteps in the mire, for the rising mud oozed swiftly in upon them, but as we at last reached firmer ground beyond the morass we all looked eagerly for them. But no slightest sign of them ever met our eyes. If the earth told a true story, then Stapleton never reached that island of refuge towards which he struggled through the fog upon that last night. Somewhere in the heart of the great Grimpen Mire, down in the foul slime of the huge morass which had sucked him in, this cold and cruel-hearted man is forever buried.[1]

Many traces we found of him in the bog-girt island where he had hid his savage ally. A huge driving-wheel and a shaft half-filled with rubbish showed the position of an abandoned mine. Beside it were the crumbling remains of the cottages of the miners, driven away no doubt by the foul reek of the surrounding swamp. In one of these a staple and chain with a quantity of gnawed bones showed where the animal had been confined. A skeleton with a tangle of brown hair adhering to it lay among the *débris*.

"A dog!" said Holmes. "By Jove, a curly-haired spaniel. Poor Mortimer will never see his pet again.[2] Well, I do not know that this place contains any secret which we have not already fathomed. He could hide his hound, but he could not hush its voice, and hence came those cries which even in daylight were not pleasant to hear. On an emergency he could keep the hound in the out-house at Merripit, but it was always a risk, and it was only on the supreme day, which he regarded as the end of all his efforts, that he dared do it. This paste in the tin is no doubt the luminous mixture with which the creature was daubed. It was suggested, of course, by the story of the family hell-hound, and by the desire to frighten old Sir Charles to death. No wonder the poor devil of a convict ran and screamed, even as our friend did, and as we ourselves might have done, when he saw such a creature bounding through the darkness of the moor upon his track. It was a cunning device, for, apart from the chance of driving your victim to his death, what peasant would venture to inquire too closely into such a creature should he get sight of it, as many have done, upon the moor? I said it in London, Watson, and I say it again now, that never yet have we helped to hunt down a more dangerous man than he who is lying yonder"—he swept his long arm towards the huge mottled expanse of green-splotched bog which stretched away until it merged into the russet slopes of the moor.

---

1 Compare the end of Major-General Heatherstone in the Hole of Cree in *The Mystery of Cloomber*.

2 Readers might puzzle about how this spaniel came to be here. Are we asked to imagine either that it crossed the Mire on its own or that the hound killed it elsewhere then brought it to its lair?

Chapter XV

A Retrospection

It was the end of November, and Holmes and I sat, upon a raw and foggy night, on either side of a blazing fire in our sitting-room in Baker Street. Since the tragic upshot of our visit to Devonshire he had been engaged in two affairs of the utmost importance, in the first of which he had exposed the atrocious conduct of Colonel Upwood in connection with the famous card scandal of the Nonpareil Club, while in the second he had defended the unfortunate Mme. Montpensier from the charge of murder which hung over her in connection with the death of her step-daughter, Mlle. Carère, the young lady who, as it will be remembered, was found six months later alive and married in New York.[1] My friend was in excellent spirits over the success which had attended a succession of difficult and important cases, so that I was able to induce him to discuss the details of the Baskerville mystery. I had waited patiently for the opportunity for I was aware that he would never permit cases to overlap,[2] and that his clear and logical mind would not be drawn from its present work to dwell upon memories of the past. Sir Henry and Dr. Mortimer were, however, in London, on their way to that long voyage which had been recommended for the restoration of his shattered nerves. They had called upon us that very afternoon, so that it was natural that the subject should come up for discussion.

"The whole course of events," said Holmes, "from the point of view of the man who called himself Stapleton was simple and direct, although to us, who had no means in the beginning of knowing the motives of his actions and could only learn part of the facts, it all appeared exceedingly complex. I have had the advantage of two conversations with Mrs. Stapleton, and the case has now been so entirely cleared up that I am not aware that there is anything which has remained a secret to us. You will find a few

---

1 Neither of these tantalizing stories appeared in print: Conan Doyle's mischievous wit.

2 What a peculiar statement: Conan Doyle has just had Watson recount a tale in which Holmes proposed precisely to allow cases to overlap—he was apparently reading Watson's reports on the Baskerville murder while solving the "blackmailing case" on behalf of "one of the most revered names in England" at Baker Street.

notes upon the matter under the heading B in my indexed list of cases."

"Perhaps you would kindly give me a sketch of the course of events from memory."

"Certainly, though I cannot guarantee that I carry all the facts in my mind. Intense mental concentration has a curious way of blotting out what has passed. The barrister who has his case at his fingers' ends and is able to argue with an expert upon his own subject finds that a week or two of the courts will drive it all out of his head once more. So each of my cases displaces the last, and Mlle. Carère has blurred my recollection of Baskerville Hall. To-morrow some other little problem may be submitted to my notice which will in turn dispossess the fair French lady and the infamous Upwood. So far as the case of the hound goes, however, I will give you the course of events as nearly as I can, and you will suggest anything which I may have forgotten.

"My inquiries show beyond all question that the family portrait did not lie, and that this fellow was indeed a Baskerville. He was a son of that Rodger Baskerville, the younger brother of Sir Charles, who fled with a sinister reputation to South America, where he was said to have died unmarried. He did, as a matter of fact, marry, and had one child, this fellow, whose real name is the same as his father's. He married Beryl Garcia, one of the beauties of Costa Rica,[1] and, having purloined a considerable sum of public money, he changed his name to Vandeleur and fled to England, where he established a school in the east of Yorkshire.[2] His reason for attempting this special line of business was that he had struck up an acquaintance with a consumptive[3] tutor upon the voyage home, and that he had used this man's ability to make the undertaking a success. Fraser, the tutor, died however, and the school which had begun well sank from disrepute into infamy. The Vandeleurs found it convenient to change their name to Stapleton, and he brought the remains of his fortune, his schemes for

---

1   Small Central American republic, between Nicaragua and Panama, with the Caribbean on the East and the Pacific on the West.

2   Charles Dickens's Wackford Squeers and the school of Dotheboys Hall, at Greta Bridge, North Yorkshire, depicted in *Nicholas Nickleby* (1838–39), made the association between remote Yorkshire schools and men of dubious morals an irresistible one in the second half of the nineteenth century.

3   Suffering from tuberculosis.

the future, and his taste for entomology to the south of England. I learned at the British Museum that he was a recognized authority upon the subject, and that the name of Vandeleur has been permanently attached to a certain moth which he had, in his Yorkshire days, been the first to describe.

"We now come to that portion of his life which has proved to be of such intense interest to us. The fellow had evidently made inquiry and found that only two lives intervened between him and a valuable estate. When he went to Devonshire his plans were, I believe, exceedingly hazy, but that he meant mischief from the first is evident from the way in which he took his wife with him in the character of his sister. The idea of using her as a decoy was clearly already in his mind, though he may not have been certain how the details of his plot were to be arranged. He meant in the end to have the estate, and he was ready to use any tool or run any risk for that end. His first act was to establish himself as near to his ancestral home as he could, and his second was to cultivate a friendship with Sir Charles Baskerville and with the neighbours.

"The baronet himself told him about the family hound, and so prepared the way for his own death. Stapleton, as I will continue to call him, knew that the old man's heart was weak and that a shock would kill him. So much he had learned from Dr. Mortimer. He had heard also that Sir Charles was superstitious and had taken this grim legend very seriously. His ingenious mind instantly suggested a way by which the baronet could be done to death, and yet it would be hardly possible to bring home the guilt to the real murderer.

"Having conceived the idea he proceeded to carry it out with considerable finesse. An ordinary schemer would have been content to work with a savage hound. The use of artificial means to make the creature diabolical was a flash of genius upon his part. The dog he bought in London from Ross and Mangles,[1] the deal-

---

1 An animal dealer, though not a real one. The "Mangles" is a touch of gruesome humour but it has been noticed that Ross Lowis Mangles, who worked for the Bengal Civil Service, was awarded the Victoria Cross, the highest medal for gallantry in British service (one of only 5 civilians ever to be so) during the Indian Mutiny in 1857. He might have been momentarily at the back of Conan Doyle's mind as he searched for a name. For more on some of the names in *The Hound*, see Donald A. Redmond, *Sherlock Holmes: A Study in Sources* (Kingston and Montreal: McGill-Queen's UP, 1982), 99–109.

ers in Fulham Road.[1] It was the strongest and most savage in their possession. He brought it down by the North Devon line and walked a great distance over the moor so as to get it home without exciting any remarks. He had already on his insect hunts learned to penetrate the Grimpen Mire, and so had found a safe hiding-place for the creature. Here he kennelled it and waited his chance.

"But it was some time coming. The old gentleman could not be decoyed outside of his grounds at night. Several times Stapleton lurked about with his hound, but without avail. It was during these fruitless quests that he, or rather his ally, was seen by peasants, and that the legend of the demon dog received a new confirmation. He had hoped that his wife might lure Sir Charles to his ruin, but here she proved unexpectedly independent. She would not endeavour to entangle the old gentleman in a sentimental attachment which might deliver him over to his enemy. Threats and even, I am sorry to say, blows refused to move her. She would have nothing to do with it, and for a time Stapleton was at a deadlock.

"He found a way out of his difficulties through the chance that Sir Charles, who had conceived a friendship for him, made him the minister of his charity in the case of this unfortunate woman, Mrs. Laura Lyons. By representing himself as a single man he acquired complete influence over her, and he gave her to understand that in the event of her obtaining a divorce from her husband he would marry her. His plans were suddenly brought to a head by his knowledge that Sir Charles was about to leave the Hall on the advice of Dr. Mortimer, with whose opinion he himself pretended to coincide. He must act at once, or his victim might get beyond his power. He therefore put pressure upon Mrs. Lyons to write this letter, imploring the old man to give her an interview on the evening before his departure for London. He then, by a specious argument, prevented her from going, and so had the chance for which he had waited.

"Driving back in the evening from Coombe Tracey he was in time to get his hound, to treat it with his infernal paint, and to bring the beast round to the gate at which he had reason to expect that he would find the old gentleman waiting. The dog, incited by its master, sprang over the wicket-gate and pursued the unfortu-

---

1 In South West London, between West Brompton and Chelsea.

nate baronet, who fled screaming down the Yew Alley. In that gloomy tunnel it must indeed have been a dreadful sight to see that huge black creature, with its flaming jaws and blazing eyes, bounding after its victim. He fell dead at the end of the alley from heart disease and terror. The hound had kept upon the grassy border while the baronet had run down the path, so that no track but the man's was visible. On seeing him lying still the creature had probably approached to sniff at him, but finding him dead had turned away again. It was then that it left the print which was actually observed by Dr. Mortimer. The hound was called off and hurried away to its lair in the Grimpen Mire, and a mystery was left which puzzled the authorities, alarmed the countryside, and finally brought the case within the scope of our observation.

"So much for the death of Sir Charles Baskerville. You perceive the devilish cunning of it, for really it would be almost impossible to make a case against the real murderer. His only accomplice was one who could never give him away, and the grotesque, inconceivable nature of the device only served to make it more effective. Both of the women concerned in the case, Mrs. Stapleton and Mrs. Laura Lyons, were left with a strong suspicion against Stapleton. Mrs. Stapleton knew that he had designs upon the old man, and also of the existence of the hound. Mrs. Lyons knew neither of these things, but had been impressed by the death occurring at the time of an uncancelled appointment which was only known to him. However, both of them were under his influence, and he had nothing to fear from them. The first half of his task was successfully accomplished but the more difficult still remained.

"It is possible that Stapleton did not know of the existence of an heir in Canada. In any case he would very soon learn it from his friend Dr. Mortimer, and he was told by the latter all details about the arrival of Henry Baskerville. Stapleton's first idea was that this young stranger from Canada might possibly be done to death in London without coming down to Devonshire at all. He distrusted his wife ever since she had refused to help him in laying a trap for the old man, and he dared not leave her long out of his sight for fear he should lose his influence over her. It was for this reason that he took her to London with him. They lodged, I find, at the Mexborough Private Hotel, in Craven Street,[1] which

---

1 Connecting The Strand with Northumberland Avenue (Sir Henry, readers will recall, was staying at the Northumberland Hotel, perhaps located either on the Avenue or Northumberland Street). See p. 79, note 2.

was actually one of those called upon by my agent in search of evidence. Here he kept his wife imprisoned in her room while he, disguised in a beard,[1] followed Dr. Mortimer to Baker Street and afterwards to the station and to the Northumberland Hotel. His wife had some inkling of his plans; but she had such a fear of her husband—a fear founded upon brutal ill-treatment—that she dare not write to warn the man whom she knew to be in danger. If the letter should fall into Stapleton's hands her own life would not be safe. Eventually, as we know, she adopted the expedient of cutting out the words which would form the message, and addressing the letter in a disguised hand. It reached the baronet, and gave him the first warning of his danger.

"It was very essential for Stapleton to get some article of Sir Henry's attire so that, in case he was driven to use the dog, he might always have the means of setting him upon his track. With characteristic promptness and audacity he set about this at once, and we cannot doubt that the boots[2] or chamber-maid of the hotel was well bribed to help him in his design. By chance, however, the first boot which was procured for him was a new one and, therefore, useless for his purpose. He then had it returned and obtained another—a most instructive incident, since it proved conclusively to my mind that we were dealing with a real hound, as no other supposition could explain this anxiety to obtain an old boot and this indifference to a new one. The more *outré* and grotesque an incident is the more carefully it deserves to be examined, and the very point which appears to complicate a case is, when duly considered and scientifically handled, the one which is most likely to elucidate it.[3]

"Then we had the visit from our friends next morning, shadowed always by Stapleton in the cab.[4] From his knowledge of our rooms and of my appearance, as well as from his general conduct, I am inclined to think that Stapleton's career of crime has been by no means limited to this single Baskerville affair. It is suggestive that during the last three years there have been four consid-

---

1   Modern English would have "with a beard."
2   The servant who cleaned and repaired the boots of guests.
3   M. Dupin, Edgar Allan Poe's detective, might have said the same. See Appendix F, pp. 271–76.
4   It is not exactly clear why Stapleton shadows Sir Henry as he does. For a summary of the bizarre theory that Dr Mortimer is in league with Stapleton, see Baring-Gould, II.105, 109.

erable burglaries in the west country, for none of which was any criminal ever arrested. The last of these, at Folkestone Court, in May, was remarkable for the cold-blooded pistolling[1] of the page, who surprised the masked and solitary burglar. I cannot doubt[2] that Stapleton recruited his waning resources in this fashion, and that for years he has been a desperate and dangerous man.

"We had an example of his readiness of resource that morning when he got away from us so successfully, and also of his audacity in sending back my own name to me through the cabman. From that moment he understood that I had taken over the case in London, and that therefore there was no chance for him there. He returned to Dartmoor and awaited the arrival of the baronet."

"One moment!" said I. "You have, no doubt, described the sequence of events correctly, but there is one point which you have left unexplained. What became of the hound when its master was in London?"

"I have given some attention to this matter and it is undoubtedly of importance. There can be no question that Stapleton had a confidant, though it is unlikely that he ever placed himself in his power by sharing all his plans with him. There was an old manservant at Merripit House, whose name was Anthony. His connection with the Stapletons can be traced for several years, as far back as the schoolmastering days, so that he must have been aware that his master and mistress were really husband and wife. This man has disappeared and has escaped from the country. It is suggestive that Anthony is not a common name in England, while Antonio is so in all Spanish or Spanish-American countries. The man, like Mrs. Stapleton herself, spoke good English, but with a curious lisping accent. I have myself seen this old man cross the Grimpen Mire by the path which Stapleton had marked out. It is very probable, therefore, that in the absence of his master it was he who cared for the hound, though he may never have known the purpose for which the beast was used.

"The Stapletons then went down to Devonshire, whither they were soon followed by Sir Henry and you. One word now as to how I stood myself at that time. It may possibly recur to your memory that when I examined the paper upon which the printed words were fastened I made a close inspection for the watermark.

---

1 Striking with a pistol (rather than being shot with it).
2 But without a shred of evidence. Conan Doyle intensifies, nonetheless, the sense of Stapleton as a wicked man.

In doing so I held it within a few inches of my eyes, and was conscious of a faint smell of the scent known as white jessamine.[1] There are seventy-five perfumes, which it is very necessary that a criminal expert should be able to distinguish from each other, and cases have more than once within my own experience depended upon their prompt recognition. The scent suggested the presence of a lady, and already my thoughts began to turn towards the Stapletons. Thus I had made certain of the hound, and had guessed[2] at the criminal before ever we went to the West country.[3]

"It was my game to watch Stapleton. It was evident, however, that I could not do this if I were with you, since he would be keenly on his guard. I deceived everybody, therefore, yourself included, and I came down secretly when I was supposed to be in London. My hardships were not so great as you imagined, though such trifling details must never interfere with the investigation of a case. I stayed for the most part at Coombe Tracey, and only used the hut upon the moor when it was necessary to be near the scene of action. Cartwright had come down with me, and in his disguise as a country boy he was of great assistance to me. I was dependent upon him for food and clean linen. When I was watching Stapleton, Cartwright was frequently watching you, so that I was able to keep my hand upon all the strings.[4]

"I have already told you that your reports reached me rapidly, being forwarded instantly from Baker Street to Coombe Tracey. They were of great service to me, and especially that one incidentally truthful piece of biography of Stapleton's. I was able to establish the identity of the man and the woman and knew at last exactly how I stood. The case had been considerably complicated through the incident of the escaped convict and the relations between him and the Barrymores. This also you cleared up in a very effective way, though I had already come to the same conclusions from my own observations.

"By the time that you discovered me upon the moor I had a complete knowledge of the whole business, but I had not a case which could go to a jury. Even Stapleton's attempt upon Sir

---

1   The more literary name for white jasmine, *Jasminum officinale*.
2   Holmes is not usually given to guessing.
3   One of the reasons, as many have observed, why Holmes must be kept out of the narrative for a substantial section.
4   Cf. p. 93.

Henry that night which ended in the death of the unfortunate convict did not help us much in proving murder against our man. There seemed to be no alternative but to catch him red-handed, and to do so we had to use Sir Henry, alone and apparently unprotected, as a bait. We did so, and at the cost of a severe shock to our client we succeeded in completing our case and driving Stapleton to his destruction. That Sir Henry should have been exposed to this is, I must confess, a reproach to my management of the case, but we had no means of foreseeing the terrible and paralyzing spectacle which the beast presented, nor could we predict the fog which enabled him to burst upon us at such short notice. We succeeded in our object at a cost which both the specialist and Dr. Mortimer assure me will be a temporary one. A long journey may enable our friend to recover not only from his shattered nerves but also from his wounded feelings. His love for the lady was deep and sincere, and to him the saddest part of all this black business was that he should have been deceived by her.[1]

"It only remains to indicate the part which she had played throughout. There can be no doubt that Stapleton exercised an influence over her which may have been love or may have been fear, or very possibly both, since they are by no means incompatible emotions. It was, at least, absolutely effective. At his command she consented to pass as his sister, though he found the limits of his power over her when he endeavoured to make her the direct accessory to murder. She was ready to warn Sir Henry so far as she could without implicating her husband, and again and again she tried to do so. Stapleton himself seems to have been capable of jealousy, and when he saw the baronet paying court to the lady, even though it was part of his own plan, still he could not help interrupting with a passionate outburst which revealed the fiery soul which his self-contained manner so cleverly concealed. By encouraging the intimacy he made it certain that Sir Henry would frequently come to Merripit House and that he would sooner or later get the opportunity which he desired. On the day of the crisis, however, his wife turned suddenly against him. She had learned something of the death of the convict, and she knew that the hound was being kept in the outhouse on the

---

1   Sir Henry could technically still marry Beryl, on the death of her husband, but her name is—within the terms of Sir Henry's upper-class society—irreparably tarnished.

evening that Sir Henry was coming to dinner. She taxed her husband with his intended crime, and a furious scene followed in which he showed her for the first time that she had a rival in his love. Her fidelity turned in an instant to bitter hatred, and he saw that she would betray him. He tied her up, therefore, that she might have no chance of warning Sir Henry, and he hoped, no doubt, that when the whole countryside put down the baronet's death to the curse of his family, as they certainly would do, he could win his wife back to accept an accomplished fact and to keep silent upon what she knew. In this I fancy that in any case he made a miscalculation, and that, if we had not been there, his doom would none the less have been sealed. A woman of Spanish blood does not condone such an injury so lightly.[1] And now, my dear Watson, without referring to my notes, I cannot give you a more detailed account of this curious case. I do not know that anything essential has been left unexplained."

"He could not hope to frighten Sir Henry to death as he had done the old uncle with his bogie[2] hound."

"The beast was savage and half-starved. If its appearance did not frighten its victim to death, at least it would paralyze the resistance which might be offered."

"No doubt. There only remains one difficulty. If Stapleton came into the succession, how could he explain the fact that he, the heir, had been living unannounced under another name so close to the property? How could he claim it without causing suspicion and inquiry?"

"It is a formidable difficulty, and I fear that you ask too much when you expect me to solve it.[3] The past and the present are within the field of my inquiry, but what a man may do in the future is a hard question to answer. Mrs. Stapleton has heard her husband discuss the problem on several occasions. There were three possible courses. He might claim the property from South America, establish his identity before the British authorities there and so obtain the fortune without ever coming to England at all, or he might adopt an elaborate disguise during the short time that he need be in London; or, again, he might furnish an accomplice with the proofs and papers, putting him in as heir, and retaining

---

1   A commonplace of late Victorian/early twentieth-century racial assumptions.

2   Not usually an adjective: implying dreaded, devilish, terrifying.

3   Indeed—and none of Holmes's three explanations is convincing.

a claim upon some proportion of his income. We cannot doubt from what we know of him that he would have found some way out of the difficulty. And now, my dear Watson, we have had some weeks of severe work, and for one evening, I think, we may turn our thoughts into more pleasant channels. I have a box for *Les Huguenots*.[1] Have you heard the De Reszkes?[2] Might I trouble you then to be ready in half an hour, and we can stop at Marcini's[3] for a little dinner on the way?"

THE END

---

1 This is meant, in the first place, to be an indication of Holmes's slightly out-of-the-way preferences: *Les Huguenots* is a 5-act opera by Giacomo Meyerbeer (1791–1864), first performed, in Paris, in February 1836. It never obtained the popularity of, for instance, the operas of Guiseppe Verdi (1813–1901) in the nineteenth century. Conan Doyle thought highly of the Huguenots throughout his life and in *The Great Boer War* (published the year before *The Hound*) he observed that their bloodline, mixed with the characteristic strength of the Dutch, produced in South Africa "one of the most rugged, virile, unconquerable races ever seen upon earth" (1). Perhaps the association in Conan Doyle's mind between Huguenot blood and unconquerable men seemed not wholly inappropriate for Sherlock Holmes's evening at the close of this adventure.

2 The Polish singers Jean De Reszke (1850–1935) and Edouard de Reszke (1853–1917). The former was one of the most distinguished tenors of the nineteenth century; between 1888 and 1900 he sang at Covent Garden, London, and from 1891 to 1901 at the Metropolitan Opera Company, New York. Edouard, a bass, débuted in Paris in 1876, and sang in London between 1880 and 1884. He was subsequently also with the Metropolitan Opera Company. See p. 239 also.

3 Fictional presumably Italian restaurant in London (pronounced, if in authentic Italian, as "Marchini's").

"Adventures of Sherlock Holmes
VIII. The Adventure of the Speckled Band"

In glancing over my notes of the seventy odd cases in which I have during the last eight years studied the methods of my friend Sherlock Holmes, I find many tragic, some comic, a large number merely strange, but none commonplace; for, working as he did rather for the love of his art than for the acquirement of wealth,[1] he refused to associate himself with any investigation which did not tend towards the unusual, and even the fantastic. Of all these varied cases, however, I cannot recall any which presented more singular features[2] than that which was associated with the well-known Surrey[3] family of the Roylotts of Stoke Moran.[4] The events in question occurred in the early days of my association with Holmes, when we were sharing rooms as bachelors in Baker-street.[5] It is possible that I might have placed them upon record before, but a promise of secrecy was made at the time, from which I have only been freed during the last month by the untimely death of the lady to whom the pledge was given. It is perhaps as well that the facts should now come to light, for I have reasons to know that there are widespread rumours as to the death of Dr. Grimesby Roylott which tend to make the matter even more terrible than the truth.

It was early in April in the year '83 that I woke one morning to find Sherlock Holmes standing, fully dressed, by the side of my bed. He was a late riser[6] as a rule, and, as the clock on the mantelpiece showed me that it was only a quarter past seven, I blinked up at him in some surprise, and perhaps just a little resentment, for I was myself regular in my habits.

---

1 One of the occasions when Conan Doyle makes Watson (or Holmes) playfully allude to the *l'art pour l'art* ("art for art's sake") doctrine of English Aestheticism, at its high point in the 1870s and 1880s. Cf. "The Adventure of the Red Circle" (1911), *CSH* 907.

2 "Singular features" is not quite the term—the narrative is full of improbabilities or impossibilities.

3 One of the prosperous "home counties," south of London.

4 There is no such place. But the name might have been suggested by Stoke d'Abernon, a village in Surrey.

5 The hyphenated form of street names was common in the nineteenth century and lingered into the twentieth.

6 Cf. p. 49, note 1 to *The Hound of the Baskervilles*.

"Very sorry to knock you up,[1] Watson," said he, "but it's the common lot this morning. Mrs. Hudson has been knocked up, she retorted upon me, and I on you."

"What is it, then—a fire?"

"No; a client. It seems that a young lady has arrived in a considerable state of excitement,[2] who insists upon seeing me. She is waiting now in the sitting-room. Now, when young ladies wander about the metropolis at this hour of the morning, and knock sleepy people up out of their beds, I presume that it is something very pressing which they have to communicate. Should it prove to be an interesting case, you would, I am sure, wish to follow it from the outset. I thought, at any rate, that I should call you and give you the chance."

"My dear fellow, I would not miss it for anything."

I had no keener pleasure than in following Holmes in his professional investigations, and in admiring the rapid deductions, as swift as intuitions, and yet always founded on a logical basis with which he unravelled the problems which were submitted to him. I rapidly threw on my clothes and was ready in a few minutes to accompany my friend down to the sitting-room. A lady dressed in black and heavily veiled, who had been sitting in the window, rose as we entered.

"Good morning, madam," said Holmes, cheerily. "My name is Sherlock Holmes. This is my intimate friend[3] and associate, Dr. Watson, before whom you can speak as freely as before myself. Ha, I am glad to see that Mrs. Hudson has had the good sense to light the fire. Pray draw up to it, and I shall order you a cup of hot coffee, for I observe that you are shivering."

"It is not cold which makes me shiver," said the woman in a low voice, changing her seat as requested.

"What then?"

"It is fear, Mr. Holmes. It is terror." She raised her veil as she spoke, and we could see that she was indeed in a pitiable state of agitation, her face all drawn and gray, with restless frightened eyes, like those of some hunted animal. Her features and figure were those of a woman of thirty, but her hair was shot with premature gray, and her expression was weary and haggard. Sherlock

---

1 I.e., "wake you up."

2 With a touch of the nineteenth-century pathological sense of "excitement": "over-strained."

3 Victorian phrase for "good friend."

Holmes ran her over with one of his quick, all-comprehensive glances.

"You must not fear," said he, soothingly, bending forward and patting her forearm. "We shall soon set matters right, I have no doubt. You have come in by train this morning, I see."

"You know me, then?"

"No, but I observe the second half of a return ticket in the palm of your left glove. You must have started early, and yet you had a good drive in a dog-cart,[1] along heavy roads, before you reached the station."

The lady gave a violent start and stared in bewilderment at my companion.

"There is no mystery, my dear madam," said he, smiling. "The left arm of your jacket is spattered with mud in no less than seven places. The marks are perfectly fresh. There is no vehicle save a dog-cart which throws up mud in that way, and then only when you sit on the left hand side of the driver."

"Whatever your reasons[2] may be, you are perfectly correct," said she. "I started from home before six, reached Leatherhead[3] at twenty past, and came in by the first train to Waterloo.[4] Sir, I can stand this strain no longer; I shall go mad if it continues. I have no one to turn to—none, save only one, who cares for me, and he, poor fellow, can be of little aid. I have heard of you, Mr. Holmes; I have heard of you from Mrs. Farintosh, whom you helped in the hour of her sore need. It was from her that I had your address.[5] Oh, sir, do you not think that you could help me, too, and at least throw a little light through the dense darkness which surrounds me? At present it is out of my power to reward you for your services, but in a month or six weeks I shall be married, with the control of my own income, and then at least you shall not find me ungrateful."

Holmes turned to his desk and, unlocking it, drew out a small case-book, which he consulted.

---

1 See p. 151, note 1.
2 She means "reasoning."
3 Leatherhead, historic market town in Surrey.
4 The first mainline station in London, opened on 11 July 1848, by the London and South Western Railway.
5 There is no character of this name in any of the Sherlock Holmes stories. It meant something to Conan Doyle, however, for it is used in *The Mystery of Cloomber* (1889).

"Farintosh," said he. "Ah yes, I recall the case; it was concerned with an opal tiara.[1] I think it was before your time, Watson.[2] I can only say, madam, that I shall be happy to devote the same care to your case as I did to that of your friend. As to reward, my profession is its own reward; but you are at liberty to defray whatever expenses I may be put to, at the time which suits you best.[3] And now I beg that you will lay before us everything that may help us in forming an opinion upon the matter."

"Alas!" replied our visitor, "the very horror of my situation lies in the fact that my fears are so vague, and my suspicions depend so entirely upon small points, which might seem trivial to another, that even he to whom of all others I have a right to look for help and advice looks upon all that I tell him about it as the fancies of a nervous woman. He does not say so, but I can read it from his soothing answers and averted eyes. But I have heard, Mr. Holmes, that you can see deeply into the manifold wickedness of the human heart. You may advise me how to walk amid the dangers which encompass me."

"I am all attention, madam."

"My name is Helen Stoner, and I am living with my stepfather, who is the last survivor of one of the oldest Saxon families in England, the Roylotts of Stoke Moran, on the western border of Surrey."

Holmes nodded his head. "The name is familiar to me," said he.

"The family was at one time among the richest in England, and the estates extended over the borders into Berkshire in the north, and Hampshire in the west. In the last century, however, four successive heirs were of a dissolute and wasteful disposition, and the family ruin was eventually completed by a gambler in the days of the Regency.[4] Nothing was left save a few acres of ground, and the two-hundred-year-old house, which is itself crushed under a heavy mortgage. The last squire dragged out his existence there, living the horrible life of an aristocratic pauper; but his only

---

1   A jewelled headband or coronet. A band of a rather different kind is the focus of this story.
2   Conan Doyle provides the explanation for why there is no chronicle of the case.
3   Holmes does not often make statements about his charges (they are fixed), though sometimes waives them altogether.
4   See p. 110, note 2.

son, my stepfather, seeing that he must adapt himself to the new conditions, obtained an advance from a relative, which enabled him to take a medical degree and went out to Calcutta, where, by his professional skill and his force of character, he established a large practice. In a fit of anger, however, caused by some robberies which had been perpetrated in the house, he beat his native butler to death and narrowly escaped a capital sentence. As it was, he suffered a long term of imprisonment and afterwards returned to England a morose and disappointed man.

"When Dr. Roylott was in India he married my mother, Mrs. Stoner, the young widow of Major-General Stoner, of the Bengal Artillery. My sister Julia and I were twins, and we were only two years old at the time of my mother's re-marriage. She had a considerable sum of money—not less than a thousand pounds a year—and this she bequeathed to Dr. Roylott entirely while we resided with him, with a provision that a certain annual sum should be allowed to each of us in the event of our marriage. Shortly after our return to England my mother died—she was killed eight years ago in a railway accident near Crewe.[1] Dr. Roylott then abandoned his attempts to establish himself in practice in London and took us to live with him in the old ancestral house at Stoke Moran. The money which my mother had left was enough for all our wants, and there seemed to be no obstacle to our happiness.

"But a terrible change came over our step-father about this time. Instead of making friends and exchanging visits with our neighbours, who had at first been overjoyed to see a Roylott of Stoke Moran back in the old family seat, he shut himself up in his house and seldom came out save to indulge in ferocious quarrels with whoever might cross his path. Violence of temper approaching to mania has been hereditary in the men of the family, and in my stepfather's case it had, I believe, been intensified by his long residence in the tropics. A series of disgraceful brawls took place, two of which ended in the police-court, until at last he became the terror of the village, and the folks would fly at his approach, for he is a man of immense strength, and absolutely uncontrollable in his anger.

"Last week he hurled the local blacksmith over a parapet into a stream, and it was only by paying over all the money which I

1 Crewe is a town with a major railway station in Cheshire in the north of England.

could gather together that I was able to avert another public exposure. He had no friends at all save the wandering gipsies, and he would give these vagabonds leave to encamp upon the few acres of bramble-covered land which represent the family estate, and would accept in return the hospitality of their tents, wandering away with them sometimes for weeks on end. He has a passion also for Indian animals, which are sent over to him by a correspondent, and he has at this moment a cheetah and a baboon,[1] which wander freely over his grounds and are feared by the villagers almost as much as their master.

"You can imagine from what I say that my poor sister Julia and I had no great pleasure in our lives. No servant would stay with us, and for a long time we did all the work of the house. She was but thirty at the time of her death, and yet her hair had already begun to whiten, even as mine has."

"Your sister is dead, then?"

"She died just two years ago, and it is of her death that I wish to speak to you. You can understand that, living the life which I have described, we were little likely to see anyone of our own age and position. We had, however, an aunt, my mother's maiden sister, Miss Honoria Westphail, who lives near Harrow,[2] and we were occasionally allowed to pay short visits at this lady's house. Julia went there at Christmas two years ago, and met there a half-pay Major of Marines, to whom she became engaged. My stepfather learned of the engagement when my sister returned and offered no objection to the marriage; but within a fortnight of the day which had been fixed for the wedding, the terrible event occurred which has deprived me of my only companion."

Sherlock Holmes had been leaning back in his chair with his eyes closed and his head sunk in a cushion, but he half opened his lids now and glanced across at his visitor.

---

1 Baboons are chiefly from Africa and Southern Asia, and adjacent islands; cheetahs from Africa. In the nineteenth century, however, they were kept in India, as Charles Darwin observed, "in large numbers for hunting" (*The Variation of Animals and Plants Under Domestication*, 2 vols [London: Murray, 1905], ii.166). In fact, cheetahs—*Acinonyx jubatus*—are not dangerous to human beings, being rather frail and lightweight, so would not make good guards. They are also diurnal so would be asleep during the night.

2 A prosperous area—with a famous public school—in the nineteenth century, now part of North West London.

"Pray be precise as to details," said he.

"It is easy for me to be so, for every event of that dreadful time is seared into my memory. The manor house is, as I have already said, very old, and only one wing is now inhabited. The bedrooms in this wing are on the ground floor, the sitting-rooms being in the central block of the buildings. Of these bedrooms the first is Dr. Roylott's, the second my sister's, and the third my own. There is no communication between them, but they all open out into the same corridor. Do I make myself plain?"

"Perfectly so."

"The windows of the three rooms open out upon the lawn. That fatal night Dr. Roylott had gone to his room early, though we knew that he had not retired to rest, for my sister was troubled by the smell of the strong Indian cigars which it was his custom to smoke. She left her room, therefore, and came into mine, where she sat for some time, chatting about her approaching wedding. At eleven o'clock she rose to leave me, but she paused at the door and looked back.

"'Tell me, Helen,' said she, 'have you ever heard anyone whistle in the dead of the night?'

"'Never,' said I.

"'I suppose that you could not possibly whistle, yourself, in your sleep?'

"'Certainly not. But why?'

"'Because during the last few nights I have always, about three in the morning, heard a low, clear whistle. I am a light sleeper, and it has awakened me. I cannot tell where it came from, perhaps from the next room, perhaps from the lawn. I thought that I would just ask you whether you had heard it.'

"'No, I have not. It must be those wretched gipsies in the plantation.'

"'Very likely. And yet if it were on the lawn, I wonder that you did not hear it also.'

"'Ah, but I sleep more heavily than you.'

"'Well, it is of no great consequence at any rate.' She smiled back at me, closed my door, and a few moments later I heard her key turn in the lock."

"Indeed," said Holmes. "Was it your custom always to lock yourselves in at night?"

"Always."

"And why?"

"I think that I mentioned to you that the doctor kept a cheetah and a baboon. We had no feeling of security unless our doors were locked."

"Quite so. Pray proceed with your statement."

"I could not sleep that night. A vague feeling of impending misfortune impressed me. My sister and I, you will recollect, were twins, and you know how subtle are the links which bind two souls which are so closely allied.[1] It was a wild night. The wind was howling outside, and the rain was beating and splashing against the windows. Suddenly, amid all the hubbub of the gale, there burst forth the wild scream of a terrified woman. I knew that it was my sister's voice. I sprang from my bed, wrapped a shawl round me, and rushed into the corridor. As I opened my door I seemed to hear a low whistle, such as my sister described, and a few moments later a clanging sound, as if a mass of metal had fallen. As I ran down the passage, my sister's door was unlocked, and revolved slowly upon its hinges. I stared at it horror-stricken, not knowing what was about to issue from it. By the light of the corridor-lamp I saw my sister appear at the opening, her face blanched with terror, her hands groping for help, her whole figure swaying to and fro like that of a drunkard. I ran to her and threw my arms round her, but at that moment her knees seemed to give way and she fell to the ground. She writhed as one who is in terrible pain, and her limbs were dreadfully convulsed. At first I thought that she had not recognized me, but as I bent over her she suddenly shrieked out in a voice which I shall never forget, 'Oh, my God! Helen! It was the band! The speckled band!' There was something else which she would fain have said, and she stabbed with her finger into the air in the direction of the doctor's room, but a fresh convulsion seized her and choked her words. I rushed out, calling loudly for my stepfather, and I met him hastening from his room in his dressing-gown. When he reached my sister's side she was unconscious, and though he poured brandy down her throat[2] and sent for medical aid from the village, all efforts were in vain, for she slowly sank and died without having recovered her consciousness. Such was the dreadful end of my beloved sister."

"One moment," said Holmes, "are you sure about this whistle and metallic sound? Could you swear to it?"

---

1 A commonplace form of folk wisdom.
2 A regular Victorian and early twentieth-century response to faints, collapses, and prostration by accidents. See also p. 196.

"That was what the county coroner asked me at the inquiry.[1] It is my strong impression that I heard it, and yet, among the crash of the gale and the creaking of an old house, I may possibly have been deceived."

"Was your sister dressed?"

"No, she was in her night-dress. In her right hand was found the charred stump of a match, and in her left a match box."

"Showing that she had struck a light and looked about her when the alarm took place. That is important. And what conclusions did the coroner come to?"

"He investigated the case with great care, for Dr. Roylott's conduct had long been notorious in the county, but he was unable to find any satisfactory cause of death. My evidence showed that the door had been fastened upon the inner side, and the windows were blocked by old-fashioned shutters with broad iron bars, which were secured every night. The walls were carefully sounded, and were shown to be quite solid all round, and the flooring was also thoroughly examined, with the same result. The chimney is wide, but is barred up by four large staples. It is certain, therefore, that my sister was quite alone when she met her end. Besides, there were no marks of any violence upon her."

"How about poison?"

"The doctors examined her for it, but without success."

"What do you think that this unfortunate lady died of, then?"

"It is my belief that she died of pure fear and nervous shock, though what it was that frightened her I cannot imagine."[2]

"Were there gipsies in the plantation at the time?"

"Yes, there are nearly always some there."

"Ah, and what did you gather from this allusion to a band—a speckled band?"

"Sometimes I have thought that it was merely the wild talk of delirium, sometimes that it may have referred to some band of people, perhaps to these very gipsies in the plantation. I do not know whether the spotted handkerchiefs which so many of them

---

1 In English law, a coroner's court, consisting of a magistrate (called the coroner) and twelve jurymen, undertake an inquest or investigation as to the cause of a death where it is required. The peculiar circumstances of Julia's death – it is *prima facie* unclear whether she has died of natural causes or by human intention – would require such an inquiry.

2 Compare the death of Sir Charles (p. 77).

wear over their heads might have suggested the strange adjective which she used."

Holmes shook his head like a man who is far from being satisfied.

"These are very deep waters," said he; "pray go on with your narrative."

"Two years have passed since then, and my life has been until lately lonelier than ever. A month ago, however, a dear friend, whom I have known for many years, has done me the honour to ask my hand in marriage. His name is Armitage—Percy Armitage—the second son of Mr. Armitage, of Crane Water,[1] near Reading.[2] My stepfather has offered no opposition to the match, and we are to be married in the course of the spring. Two days ago some repairs were started in the west wing of the building, and my bedroom wall has been pierced, so that I have had to move into the chamber in which my sister died, and to sleep in the very bed in which she slept. Imagine, then, my thrill of terror when last night, as I lay awake, thinking over her terrible fate, I suddenly heard in the silence of the night the low whistle which had been the herald of her own death. I sprang up and lit the lamp, but nothing was to be seen in the room. I was too shaken to go to bed again, however, so I dressed, and as soon as it was daylight I slipped down, got a dog-cart at the 'Crown' Inn, which is opposite, and drove to Leatherhead, from whence I have come on this morning with the one object of seeing you and asking your advice."

"You have done wisely," said my friend. "But have you told me all?"

"Yes, all."

"Miss Roylott, you have not. You are screening your stepfather."

"Why, what do you mean?"

For answer Holmes pushed back the frill of black lace which fringed the hand that lay upon our visitor's knee. Five little livid spots, the marks of four fingers and a thumb, were printed upon the white wrist.

"You have been cruelly used," said Holmes.

---

1 A name half-suggested by the artist and illustrator, Walter Crane (1845–1915)?

2 A large town in Berkshire (non-UK readers will want to know that this name is pronounced "redding").

The lady coloured deeply and covered over her injured wrist. "He is a hard man," she said, "and perhaps he hardly knows his own strength."

There was a long silence, during which Holmes leaned his chin upon his hands and stared into the crackling fire.

"This is a very deep business," he said at last. "There are a thousand details which I should desire to know before I decide upon our course of action. Yet we have not a moment to lose. If we were to come to Stoke Moran to-day, would it be possible for us to see over these rooms without the knowledge of your stepfather?"

"As it happens, he spoke of coming into town to-day upon some most important business. It is probable that he will be away all day, and that there would be nothing to disturb you. We have a house-keeper now, but she is old and foolish, and I could easily get her out of the way."

"Excellent. You are not averse to this trip, Watson?"

"By no means."

"Then we shall both come. What are you going to do yourself?"

"I have one or two things which I would wish to do now that I am in town. But I shall return by the twelve o'clock train, so as to be there in time for your coming."

"And you may expect us early in the afternoon. I have myself some small business matters to attend to. Will you not wait and breakfast?"

"No, I must go. My heart is lightened already since I have confided my trouble to you. I shall look forward to seeing you again this afternoon." She dropped her thick black veil over her face and glided from the room.

"And what do you think of it all, Watson?" asked Sherlock Holmes, leaning back in his chair.

"It seems to me to be a most dark and sinister business."

"Dark enough and sinister enough."

"Yet if the lady is correct in saying that the flooring and walls are sound, and that the door, window, and chimney are impassable, then her sister must have been undoubtedly alone when she met her mysterious end."

"What becomes, then, of these nocturnal whistles, and what of the very peculiar words of the dying woman?"

"I cannot think."

"When you combine the ideas of whistles at night, the presence of a band of gipsies who are on intimate terms with this old doctor, the fact that we have every reason to believe that the doctor has an interest in preventing his stepdaughter's marriage, the dying allusion to a band, and, finally, the fact that Miss Helen Stoner heard a metallic clang, which might have been caused by one of those metal bars that secured the shutters falling back into its place, I think that there is good ground to think that the mystery may be cleared along those lines."

"But what, then, did the gipsies do?"

"I cannot imagine."

"I see many objections to any such theory."

"And so do I. It is precisely for that reason that we are going to Stoke Moran this day. I want to see whether the objections are fatal, or if they may be explained away. But what in the name of the devil!"

The ejaculation had been drawn from my companion by the fact that our door had been suddenly dashed open, and that a huge man had framed himself in the aperture. His costume was a peculiar mixture of the professional and of the agricultural, having a black top-hat, a long frock-coat, and a pair of high gaiters,[1] with a hunting-crop[2] swinging in his hand. So tall was he that his hat actually brushed the cross bar of the doorway, and his breadth seemed to span it across from side to side. A large face, seared with a thousand wrinkles, burned yellow with the sun, and marked with every evil passion, was turned from one to the other of us, while his deep-set, bile-shot eyes, and his high, thin, fleshless nose, gave him somewhat the resemblance to a fierce old bird of prey.[3]

"Which of you is Holmes?" asked this apparition.

"My name, sir; but you have the advantage of me," said my companion quietly.

"I am Dr. Grimesby Roylott, of Stoke Moran."

"Indeed, Doctor," said Holmes blandly. "Pray take a seat."

"I will do nothing of the kind. My stepdaughter has been here—I have traced her. What has she been saying to you?"

"It is a little cold for the time of the year," said Holmes.

---

1 Cloth or leather covering of the ankle or lower leg.

2 See p. 141, note 1.

3 Character is marked on the face—a conventional nineteenth-century assumption.

"What has she been saying to you?" screamed the old man furiously.

"But I have heard that the crocuses promise well," continued my companion imperturbably.

"Ha! You put me off, do you?" said our new visitor, taking a step forward and shaking his hunting-crop. "I know you, you scoundrel! I have heard of you before. You are Holmes, the meddler."

My friend smiled.

"Holmes, the busybody!"

His smile broadened.

"Holmes, the Scotland Yard Jack-in-office!"[1]

Holmes chuckled heartily. "Your conversation is most entertaining," said he. "When you go out close the door, for there is a decided draught."

"I will go when I have said my say. Don't you dare to meddle with my affairs. I know that Miss Stoner has been here. I traced her! I am a dangerous man to fall foul of! See here." He stepped swiftly forward, seized the poker, and bent it into a curve with his huge brown hands.

"See that you keep yourself out of my grip," he snarled, and hurling the twisted poker into the fireplace he strode out of the room.

"He seems a very amiable person," said Holmes, laughing. "I am not quite so bulky, but if he had remained I might have shown him that my grip was not much more feeble than his own." As he spoke he picked up the steel poker and, with a sudden effort, straightened it out again.

"Fancy his having the insolence to confound me with the official detective force! This incident gives zest to our investigation, however, and I only trust that our little friend will not suffer from her imprudence in allowing this brute to trace her. And now, Watson, we shall order breakfast, and afterwards I shall walk down to

---

1   Scotland Yard was the head-quarters of the Metropolitan Police (London) situated from 1829 to 1890 in Great Scotland Yard, near to Northumberland Street (see p. 79, note 2); from 1890–1967 it was at New Scotland Yard on the Thames Embankment. Holmes, as he later remarks, is amused to be associated with the professional force as he is habitually ahead of them in solving crime and often scornful of their efforts.

Doctors' Commons,[1] where I hope to get some data[2] which may help us in this matter."

It was nearly one o'clock when Sherlock Holmes returned from his excursion. He held in his hand a sheet of blue paper, scrawled over with notes and figures.

"I have seen the will of the deceased wife," said he. "To determine its exact meaning I have been obliged to work out the present prices of the investments with which it is concerned. The total income, which at the time of the wife's death was little short of £1,100, is now, through the fall in agricultural prices, not more than £750. Each daughter can claim an income of £250, in case of marriage. It is evident, therefore, that if both girls had married, this beauty would have had a mere pittance, while even one of them would cripple him to a very serious extent. My morning's work has not been wasted, since it has proved that he has the very strongest motives for standing in the way of anything of the sort. And now, Watson, this is too serious for dawdling, especially as the old man is aware that we are interesting ourselves in his affairs; so if you are ready, we shall call a cab and drive to Waterloo. I should be very much obliged if you would slip your revolver into your pocket. An Eley's No. 2[3] is an excellent argument with gentlemen who can twist steel pokers into knots. That and a tooth-brush are, I think, all that we need."

At Waterloo we were fortunate in catching a train for Leatherhead, where we hired a trap[4] at the station inn and drove for four or five miles through the lovely Surrey lanes. It was a perfect day, with a bright sun and a few fleecy clouds in the heavens. The trees and wayside hedges were just throwing out their first green shoots, and the air was full of the pleasant smell of the moist earth. To me at least there was a strange contrast between the sweet promise of the spring and this sinister quest upon which we were engaged. My companion sat in the front of the trap, his

---

1 London legal society formed in 1509 (of Doctors of the Law) and dissolved in 1858; its buildings were taken down in 1867. The second edition of *OED* sensibly notes "Literary references to Doctors' Commons in later times usually refer to the registration or probate of wills, to marriage licences, or to proceedings for divorce."

2 Holmes's use of this word—to mean "facts"—is rather new. *OED*'s first instance is 1899.

3 Eley, the munitions company, was established in 1828.

4 A small, usually two-wheeled carriage.

arms folded, his hat pulled down over his eyes, and his chin sunk upon his breast, buried in the deepest thought. Suddenly, however, he started, tapped me on the shoulder, and pointed over the meadows

"Look there!" said he.

A heavily timbered park stretched up in a gentle slope, thickening into a grove at the highest point. From amid the branches there jutted out the gray gables and high roof-tree of a very old mansion.

"Stoke Moran?" said he.

"Yes, sir, that be the house of Dr. Grimesby Roylott," remarked the driver.[1]

"There is some building going on there," said Holmes; "that is where we are going."

"There's the village," said the driver, pointing to a cluster of roofs some distance to the left; "but if you want to get to the house, you'll find it shorter to get over this stile,[2] and so by the foot-path over the fields. There it is, where the lady is walking."

"And the lady, I fancy, is Miss Stoner," observed Holmes, shading his eyes. "Yes, I think we had better do as you suggest."

We got off, paid our fare, and the trap rattled back on its way to Leatherhead.

"I thought it as well," said Holmes as we climbed the stile, "that this fellow should think we had come here as architects, or on some definite business. It may stop his gossip. Good-afternoon, Miss Stoner. You see that we have been as good as our word."

Our client of the morning had hurried forward to meet us with a face which spoke her joy. "I have been waiting so eagerly for you," she cried, shaking hands with us warmly. "All has turned out splendidly. Dr. Roylott has gone to town, and it is unlikely that he will be back before evening."

"We have had the pleasure of making the Doctor's acquaintance," said Holmes, and in a few words he sketched out what had occurred. Miss Stoner turned white to the lips as she listened.

"Good heavens!" she cried, "he has followed me, then."

"So it appears."

---

1 "That *be*" is a standard, clichéd, representation of rural (particularly southern/south-western) speech.

2 Wooden construction of steps that enables human beings but not animals to cross low field walls.

"He is so cunning that I never know when I am safe from him.[1] What will he say when he returns?"

"He must guard himself, for he may find that there is someone more cunning than himself upon his track. You must lock yourself up from him to-night. If he is violent, we shall take you away to your aunt's at Harrow. Now, we must make the best use of our time, so kindly take us at once to the rooms which we are to examine."

The building was of gray, lichen-blotched stone, with a high central portion and two curving wings, like the claws of a crab, thrown out on each side. In one of these wings the windows were broken and blocked with wooden boards, while the roof was partly caved in, a picture of ruin. The central portion was in little better repair, but the right-hand block was comparatively modern, and the blinds in the windows, with the blue smoke curling up from the chimneys, showed that this was where the family resided. Some scaffolding had been erected against the end wall, and the stone-work had been broken into, but there were no signs of any workmen at the moment of our visit. Holmes walked slowly up and down the ill-trimmed lawn and examined with deep attention the outsides of the windows.

"This, I take it, belongs to the room in which you used to sleep, the centre one to your sister's, and the one next to the main building to Dr. Roylott's chamber?"

"Exactly so. But I am now sleeping in the middle one."

"Pending the alterations, as I understand. By the way, there does not seem to be any very pressing need for repairs at that end wall."

"There were none. I believe that it was an excuse to move me from my room."

"Ah! that is suggestive. Now, on the other side of this narrow wing runs the corridor from which these three rooms open. There are windows in it, of course?"

"Yes, but very small ones. Too narrow for anyone to pass through."

"As you both locked your doors at night, your rooms were unapproachable from that side. Now, would you have the kindness to go into your room and bar your shutters?"

Miss Stoner did so, and Holmes, after a careful examination

---

1 It does not seem that cunning simply to have followed Miss Stoner—but she is becoming over-strained.

through the open window, endeavoured in every way to force the shutter open, but without success. There was no slit through which a knife could be passed to raise the bar. Then with his lens he tested the hinges, but they were of solid iron, built firmly into the massive masonry. "Hum!" said he, scratching his chin in some perplexity, "my theory certainly presents some difficulties. No one could pass these shutters if they were bolted. Well, we shall see if the inside throws any light upon the matter."

A small side door led into the whitewashed corridor from which the three bedrooms opened. Holmes refused to examine the third chamber, so we passed at once to the second, that in which Miss Stoner was now sleeping, and in which her sister had met with her fate. It was a homely little room, with a low ceiling and a gaping fireplace, after the fashion of old country-houses. A brown chest of drawers stood in one corner, a narrow white-counterpaned[1] bed in another, and a dressing-table on the left-hand side of the window. These articles, with two small wicker-work chairs, made up all the furniture in the room save for a square of Wilton carpet[2] in the centre. The boards round and the panelling of the walls were of brown, worm-eaten oak, so old and discoloured that it may have dated from the original building of the house. Holmes drew one of the chairs into a corner and sat silent, while his eyes travelled round and round and up and down, taking in every detail of the apartment.

"Where does that bell communicate with?" he asked at last pointing to a thick belt-rope which hung down beside the bed, the tassel actually lying upon the pillow.

"It goes to the housekeeper's room."

"It looks newer than the other things?"

"Yes, it was only put there a couple of years ago."

"Your sister asked for it, I suppose?"

"No, I never heard of her using it. We used always to get what we wanted for ourselves."

"Indeed, it seemed unnecessary to put so nice a bell-pull there. You will excuse me for a few minutes while I satisfy myself as to this floor." He threw himself down upon his face with his lens in his hand and crawled swiftly backward and forward, examining

---

1 A counterpane is a quilt, the outer covering of a bed, generally more or less ornamental, being woven in a raised pattern, quilted, or made of patch-work (*OED*).

2 Cut-pile carpet first manufactured in Wilton, Wiltshire.

minutely the cracks between the boards. Then he did the same with the wood-work with which the chamber was panelled. Finally he walked over to the bed and spent some time in staring at it and in running his eye up and down the wall. Finally he took the bell-rope in his hand and gave it a brisk tug.

"Why, it's a dummy," said he.

"Won't it ring?"

"No, it is not even attached to a wire. This is very interesting. You can see now that it is fastened to a hook just above where the little opening for the ventilator is."

"How very absurd! I never noticed that before."

"Very strange!" muttered Holmes, pulling at the rope. "There are one or two very singular points about this room. For example, what a fool a builder must be to open a ventilator into another room, when, with the same trouble, he might have communicated with the outside air!"

"That is also quite modern," said the lady.

"Done about the same time as the bell-rope?" remarked Holmes.

"Yes, there were several little changes carried out about that time."

"They seem to have been of a most interesting character—dummy bell-ropes, and ventilators which do not ventilate. With your permission, Miss Stoner, we shall now carry our researches into the inner apartment."

Dr. Grimesby Roylott's chamber was larger than that of his stepdaughter, but was as plainly furnished. A camp-bed, a small wooden shelf full of books, mostly of a technical character, an armchair beside the bed, a plain wooden chair against the wall, a round table, and a large iron safe were the principal things which met the eye. Holmes walked slowly round and examined each and all of them with the keenest interest.

"What's in here?" he asked, tapping the safe.

"My stepfather's business papers."

"Oh! you have seen inside, then?"

"Only once, some years ago. I remember that it was full of papers."

"There isn't a cat in it, for example?"

"No. What a strange idea!"

"Well, look at this!" He took up a small saucer of milk which stood on the top of it.

"No; we don't keep a cat. But there is a cheetah and a baboon."

"Ah, yes, of course! Well, a cheetah is just a big cat, and yet a saucer of milk does not go very far in satisfying its wants, I daresay. There is one point which I should wish to determine." He squatted down in front of the wooden chair and examined the seat of it with the greatest attention.

"Thank you. That is quite settled," said he, rising and putting his lens in his pocket. "Hullo! Here is something interesting!"

The object which had caught his eye was a small dog lash hung on one corner of the bed. The lash, however, was curled upon itself and tied so as to make a loop of whipcord.

"What do you make of that, Watson?"

"It's a common enough lash. But I don't know why it should be tied."

"That is not quite so common, is it? Ah, me! it's a wicked world, and when a clever man turns his brains to crime it is the worst of all. I think that I have seen enough now, Miss Stoner, and with your permission we shall walk out upon the lawn."

I had never seen my friend's face so grim or his brow so dark as it was when we turned from the scene of this investigation. We had walked several times up and down the lawn, neither Miss Stoner nor myself liking to break in upon his thoughts before he roused himself from his reverie.

"It is very essential, Miss Stoner," said he, "that you should absolutely follow my advice in every respect."

"I shall most certainly do so."

"The matter is too serious for any hesitation. Your life may depend upon your compliance."

"I assure you that I am in your hands."

"In the first place, both my friend and I must spend the night in your room."[1]

Both Miss Stoner and I gazed at him in astonishment.

"Yes, it must be so. Let me explain. I believe that that is the village inn over there?"

"Yes, that is the 'Crown.'"[2]

"Very good. Your windows would be visible from there?"

"Certainly."

"You must confine yourself to your room, on pretence of a headache, when your stepfather comes back. Then when you hear

---

1 In the decorum of daily society, an extraordinary proposal that would compromise Miss Stoner gravely.
2 A common name for an English inn or public house.

him retire for the night, you must open the shutters of your window, undo the hasp, put your lamp there as a signal to us, and then withdraw quietly with everything which you are likely to want into the room which you used to occupy. I have no doubt that, in spite of the repairs, you could manage there for one night."

"Oh, yes, easily."

"The rest you will leave in our hands."

"But what will you do?"

"We shall spend the night in your room, and we shall investigate the cause of this noise which has disturbed you."

"I believe, Mr. Holmes, that you have already made up your mind," said Miss Stoner, laying her hand upon my companion's sleeve.

"Perhaps I have."

"Then for pity's sake tell me what was the cause of my sister's death."

"I should prefer to have clearer proofs before I speak."

"You can at least tell me whether my own thought is correct, and if she died from some sudden fright."

"No, I do not think so. I think that there was probably some more tangible cause. And now, Miss Stoner, we must leave you for if Dr. Roylott returned and saw us, our journey would be in vain. Good-bye, and be brave, for if you will do what I have told you, you may rest assured that we shall soon drive away the dangers that threaten you."

Sherlock Holmes and I had no difficulty in engaging a bedroom and sitting-room at the "Crown" Inn. They were on the upper floor, and from our window we could command a view of the avenue gate, and of the inhabited wing of Stoke Moran Manor House. At dusk we saw Dr. Grimesby Roylott drive past, his huge form looming up beside the little figure of the lad who drove him. The boy had some slight difficulty in undoing the heavy iron gates, and we heard the hoarse roar of the doctor's voice and saw the fury with which he shook his clinched fists at him. The trap drove on, and a few minutes later we saw a sudden light spring up among the trees as the lamp was lit in one of the sitting-rooms.

"Do you know, Watson," said Holmes as we sat together in the gathering darkness, "I have really some scruples as to taking you to-night. There is a distinct element of danger."

"Can I be of assistance?"

"Your presence might be invaluable."

"Then I shall certainly come."

"It is very kind of you."

"You speak of danger. You have evidently seen more in these rooms than was visible to me."

"No, but I fancy that I may have deduced a little more. I imagine that you saw all that I did."

"I saw nothing remarkable save the bell-rope, and what purpose that could answer I confess is more than I can imagine."

"You saw the ventilator, too?"

"Yes, but I do not think that it is such a very unusual thing to have a small opening between two rooms. It was so small that a rat could hardly pass through."

"I knew that we should find a ventilator before ever we came to Stoke Moran."

"My dear Holmes!"

"Oh, yes, I did. You remember in her statement she said that her sister could smell Dr. Roylott's cigar. Now, of course that suggested at once that there must be a communication between the two rooms. It could only be a small one, or it would have been remarked upon at the coroner's inquiry. I deduced a ventilator."

"But what harm can there be in that?"

"Well, there is at least a curious coincidence of dates. A ventilator is made, a cord is hung, and a lady who sleeps in the bed dies. Does not that strike you?"

"I cannot as yet see any connection."

"Did you observe anything very peculiar about that bed?"

"No."

"It was clamped to the floor. Did you ever see a bed fastened like that before?"

"I cannot say that I have."

"The lady could not move her bed. It must always be in the same relative position to the ventilator and to the rope—or so we may call it, since it was clearly never meant for a bell-pull."

"Holmes," I cried, "I seem to see dimly what you are hinting at. We are only just in time to prevent some subtle and horrible crime."

"Subtle enough and horrible enough. When a doctor does go wrong, he is the first of criminals. He has nerve and he has knowledge. Palmer and Pritchard[1] were among the heads of their profession. This man strikes even deeper, but I think, Watson, that we shall be able to strike deeper still. But we shall have horrors enough before the night is over; for goodness' sake let us have a quiet pipe and turn our minds for a few hours to something more cheerful."

About nine o'clock the light among the trees was extinguished, and all was dark in the direction of the Manor House. Two hours passed slowly away, and then, suddenly, just at the stroke of eleven, a single bright light shone out right in front of us.

"That is our signal," said Holmes, springing to his feet; "it comes from the middle window."

As we passed out he exchanged a few words with the landlord, explaining that we were going on a late visit to an acquaintance, and that it was possible that we might spend the night there. A moment later we were out on the dark road, a chill wind blowing in our faces, and one yellow light twinkling in front of us through the gloom to guide us on our sombre errand.

There was little difficulty in entering the grounds, for unrepaired breaches gaped in the old park wall. Making our way among the trees, we reached the lawn, crossed it, and were about to enter through the window when out from a clump of laurel bushes there darted what seemed to be a hideous and distorted child, who threw itself upon the grass with writhing limbs and then ran swiftly across the lawn into the darkness.

"My God!" I whispered; "did you see it?"

Holmes was for the moment as startled as I. His hand closed like a vice upon my wrist in his agitation. Then he broke into a low laugh and put his lips to my ear.

"It is a nice household," he murmured. "That is the baboon."

I had forgotten the strange pets which the doctor affected. There was a cheetah, too; perhaps we might find it upon our shoulders at any moment. I confess that I felt easier in my mind when, after following Holmes's example and slipping off my

---

1 Dr William Palmer, the "Rugeley Poisoner," was hanged outside Stafford Jail in June 1856 for murder. He was convicted of a single killing but may have poisoned several others (if not the 16 that was the highest estimate). He had been more a horse-racing enthusiast than a medic. Dr Edward Pritchard was executed in Glasgow in 1865 having been found guilty of the murder of his wife and mother-in-law. Neither of these local doctors could be described at all as at the "heads of their profession."

shoes, I found myself inside the bedroom. My companion noise-lessly closed the shutters, moved the lamp onto the table, and cast his eyes round the room. All was as we had seen it in the daytime. Then creeping up to me and making a trumpet of his hand, he whispered into my ear again so gently that it was all that I could do to distinguish the words:

"The least sound would be fatal to our plans."

I nodded to show that I had heard.

"We must sit without light. He would see it through the venti-lator."

I nodded again.

"Do not go asleep;[1] your very life may depend upon it. Have your pistol ready in case we should need it. I will sit on the side of the bed, and you in that chair."

I took out my revolver and laid it on the corner of the table.

Holmes had brought up a long thin cane, and this he placed upon the bed beside him. By it he laid the box of matches and the stump of a candle. Then he turned down the lamp, and we were left in darkness.

How shall I ever forget that dreadful vigil? I could not hear a sound, not even the drawing of a breath, and yet I knew that my companion sat open-eyed, within a few feet of me, in the same state of nervous tension in which I was myself. The shutters cut off the least ray of light, and we waited in absolute darkness. From outside came the occasional cry of a night-bird, and once at our very window a long drawn catlike whine,[2] which told us that the cheetah was indeed at liberty. Far away we could hear the deep tones of the parish clock, which boomed out every quarter of an hour. How long they seemed, those quarters! Twelve struck, and one, and two, and three, and still we sat waiting silently for whatever might befall.

Suddenly there was the momentary gleam of a light up in the direction of the ventilator, which vanished immediately, but was succeeded by a strong smell of burning oil and heated metal. Someone in the next room had lit a dark lantern. I heard a gen-tle sound of movement, and then all was silent once more, though the smell grew stronger. For half an hour I sat with straining ears. Then suddenly another sound became audible—a very gentle,

---

1 Modern English would require "Do not go to sleep."
2 The cheetah does not roar but makes all kinds of barks, yelps, and
squeals; it can also produce high-pitched chirping sounds and whines.

soothing sound, like that of a small jet of steam escaping continually from a kettle. The instant that we heard it, Holmes sprang
from the bed, struck a match, and lashed furiously with his cane
at the bell-pull.

"You see it, Watson?" he yelled. "You see it?"

But I saw nothing.[1] At the moment when Holmes struck the
light I heard a low, clear whistle, but the sudden glare flashing
into my weary eyes made it impossible for me to tell what it was
at which my friend lashed so savagely. I could, however, see that
his face was deadly pale and filled with horror and loathing.

He had ceased to strike and was gazing up at the ventilator
when suddenly there broke from the silence of the night the most
horrible cry to which I have ever listened. It swelled up louder
and louder, a hoarse yell of pain and fear and anger all mingled
in the one dreadful shriek. They say that away down in the village,
and even in the distant parsonage, that cry raised the sleepers
from their beds. It struck cold to our hearts, and I stood gazing at
Holmes, and he at me, until the last echoes of it had died away
into the silence from which it rose.

"What can it mean?" I gasped.

"It means that it is all over," Holmes answered. "And perhaps,
after all, it is for the best. Take your pistol, and we will enter Dr.
Roylott's room."

With a grave face he lit the lamp and led the way down the corridor. Twice he struck at the chamber door without any reply
from within. Then he turned the handle and entered, I at his
heels, with the cocked pistol in my hand.

It was a singular sight which met our eyes. On the table stood
a dark-lantern with the shutter half open, throwing a brilliant
beam of light upon the iron safe, the door of which was ajar.
Beside this table, on the wooden chair, sat Dr. Grimesby Roylott
clad in a long gray dressing-gown, his bare ankles protruding
beneath, and his feet thrust into red heelless Turkish slippers.
Across his lap lay the short stock with the long lash which we had
noticed during the day. His chin was cocked upward and his eyes
were fixed in a dreadful, rigid stare at the corner of the ceiling.
Round his brow he had a peculiar yellow band, with brownish

---

1   Sidney Paget, illustrating this moment in *The Strand* edition, shows
Holmes lashing furiously with his cane but the snake is not visible. It is a
neat visual counterpart to Watson's inability to see the creature.

speckles, which seemed to be bound tightly round his head. As we entered he made neither sound nor motion.

"The band! the speckled band!" whispered Holmes.

I took a step forward. In an instant his strange headgear began to move, and there reared itself from among his hair the squat diamond-shaped head and puffed neck of a loathsome serpent.

"It is a swamp adder!"[1] cried Holmes, "—the deadliest snake in India. He has died within ten seconds of being bitten.[2] Violence does, in truth, recoil upon the violent, and the schemer falls into the pit[3] which he digs for another. Let us thrust this creature back into its den, and we can then remove Miss Stoner to some place of shelter and let the county police know what has happened."

As he spoke he drew the dog-whip swiftly from the dead man's lap, and throwing the noose round the reptile's neck he drew it from its horrid perch and, carrying it at arm's length, threw it into the iron safe, which he closed upon it.

Such are the true facts of the death of Dr. Grimesby Roylott, of Stoke Moran. It is not necessary that I should prolong a narrative which has already run to too great a length by telling how we broke the sad news to the terrified girl, how we conveyed her by the morning train to the care of her good aunt at Harrow, of how the slow process of official inquiry came to the conclusion that the doctor met his fate while indiscreetly playing with a

---

1   There is no such animal. Baring-Gould, I.263–6, assesses possible iden- tifications but concludes that there is none that "satisfies all the require- ments of the speckled band," (266). No one has changed this judge- ment. Conan Doyle produced a dramatic version of "The Speckled Band" which was very successful. In his autobiography he records the amusing consequences of endeavouring to work with a real snake which was not, of course, the fabled swamp adder. "We had a fine rock boa," he commented, "to play the title-rôle, a snake which was the pride of my heart, so one can imagine my disgust when I saw that one critic ended his disparaging review by the words 'The crisis of the play was produced by the appearance of a palpably artificial serpent.' I was inclined to offer him a goodly sum if he would undertake to go to bed with it," (*Memo- ries and Adventures*, 101–02).

2   Strangely unlike its first victim, of course.

3   Cf. Ecclesiastes 10.8: "He that diggeth a pit, shall fall into it; and who so breaketh an hedge, a serpent shall bite him"; and Matthew 26.52: "Then said Jesus unto him, Put up again thy sword into his place: for all they that take the sword, shall perish with the sword."

dangerous pet.[1] The little which I had yet to learn of the case was told me by Sherlock Holmes as we travelled back next day.

"I had," said he, "come to an entirely erroneous conclusion which shows, my dear Watson, how dangerous it always is to reason from insufficient data. The presence of the gipsies, and the use of the word "band," which was used by the poor girl, no doubt to explain the appearance which she had caught a hurried glimpse of by the light of her match, were sufficient to put me upon an entirely wrong scent.[2] I can only claim the merit that I instantly reconsidered my position when, however, it became clear to me that whatever danger threatened an occupant of the room could not come either from the window or the door. My attention was speedily drawn, as I have already remarked to you, to this ventilator, and to the bell-rope which hung down to the bed. The discovery that this was a dummy, and that the bed was clamped to the floor, instantly gave rise to the suspicion that the rope was there as a bridge for something passing through the hole and coming to the bed. The idea of a snake instantly occurred to me, and when I coupled it with my knowledge that the doctor was furnished with a supply of creatures from India, I felt that I was probably on the right track. The idea of using a form of poison which could not possibly be discovered by any chemical test was just such a one as would occur to a clever and ruthless man who had had an Eastern training.[3] The rapidity with which such a poison would take effect would also, from his point of view, be an advantage. It would be a sharp-eyed coroner, indeed, who could distinguish the two little dark punctures which would show where the poison fangs had done their work. Then I thought of the whistle. Of course he must recall the snake before the morning light revealed it to the victim.[4]

---

1   Conan Doyle's Holmes stories assume remarkable incompetence on the part of officials, especially local police and coroners' courts.

2   One of Holmes's many hunting metaphors.

3   The East is mysteriously associated with forms of (dangerous) knowledge unknown to the West. See Introduction, p. 32.

4   Snakes are without external ears and largely deaf to human noise—experts disagree, but it seems that, at the very best, it would have been exceptionally difficult to train a snake to respond to a whistle. To train it to return home from another room through a ventilator at the sound of a whistle is, however, plainly absurd. And then there is another problem. A large snake would not willingly climb up and then down a rope (let alone in response to a sound it could not hear); a small snake such as this one would simply be unable to do so as its motion would be wholly unsuited to it.

He had trained it, probably by the use of the milk which we saw,[1] to return to him when summoned. He would put it through this ventilator at the hour that he thought best, with the certainty that it would crawl down the rope and land on the bed. It might or might not bite the occupant, perhaps she might escape every night for a week, but sooner or later she must fall a victim.[2]

"I had come to these conclusions before ever I had entered his room. An inspection of his chair showed me that he had been in the habit of standing on it, which of course would be necessary in order that he should reach the ventilator. The sight of the safe, the saucer of milk, and the loop of whipcord were enough to finally dispel any doubts which may have remained. The metallic clang heard by Miss Stoner was obviously caused by her stepfather hastily closing the door of his safe upon its terrible occupant.[3] Having once made up my mind, you know the steps which I took in order to put the matter to the proof. I heard the creature hiss as I have no doubt that you did also, and I instantly lit the light and attacked it."

"With the result of driving it through the ventilator."[4]

"And also with the result of causing it to turn upon its master at the other side. Some of the blows of my cane came home and roused its snakish temper, so that it flew upon the first person it saw. In this way I am no doubt indirectly responsible for Dr. Grimesby Roylott's death, and I cannot say that it is likely to weigh very heavily upon my conscience."[5]

---

1 Snakes do not drink milk by choice.

2 A poisonous snake would only attack a sleeper if it thought it was endangered which seems unlikely in such a circumstance, to say the least. See Introduction pp. 20–22.

3 One assumes this safe has some ventilation or the snake would have suffocated. Even given air, it is unlikely to have thrived in darkness for long.

4 Conan Doyle describes what sounds an extremely risky strategy. The beaten snake would have been more likely to have attacked Holmes than obediently returned through the ventilator.

5 Holmes's plays the bringer of justice himself here rather than the courts. He metes out his own sentence of death too. See Introduction, pp. 28–32. Rather ironically, the reader of this adventure in *The Strand* would, on turning the page for the next article, find the first part of Sir John Lubbock's "Beauty in Nature": a reminder of the disruptive, composite forms of reading that serialization created.

Appendix A: "Curiosities," The Strand Magazine 21 (April 1901), 477–80

[*The Strand Magazine* was a very successful mixture of serialized fiction (often with an emphasis on adventure and romance) and factual articles. Many of the latter had an element of modern appeal—they were, for instance, about celebrities, curious new inventions, crime, developments in science. Nothing scandalous was reproduced—this was a respectable journal—but there was a taste for the mildly sensational in some articles. In the edition for April 1901, while Conan Doyle was writing *The Hound of the Baskervilles*, articles included Conan Doyle's own "Strange Studies from Life: II. The Love Affair of George Vincent Parker," which was part of his series of "studies of criminal psychology [...] from the actual history of crime"; "Some Personal Characteristics of Queen Victoria" (*The Strand* was respectful of monarchy); Robert Barr's "A Romance of the Middle Ages"; Sir Robert Ball's discussion of "Comets"; an instalment of H.G. Wells's *The First Men in the Moon* (see Introduction 19–20); some light parliamentary satire; one of John Arthur Barry's "Sea Stories"; and a piece on "What is the Greatest Achievement in Music?" This included, by the way, a contribution from Jean de Reszke, one of the singers whom Holmes invites Watson to hear at the end of *The Hound*.[1]

At the end of editions of *The Strand* came a section entitled "Curiosities" where readers' letters and photographs were published. This section—still intriguing after a century—responded to the now widespread possession of affordable and easily-manageable cameras and to the oddities that they both recorded and sometimes created. The pages reproduced below

---

1 There is a photograph of Jean de Reszke on p. 431 of the article. As with the typewriters (see note 2 on p. 155) Conan Doyle wrote *The Hound of the Baskervilles*—and his other Holmes adventures—very much conscious of the publication in which it would appear and its interests.

are typical of a "Curiosities" section and remind the reader of the way in which *The Strand* privileged the odd, unusual, sometimes even the appearance of the supernatural ("ghost photographs" were a regular feature of these pages). *The Hound* and "The Speckled Band" were "Curiosities" in their own way and part of *The Strand*'s interest in the out-of-the-way and peculiar. Visual puzzles—most obviously the typed letter on p. 480 (244) from Mr O'Donoghue—chimed with the kind of detecting that Conan Doyle offered and exemplified in Holmes. In part of an instalment readers could find themselves contemplating Holmes solving the puzzle of a walking stick and later puzzling in their own right over a picture of something improbable that had nonetheless been—apparently—authenticated.]

A FREAK OF AN EXPLOSION.

Mr. le Moyne L. Parkinson, of Beaver Falls, Pa., sends a curious instance of a lucky escape from the effects of a terrible explosion. He says: " Part of the stone foundation of this frame house was blown out, the rear of building completely blown away, and the front extended out in an obtuse angle, while, strange to relate, the family and visitors were not injured in the least. The photograph shows a heavy leather couch turned upside down and sticking in the ceiling, caused by the force of the explosion."

WHEN IS AN EGG NOT AN EGG?

Miss Clara Tilling, of Highfield, West-moreland Road, Bromley, Kent, is the fortunate possessor of an extraordinary egg, or, to be more accurate, eggs, for the curiosity in her possession consists of two perfectly formed eggs found one within the other. This extraordinary find was laid on Michael-mas Day, September 29th, 1900, by a Plymouth Rock hen. It weighed 6oz., and was larger than that of a goose. When it was blown an ordinary egg was found float-

ing in the white of the large one, which had no yolk. The inner egg had the usual white and yolk, and the shell of the outer one was very thin. The hen had not laid for four days before the occurrence, and has not laid since.

HOW DID IT GET THERE?

Mr. R. C. Hardman, of Meadhurst, Uppingham, has been the fortunate finder of a coin dated 1397 embedded in a lump of coal, which formed part and parcel of a ton of that useful commodity bought at current prices.

NATURE'S LITTLE JOKE.

The weird picture shown above was sent to us by Mr. John Bee, of Avonville, Albert Street, Kew, Melbourne. It represents a curious old gum tree in the paddock at the back of Mr. Bee's house. The cow happened to be walking past when Mr. Bee took the snap-shot, and the curious though unexpected result shown here was noticed only on developing.

THE WOODEN HAND OF NATURE.

This hand-like curiosity was taken from a branch of a tree grown in the Cairns District, Queensland, and was obtained from Ranger Duffen on a recent visit to the north by Mr. L. Board, the Inspector of State Forests, who kindly sent the photograph to us.

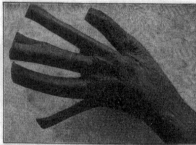

A CURIOUS BEE STORY.

An admirer of THE STRAND sends the next picture from New Rochelle, N.Y. It appears that while repairing his sail-boat in the spring he noticed a hole bored in the mast, and on opening it found this nest of bees. The mother-bee had bored out a tunnel about 8in. in length, boring both forward and back, making the entrance in the middle of the tunnel. She then laid four eggs, walling up each within a space by a partition formed of the sawdust made in boring the tunnel. This partition was a thin but a very firm and tough membrane. When found, three of the eggs had developed into bees, perfectly formed, but white; the fourth was still in the pupa form, and the mother-bee was lying outside the last wall, dead.

Shortly the two oldest bees died, the third and the fourth, the pupa, developed into bees; they laid on their backs and slowly changed to brown and finally black, beautiful bees; the only signs of life noticeable for days was a vibratory oscillation sideways when the stick was moved or shaken. Each compartment had a store of little black seed in it when found. When the remaining two bees were fully grown they were fed with a little sugar and water, which they ate greedily. They grew strong enough to walk, and finally one day were put out in the fresh air, and on learning the strength of their wings flew away. Several puzzling questions were suggested during these interesting developments. Does the mother-bee always die and block the entrance to her prospective family's home? Again, how does the oldest bee, which is the farthest from the entrance, make its way out, and how does this wonderful mother-bee make her partition so delicate and yet so strong?

A REVERSIBLE DATE.

1061. In this year reigned King Edward the Confessor, the first English Sovereign of that name and one of the best of English kings. Turn the figures upside down and you obtain 1901. In this year reigns Edward VII. The above type is taken from a January calendar, and sent by Mr. J. H. Helps, Beechwood, Tyne Road, Bristol.

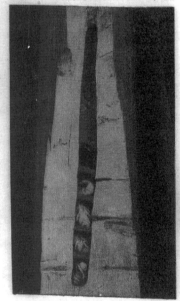

CAUGHT!

This dog tried to jump a fence; much to his amazement, however, he found himself, though unhurt, a prisoner between the spikes in the manner shown. Since when he has jumped no other. Photo. by Mr. A. H. Shorey, 76, Redpath Street, Montreal.

attaching masts to the front framework of their bicycles. Hoisting the sails they jumped on and let the wind carry them. Frequently the wheelmen can coast at a speed of from twenty to twenty-five miles an hour. In the contest illustrated the automobile won by only a few lengths." So writes Mr. D. A. Willey, of Baltimore.

A "RIGHT"-MINDED DOG.

Miss Mildred Hunter, of 30, Clarence Square, Gosport, sends a pretty dog story, together with a photo. of her pet, who, to say the least of it, is a very clever dog indeed. Miss Hunter says : "I send you a photo. of my fox-terrier dog, who will refuse all food if

AN AERATED VANDAL.

Mr. J. Ross McMillan, in sending the next photograph, says : "I send you the photograph of an injured picture hanging in my house, 16, Bon Accord Square, Dublin. An ordinary sized soda-water bottle was left standing on the dining-room table on retiring at night, and in the morning the splintered pieces of the bottle were found strewn round the room, the head of the bottle being lodged, as you will see by the photograph, in the picture. The piece which has thus injured the picture measures 6in. long."

SAIL-BIKE v. MOTOR.

"This is what might be called a twentieth century race, and it is undoubtedly the first photograph ever published of a contest between an automobile and a bicycle 'under sail.' The affair came off recently at Ormond, Fla. Here the beach along the coast is so smooth and hard that it has long been a favourite place for trotting horses and for taking bicycle trips. This winter several 'mobile' owners brought their machines with them. Taking advantage of a favourable wind, two of the wheelmen 'rigged up' sails by

offered in the left hand. In the picture he is being tempted with a piece of biscuit of which he is par-

ticularly fond, and you can see from his appearance that it is not because he is dainty that he will not take it, but that he is only waiting for it to be changed to the right hand, when he will snap it up at once. However you may try to deceive him he recognises the left hand at once, unless you stand back to him, and then he is not certain."

AN ACCIDENTAL PUZZLE.

Mr. Jos. O'Donoghue, of Dingle, Ireland, writes: "Inclosed please find a letter for your 'Curiosities.' It is a copy of a letter written by me to a firm asking for their latest catalogue. The figure shift-key of the typewriter got out of order, with the result that neither shift-key would work. I wrote the *facsimile* of the letter without knowing it until almost finished, then I decided to complete it for your Magazine. It will make an excellent puzzle for your readers to solve." Perhaps our readers will try. It is not at all difficult.

UMBRELLA-STICK HEROES.

A dozen years ago or more an enterprising firm of umbrella-stick manufacturers struck on the novel idea of placing umbrellas on the market the handle of which should contain the profile of some notable personage. The design was duly registered, but, for some reason or other, the sale was not large. Now that hero worship is at concert pitch something of the kind might possibly "catch on." Some ladies, for instance, might like to carry about with them either Bobs or that general favourite known as B.-P., not to mention selections from scores of others. No

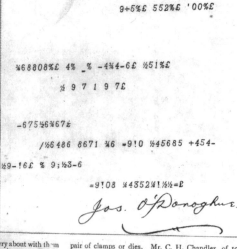

pair of clamps or dies. Mr. C. H. Chandler, of 10, Allison Road, Harringay, N., is responsible for this interesting contribution.

one will fail to recognise in the above photograph the outline of the late Mr. W. E. Gladstone's face, and it will be noticed that the ever-familiar collar is particularly prominent. The handle is made of composition, and the result is obtained by means of a

WHAT THE KETTLE DID.

Our next photograph shows how necessary it is for good housewives to make adequate provision for the prevention of accumulation of lime and fur in the kettle, which plays such an important part in every

household. The marble which may be plainly seen in the photo. was placed in a kettle some three months ago, and has gathered, ever since the first day of its incarceration, a coating of lime and fur, which has increased daily to the extraordinary proportions shown in the photograph. The use of this marble has been the cause of considerable saving of fuel by its having collected the lime which would otherwise have formed a coating on the inside of the kettle. Mr. Albert J. Judd, of 36, Clifford Street, Watford, Herts, sends this contribution.

Appendix B: From Francis Galton, "Composite Portraits, made by combining those of many different persons into a single resultant figure," Journal of the Anthropological Institute of Great Britain and Ireland 8 (1879): 132–44

[*The Hound of the Baskervilles* ruminates on questions of hereditary, bloodline, and biological determinism (see Introduction, pp. 23–27). It was a widely-discussed matter at the end of the century. Francis Galton (1822–1911), a cousin of Darwin, scientist and eugenicist, considered the issues from a quasi-scientific point of view and his work was predicated on an assumption, derived from Darwin, about the hereditary nature of characteristics. He thought, as the extract from his important book *Hereditary Genius* in Appendix C shows, 251–54—that special abilities in human beings, as well as their lack of them, were biologically determined. It was part of the basis of his later belief in eugenics. Similarly, he supported the idea that criminality was a hereditary characteristic which was evident even in the physical form of the criminal's body. Using the technical procedures of composite photography described in this revealing essay from the newly founded *Journal of the Anthropological Institute*, Galton proposed that it was possible to discern the archetype of the criminal face (one thinks of Selden in *The Hound* as a kind of *imagined* archetype—or at least stereotype—of the criminal). In looking at this "ideal" form, Galton argued that one saw the generalized image of criminal selfhood, an ancestrally determined identity that passed from generation to generation. *The Hound* cannot fully commit itself to the same view of human development and determinism that sustained Galton's thinking but is in dialogue with it.]

[...] I submit to the Anthropological Institute my first results in carrying out a process that I suggested last August in my presidential address to the Anthropological Subsection of the British Association at Plymouth, in the following words:—

"Having obtained drawings or photographs of several persons alike in most respects, but differing in minor details, what sure method is there of extracting the typical characteristics from them? I may mention a plan which had occurred both to Mr. Herbert Spencer[1] and myself, the principle of which is to superimpose optically the various drawings, and to accept the aggregate result. Mr. Spencer suggested to me in conversation that the drawings reduced to the same scale might be traced on separate pieces of transparent paper and secured one upon another, and then held between the eye and the light. I have attempted this with some success. My own idea was to throw faint images of the several portraits, in succession, upon the same sensitised photographical plate. I may add that it is perfectly easy to superimpose optically two portraits by means of a stereoscope, and that a person who is used to handle instruments will find a common double eyeglass fitted with stereoscopic lenses to be almost as effectual and far handier than the boxes sold in shops."

Mr. Spencer, as he informed me had actually devised an instrument, many years ago, for tracing mechanically, longitudinal, transverse, and horizontal sections of heads on transparent paper, intending to superimpose them, and to obtain an average result by transmitted light.

Since my Address was published, I have caused trials to be made, and have found, as a matter of fact, that the photographic process of which I there spoke enables us to obtain with mechanical precision a generalised picture; one that represents no man in particular, but portrays an imaginary figure possessing the average features of any given group of men. These ideal faces have a surprising air of reality. Nobody who glanced at one of them for the first time, would doubt its being the likeness of a living person, yet, as I have said, it is no such thing; it is the portrait of a type and not of an individual.

I began by collecting photographs of the persons with whom I propose to deal. They must be similar in attitude and size, but no exactness is necessary in either of these respects. Then, by a simple contrivance, I make two pinholes in each of them, to enable me to hang them up one in front of the other, like a pack of cards, upon the same pair of pins, in such a way that the eyes of all the portraits shall be as nearly as possible superimposed; in which case

---

1 Herbert Spencer (1820–1903), social theorist, philosopher, psychologist, and investigator of the new "science" of sociology.

the remainder of the features will also be superimposed nearly enough. These pinholes correspond to what are technically known to printers as "register marks." They are easily made: A slip of brass or card has an aperture cut out of its middle, and threads are stretched from opposite sides, making a cross. Two small holes are drilled in the plate, one on either side of the aperture. The slip of brass is laid on the portrait with the aperture over its face. It is turned about until one of the cross threads cuts the pupils of both the eyes, and it is further adjusted until the other thread divides the interval between the pupils in two equal parts. Then it is held firmly, and a prick is made through each of the holes.

The portraits being thus arranged, a photographic camera is directed upon them. Suppose there are eight portraits in the pack, and that under existing circumstances it would require an exposure of eighty seconds to give an exact photographic copy of any one of them. The general principle of proceeding is this, subject in practice to some variation of details, depending on the different brightness of the several portraits. We throw the image of each of the eight portraits in turn upon the same part of the sensitised plate for ten seconds. Thus, portrait No. 1 is in the front of the pack; we take the cap off the object glass of the camera for ten seconds, and afterwards replace it. We then remove No. 1 from the pins, and No. 2 appears in the front; we take off the cap a second time for ten seconds, and again replace it. Next we remove No. 2 and No. 3 appears in the front, which we treat as its predecessors, and so we go on to the last of the pack. The sensitised plate will now have had its total exposure of eighty seconds; it is then developed, and the print taken from it is the generalised picture of which I speak. It is a composite of eight component portraits. Those of its outlines are sharpest and darkest that are common to the largest number of the components; the purely individual peculiarities leave little or no visible trace. The latter being necessarily disposed equally on both sides of the average, the outline of the composite is the average of all the components. It is a band and not a fine line, because the outlines of the components are seldom exactly superimposed. The band will be darkest in its middle whenever the component portraits have the same general type of features, and its breadth, or amount of blur, will measure the tendency of the components to deviate from the common type. This is so for the very same reason that the shot-marks on a target are more thickly disposed near the bulls-eye than away from it, and in a greater degree as the marksmen are more skilful. All that has been said of the outlines is equally true as regards the shadows; the result being that the composite represents an averaged figure, whose lineaments have been softly drawn. The eyes come out with appropriate distinctness, owing to the mechanical conditions under which the components were hung.

A composite portrait represents the picture that would rise before the mind's eye of a man who had the gift of pictorial imagination in an exalted degree. But the imaginative power even of the highest artists is far from precise, and is so apt to be biased by special cases that may have struck their fancies, that no two artists agree in any of their typical forms. The merit of the photographic composite is its mechanical precision, being subject to no errors beyond those incidental to all photographic productions.

I submit several composites made for me by Mr. H. Reynolds. The first set of portraits are those of criminals convicted of murder, manslaughter, or robbery accompanied with violence. It will be observed that the features of the composites are much better looking than those of the components. The special villainous irregularities in the latter have disappeared, and the common humanity that underlies them has prevailed. They represent, not the criminal, but the man who is liable to fall into crime. All composites are better looking than their components, because the averaged portrait of many persons is free from the irregularities that variously blemish the looks of each of them.

I selected these for my first trials because I happened to possess a large collection of photographs of criminals, through the kindness of Sir Edmund Du Cane, the Director-General of Prisons,[1] for the purpose of investigating criminal types. They were peculiarly adapted to my present purpose, being all made of about the same size, and taken in much the same attitudes. It was while endeavouring to elicit the principal criminal types by methods of optical superimposition of the portraits, such as I had frequently employed with maps and meteorological traces, that the idea of composite figures first occurred to me.

---

1   Sir Edmund Du Cane (1830–1903), British prison administrator. Du Cane did not believe in *innate* criminality and, particularly in relation to young offenders, thought that some reformation was possible. Such a view had substantial consequences on the direction of British penal policy in the second half of the nineteenth century, helping the institution of brutal "reformist" and deterrent prison systems. Though differing from Galton in understanding the origins of criminality, he was a close friend, and encouraged him in the study of criminals' facial features.

[...] The use of composite portraits are many. They give us typical pictures of different races of men, if derived from a large number of individuals of those races taken at random. An assurance of the truth of any of our pictorial deductions is to be looked for in their substantial agreement when different batches of components have been dealt with, this being a perfect test of truth in all statistical conclusions. Again, we may select prevalent or strongly-marked types from among the men of the same race. [...]

The last use of the process that I shall mention is of great interest as regards inquiries into the hereditary transmission of features, as it enables us to compare the average features of the produce with those of the parentage. A composite of all the brothers and sisters in a large family would be an approximation to what the average of the produce would probably be if the family were indefinitely increased in number, but the approximation would be closer if we also took into consideration those of the cousins who inherited the family likeness. As regards the parentage, it is by no means sufficient to take a composite of the two parents; the four grandparents and the uncles and aunts on both sides should be also included. Some statistical inquiries I published on the distribution of ability in families give provisional data for determining the weight to be assigned in the composite to the several degrees of relationship. I should, however, not follow those figures in the present case, but would rather suggest, for the earlier trials, first to give equal "weights" to the male and female sides; thus the father and a brother of the male parent would count equally with the father and a brother of the female parent. Secondly, I should "weight" each parent as four, and each grandparent and each uncle and aunt as one; again, I should weight each brother and sister as four, and each of those cousins as one who inherited any part of the likeness of the family in question. The other cousins I should disregard [...]

Appendix C: From Francis Galton, Hereditary Genius: An Inquiry into its Laws and Consequences, 2nd ed (London: Macmillan, 1892)

[Francis Galton's work in hereditary acquirement also included this substantial study of the nature of inherited ability, first published in 1869, and in a second edition, with a new Preface, in 1892. The argument of the book is, in outline, that there is a fixed limit to the powers of will and environment to modify what has been inherited through biology. These extracts should be read alongside the essay on "Composite Portraits," in Appendix B. Galton's ideas had significant consequences for the nature of education policy at the beginning of the twentieth century and his assertion in the "Introduction" that it is humanity's duty to maximize the benefits of its biological past crucially moved science into social policy. This notion of maximization, for him, provided the ethical foundation for eugenics. *The Hound* considers similar issues of biological legacies although it offers a far more complicated model of the operation of inheritance and declines, in the end, to commit itself to Galton's position.]

From "Introductory Chapter"

[...] I propose to show in this book that a man's natural abilities are derived by inheritance, under exactly the same limitations as are the form and physical features of the whole organic world. Consequently, as it is easy, notwithstanding those limitations, to obtain by careful selection a permanent breed of dogs or horses gifted with peculiar powers of running, or of doing anything else, so it would be quite practicable to produce a highly-gifted race of men by judicious marriages during several consecutive generations.[1] I shall show that social agencies of an ordinary character, whose influences are little suspected, are at this moment working towards the degradation of human nature, and that others are

---

1   Galton is echoing the language of Charles Darwin's *The Origin of Species* (1859) in this opening.

working towards its improvement. I conclude that each generation has enormous power over the natural gifts of those that follow, and maintain that it is a duty we owe to humanity to investigate the range of that power, and to exercise it in a way that, without being unwise towards ourselves, shall be most advantageous to future inhabitants of the earth. [...]

From Chapter 3, "Classification of Men According to their Natural Gifts"

[...] I have no patience with the hypothesis occasionally expressed, and often implied, especially in tales written to teach children to be good, that babies are born pretty much alike, and that the sole agencies in creating differences between boy and boy, and man and man, are steady application and moral effort. It is in the most unqualified manner that I object to pretensions of natural equality. The experiences of the nursery, the school, the University, and of professional careers, are a chain of proofs to the contrary. I acknowledge freely the great power of education and social influences in developing the active powers of the mind, just as I acknowledge the effect of use in developing the muscles of a blacksmith's arm, and no further. Let the blacksmith labour as he will, he will find there are certain feats beyond his power that are well within the strength of a man of herculean make, even although the latter may have led a sedentary life. Some years ago, the Highlanders held a grand gathering in Holland Park,[1] where they challenged all England to compete with them in their games of strength. The challenge was accepted, and the well-trained men of the hills were beaten in the foot-race by a youth who was stated to be a pure Cockney, the clerk of a London banker.

Everybody who has trained himself to physical exercises discovers the extent of his muscular powers to a nicety. When he begins to walk, to row, to use the dumb bells, or to run, he finds to his great delight that his thews[2] strengthen, and his endurance of fatigue increases day after day. So long as he is a novice, he perhaps flatters himself there is hardly an assignable limit to the education of his muscles; but the daily gain is soon discovered to diminish, and at last it vanishes altogether. His maximum perfor-

---

1 The largest park in what is now the Royal Borough of Kensington and Chelsea in London.
2 Muscular force.

mance becomes a rigidly determinate quantity. He learns to an inch, how high or how far he can jump, when he has attained the highest state of training. He learns to half a pound, the force he can exert on the dynamometer,[1] by compressing it. He can strike a blow against the machine used to measure impact, and drive its index to a certain graduation, but no further. So it is in running, in rowing, in walking, and in every other form of physical exertion. There is a definite limit to the muscular powers of every man, which he cannot by any education or exertion overpass.

This is precisely analogous to the experience that every student has had of the working of his mental powers. The eager boy, when he first goes to school and confronts intellectual difficulties, is astonished at his progress. He glories in his newly-developed mental grip and growing capacity for application, and, it may be, fondly believes it to be within his reach to become one of the heroes who have left their mark upon the history of the world. The years go by; he competes in the examinations of school and college, over and over again with his fellows, and soon finds his place among them. He knows he can beat such and such of his competitors; that there are some with whom he runs on equal terms, and others whose intellectual feats he cannot even approach. Probably his vanity still continues to tempt him, by whispering in a new strain. It tells him that classics, mathematics, and other subjects taught in universities, are mere scholastic specialities, and no test of the more valuable intellectual powers. It reminds him of numerous instances of persons who had been unsuccessful in the competitions of youth, but who had shown powers in after-life that made them the foremost men of their age. Accordingly, with newly furbished hopes, and with all the ambition of twenty-two years of age, he leaves his University and enters a larger field of competition. The same kind of experience awaits him here that he has already gone through. Opportunities occur—they occur to every man—and he finds himself incapable of grasping them. He tries, and is tried in many things. In a few years more, unless he is incurably blinded by self-conceit, he learns precisely of what performances he is capable, and what other enterprises lie beyond his compass. When he reaches mature life, he is confident only within certain limits, and knows,

---

1 *OED* says "A name of instruments of various kinds for measuring the amount of energy exerted by an animal, or expended by a motor or other engine in its work, or by the action of any mechanical force."

or ought to know, himself just as he is probably judged of by the world, with all his unmistakeable weakness and all his undeniable strength. He is no longer tormented into hopeless efforts by the fallacious promptings of overweening vanity, but he limits his undertakings to matters below the level of his reach, and finds true moral repose in an honest conviction that he is engaged in as much good work as his nature has rendered him capable of performing. [...]

Appendix D: From Jack London, The People of the Abyss (New York: Macmillan, 1903). Also published by Isbister, London, in the same year.

[One of the subdued preoccupations of *The Hound* is atavism and the return to primitive states of being. Conan Doyle was not the only writer at this period to be interested in varieties of the primitive. There was, of course, an element of this in Galton's work (245–53). In anthropology, it was a matter of significance (see the extracts from Edward Tylor, 283–87) and in fiction and journalistic writing states of human primitivism, and atavistic reversals, were variously probed. Reversions to pre-civilized states were, most memorably, treated in R. L. Stevenson's *The Strange Case of Dr Jekyll and Mr Hyde* (1886) and Joseph Conrad's *Heart of Darkness* (1899)—but not here alone. The US novelist and prose writer Jack London (1876–1916) achieved his first major success shortly after the publication of *The Hound* with the bestseller *The Call of the Wild* (1903). This narrated a journey "into the primitive" (to use the title of the first chapter) and the powerful atavistic reversion of Buck, its canine hero, from civilized southerner to the wild Ghost-dog of the north. It was a transformation that gave Buck a savage integrity; it was both brutalising and a passage to a more authentic state of being. Clemence Housman's *The Were-Wolf* (1896) had considered a different form of human transformation to a brutish state and proposed a Christianized version of a were-wolf narrative in which a man dies to save his brother from White Fell, a beautiful woman who is in truth a great white wolf. Criminal atavism—narratives of debasement and decline into criminal states of being—formed the drive of Frank Norris's *McTeague* (1899) and *Vandover the Brute* (written at the end of the century but published in 1914).

Among the plural imaginative journeys "into the primitive," there were provocative redefinitions of what constituted primitivism, radically different from these. In 1902, Jack London had spent two months in the late summer and early autumn in the East End of London, an area of working-class houses and slums which was a common subject of philanthropic and journalistic interest in the second half of the nineteenth century. Its poverty and the hardships of East End life, only a few miles away from the prosperous heart of the capital, had gradually obtained a curiously inverted kind of glamour. Jack London's experiences were recounted in 1903 in *The People of the Abyss*, a volume that grimly developed the Victorian tradition of investigative city journalism—such as Henry Mayhew's *London Labour and the London Poor* (2 vols., 1851)—and late Victorian inquiring fictions of East End poverty such as Walter Besant's *All Sorts and Conditions of Men* (1882). Here, London offered a fresh perspective on man's decline into primitive states, quite different from Norris or Conan Doyle, and understood to be about dehumanization consequent on poverty. In *The People of the Abyss*, the affluent writer masquerades as a pauper in order to learn the nature of East End life (the link with Besant is plain) and, in the narrative of human squalor and existence as ill-treated animals, London finds sympathy for the poor and outraged disgust on their behalf. *The People of the Abyss* is a grim account of men living in a primeval state in England (not in Neolithic huts but in the capital city) at the beginning of the twentieth century—Orwell would return to this territory in *Down and Out in Paris and London* (1933). It offers a sharply different view of the cultural preoccupation with life below the limits of civilization that is evident in a remarkably different form in *The Hound* and other turn-of-the-century writing.]

From "The Carter and the Carpenter"[1]

[...] The Carter, with his clean-cut face, chin beard, and shaved upper lip, I should have taken in the United States for anything from a master workman to a well-to-do farmer. The Carpenter—well, I should have taken him for a carpenter. He looked it, lean and wiry, with shrewd, observant eyes, and hands that had grown twisted to the handles of tools through forty-seven years' work at the trade. The chief difficulty with these men was that they were old, and that their children, instead of growing up to take care of them, had died. Their years had told on them, and they had been forced out of the whirl of industry by the younger and stronger competitors who had taken their places.

---

1 Is there an ironic, deliberately incongruous glance in this title to Lewis Carroll's "The Walrus and the Carpenter" (1872)?

These two men, turned away from the casual ward of Whitechapel Workhouse, were bound with me for Poplar Workhouse. Not much of a show, they thought, but to chance it was all that remained to us. It was Poplar, or the streets and night. Both men were anxious for a bed, for they were "about gone," as they phrased it. The Carter, fifty-eight years of age, had spent the last three nights without shelter or sleep, while the Carpenter, sixty-five years of age, had been out five nights.

But, O dear, soft people, full of meat and blood, with white beds and airy rooms waiting you each night, how can I make you know what it is to suffer as you would suffer if you spent a weary night on London's streets! Believe me, you would think a thousand centuries had come and gone before the east paled into dawn; you would shiver till you were ready to cry aloud with the pain of each aching muscle; and you would marvel that you could endure so much and live. Should you rest upon a bench, and your tired eyes close, depend upon it the policeman would rouse you and gruffly order you to "move on." You may rest upon the bench, and benches are few and far between; but if rest means sleep, on you must go, dragging your tired body through the endless streets. Should you, in desperate slyness, seek some forlorn alley or dark passageway and lie down, the omnipresent policeman will rout you out just the same. It is his business to rout you out. It is a law of the powers that be that you shall be routed out.

But when the dawn came, the nightmare over, you would hale you home to refresh yourself, and until you died you would tell the story of your adventure to groups of admiring friends. It would grow into a mighty story. Your little eight-hour night would become an Odyssey and you a Homer.

Not so with these homeless ones who walked to Poplar Workhouse with me. And there are thirty-five thousand of them, men and women, in London Town this night. Please don't remember it as you go to bed; if you are as soft as you ought to be you may not rest so well as usual. But for old men of sixty, seventy, and eighty, ill-fed, with neither meat nor blood, to greet the dawn unrefreshed, and to stagger through the day in mad search for crusts, with relentless night rushing down upon them again, and to do this five nights and days—O dear, soft people, full of meat and blood, how can you ever understand?

I walked up Mile End Road between the Carter and the Carpenter. Mile End Road is a wide thoroughfare, cutting the heart of East London, and there were tens of thousands of people abroad on it. I tell you this so that you may fully appreciate what I shall describe in the next paragraph. As I say, we walked along, and when they grew bitter and cursed the land, I cursed with them, cursed as an American waif would curse, stranded in a strange and terrible land. And, as I tried to lead them to believe, and succeeded in making them believe, they took me for a "seafaring man," who had spent his money in riotous living, lost his clothes (no unusual occurrence with seafaring men ashore), and was temporarily broke while looking for a ship. This accounted for my ignorance of English ways in general and casual wards in particular, and my curiosity concerning the same.

The Carter was hard put to keep the pace at which we walked (he told me that he had eaten nothing that day), but the Carpenter, lean and hungry, his grey and ragged overcoat flapping mournfully in the breeze, swung on in a long and tireless stride which reminded me strongly of the plains wolf or coyote.[1] Both kept their eyes upon the pavement as they walked and talked, and every now and then one or the other would stoop and pick something up, never missing the stride the while. I thought it was cigar and cigarette stumps they were collecting, and for some time took no notice. Then I did notice.

From the slimy sidewalk, they were picking up bits of orange peel, apple skin, and grape stems, and they were eating them. The pips of green gage plums they cracked between their teeth for the kernels inside. They picked up stray crumbs of bread the size of peas, apple cores so black and dirty one would not take them to be apple cores, and these things these two men took into their mouths, and chewed them, and swallowed them; and this, between six and seven o'clock in the evening of August 20, year of our Lord 1902, in the heart of the greatest, wealthiest, and most powerful empire the world has ever seen.

These two men talked. They were not fools, they were merely old. And, naturally, their guts a-reek with pavement offal, they talked of bloody revolution. They talked as anarchists, fanatics, and madmen would talk. And who shall blame them? In spite of my three good meals that day, and the snug bed I could occupy if I wished, and my social philosophy, and my evolutionary belief in the slow development and metamorphosis of things—in spite of all this, I say, I felt impelled to talk rot with them or hold my

---

1 Such creatures interested London deeply; 1903, of course, saw the publication of *The Call of the Wild*.

tongue. Poor fools! Not of their sort are revolutions bred. And when they are dead and dust, which will be shortly, other fools will talk bloody revolution as they gather offal from the spittle-drenched sidewalk along Mile End Road to Poplar Workhouse.

Being a foreigner, and a young man, the Carter and the Carpenter explained things to me and advised me. Their advice, by the way, was brief, and to the point; it was to get out of the country. "As fast as God'll let me," I assured them; "I'll hit only the high places, till you won't be able to see my trail for smoke." They felt the force of my figures, rather than understood them, and they nodded their heads approvingly.

"Actually make a man a criminal against 'is will," said the Carpenter. "'Ere I am, old, younger men takin' my place, my clothes getting' shabbier an' shabbier, an' makin' it 'arder every day to get a job. I go to the casual ward for a bed. Must be there by two or three in the afternoon or I won't get in. You saw what happened to-day. What chance does that give me to look for work? S'pose I do get into the casual ward? Keep me in all day to-morrow, let me out mornin' o' next day. What then? The law sez I can't get in another casual ward that night less'n ten miles distant. Have to hurry an' walk to be there in time that day. What chance does that give me to look for a job? S'pose I don't walk. S'pose I look for a job? In no time there's night come, an' no bed. No sleep all night, nothin' to eat, what shape am I in the mornin' to look for work? Got to make up my sleep in the park somehow" (the vision of Christ's Church, Spitalfield, was strong on me) "an' get something to eat. An' there I am! Old, down, an' no chance to get up."

"Used to be a toll-gate 'ere," said the Carter. "Many's the time I've paid my toll 'ere in my cartin' days."

"I've 'ad three 'a'penny[1] rolls in two days," the Carpenter announced, after a long pause in the conversation. "Two of them I ate yesterday, an' the third to-day," he concluded, after another long pause.

"I ain't 'ad anything to-day," said the Carter. "An' I'm fagged out. My legs is hurtin' me something fearful."

"The roll you get in the 'spike' is that 'ard you can't eat it nicely with less'n a pint of water," said the Carpenter, for my benefit. And, on asking him what the "spike" was, he answered, "The casual ward. It's a cant word, you know."

---

1 Halfpenny (very cheap).

But what surprised me was that he should have the word "cant" in his vocabulary, a vocabulary that I found was no mean one before we parted.

I asked them what I might expect in the way of treatment, if we succeeded in getting into the Poplar Workhouse, and between them I was supplied with much information. Having taken a cold bath on entering, I would be given for supper six ounces of bread and "three parts of skilly." "Three parts" means three-quarters of a pint, and "skilly" is a fluid concoction of three quarts of oatmeal stirred into three buckets and a half of hot water.

"Milk and sugar, I suppose, and a silver spoon?" I queried.

"No fear. Salt's what you'll get, an' I've seen some places where you'd not get any spoon. 'Old 'er up an' let 'er run down, that's 'ow they do it."

"You do get good skilly at 'Ackney," said the Carter.

"Oh, wonderful skilly, that," praised the Carpenter, and each looked eloquently at the other.

"Flour an' water at St. George's in the East," said the Carter.

The Carpenter nodded. He had tried them all.

"Then what?" I demanded

And I was informed that I was sent directly to bed. "Call you at half after five in the mornin',' an' you get up an' take a 'sluice'— if there's any soap. Then breakfast, same as supper, three parts o'skilly an' a six-ounce loaf."

"'Tisn't always six ounces," corrected the Carter.

"'Tisn't, no; an' often that sour you can 'ardly eat it. When first I started I couldn't eat the skilly nor the bread, but now I can eat my own an' another man's portion."

"I could eat three other men's portions," said the Carter. "I 'aven't 'ad a bit this blessed day."

"Then what?"

"Then you've got to do your task, pick four pounds of oakum,[1] or clean an' scrub, or break ten to eleven hundredweight o' stones.[2] I don't 'ave to break stones; I'm past sixty, you see. They'll make you do it, though. You're young an' strong."

"What I don't like," grumbled the Carter, "is to be locked up in a cell to pick oakum. It's too much like prison."[3]

---

1 Unpicked rope (to be mixed later with tar as a waterproof protection, usually in ship building and maintenance).
2 For the road-building trade.
3 Where oakum picking and stone-breaking were indeed standard forms of labour.

"But suppose, after you've had your night's sleep, you refuse to pick oakum, or break stones, or do any work at all?" I asked.

"No fear you'll refuse the second time; they'll run you in," answered the Carpenter.

"Wouldn't advise you to try it on, my lad."

"Then comes dinner," he went on. "Eight ounces of bread, one and a 'arf ounces of cheese, an' cold water. Then you finish your task an' 'ave supper, same as before, three parts o' skilly an' six ounces o' bread. Then to bed, six o'clock, an' next mornin' you're turned loose, provided you've finished your task."

We had long since left Mile End Road, and after traversing a gloomy maze of narrow, winding streets, we came to Poplar Workhouse. On a low stone wall we spread our handkerchiefs, and each in his handkerchief put all his worldly possessions, with the exception of the "bit o' baccy" down his sock. And then, as the last light was fading from the drab-coloured sky, the wind blowing cheerless and cold, we stood, with our pitiful little bundles in our hands, a forlorn group at the workhouse door.

Three working girls came along, and one looked pityingly at me; as she passed I followed her with my eyes, and she still looked pityingly back at me. The old men she did not notice. Dear Christ, she pitied me, young and vigorous and strong, but she had no pity for the two old men who stood by my side! She was a young woman, and I was a young man, and what vague sex promptings impelled her to pity me put her sentiment on the lowest plane. Pity for old men is an altruistic feeling, and besides, the workhouse door is the accustomed place for old men. So she showed no pity for them, only for me, who deserved it least or not at all. Not in honour do grey hairs go down to the grave in London Town.

On one side the door was a bell handle, on the other side a press button.

"Ring the bell," said the Carter to me.

And just as I ordinarily would at anybody's door, I pulled out the handle and rang a peal.

"Oh! Oh!" they cried in one terrified voice. "Not so 'ard!"

I let go, and they looked reproachfully at me, as though I had imperilled their chance for a bed and three parts of skilly. Nobody came. Luckily it was the wrong bell, and I felt better.

"Press the button," I said to the Carpenter.

"No, no, wait a bit," the Carter hurriedly interposed.

From all of which I drew the conclusion that a poorhouse

porter, who commonly draws a yearly salary of from seven to nine pounds, is a very finicky and important personage, and cannot be treated too fastidiously by—paupers.

So we waited, ten times a decent interval, when the Carter stealthily advanced a timid forefinger to the button, and gave it the faintest, shortest possible push. I have looked at waiting men where life or death was in the issue; but anxious suspense showed less plainly on their faces than it showed on the faces of these two men as they waited on the coming of the porter.

He came. He barely looked at us. "Full up," he said and shut the door.

"Another night of it," groaned the Carpenter. In the dim light the Carter looked wan and grey.

Indiscriminate charity is vicious, say the professional philanthropists. Well, I resolved to be vicious.

"Come on; get your knife out and come here," I said to the Carter, drawing him into a dark alley.

He glared at me in a frightened manner, and tried to draw back. Possibly he took me for a latter-day Jack-the-Ripper,[1] with a penchant for elderly male paupers. Or he may have thought I was inveigling him into the commission of some desperate crime. Anyway, he was frightened.

It will be remembered, at the outset, that I sewed a pound inside my stoker's singlet under the armpit. This was my emergency fund, and I was now called upon to use it for the first time.

Not until I had gone through the acts of a contortionist, and shown the round coin sewed in, did I succeed in getting the Carter's help. Even then his hand was trembling so that I was afraid he would cut me instead of the stitches, and I was forced to take the knife away and do it myself. Out rolled the gold piece, a fortune in their hungry eyes; and away we stampeded for the nearest coffee-house.

Of course I had to explain to them that I was merely an investigator, a social student, seeking to find out how the other half lived. And at once they shut up like clams. I was not of their kind; my speech had changed, the tones of my voice were different, in short, I was a superior, and they were superbly class conscious.

"What will you have?" I asked, as the waiter came for the order.

---

1 Unidentified murderer whose vicious crimes against women in the Whitechapel area of London in 1888 gave him an international infamy.

"Two slices an' a cup of tea," meekly said the Carter.

"Two slices an' a cup of tea," meekly said the Carpenter.

Stop a moment, and consider the situation. Here were two men, invited by me into the coffee-house. They had seen my gold piece, and they could understand that I was no pauper. One had eaten a ha'penny roll that day, the other had eaten nothing. And they called for "two slices an' a cup of tea!" Each man had given a tu'penny order. "Two slices," by the way, means two slices of bread and butter.

This was the same degraded humility that had characterised their attitude toward the poorhouse porter. But I wouldn't have it. Step by step I increased their order—eggs, rashers of bacon, more eggs, more bacon, more tea, more slices and so forth—they denying wistfully all the while that they cared for anything more, and devouring it ravenously as fast as it arrived.

"First cup o' tea I've 'ad in a fortnight," said the Carter.

"Wonderful tea, that," said the Carpenter.

They each drank two pints of it, and I assure you that it was slops. It resembled tea less than lager beer resembles champagne. Nay, it was "water-bewitched," and did not resemble tea at all.

It was curious, after the first shock, to notice the effect the food had on them. At first they were melancholy, and talked of the divers times they had contemplated suicide. The Carter, not a week before, had stood on the bridge and looked at the water, and pondered the question. Water, the Carpenter insisted with heat, was a bad route. He, for one, he knew, would struggle. A bullet was "'andier," but how under the sun was he to get hold of a revolver? That was the rub.

They grew more cheerful as the hot "tea" soaked in, and talked more about themselves. The Carter had buried his wife and children, with the exception of one son, who grew to manhood and helped him in his little business. Then the thing happened. The son, a man of thirty-one, died of the smallpox. No sooner was this over than the father came down with fever and went to the hospital for three months. Then he was done for. He came out weak, debilitated, no strong young son to stand by him, his little business gone glimmering, and not a farthing. The thing had happened, and the game was up. No chance for an old man to start again. Friends all poor and unable to help. He had tried for work when they were putting up the stands for the first Coronation parade. "An' I got fair sick of the answer: 'No! no! no!' It rang in my ears at night when I tried to sleep, always the same, 'No! no!

no!'" Only the past week he had answered an advertisement in Hackney, and on giving his age was told, "Oh, too old, too old by far."

The Carpenter had been born in the army, where his father had served twenty-two years. Likewise, his two brothers had gone into the army; one, troop sergeant-major of the Seventh Hussars, dying in India after the Mutiny;[1] the other, after nine years under Roberts[2] in the East, had been lost in Egypt. The Carpenter had not gone into the army, so here he was, still on the planet.

"But 'ere, give me your 'and," he said, ripping open his ragged shirt. "I'm fit for the anatomist, that's all. I'm wastin' away, sir, actually wastin' away for want of food. Feel my ribs an' you'll see."

I put my hand under his shirt and felt. The skin was stretched like parchment over the bones, and the sensation produced was for all the world like running one's hand over a washboard.

"Seven years o' bliss I 'ad," he said. "A good missus and three bonnie lassies. But they all died. Scarlet fever took the girls inside a fortnight."

"After this, sir," said the Carter, indicating the spread, and desiring to turn the conversation into more cheerful channels; "after this, I wouldn't be able to eat a workhouse breakfast in the morning."

"Nor I," agreed the Carpenter, and they fell to discussing belly delights and the fine dishes their respective wives had cooked in the old days.

"I've gone three days and never broke my fast," said the Carter.

"And I, five," his companion added, turning gloomy with the memory of it. "Five days once, with nothing on my stomach but a bit of orange peel, an' outraged nature wouldn't stand it, sir, an' I near died. Sometimes, walkin' the streets at night, I've ben that desperate I've made up my mind to win the horse or lose the saddle. You know what I mean, sir—to commit some big robbery. But

---

1   The Indian Mutiny (Uprising) was a serious assault on British authority in India in 1857 and led to wide modifications in colonial governance.

2   That is, under Frederick Sleigh Roberts, first Earl Roberts (1832–1914), who commanded British forces with distinction in India and South Africa in the second half of the nineteenth century. Between 1900 and 1904, he was Commander-in-Chief of the British Army.

when mornin' come, there was I, too weak from 'unger an' cold to 'arm a mouse."

As their poor vitals warmed to the food, they began to expand and wax boastful, and to talk politics. I can only say that they talked politics as well as the average middle-class man, and a great deal better than some of the middle-class men I have heard. What surprised me was the hold they had on the world, its geography and peoples, and on recent and contemporaneous history. As I say, they were not fools, these two men. They were merely old, and their children had undutifully failed to grow up and give them a place by the fire.

One last incident, as I bade them good-bye on the corner, happy with a couple of shillings in their pockets and the certain prospect of a bed for the night. Lighting a cigarette, I was about to throw away the burning match when the Carter reached for it. I proffered him the box, but he said, "Never mind, won't waste it, sir." And while he lighted the cigarette I had given him, the Carpenter hurried with the filling of his pipe in order to have a go at the same match.

"It's wrong to waste," said he.

"Yes," I said, but I was thinking of the wash-board ribs over which I had run my hand.

Appendix E: Crime reporting from The Times, *14 April 1901*

[Middle-class readers at the turn of the century were by no means insulated from the details of daily crime. The popular press—unconfined by the *sub judice* laws that currently govern British newspaper reports of crimes before and during a trial—could be sensationalist in its reporting of law-breaking in later nineteenth and early twentieth century. Most notoriously sensational, of course, was the Jack the Ripper reporting in 1888–89. But detailed accounts of the most ordinary of crimes were available at the turn of the century to the most educated of readers. *The Times*, the leading quality newspaper, carried in many editions extensive reports of police and court proceedings, often with detailed information about injuries and suffering. Reproduced below is a portion of the routine crime reportage from a randomly chosen edition of *The Times* published during the time that Conan Doyle was writing *The Hound*. It is offered as representative of regular crime journalism in the middle-class press and a reminder that early twentieth-century readers even of *The Times*—which plays, of course, a momentary but significant role in the plot of *The Hound*—had a wealth of information about day-to-day offences, the processes of their detection, and of the subsequent trials and verdicts. Conan Doyle, and his fellow detective writers at the turn of the century, wrote in an environment in which accounts of the minutiae, and sordidness, of commonplace criminal activity, were widely available. Crime was part of the news, a feature of the circulation of contemporary knowledge.]

[...] At WORSHIP-STREET, WILLIAM JOSEPH WILSON, 26, potman,[1] living in Mansfield-street, Kingsland, was charged on remand with feloniously wounding Arthur Alfred Maddock by stabbing him in the face with a carving knife. Mr. Margetts, solicitor, defended. The prosecutor is manager of the publichouse at which prisoner was potman—the Durham Arms, Hackney-road—and moreover they are brothers-in-law. On the 8th inst., they had some words as to the prisoner's neglecting his work, and

---

1   A man employed in a pub to serve the drinks and collect the glasses.

the prisoner went out and returned the worse for drink and was then told by the prosecutor to go home. He is said to have retorted that he would leave, and was told he could do so. The prosecutor went into the bar and heard his wife expostulating with the prisoner and presently sounds of a scuffle. He ran in, and then found that his wife was on the floor in the parlour and the prisoner over her striking her with his fists. On his pulling the prisoner off, the latter stood up and rushed to the table, where he seized a carving knife and plunged it into the prosecutor's face on the left side. Mr. Margetts, in cross-examination, elicited that the table in the parlour was laid for dinner and the knife handy. The act was a sudden one. Dr. Linnell, of the London Hospital, said the weapon entered the face just below the upper maxillary and penetrated downwards through the soft palate to the tonsils and into the mouth for about 4 in. At one time the prosecutor's life was despaired of and his deposition taken. The prisoner was committed for attempted murder to the Central Criminal Court.

At WESTMINSTER, Dr. SIDNEY SMITH, of Wandsworth-bridge-road, appeared in answer to his bail, on remand, charged with causing the death of Florence Bromley Smith, at Chelsea, by unlawful operation. Mr. Mathews, for the Public Prosecutor, in applying for a further adjournment on the ground that the coroner's inquiry was unfinished, said that the case would occupy the Court at least two days—probably three. Mr. Shell remanded the defendant for another fortnight on £500 bail, in addition to his recognizance in a like amount.

At LAMBETH, JOHN MCNALLY, 22, a labourer, of White Hart-street, Kennington, was charged before Mr. Hopkins with assaulting his wife and an omnibus driver named James Muir. Mrs. McNally said the prisoner and herself were married four years ago. In the early hours of Thursday morning she was standing in White Hart-street when the prisoner struck her several blows with his fist and blacked her eye. When he got drunk he always assaulted her. She had been afraid to come to the court before. Mr. Muir said he was passing along White Hart-street and saw the last witness leaning against some railings, but passed on without taking any notice. The prisoner came behind him and knocked him down, and when he got up struck him again. Mr. Hopkins.—What did he strike you for? Witness.—For no reason. I never saw this man before in my life. Mr. Hopkins.—Did he say why he struck you? Witness.—He did not say a word. Prisoner.— Me and my wife were having a few words, and I asked him what he wanted to interfere for. Police-constable Deeves, 302 L, said he found the woman with her face streaming with blood, and Muir lying on the ground. Mr. Hopkins (to accused).—What have you got to say for yourself? Prisoner.—Nothing, Mr. Hopkins,—Very well, you can stay in prison, with hard labour, for three months.

At CLERKENWELL, CHARLES HUTCHINSON PHILLIPS, *alias* GEORGE GEARD, 38, a perfumer, of Windsor-road, Holloway, was charged on remand with uttering to Hugh Barrington Simeon a forged acceptance to an order for the payment of £65 12s. 6d. with intent to defraud. There were also three other charges preferred against the prisoner for forging his father's and mother's names and also that of a Mr. Frith to bills of acceptance. When the warrant was read over to him, he said "I admit writing my mother's name for £150 and also my father's name to several bills." Mr. Chapman committed the prisoner for trial [...]

Appendix F: From Edgar Allan Poe, "The Murders in the Rue Morgue," Graham's Magazine 18 (April 1841), 166–79

[Conan Doyle always drew attention to the influence of Dr Joseph Bell on the character of Sherlock Holmes (see 31 and note 1 on p. 21). Important though Bell was, Conan Doyle's habitual account of the detective's genesis deflected attention away from a more obvious literary precursor: Edgar Allan Poe's eccentric, unsociable, brilliant, and sometimes rather creepy detective, Monsieur C. Auguste Dupin. Dupin's methods are similar to Holmes's: both present themselves as wholly logical in their patient deductions, both collect details of forensic evidence to reconstruct the nature of the crime, both compare their own deductive principles against the blindness of the official police, both are proud to present their conclusions as the result of a special kind of *mental* work. Both also, as discussed on pp. 49–50, note 6, have a local habit of reading their companion's thoughts as if by supernatural powers but in fact by—implausibly—careful observation. "The Murders in the Rue Morgue" is Poe's most celebrated Dupin short story, a tale in which a savagely violent crime seems, for a long time, to have no possible explanation (as in Stapleton's treatment of his wife and Dr Roylott's of his step-daughters, the subject involves ferocious violence towards women). Below is reproduced a portion of this famous tale as an instance of the kind of *literary* environment in which one can read "The Speckled Band" and *The Hound* (the perpetrator of the crimes in Poe's story turns out to be intriguingly related to that in *The Hound* too), and a glimpse of Sherlock Holmes's textual origins. Conan Doyle remarked in *Through the Magic Door* that, together with Poe's "Gold Bug," it was impossible to see how "['The Murders in the Rue Morgue'] could be bettered,"[1] and he hailed Poe as "the master of all"[2] among short story writers. This extract is part of Dupin's long explanation of his methods and

---

1 Conan Doyle, *Through the Magic Door* (n.p.p.: Quiet Vision, 2000), 77.
2 Ibid., 76.

deductions in relation to the crime which makes clear his similarities (and differences) to Holmes.

Readers will need to know the context. Madame L'Espanaye has been found dead in the courtyard of her apartment in the Quartier St Roch in Paris, so viciously attacked that her head has been almost severed. Inside her rooms, her daughter's body is also discovered, forced, after being violently throttled, far up the chimney over the fireplace. The criminal appears, from the savagery and strength required to commit these crimes, to possess superhuman powers. Witness testimonials are reproduced in the newspapers, many remarking on a heated discussion heard as they approached the apartment in response to agonized screams. Each person offers different identifications of the language of one of the voices in the dispute. Further facts compound the difficulties of the case. Close investigation of the room, and particularly its windows and doors, offers no explanation for the exit route of the criminal or criminals: no one, it appears, could have escaped from the room without meeting the witnesses climbing the stairs. The police are shocked and baffled. The crime seems inexplicable. But Dupin, having acquired evidence from both newspapers and a personal investigation of the scene, has begun to form a startling and brilliantly deduced explanation. Here, then, is part of his account to his bewildered companion. Neither the extract nor my annotation gives away the solution to the crime.]

[...] "I am now awaiting," continued he, looking toward the door of our apartment—"I am now awaiting a person who, although perhaps not the perpetrator of these butcheries, must have been in some measure implicated in their perpetration. Of the worst portion of the crimes committed, it is probable that he is innocent. I hope that I am right in this supposition; for upon it I build my expectation of reading the entire riddle. I look for the man here—in this room—every moment. It is true that he may not arrive; but the probability is that he will. Should he come, it will be necessary to detain him. Here are pistols; and we both know how to use them when occasion demands their use."

I took the pistols, scarcely knowing what I did, or believing what I heard, while Dupin went on, very much as if in a soliloquy. I have already spoken of his abstract manner at such times. His discourse was addressed to myself; but his voice, although by no means loud, had that intonation which is commonly employed in speaking to some one at a great distance. His eyes, vacant in expression, regarded only the wall.

"That the voices heard in contention," he said, "by the party upon the stairs, were not the voices of the women themselves, was fully proved by the evidence. This relieves us of all doubt upon the question whether the old lady could have first destroyed the daughter, and afterward have committed suicide. I speak of this point chiefly for the sake of method; for the strength of Madame L'Espanaye would have been utterly unequal to the task of thrusting her daughter's corpse up the chimney as it was found; and the nature of the wounds upon her own person entirely precludes the idea of self-destruction. Murder, then, has been committed by some third party; and the voices of this third party were those heard in contention. Let me now advert—not to the whole testimony respecting these voices—but to what was peculiar in that testimony. Did you observe any thing peculiar about it?"

I remarked that, while all the witnesses agreed in supposing the gruff voice to be that of a Frenchman, there was much disagreement in regard to the shrill, or, as one individual termed it, the harsh voice.

"That was the evidence itself," said Dupin, "but it was not the peculiarity of the evidence. You have observed nothing distinctive. Yet there was something to be observed. The witnesses, as you remarked, agreed about the gruff voice; they were here unanimous. But in regard to the shrill voice, the peculiarity is—not that they disagreed—but that, while an Italian, an Englishman, a Spaniard, a Hollander, and a Frenchman attempted to describe it, each one spoke of it as that of a foreigner. Each is sure that it was not the voice of one of his own countrymen. Each likens it—not to the voice of an individual of any nation with whose language he is conversant—but the converse. The Frenchman supposes it is the voice of a Spaniard, and 'might have distinguished some words had he been acquainted with the Spanish.' The Dutchman maintains it to have been that of a Frenchman; but we find it stated that 'not understanding French this witness was examined through an interpreter.' The Englishman thinks it the voice of a German, and 'does not understand German.' The Spaniard 'is sure' that it was that of an Englishman, but 'judges by the intonation' altogether, 'as he has no knowledge of the English.' The Italian believes it the voice of a Russian, but 'has never conversed with a native of Russia.' A second Frenchman differs, moreover, with the first, and is positive that the voice was that of an Italian; but, not being cognizant of that tongue, is, like the Spaniard, 'convinced by the intonation.' Now, how strangely unusual must that voice have really been, about which such testimony as this could have been elicited!—in whose tones, even, denizens of the five great divisions of Europe could recognize nothing familiar! You will say that it might have been the voice of an Asiatic—of an African. Neither Asiatics nor Africans abound in Paris; but, without denying the inference, I will now merely call your attention to three points. The voice is termed by one witness 'harsh rather than shrill.' It is represented by two others to have been 'quick and unequal.' No words—no sounds resembling words—were by any witness mentioned as distinguishable.

"I know not," continued Dupin, "what impression I may have made, so far, upon your own understanding; but I do not hesitate to say that legitimate deductions even from this portion of the testimony—the portion respecting the gruff and shrill voices—are in themselves sufficient to engender a suspicion which should give direction to all farther progress in the investigation of the mystery. I said 'legitimate deductions'; but my meaning is not thus fully expressed. I designed to imply that the deductions are the sole proper ones, and that the suspicion arises inevitably from them as the single result. What the suspicion is, however, I will not say just yet. I merely wish you to bear in mind that, with myself, it was sufficiently forcible to give a definite form—a certain tendency—to my inquiries in the chamber.

"Let us now transport ourselves, in fancy, to this chamber. What shall we first seek here? The means of egress employed by the murderers. It is not too much to say that neither of us believe in praeternatural events. Madame and Mademoiselle L'Espanaye were not destroyed by spirits. The doers of the deed were material and escaped materially. Then how? Fortunately there is but one mode of reasoning upon the point, and that mode must lead us to a definite decision. Let us examine, each by each, the possible means of egress. It is clear that the assassins were in the room where Mademoiselle L'Espanaye was found, or at least in the room adjoining, when the party ascended the stairs. It is, then, only from these two apartments that we have to seek issues. The police have laid bare the floors, the ceiling, and the masonry of the walls, in every direction. No secret issues could have escaped their vigilance. But, not trusting to their eyes, I examined with my own. There were, then, no secret issues. Both doors leading from the rooms into the passage were securely locked, with the keys inside. Let us turn to the chimneys. These, although of ordinary width for some eight or ten feet above the hearths, will not admit, throughout their extent, the body of a large cat. The impossibility of egress, by means already stated, being thus absolute, we are reduced to the windows. Through those of the front room no one could have escaped without notice from the crowd in the street. The murderers must have passed, then, through those of the back room. Now, brought to this conclusion in so unequivocal a manner as we are, it is not our part, as reasoners, to reject it on account of apparent impossibilities. It is only left for us to prove that these apparent 'impossibilities' are, in reality, not such.

"There are two windows in the chamber. One of them is unobstructed by furniture, and is wholly visible. The lower portion of the other is hidden from view by the head of the unwieldy bedstead which is thrust close up against it. The former was found securely fastened from within. It resisted the utmost force of those who endeavor to raise it. A large gimlet-hole had been pierced in its frame to the left, and a very stout nail was found fitted therein, nearly to the head. Upon examining the other window, a similar nail was seen similarly fitted in it; and a vigorous attempt to raise this sash failed also. The police were now entirely satisfied that egress had not been in these directions. And, therefore, it was thought a matter of supererogation to withdraw the nails and open the windows.

"My own examination was somewhat more particular, and was so for the reason I have just given—because here it was, I knew, that all apparent impossibilities must be proved to be not such in reality.

"I proceeded to think thus—*a posteriori*.[1] The murderers did escape from one of these windows. This being so, they could not have re-fastened the sashes from the inside, as they were found fastened;—the consideration which put a stop, through its obviousness, to the scrutiny of the police in this quarter. Yet the sashes were fastened. They must, then, have the power of fastening themselves. There was no escape from this conclusion. I stepped to the unobstructed casement, withdrew the nail with some difficulty, and attempted to raise the sash. It resisted all my efforts, as I had anticipated. A concealed spring must, I now knew, exist; and this corroboration of my idea convinced me that my premises, at least, were correct, however mysterious still appeared the circumstances attending the nails. A careful search soon brought to light the hidden spring. I pressed it, and, satisfied with the discovery, forbore to upraise the sash.

---

1 Of an argument that works backwards from affects to causes.

"I now replaced the nail and regarded it attentively. A person passing out through this window might have reclosed it, and the spring would have caught—but the nail could not have been replaced. The conclusion was plain, and again narrowed in the field of my investigations. The assassins must have escaped through the other window. Supposing, then, the springs upon each sash to be the same, as was probable, there must be found a difference between the nails, or at least between the modes of their fixture. Getting upon the sacking of the bedstead, I looked over the head-board minutely at the second casement. Passing my hand down behind the board, I readily discovered and pressed the spring, which was, as I had supposed, identical in character with its neighbor. I now looked at the nail. It was as stout as the other, and apparently fitted in the same manner—driven in nearly up to the head.

"You will say that I was puzzled; but, if you think so, you must have misunderstood the nature of the inductions. To use a sporting phrase, I had not been once 'at fault.' The scent had never for an instant been lost. There was no flaw in any link in the chain. I had traced the secret to its ultimate result,—and that result was the nail. It had, I say, in every respect, the appearance of its fellow in the other window; but this fact was an absolute nullity (conclusive as it might seem to be) when compared with the consideration that here, at this point, terminated the clew. 'There must be something wrong,' I said, 'about the nail.' I touched it; and the head, with about a quarter of an inch of the shank, came off in my fingers. The rest of the shank was in the gimlet-hole, where it had been broken off. The fracture was an old one (for its edges were incrusted with rust), and had apparently been accomplished by the blow of a hammer, which had partially imbedded, in the top of the bottom sash, the head portion of the nail. I now carefully replaced this head portion in the indentation whence I had taken it, and the resemblance to a perfect nail was complete—the fissure was invisible. Pressing the spring, I gently raised the sash for a few inches; the head went up with it, remaining firm in its bed. I closed the window, and the semblance of the whole nail was again perfect.

"This riddle, so far, was now unriddled. The assassin had escaped through the window which looked upon the bed. Dropping of its own accord upon his exit (or perhaps purposely closed), it had become fastened by the spring; and it was the retention of this spring which had been mistaken by the police for that of the nail,—farther inquiry being thus considered unnecessary.

"The next question is that of the mode of descent["] [...]

Appendix G: From Adam Badeau, "The Land," Aristocracy in England (New York: Harper, 1886 [first published 1885]), 230–37

[Adam Badeau (1831–95) served as an officer under General Ulysses S. Grant (retiring with the rank of Brigadier General) and subsequently as a diplomat in England and Cuba. Badeau's visits to England led to the publication, in 1885, of his somewhat intemperate, not to say moaning or, in that distinctively British sense, *whinging* reflections on the state of the English aristocracy at the end of the nineteenth century. This chapter specifically on landownership, nonetheless, brings into focus some of the political issues about the aristocracy's precariousness worth taking seriously. Conan Doyle's *Hound* thought also about the state of the aristocracy—but from a very different perspective. Badeau's views, powerfully articulated but with disablingly simplistic logic, were shaped, certainly, by a number of uninvestigated assumptions from his own culture. He did not make much attempt to understand the distinctive qualities of English national life before advocating their reform along American lines.[1] His main point here, however, is one that connects him with an issue pertinent for readers of *The Hound*. He sees the aristocracy approaching collapse. For him, the discrepancy between landed wealth and the poverty of the (rural) poor is an overwhelming indictment of the place of the privileged rich in British political life. Towards the end of the chapter, Badeau also begins to imply the moral blindness, the self-interested strategies of inertia, of the aristocrats. He senses a system—as he understands it—incapable now of long survival and an aristocracy approaching the end of its traditional role in British society.

The landed families depicted in *The Hound of the Baskervilles* and "The Adventure of the Speckled Band" are in jeopardy too. Both Badeau and Conan Doyle, albeit from very different per-

---

1 Badeau implies, for instance, that much distress among the English poor would be solved if they owned (and, presumably, did not have to pay for) their own land rather than renting it from landowners.

spectives, contemplate a system in danger. But, of course, *The Hound* works—if not wholly convincingly—to restore it. The Baskerville family's decline is to do with a gradual depletion of capital linked with a more general idea of the withering of bloodlines and the corruption of stock; in "The Speckled Band," that decay is figured in terms of gradual moral degeneration. In neither is the danger to the upper classes the result of political desires to redistribute their possessions. But both Badeau and Conan Doyle, from their alternative political viewpoints, record at the broadest of levels something of the same cultural concern as, at the close of the nineteenth century, the future of the once ruling classes, the ancient families, the titled landowners, the squires, baronets, and the aristocracy proper, became a matter of debate.

Badeau anticipates the abolition of the English aristocracy as it then operated and the democratization of landownership. Conan Doyle offers another view in *The Hound* of how the old landed interests may still work even at the end of the nineteenth century, if properly managed, in the interest of all. Holmes acts to protect the rural squirearchy of Dartmoor, but not for the personal advantage of Sir Henry. The model of the baronet's role in that local economy is one of responsibility; Sir Henry's philanthropy, altruism, and conscientiousness will make secure the local society around him. This hierarchical model functions—or will function, the novel suggests we should believe, once Sir Henry has recovered from the loss of Beryl—in a way Badeau's political paradigm cannot bring itself to imagine.]

[...] The landed property of England covers 72,000,000 acres. It is worth ten thousand millions of dollars, and yields an annual rent, independent of mines, of three hundred and thirty millions. One-fourth of this territory, exclusive of that held by the owners of less than an acre, is in the hands of 1,200 proprietors, and a second fourth is owned by 6,200 others; so that half of the entire country is held by 7,400 individuals. The population is 34,000,000. The peers, not six hundred in number, own more than one-fifth of the kingdom; they possess 14,000,000 acres of land, worth two thousand millions of dollars, with an annual rental of $66,000,000.

Next to Belgium, England is the most thickly populated country in the world, but the Duke of Devonshire has one estate of 83,000 acres and another of 11,000; the Duke of Bedford one of 33,000; the Duke of Portland owns 53,000 acres, the Duke of

Northumberland 181,000, and in every county there are properties ranging from 10,000 to 30,000 acres in the possession of the lords. Seven persons own one-seventh of Buckinghamshire, which has a population of 175,000 and an acreage of 450,000. Cambridge has a population of 149,000, and five persons own one-ninth of the land and receive one thirteenth of the rental. In Cheshire the population is 561,000, and sixteen persons own two-sevenths of the land, which is 602,000 acres in extent.

In Ireland the situation is similar. In the province of Munster eleven persons own one-eleventh of the land. In Ulster, a noble marquis, the grandson of George IV.'s mistress, owns 122,300 acres; the natural son of another marquis, who was probably the worst Englishman that ever lived, owns 58,000, and still another marquis, married to a woman of the town now living, owns 34,000. In Connaught two persons own 274,000 acres, and besides these Viscount Dillon holds 83,000 and the Earl of Lucan 60,000. Lord Fitzwilliam has an estate of 89,000 acres, the Duke of Leinster one of 67,000, Lord Kenmare one of 91,000 and another of 22,000, Lord Bantry one of 69,000, Lord Landsdowne one of 91,000, another of 13,000, and another of 9,000; Lord Downshire one of 26,000, one of 15,000, and another of 64,000; Lord Leitrim three of 54,000, 22,000, and 18,000 respectively. The Duke of Devonshire, in addition to his enormous English properties, has one Irish estate of 32,000 acres and another of 27,000. His eldest son is the Marquis of Hartington, recently the leader of the Liberal party in England, but his lordship was unable to follow Mr. Gladstone in his endeavors to bring peace and prosperity to Ireland.[1] Like the young man of Scripture, he went away sorrowing, "for he had great possessions."[2]

Scotland, however, is the paradise of the peers. The county of Sutherland contains 1,299,253 acres, of which the Duke of Sutherland owns 1,176,343. The population of the county is 24,317 souls. Six other potentates hold over 100,000 acres among them, leaving exactly 5,295 acres for the remaining 24,310 inhabitants. There, are, however, only 85 of these with more than an acre apiece.

Among the other great proprietors in Scotland are the Duchess of Sutherland, who owns an estate of 149,000 acres in

1 The Prime Minister, William Ewart Gladstone (1809–98), had left office in June 1885—the year Badeau's book was first published—with his plans for Home Rule in Ireland unachieved.
2 See Matthew 19. 16–26.

her own right, and the Earl of Fife, who has one of 140,000, another of 72,000, and another of 40,000. The Duke of Richmond has one of 155,000 and another of 69,000; the Earl of Seafield (the head of the Grants), one of 96,000, one of 48,000, and one of 16,000; the Earl of Breadalbane owns 193,000 and 179,000 acres; the Duke of Hamilton, 102,000 and 45,000; the Duke of Buccleugh, 253,000, 104,000, and 60,000. The Duke of Argyll is comparatively poor; he owns only 168,000 acres, while the Queen's estate of Balmoral is a modest little property of 25,000 acres. In Inverness-shire twenty men own 2,000,000 acres among them, and in Aberdeenshire twenty-three "lords and gentlemen" own more than half the county, though the population is 244,000. The greater part of all this territory is devoted to the sports of the aristocracy, for whom Scotland is only one great playground.[1]

Three-fourths of these noble landlords inherit their estates either from grasping robbers of the Norman type or Cromwellian[2] conquest, or from women who sold their beauty and their virtue to kings or panders, or from politicians of the stamp of Aaron Burr[3] or Alderman Jaehne.[4] Walpole and Pitt[5] were the most lavish distributors of coronets England ever had, and one of these notoriously bought with money and titles the very Irish Union which is certain soon to be dissolved, while the other was the author of the famous maxim in English politics, "Every man has his price."[6]

The great landowners themselves seldom cultivate more than a little piece of soil, sufficient for the requirements of a single establishment. The arable and pasture land of the kingdom is let out to 1,160,000 tenant farmers, 70 per cent. of whom hold [fewer] than 50 acres each, 12 per cent. between 50 and 100 acres, and only 18 per cent. more than 100 acres apiece. In all the

---

1 That is to say, regarded merely as a place to hunt and, to a lesser extent, fish.

2 Oliver Cromwell (1599–1658), Lord Protector of England (1653–58) during the period of the Republic following the Civil War.

3 Aaron Burr Jnr (1756–1836), American politician, soldier, dueller (he shot Alexander Hamilton): the object of much dislike and rumour.

4 One of the corrupt aldermen involved in the Broadway surface road and Broadway Surface Railway Company scandal in New York, which was exposed in 1885.

5 Robert Walpole, first earl of Orford (1676–1745), British prime minister; William Pitt the Younger, British premier 1783–1801 and 1804–06.

6 A phrase often attributed to Walpole.

kingdom only 600 farmers are little better off than their own laborers, but in the aggregate they employ a capital of $2,000,000,000. With the laborers they constitute one-tenth of the working population of the country.

The laborers have not capital but the furniture of their dwellings, unless the strength of their bodies and the hard experience of toil may be considered capital. Their wages are insufficient to maintain them, and the consequence is there are a million of paupers to be supported by the State. They have, of course, no independence, and are in reality serfs of the soil. They rarely leave the parish in which they were born; until recently, if they did so they forfeited the right to relief when destitute, or to the almshouse, which every peasant looks to as the end of his laborious life. They never save; they have insufficient food; in many parts of the country their stature is dwarfish, their gait slow and sluggish, like their minds. They have no education; their only pleasure is drink. Above all, they have no possibility of bettering themselves. But it is upon their poverty, degradation, and misery that the grandeur and luxury of the aristocracy are founded. One is the direct cause of the other.

In 1880 the average wages of the agricultural laborer, the man who worked the two thousand million acres of land and produced the three hundred and thirty millions of revenue, was fourteen English shillings a week, or about fifty cents a day. Out of this he had to pay his rent to the earl or the duke, which was two English shillings, or fifty cents, a week. Bread was three cents a pound, meat eighteen cents, and butter one shilling and eight pence, about forty cents. So his fifty cents a day would not buy many pounds of meat or butter, if the family was large. For there were shoes to be got for all, clothes, fuel, lights, as well as food, all out of fourteen shillings a week, and in sight of the castle of my lord, who was rich solely because the hind was poor.

The ordinary cottage of the English labourer has but two rooms, and when the married man has a family of nearly or quite grown sons and daughters they often all sleep in one room, and not unfrequently in the same bed. The great majority of cottages are wretchedly built, often on very unhealthy sites, miserably small, very low, badly drained, and they scarcely ever have a cellar or a space under the roof above the room on the lower floor. They are fit abodes for a peasantry pauperized and demoralized by the utter helplessness of their condition.

The first summer that I spent in England I visited two splendid mansions in the south whose owners were earls. One of these showed me a hall in his castle that was restored in the time of

Henry V., and other was of the family of that Count Robert of Paris who sat for an hour on the throne of Constantinople.[1] Both of these nobles were personally estimable, and even religious men, who undoubtedly supposed they were doing their duty in that state of life to which it had pleased God to call them. I knew of exalted and beautiful traits in the character of each that would extort the admiration of honourable men everywhere.

While I was visiting them, I attended the meetings of the British Association for the Advancement of Science, held in a neighbouring town. Large parties went in each day from the palatial and luxurious abodes of the nobility, to be present at the sessions, at which an earl presided; and nearly a score of high-placed proprietors attended what interested me most of all, the sittings of the Department of Political and Social Economy. The magnates were engaged for several days discussing the condition of the English poor. I heard viscounts and baronets and bishops and earls lamenting the misery and depravity, the poverty and low wages of the wretches who lived on their estates. I heard them admit that in their part of the country a shilling a day was often the wages of a strong, healthy man, who had a wife and six or seven children to support, out of which, I heard them say, at least a shilling a week was deducted for rent. I heard that whole families occupied a single bed-room, I heard of the ignorance and stolidity, often the brutality, of the English peasants, of whom there are several millions.

Not all are in this extreme condition, but all are degraded and demoralized; and I have heard English noblemen declare that, as a class, they are more brutish—that was the word—than any other peasantry in the world. The worst things I have told are neither exceptional nor rare. I went back to the stately halls, where forty or fifty guests were feasted each night off silver, and where the very servants were ten times better fed and clad and housed than the best off of the lower class outside; where the poor crowded around the charitable kitchen gate, literally glad to feed on the crumbs that feel from the rich man's table; and I wondered what would be the end—and the how long it would be deferred—of the aristocracy of England. [...]

---

1 See Sir Walter Scott, *Count Robert of Paris* (1832), a novel set during the reign of the Byzantine Emperor Alexius Comnenus (1081–1118) and concerning the First Crusade. Conan Doyle wrote about this novel enthusiastically in *Through the Magic Door*, pp. 24–25 (ch 2).

Appendix H: From Edward B. Tylor, "The Development of Culture," Primitive Culture: Researches into the Development of Mythology, Philosophy, Religion, Language, Art, and Custom, *2nd ed, 2 vols (London: Murray, 1873 [first published 1871])*

[Edward Tylor's *Primitive Culture* (1871) was a defining work of nineteenth-century ethnography that attempted a major survey of the conditions and development of tribal or so-called "savage" peoples. In this extract, Tylor first offers, then proceeds to query, a conventional model of the development of peoples from primitive to civilized. Advanced societies are not in everything better than primeval, he argues, despite what many think, and in important ways the civilized have forgotten values that the primitive cherish (tolerance, for instance, is particularly admired by the Creek Indians, Tylor wryly observes, when the West has a striking history of forgetting it). Moreover, civilized societies can degenerate, and they often have—Tylor was particularly interested in this—so-called "survivals," the vestiges of primitive life existing clearly within them. The relationship between the primitive and the civilized, the degeneration of the former, and the survival of the savage even in modern societies connect Tylor's consequential book with multiple imaginative engagements of *The Hound* and "The Speckled Band."]

[...] In taking up the problem of the development of culture as a branch of ethnological research, a first proceeding is to obtain a means of measurement. Seeking something like a definite line along which to reckon progression and retrogression in civilization, we may apparently find it best in the classification of real tribes and nations, past and present. Civilization actually existing among mankind in different grades, we are enabled to estimate and compare it by positive examples. The educated world of Europe and America practically settles a standard by simply placing its own nations at one end of the social series and savage tribes at the other, arranging the rest of mankind between these limits according as they correspond more closely to savage or to cultured life. The principal criteria of classification are the absence or presence, high or low development, of the industrial arts, especially metal-working, manufacture of implements and vessels, agriculture, architecture, &c., the extent of scientific knowledge, the definiteness of moral principles, the condition of religious belief and ceremony, the degree of social and political organization, and so forth. Thus, on the definite basis of compared facts, ethnographers are able to set up at least a rough scale of civilization. Few would dispute that the following races are arranged rightly in order of culture:—Australian, Tahitian, Aztec, Chinese, Italian. By treating the development of civilization on this plain ethnographic basis, many difficulties may be avoided which have embarrassed its discussion. This may be seen by a glance at the relation which theoretical principles of civilization bear to the transitions to be observed as matter[s] of fact between the extremes of savage and cultured life.

From an ideal point of view, civilization may be looked upon as the general improvement of mankind by higher organization of the individual and of society, to the end of promoting at once man's goodness, power, and happiness. This theoretical civilization does in no small measure correspond with actual civilization, as traced by comparing savagery with barbarism, and barbarism with modern educated life. So far as we take into account only material and intellectual culture, this is especially true. Acquaintance with the physical laws of the world, and the accompanying power of adapting nature to man's own ends, are, on the whole, lowest among savages, mean among barbarians, and highest among modern educated nations. Thus a transition from the savage state to our own would be, practically, that very progress of art and knowledge which is one main element in the development of culture.

But even those students who hold most strongly that the general course of civilization, as measured along the scale of races from savages to ourselves, is progress towards the benefit of mankind, must admit many and manifold exceptions. Industrial and intellectual culture by no means advances uniformly in all its branches, and in fact excellence in various of its details is often obtained under conditions which keep back culture as a whole. It is true that these exceptions seldom swamp the general rule; and the Englishman, admitting that he does not climb trees like the wild Australian, nor track game like the savage of the Brazilian forest, nor compete with the ancient Etruscan[1] and the modern Chinese in delicacy of goldsmith's work and ivory carving, nor reach the classic Greek level of oratory and sculpture, may yet claim for himself a general condition above any of these races. But there actually have to be taken into account developments of science and art which tend directly against culture. To have learnt to give poison secretly and effectually, to have raised a corrupt literature to pestilent perfection, to have organized a successful scheme to arrest free enquiry and proscribe free expression, are works of knowledge and skill whose progress toward their goal has hardly conduced to the general good. Thus, even in comparing mental and artistic culture among several peoples, the balance of good and ill is not quite easy to strike.

If not only knowledge and art, but at the same time moral and political excellence, be taken into consideration, it becomes yet harder to reckon on an ideal scale the advance or decline from state to stage of culture. In fact, a combined intellectual and moral measure of [the] human condition is an instrument which no student has as yet learnt properly to handle. Even granting that intellectual, moral, and political life may, on a broad view, be seen to progress together, it is obvious that they are far from advancing with equal steps. It may be taken as man's rule of duty in the world, that he shall strive to know as well as he can find out, and to do as well as he knows how. But the parting asunder of these two great principles, that separation of intelligence from virtue which accounts for so much of the wrong-doing of mankind, is continually seen to happen in the great movements of civilization. As one conspicuous instance of what all history stands to prove, if we study the early ages of Christianity, we may see men with minds pervaded by the new religion of duty, holiness, and love, yet at the same time actually falling away in intellectual life, thus at once vigorously grasping one half of civilization, and contemptuously casting off the other. Whether in high ranges or in low of human life, it may be seen that advance of culture seldom results at once in unmixed good. Courage, honesty, generosity, are virtues which may suffer, at least for a time, by the development of a sense of value of life and property. The savage who adopts something of foreign civilization too often loses his ruder virtues without gaining an equivalent. The white invader or

---

1 ·Etruria is an ancient area of northern Italy.

colonist, though representing on the whole a higher moral standard than the savage he improves or destroys, often represents his standard very ill, and at best can hardly claim to substitute a life stronger, nobler, and purer at every point than that which he supersedes. The onward movement from barbarism has dropped behind it more than one quality of barbaric character, which cultured modern men look back on with regret, and will even strive to regain by futile attempts to stop the course of history, and restore the past in the midst of the present. So it is with social institutions. The slavery recognized by savage and barbarous races is preferable in kind to that which existed for centuries in late European colonies. The relation of the sexes among many savage tribes is more healthy than among the richer classes of the Mahommedan world. As a supreme authority of government, the savage councils of chiefs and elders compare favourably with the unbridled despotism under which so many cultured races have groaned. The Creek Indians, asked concerning their religion, replied that where agreement was not to be had, it was best to "let every man paddle his canoe his own way:" and after long ages of theological strife and persecution, the modern world seems coming to think these savages not far wrong.

★ ★ ★

In the various branches of the problem which will henceforward occupy our attention, that of determining the relation of the mental condition of savages to that of civilized men, it is an excellent guide and safeguard to keep before our minds the theory of development in the material arts. Throughout all the manifestations of the human intellect, facts will be found to fall into their places on the same general lines of evolution. The notion of the intellectual state of savages as resulting from decay of previous high knowledge, seems to have as little evidence in its favour as that stone celts[1] are the degenerate successors of Sheffield axes, or earthen grave-mounds degraded copies of Egyptian pyramids. The study of savage and civilized life alike avail us to trace in the early history of the human intellect, not gifts of transcendental wisdom, but rude shrewd sense taking up the facts of common life and shaping from them schemes of primitive philosophy. It

---

1 Implements with a chisel-shaped edge found in the habitations of prehistoric man.

will be seen again and again, by examining such topics as language, mythology, custom, religion, that savage opinion is in a more or less rudimentary state, while the civilized mind still bears vestiges, neither few nor slight, of a past condition from which savages represent the least, and civilized men the greatest advance. Throughout the whole vast range of the history of human thought and habit, while civilization has to contend not only with survival from lower levels, but also with degeneration within its own borders, it yet proves capable of overcoming both and taking its own course. History within its proper field, and ethnography over a wider range, combine to show that the institutions which can best hold their own in the world gradually supersede the less fit ones, and that this incessant conflict determines the general resultant course of culture. I will venture to set forth in mythic fashion how progress, aberration, and retrogression in the general course of culture contrast themselves in my own mind. We may fancy ourselves looking on Civilization, as in personal figure she traverses the world; we see her lingering or resting by the way, and often deviating into paths that bring her toiling back to where she had passed by long ago; but, direct or devious, her path lies forward, and if now and then she tries a few backward steps, her walk soon falls into a helpless stumbling. It is not according to her nature, her feet were not made to plant uncertain steps behind her, for both in her forward view and in her onward gait she is of truly human type. [...]

Appendix I: From Arthur Conan Doyle, The New Revelation (London: Hodder and Stoughton, 1918)

[Dedicated to "all the brave men and women, humble or learned, who have had the moral courage during seventy years to face ridicule or worldly disadvantage in order to testify to an all-important truth," Conan Doyle's *The New Revelation* (1918) was his first substantial statement on spiritualism in print. He had been studying the possibilities of life beyond death and of communication from beyond the grave for most of his adult life and had attended hundreds of séances. In this book, he announced climactically that he had "finally declared myself to be satisfied with the evidence" (*New Revelation*, 16), and thereafter his career would be dedicated to communicating the vital truths, as he saw it, of spiritualism. The extract reproduced below is part of the result of what he called "The Search" which had occupied much of his life and during which he believed he had applied the rigorous standards of scientific proof to the amassed evidence of the spiritualists. Here—and now as a believer—he discusses the consistency of information gleaned from the returning dead about the first stages of life on the Other Side, and how this might constitute a statement about Spiritland in general (and, specifically, an argument against the existence of a Christian hell). It is easy to think of Sherlock Holmes as the antithesis to the spiritualist side of Conan Doyle's mind, and there is an element of truth in this. But the relationship is, in its fullness, more complex. Holmes, at one level, helped dramatize some of Conan Doyle's inner anxieties before he was fully committed to spiritualism about the relation between science and the supernatural—*The Hound* is etched with this process of thinking (see Introduction, pp. 33–39)—and, more obviously, Conan Doyle always saw himself applying meticulous, scientific, *Holmesian* standards of analysis to the evidence for the *revenants*. He never regarded himself as having abandoned scientific rigour. In this extract, one hears the voice of a scientific reasoner, which is not unlike the detective, applied to none of the mere problems of terrestrial crime but to the extraordinary possibilities—certainties, now, for Holmes's creator—of life beyond the grave.]

[...] Now, leaving this large and possibly contentious subject of the modifications which such new revelations must produce in Christianity,[1] let us try to follow what occurs to man after death. The evidence on this point is fairly full and consistent. Messages from the dead have been received in many lands at various times, mixed up with a good deal about this world, which we could verify. When messages come thus, it is only fair, I think, to suppose that if what we can test is true, then what we cannot test is true also. When in addition we find a very great uniformity in the messages and an agreement as to details which are not at all in accordance with any pre-existing scheme of thought, then I think the presumption of truth is very strong. It is difficult to think that some fifteen or twenty messages from various sources of which I have personal notes, all agree, and yet are all wrong, nor is it easy to suppose that spirits can tell the truth about our world but untruth about their own.

I received lately, in the same week, two accounts of life in the next world, one received through the hand of the near relative of a high dignitary of the Church, while the other came through the wife of a working mechanician in Scotland. Neither could have been aware of the existence of the other, and yet the two accounts are so alike as to be practically the same.

The message upon these points seems to me to be infinitely reassuring, whether we regard our own fate or that of our friends. The departed all agree that passing is usually both easy and painless, and followed by an enormous reaction of peace and ease. The individual finds himself in a spirit body, which is the exact counterpart of his old one, save that all disease, weakness, or deformity has passed from it. This body is standing or floating beside the old body, and conscious both of it and of the surrounding people. At this moment the dead man is nearer to matter than he will ever be again, and hence it is that at that moment the greater part of those cases occur where, his thoughts having turned to someone in the distance, the spirit body went with the thoughts and was manifest to the person. Out of some 250 cases

---

1 The subject of Chapter II, "The Revelation."

carefully examined by Mr. Gurney,[1] 134 of such apparitions were actually at this moment of dissolution, when one could imagine that the new spirit body was possibly so far material as to be more visible to a sympathetic human eye than it would later become.

These cases, however, are very rare in comparison with the total number of deaths. In most cases I imagine that the dead man is too preoccupied with his own amazing experience to have much thought for others. He soon finds, to his surprise, that though he endeavours to communicate with those whom he sees, his ethereal voice and his ethereal touch are equally unable to make any impression upon those human organs which are only attuned to coarser stimuli. It is a fair subject for speculation, whether a fuller knowledge of those light rays which we know to exist on either side of the spectrum, or of those sounds which we can prove by the vibrations of a diaphragm to exist, although they are too high for mortal ear, may not bring us some further psychical knowledge. Setting that aside, however, let us follow the fortunes of the departing spirit. He is presently aware that there are others in the room besides those who were there in life, and among these others, who seem to him as substantial as the living, there appear familiar faces, and he finds his hand grasped or his lips kissed by those whom he had loved and lost. Then in their company, and with the help and guidance of some more radiant being who has stood by and waited for the newcomer, he drifts to his own surprise through all solid obstacles and out upon his new life.

This is a definite statement, and this is the story told by one after the other with a consistency which impels belief. It is already very different from any old theology. The Spirit is not a glorified angel or goblin damned, but it is simply the person himself, containing all his strength and weakness, his wisdom and his folly, exactly as he has retained his personal appearance. We can well believe that the most frivolous and foolish would be awed into decency by so tremendous an experience, but impressions soon become blunted, the old nature may soon reassert itself in new surroundings, and the frivolous still survive, as our *séance* rooms can testify.

And now, before entering upon his new life, the new Spirit has a period of sleep which varies in its length, sometimes hardly

---

1   Edmund Gurney (1847–88), Fellow of Trinity College, Cambridge, and psychical researcher; co-author with F.W.H. Myers and Frank Podmore of *Phantasms of the Living*, 2 vols (1886).

existing at all, at others extending for weeks or months. Raymond said that his lasted for six days.[1] That was the period also in a case of which I had some personal evidence. Mr. Myers,[2] on the other hand, said that he had a very prolonged period of unconsciousness. I could imagine that the length is regulated by the amount of trouble or mental preoccupation of this life, the longer rest giving the better means of wiping this out. Probably the little child would need no such interval at all. This, of course, is pure speculation, but there is a considerable consensus of opinion as to the existence of a period of oblivion after the first impression of the new life and before entering upon its duties.

Having wakened from this sleep, the spirit is weak, as the child is weak after earth birth. Soon, however, strength returns and the new life begins. This leads us to the consideration of heaven and hell. Hell, I may say, drops out altogether, as it has long dropped out of the thoughts of every reasonable man. This odious conception, so blasphemous in its view of the Creator, arose from the exaggerations of Oriental phrases, and may perhaps have been of service in a coarse age where men were frightened by fires, as wild beasts are scared by the travellers. Hell as a permanent place does not exist. But the idea of punishment, of purifying chastisement, in fact of Purgatory, is justified by the reports from the other side. Without such punishment there could be no justice in the Universe, for how impossible it would be to imagine that the fate of a Rasputin[3] is the same as that of a Father Damien.[4] The punishment is very certain and very serious, though in its less severe forms it only consists in the fact that the grosser souls are in lower spheres with a knowledge that their own deeds have placed them there, but also with the hope that expiation and the help of those

---

1 See Oliver Lodge, *Raymond: or, Life and Death: With Examples of the Evidence for Survival of Memory and Affection after Death* (1916).

2 Frederic William Henry Myers (1843–1901), psychical researcher and essayist, and one of the founders of the Society for Psychical Research.

3 Grigori Rasputin (1869?–1916), man of religion (*starets*), apparent faith healer, and friend of the Romanovs, the Russian Royal Family. He was murdered, it seems, by forces anxious to stop his growing influence with the Czar's family (there is evidence that those forces included British Intelligence). Rasputin was widely known in England as a "wicked monk," a drunkard, frequenter of prostitutes, and manipulator of royalty.

4 Father Damien, Joseph de Veuster (1840–89), was a Belgian Catholic missionary priest who worked among those suffering from leprosy on the Hawaiian island of Molokai until succumbing to the disease himself.

above them will educate them and bring them level with the others. In this saving process the higher spirits find part of their employment. Miss Julia Ames in her beautiful posthumous book, says in memorable words: "The greatest joy of Heaven is emptying Hell."[1]

Setting aside those probationary spheres, which should perhaps rather be looked upon as a hospital for weakly souls than as a penal community, the reports from the other world are all agreed as to the pleasant conditions of life in the beyond. They agree that like goes to like, that all who love or who have interests in common are united, that life is full of interest and of occupation, and that they would by no means desire to return. All of this is surely tidings of great joy, and I repeat that it is not a vague faith or hope, but that it is supported by all the laws of evidence which agree that where many independent witnesses give a similar account, that account has a claim to be considered a true one. If it were an account of glorified souls purged instantly from all human weakness and of a constant ecstasy of adoration round the throne of the all powerful, it might well be suspected as being the mere reflection of that popular theology which all the mediums had equally received in their youth. It is, however, very different to any pre-existing system. It is also supported, as I have already pointed out, not merely by the consistency of the accounts, but by the fact that the accounts are the ultimate product of a long series of phenomena, all of which have been attested as true by those who have carefully examined them.

In connection with the general subject of life after death, people may say we have got this knowledge already through faith. But faith, however beautiful in the individual, has always in collective bodies been a very two-edged quality. All would be well if every faith were alike and the intuitions of the human race were constant. We know that it is not so. Faith means to say that you entirely believe a thing which you cannot prove. One man says: "My faith is *this*." Another says: "My faith is *that*." Neither can prove it, so they wrangle for ever, either mentally or in the old days physically. If one is stronger than the other, he is inclined to persecute him just to twist him round to the true faith. Because Philip the Second's faith was strong and clear he, quite logically,

---

1 From Julia [Julia A. Ames], *Letters from Julia; or, Light from the Borderland, a series of messages ... received by automatic writing, etc.* (London: Grant Richards, 1898).

killed a hundred thousand Lowlanders[1] in the hope that their fellow countrymen would be turned to the all-important truth. Now, if it were recognised that it is by no means virtuous to claim what you could not prove, we should then be driven to observe facts, to reason from them,[2] and perhaps reach common agreement. That is why this psychical movement appears so valuable. Its feet are on something more solid than texts or traditions or intuitions. It is religion from the double point of view of both worlds up to date, instead of the ancient traditions of one world.

We cannot look upon this coming world as a tidy Dutch garden of a place which is so exact that it can easily be described. It is probable that those messengers who come back to us are all, more or less, in one state of development and represent the same wave of life as it recedes from our shores. Communications usually come from those who have not long passed over, and tend to grow fainter, as one would expect. It is instructive in this respect to notice that Christ's reappearances to his disciples or to Paul, are said to have been within a very few years of his death, and that there is no claim among the early Christians to have seen him later. The cases of spirits who give good proof of authenticity and yet have passed some time are not common. There is, in Mr. Dawson Roger's life, a very good case of a spirit who called himself Manton, and claimed to have been born at Lawrence Lydiard and buried at Stoke Newington in 1677. It was clearly shown afterwards that there was such a man, and that he was Oliver Cromwell's chaplain.[3] So far as my own reading goes, this is the oldest spirit who is on record as returning, and generally they are quite recent. Hence, one gets all one's views from the one generation, as it were, and we cannot take them as final, but only as partial. How spirits may see things in a different light as they progress in the other world is shown by Miss Julia Ames, who was deeply impressed at first by the necessity of forming a bureau of commu-

---

1   The Catholic monarch Philip II of Spain (1527–98) was brutal in his suppression of Protestantism.

2   The scientific spirit—and something like the voice of Holmes—in defence of spiritualism's empirical credibility.

3   Thomas Manton (1620–77), nonconformist (Calvinist) minister, born at Lydeard St Lawrence in Somerset, was later minister at Stoke Newington (now an area of North East London); during the Civil War he preached before the Commons and was closely associated with the Protectorate.

nication, but admitted, after fifteen years, that not one spirit in a million among the main body upon the further side ever wanted to communicate with us at all since their own loved ones had come over. She had been misled by the fact that when she first passed over everyone she met was newly arrived like herself.

Thus the account we give may be partial, but still such as it is it is very consistent and of extraordinary interest, since it refers to our own destiny and that of those we love. All agree that life beyond is for a limited period, after which they pass on to yet other phases, but apparently there is more communication between these phases than there is between us and Spiritland. The lower cannot ascend, but the higher can descend at will. The life has a close analogy to that of this world at its best. It is pre-eminently a life of the mind, as this is of the body. Preoccupations of food, money, lust, pain, etc., are of the body and are gone. Music, the Arts, intellectual and spiritual knowledge, and progress have increased. The people are clothed, as one would expect, since there is no reason why modesty should disappear with our new forms. These new forms are the absolute reproduction of the old ones at their best, the young growing up and the old reverting until all come to the normal. People live in communities, as one would expect if like attracts like, and the male spirit still finds his true mate though there is no sexuality in the grosser sense and no childbirth. Since connections still endure, and those in the same state of development keep abreast, one would expect that nations are still roughly divided from each other, though language is no longer a bar, since thought has become a medium of conversation. [...]

Selected Further Reading and Filmography

Arthur Conan Doyle
General

Bibliography

Green, Richard Lancelyn and John Michael Gibson. *A Bibliography of A. Conan Doyle*. Foreword by Graham Greene. Oxford: Clarendon, 1983. Published in the Soho Bibliography Series.

Autobiography and Biography

Conan Doyle, Arthur. *Memories and Adventures*. 1924. Oxford: Oxford UP, 1989.

Pearson, Hesketh. *Conan Doyle, His Life and Art*. London: Methuen, 1943.

Conan Doyle, Adrian. *The True Conan Doyle*. Preface by General Sir Hubert Gough. London: Murray, 1945.

Carr, John Dickson. *The Life of Sir Arthur Conan Doyle*. London: Murray, 1949.

Jones, Kelvin I. *Conan Doyle and the Spirits: The Spiritualist Career of Sir Arthur Conan Doyle*. Northamptonshire: Aquarian, 1989.

Coren, Michael. *Conan Doyle*. London: Bloomsbury, 1995.

Editions

Conan Doyle, Arthur. *The Hound of the Baskervilles*. Edited, and with an introduction and afterword, by John Fowles. London: Murray/Cape, 1974.

——. *The Hound of the Baskervilles*. Ed. W. W. Robson. Oxford: Oxford UP, 1993.

——. *The Hound of the Baskervilles*. Ed. Christopher Frayling. Harmondsworth: Penguin, 2001.

——. *The New Annotated Sherlock Holmes: The Complete Short*

Stories. Ed. Leslie S. Klinger. Introduction by John le Carré. 2 vols. New York: Norton, 2004.

Topography

Baring-Gould, Sabine. *Devon.* 1899. London: Mott, 1983.
Weller, Philip. *The Dartmoor Locations of* The Hound of the Baskervilles: *A Practical Guide to the Sherlock Holmes Locations.* 2nd ed. Hornsea: Sherlock Publications, 1992.

The Hound and other adventures

Commentaries

Baring-Gould, William S., ed. *The Annotated Sherlock Holmes.* 2 vols. London: Murray, 1968.
Dakin, D. Martin. *A Sherlock Holmes Commentary.* Newton Abbot: David and Charles, 1972.

Criticism

Barsham, Diana. *Arthur Conan Doyle and the Meaning of Masculinity.* Aldershot and Burlington, VT: Ashgate, 2000.
Carey, John. *Pure Pleasure: A Guide to the Twentieth Century's Most Enjoyable Books.* London: Faber, 2000.
Fisher, Benjamin F. "*The Hound of the Baskervilles* 100 Years After: A Review Essay." *English Literature in Transition (1880–1920)* 47 (2004): 181–90.
Frank, Lawrence. *Victorian Detective Fiction and the Nature of Evidence: The Scientific Investigations of Poe, Dickens, and Doyle.* Basingstoke: Palgrave Macmillan, 2003.
Hendershot, Cyndy. "The Animal Without: Masculinity and Imperialism in *The Island of Doctor Moreau* and *The Adventure of the Speckled Band.*" *Nineteenth Century Studies* 10 (1996): 1–32.
Jann, Rosemary. *The Adventures of Sherlock Holmes: Detecting Social Order.* New York: Twayne, 1995.
Kerrigan, John. *Revenge Tragedy from Aeschylus to Armegeddon.* Oxford: Clarendon, 1996.
Kestner, Joseph. *Sherlock's Men: Masculinity, Conan Doyle and Cultural History.* Aldershot and Burlington, VT: Ashgate, 1997.

——. *Sherlock's Sisters: The British Female Detective, 1864–1913*. Aldershot and Burlington, VT: Ashgate, 2003.

Orel, Harold, ed. *Critical Essays on Sir Arthur Conan Doyle*. New York: Hall, 1992.

Ousby, Ian. *Bloodhounds of Heaven: The Detective in English Fiction from Godwin to Doyle*. Cambridge, MA: Harvard UP, 1976.

Redmond, Donald A. *Sherlock Holmes: A Study in Sources*. Kingston and Montreal: McGill-Queen's UP, 1982.

Alan Smith, "Mire, *bog*, and Hell in *The Hound of the Baskervilles*." *Victorian Newsletter* 94 (1998): 42–44.

Thomas, Ronald R. *Detective Fiction and the Rise of Forensic Science*. Cambridge: Cambridge UP, 1999.

Wynne, Catherine. *The Colonial Conan Doyle: British Imperialism, Irish Nationalism, and the Gothic*. Westport: Greenwood, 2002.

Selected Film Versions of *The Hound*

A useful account of visual versions of the Holmes narratives is to be found in Michael Pointer, *The Pictorial History of Sherlock Holmes* (Swindon: Smith, 1991).

The Hound of the Baskervilles. Screenplay by Ernest Pascal. Dir. Sidney Lanfield. Perf. Basil Rathbone, Nigel Bruce, Richard Greene, and Lionel Atwill. Twentieth Century Fox, 1939. Now available as Orbit Media DVD.

The Hound of the Baskervilles. Screenplay by Peter Bryan. Dir. Terence Fisher. Perf. Peter Cushing, André Morell, Christopher Lee, Francis de Wolff. Hammer Studios, 1959. Now available as MGM Home Entertainment DVD.

The Hound of the Baskervilles. Perf. Peter Cushing and Nigel Stock. A 2-part BBC movie. 1968. Now available as BBC Worldwide Publishing DVD.

The Hound of the Baskervilles. Screenplay by Peter Cooke, Dudley Moore, and Paul Morrissey. Dir. Paul Morrissey. Perf. Dudley Moore, Peter Cooke, Denholm Elliott, Terry-Thomas, Kenneth Williams. Michael White Ltd., 1977. This was produced as a comedy, and is now available as Prism Leisure Corporation DVD.

The Hound of the Baskervilles. Dir. Douglas Hickox. Perf. Ian Richardson, Martin Shaw, Donald Churchill. Sy Weintraub, 1983. Now available as Ilc Prime DVD.

The Hound of the Baskervilles. Dir. Peter Hammond. Perf. Jeremy

Brett, Edward Hardwicke, Ronald Pickup, Kristoffa Tabori. ITV, 1988. Now available as Cinema Club DVD.

The Hound of the Baskervilles. Screenplay by Allan Cubitt. Dir. David Attwood. Perf. Richard Roxburgh, Ian Hart, Richard E. Grant, John Nettles, Geraldine James. 2003. This BBC Television edition is now available on BBC Worldwide Publishing DVD. The companion website http://www.pbs.org/wgbh/masterpiece/hound/index.html is limited and inaccurate.

Websites

There are many with the familiar wide range of quality; a good starting point is http://www.tc.umn.edu/~bergq003/holmes/

Other

An engaging contemporary response to Sherlock Holmes and *The Hound of the Baskervilles* is Mark Haddon, *The Curious Incident of the Dog in the Night-time* (London: Cape, 2003). Umberto Eco in his great 1983 post-modern mystery novel published in English as *The Name of the Rose*, trans. William Weaver [New York: Picador, 1986] salutes *The Hound* by naming his Franciscan detective Baskerville.

from the publisher

A name never says it all, but the word "broadview" expresses a good deal of the philosophy behind our company. We are open to a broad range of academic approaches and political viewpoints. We pay attention to the broad impact book publishing and book printing has in the wider world; we began using recycled stock more than a decade ago, and for some years now we have used 100% recycled paper for most titles. As a Canadian-based company we naturally publish a number of titles with a Canadian emphasis, but our publishing program overall is internationally oriented and broad-ranging. Our individual titles often appeal to a broad readership too; many are of interest as much to general readers as to academics and students.

Founded in 1985, Broadview remains a fully independent company owned by its shareholders—not an imprint or subsidiary of a larger multinational.

If you would like to find out more about Broadview and about the books we publish, please visit us at **www.broadviewpress.com**. And if you'd like to place an order through the site, we'd like to show our appreciation by extending a special discount to you: by entering the code below you will receive a 20% discount on purchases made through the Broadview website.

Discount code: **broadview20%**

Thank you for choosing Broadview.

Please note: this offer applies only to sales of bound books within the United States or Canada.

LIST
of products used:

1,400 lb(s) of Rolland Enviro100 Print
100% post-consumer

RESULTS
Based on the Cascades products you selected
compared to products in the industry made with
100% virgin fiber, your savings are:

 12 trees

 11,582 gal. US of water
125 days of water consumption

 1,464 lbs of waste
14 waste containers

 3,806 lbs CO2
7,217 miles driven

 18 MMBTU
90,263 60W light bulbs for one hour

 11 lbs NOx
emissions of one truck during 16
days